Hidden Truths

A Secret Identity Romance Collection

Alison Reid

Hidden Truths – A Secret Identity Romance Collection

by Alison Reid

This is a work of fiction. Names, characters, businesses, places, events, and incidents are either the products of the author's imagination or used in a fictitious manner. Any resemblance to actual persons, living or dead, or actual events is purely coincidental.

ISBN: 978-1-7644837-9-7

First edition

Independently published

Introduction to…

Hidden Truths

A Secret Identity Romance Collection

Some loves begin with a lie… and survive only if the truth is strong enough.

Hidden Truths is a curated romance collection featuring emotionally charged standalone love stories built around secret identities, hidden agendas, and the moment everything comes crashing down.

In these novels, powerful men step into the shadows—posing as strangers, protectors, or ordinary men—to escape expectation, test loyalty, or protect the people they love. But when desire turns real and the truth is revealed, hearts are broken, trust is shattered, and love must prove it was never a lie at all.

Written in the spirit of classic Mills & Boon with a modern edge, each story delivers intense emotion, swoon-worthy heroes, resilient heroines, and deeply satisfying redemption arcs. Every romance is a complete standalone, with no cheating and a guaranteed happily-ever-after.

If you love secret billionaires, undercover protectors, forced proximity, emotional revelations, and romance where love survives deception, Hidden Truths belongs on your shelf.

Table of Contents

After the Storm

Alison Reid

A complete standalone romance

Previously published individually

Chapter One

"Jeremy, are you okay? You sound… angry," Rachel asked cautiously, pressing the phone tighter to her ear as if closeness could be conjured by will alone.

A heavy silence followed. One heartbeat. Two.

Then, a sharp sigh crackled through the line—exasperated and clipped.

"I have to go, Rach. I'll call you on Saturday."

Rachel blinked. Saturday? Her brows drew together. It was Sunday.

She shifted upright on the edge of her bed, clutching the phone with both hands, her back tense. "Is everything okay?" she asked, voice softer now. "With us, I mean?"

Another pause.

Then his voice came again—flat, mechanical. Like someone reading a line off a script. "Of course it is. I'm just busy."

She waited for something more—a laugh, a touch of affection, even the warmth that used to linger at the end of his sentences.

But there was nothing.

"Jeremy—"

"I've got to go."

The line went dead.

Rachel slowly lowered the phone, staring at the dark screen as if it might blink back to life, and explain what had just happened. Her stomach twisted with unease, her heart a slow thud of dread in her chest.

What the hell was that?

She exhaled, the breath catching slightly in her throat, and tossed the phone beside her on the bed. The rhythmic crash of waves outside her window should have calmed her. Instead, it made the silence in the room feel cavernous.

She was alone.

Not just physically, but in that deep, aching way that crept up on you when the person who was supposed to care just… didn't.

She stared out at the ocean beyond the glass doors; the horizon painted in strokes of gold and coral. It was stunning. Breathtaking. But instead of peace, all she felt was that hollow, sinking weight settling deep in her chest.

Something's wrong.

She'd felt it for weeks now—quietly at first, then louder, more insistent. Doubt had begun whispering to her in the in-between moments. During phone calls that ended too fast. During texts that came hours late, without warmth. She had ignored the signs, rationalised them away.

He's busy. He's under pressure. Long-distance is hard.

But something deeper told her it wasn't just distance.

He's pulling away.

And maybe—just maybe—he already had.

She'd first started questioning the engagement a month ago, when the silences became longer than the conversations. But she hadn't wanted to make any rash decisions, not without seeing him face to face. She had clung to the version of him who had swept her off her feet—flowers at her door, whirlwind weekends in Paris, candlelit dinners with laughter and promise.

The version who had dropped to one knee and asked her to spend the rest of her life with him.

It had been a surprise. A beautiful one, at the time.

But now, the memory felt like a photo that had begun to fade around the edges—blurred, washed out.

Rachel rubbed her hands over her face, dragging her fingers through her hair as the ache behind her eyes sharpened.

They weren't just separated by geography. They were separated by something far deeper.

And maybe… they always had been.

She had taken the job at the eco-resort because it felt like a dream. Three months on an island paradise, working as a singer and dancer, performing under the stars, waking up to ocean breezes and something that felt like freedom. It was an incredible opportunity—good pay, free accommodation, and a chance to step out of her routine and into something alive.

And if she was being completely honest, she'd taken it partly because she needed space. From the city. From expectations. From Jeremy.

From the version of herself she wasn't sure fit anymore.

Now, as she sat bathed in the soft glow of the island sunset, Rachel felt the weight of the question she'd been avoiding press down with new clarity.

Did she really want to marry Jeremy?

Or had she simply been clinging to a promise made in the rush of infatuation—because it was easy, familiar, expected?

The silence in the room, once peaceful, now felt suffocating. The steady rhythm of waves outside her window no longer soothed her nerves. Instead, it underscored the emptiness inside her—the gnawing uncertainty that had slowly grown roots.

She glanced down at her phone on the bed, still dark, still silent. No messages. No call back.

Her heart ached, not just from the distance between them, but from the growing suspicion that maybe—just maybe—they had never truly been close at all.

She drew in a breath, pushing to her feet. Her mind drifted, unbidden, to her arrival here—her first day. When everything had felt wide open, full of promise.

She remembered it with vivid clarity.

After the long-haul flight from London to Mahé, she'd been jet-lagged and bleary-eyed, her muscles stiff from cramped seats and airport waiting lounges. Exhaustion clung to her like a second skin. But beneath it, a quiet thrill had throbbed through her veins.

The moment she stepped off the plane and into the thick, fragrant heat of the Seychelles air, something inside her had shifted.

The scent of salt, frangipani, and sun-warmed earth had filled her lungs. The sky was a clear, impossible blue, and the sun wrapped around her like silk.

She'd boarded a boat at the harbour, the dock buzzing with cheerful staff and the melodic lilt of Creole. As the boat sliced through the glittering turquoise waves, she'd watched Mahé fade behind her, replaced by the breathtaking silhouette of the island that would soon become her world.

Silhouette Island had felt like something out of a dream.

Rising out of the ocean like an emerald jewel, the island's thick rainforest blanketed the mountains that loomed above, their mist-covered peaks giving the whole place an air of mystery and magic. The scent of blooming hibiscus and salt hung in the breeze, swirling together in a fragrance that made her head spin.

When she'd stepped onto the wooden dock, barefoot and wide-eyed, she had felt it immediately—that hum of life beneath her feet. The sense that this place was alive, not just with nature, but with something deeper. A pulse. A soul.

The beach shimmered under the midday sun, white sand warm and powder-soft, stretching like a ribbon along the coast. The ocean, impossibly clear, shifted in shades of aquamarine and sapphire, each wave a quiet invitation.

But it wasn't just the beach or the sea that captivated her.

It was the island's heart.

In the days that followed, she'd explored the jungle trails that wove through towering banyans and swaying palms. Giant ferns unfurled like green lace in the filtered sunlight, and orchids bloomed in wild bursts of colour along hidden paths. Birds she didn't know the names of darted overhead, their cries echoing through the canopy in joyful song.

She'd found secret waterfalls tucked between moss-covered rocks, their cool water cascading over smooth stones in silver ribbons. She had wandered barefoot along jungle paths, let the rain soak through her hair, tasted tropical fruit plucked straight from the tree.

And in the quiet moments—in the stillness between performances or just after dusk when the stars lit up the sky—she had felt something she hadn't felt in a long time.

Freedom.

Here, she wasn't Rachel-the-fiancée, or Rachel-the-woman-waiting-for-someone-to-call. She was simply Rachel.

Untethered. Whole.

The island had reminded her of who she was before expectations before compromises.

Before Jeremy.

She had fallen in love with it instantly—not just for its beauty, but for what it awakened in her. A sense of possibility. A sense of self.

And now, as the sun dipped lower beyond the horizon and painted the ocean in streaks of fire and gold, Rachel sat in the glow of it all, feeling that familiar pull again.

She didn't want to spend the rest of her life wondering if she'd settled.

She didn't want to marry a man who didn't see her.

Because here—on this island—she had finally started to see herself.

On her days off, Rachel would slip away from the bustle of the resort and disappear into the island's untamed beauty. No schedule. No destination. Just her and the trail.

She wandered for hours beneath canopies of green, letting the jungle lead her. Twisting footpaths carried her through ancient groves where sunlight pierced the foliage in golden shafts, lighting up patches of wild orchids and dew-soaked leaves. Ferns brushed her ankles, and the earthy scent of rain-soaked soil clung to her skin.

Sometimes she found herself standing before hidden waterfalls, their crystalline streams tumbling over mossy rocks into clear, cool pools. She'd sit there for what felt like forever, dipping her toes into the water, letting the soft roar of falling water drown out everything else.

The beaches, though—those became her sanctuary.

She'd walk the shoreline barefoot, her toes sinking into warm, sun-baked sand. The sun would kiss her skin as the sea breeze tangled through her hair. She loved to wade into the shallows, the tide swirling around her calves like a lover's touch, the water glittering with light. Here, she felt untethered. Light. As though the weight she'd carried for so long had finally slipped from her shoulders.

London had never suited her—not really. It had always felt too cold, too grey, too rushed. The crowded trains. The honking horns. The drizzling skies. The rigid roles everyone played. Back there, she was always running—toward deadlines, toward expectations, toward a future that someone else had sketched out for her.

But here?

Here, she could breathe.

And for the first time in years, she wasn't sure she wanted to go back.

Still, even in paradise, a quiet tension tugged at the edges of her joy—a creeping unease that whispered to her in moments of silence. Her life back home was unravelling, and no amount of turquoise water or tropical sun could completely silence the truth of it.

Rachel had always found clarity in music and movement. On the island, she poured herself into both. She was the lead dancer in the resort's nighttime shows, performing under open skies, her body moving to rhythms that stirred something deep within her.

The stage was nestled in a clearing near the beach, ringed with lanterns and flickering torches that cast a golden glow on everything they touched. Each night, she danced barefoot on the wooden platform as the sound of drums and island guitars swelled around her. The warm sea breeze brushed against her skin, mingling with the applause and the scent of salt and frangipani.

When she danced, she felt alive. She felt seen.

And for those fleeting hours, the world beyond the island disappeared. There was no London. No unanswered texts. No Jeremy.

Just the beat. Just her.

The other dancers had embraced her from the start. Their camaraderie was effortless—shared meals after late shows, laughter around bonfires on the beach, spontaneous dips in the ocean in full costume. They weren't just colleagues; they had become her island family.

The guests adored the performances. Some clapped politely, others offered compliments in passing. And every now and then, Rachel would catch a stranger's gaze lingering longer than expected—spellbound by the way she moved, as if she were something otherworldly.

But even in those dazzling, dreamlike moments, something coiled inside her.

Because this was temporary.

In just over a week, she'd be boarding a plane back to London. Back to chilly mornings and crowded tubes. Back to polite conversations that didn't quite mean anything. Back to a man she hadn't spoken to in days—a fiancé who felt more like a distant acquaintance with each passing call.

Back to a wedding she couldn't picture anymore.

The thought made her stomach knot.

She'd tried so hard to hold on to what they once were. But now, every time she thought about Jeremy—his clipped tone, his disinterest, the way she felt like a ghost in his world—a quiet voice whispered that maybe what they had wasn't what she wanted.

And maybe… it never had been.

When Jeremy had proposed, it had felt right.

It had been thrilling—sweeping her up in a whirlwind of champagne nights and whispered promises. The kind of love story she had dreamed about in her early twenties when everything felt possible and forever seemed only one decision away.

A romantic gesture from a man who checked all the right boxes: ambitious, charming, successful. A man who said all the right things.

But dreams, Rachel had learnt, had a way of shifting. Of revealing hairline cracks beneath polished surfaces. And lately, when she thought about Jeremy—not the memory of him, but the real, present version—she didn't feel excitement.

She felt doubt.

Did she love him the way she was supposed to?

The way a woman should love the man she was about to marry.

She wanted the answer to be yes. She wanted to believe that the strange heaviness in her chest was just a byproduct of the distance, the long calls that turned into short ones, the different time zones, the quiet unravelling of what they used to be. She wanted to believe it was temporary.

But deep down, beneath the carefully constructed excuses, she wasn't sure anymore.

And that truth scared her far more than the silence on the other end of the phone ever could.

She glanced at the clock.

Time to get ready.

With a soft sigh, Rachel pushed the thoughts aside—shoving them into that mental drawer she kept for things she wasn't ready to face—and stood. She crossed the cool tile floor of her bungalow and stepped into the bathroom, letting the door swing shut behind her.

Chapter Two

The warm spray of the shower welcomed her like a gentle embrace. She tilted her head back, letting the water cascade over her body, over the tight line of her shoulders, down her back. The tension she'd been holding there slowly began to melt.

She lingered longer than she needed to, letting the steady rhythm of the water drum against her skin. It was a simple thing, standing there in the steam, surrounded by the scent of coconut and frangipani, but it grounded her. It stripped away the noise—the voices in her head, the ache in her chest—and left only the moment.

There were no thoughts of wedding invitations or unanswered calls. No wondering where Jeremy was or why he no longer felt like home.

There was only this: water, warmth, breath. The faint, distant hum of the ocean just beyond her window.

When she finally stepped out, the air was thick with heat and lavender-scented mist. She wrapped herself in a towel and stood for a moment, staring at her reflection in the mirror. Her cheeks were flushed, her skin glowing from the steam. But it was her eyes she studied most—their grey depths slightly shadowed, searching.

She wasn't the same woman who had said yes to Jeremy's proposal.

She wasn't even sure who that woman had been anymore.

Rachel reached for the hairdryer, the noise filling the bathroom like a comforting shield. Her long, golden-blonde waves dried quickly in the island heat, the strands falling past her waist in glossy sheets. When they were nearly dry, she gathered them into a sleek, tight bun, smoothing each section with careful precision.

Her movements were practiced. Intentional.

Every tug and twist was part of the transformation—from woman with doubts to performer with purpose.

The show required focus. Control. Strength. Her bun had to hold through every leap, every spin, every moment she gave to the stage. No loose ends. No distractions.

She secured the final pin, her fingers lingering at the nape of her neck.

Tonight, she would dance. She would let the music move through her. And for a little while, she wouldn't have to think about London. Or Jeremy. Or the life waiting for her at the end of this island dream.

Just rhythm. Just movement. Just now.

Tonight was expected to be a full house.

A new boatload of guests had arrived that afternoon—fresh-faced honeymooners, seasoned travellers, families chasing the glow of paradise—and the staff had buzzed all day in anticipation. The first evening always mattered. It was the opening note of the island's song, the moment where strangers were invited to surrender to the rhythm, the beauty, the illusion. The resort prided itself on its entertainment, and Rachel knew the power of her role.

She didn't just perform. She set the tone. She was the heartbeat of the show.

Crossing her bungalow's small dressing space, she slid open the wardrobe doors. Inside hung a kaleidoscope of fabrics—flowing skirts in sun-drenched colours, sheer panels that caught the wind, beadwork that glittered under lantern light. Each piece was more than a costume; it was a story waiting to be told.

She paused, fingers brushing over a rich garnet silk before settling on tonight's choice: a two-piece ensemble in deep sapphire blue. The fabric was featherlight and fluid, designed to ripple like water with every step, every spin. The skirt dipped low on her hips, edged with delicate silver beading that shimmered like starlight. The top was fitted and cropped, embroidered with intricate silver thread that gleamed under stage lights.

It was sensual. Regal. A visual echo of the sea after dusk.

She slipped into the outfit, adjusting the beaded waistband until it sat just right. Her fingers smoothed over the fabric with practiced ease, but something about the act felt different tonight—more deliberate, more weighted.

In front of the mirror, she reached for her makeup kit. Her hands moved on autopilot, though her thoughts lingered elsewhere.

Stage makeup was its own kind of mask—bolder than her everyday face, designed to captivate from meters away. She swept a smoky shadow over her lids, winged her eyeliner with precision, and coated her lashes in thick black. A touch of shimmering highlighter kissed her cheekbones. Her lips she stained in a deep, sultry red—a colour that said power, presence, performance.

By the time she was finished, the transformation was complete.

The woman in the mirror stared back at her, confident and poised. A dancer. A siren. A living piece of the island's magic.

But behind the kohl-lined eyes and radiant skin, Rachel saw the shadow of her unease—quiet but constant. The weight of the choices she wasn't ready to make. The life in London waiting for her like an unopened letter. A fiancé she barely recognised anymore.

She pressed her palms to the edge of the vanity, grounding herself.

Not now.

Tonight, there were no questions. No ring on her finger. No city waiting with cool skies and colder realities. There was only music, and light, and the way her body came alive when she danced.

Drawing in a slow breath, she turned from the mirror, the soft chime of her skirt's beadwork following her like a whisper.

Outside, the air was thick with the scent of jasmine and ocean breeze. The open-air theatre came into view as she wound through the lush resort paths—lanterns glowing amber against the encroaching dusk, the murmurs of anticipation growing louder.

Guests were already gathering in the tiered seating area, their conversations low and eager. Candles flickered on the tables, casting gold against crystal glasses and white linen. The stage waited, quiet for now, lit only by strings of overhead lights that swayed in the evening breeze.

Rachel's heart beat in time with the waves.

Tonight, she would lose herself in the dance.

And for a little while, everything else—London, Jeremy, the choices looming at the edge of her island dream—could wait.

The open-air theatre sat like a jewel nestled in the heart of the resort, cradled by swaying palm trees and framed by the dark silhouette of the rainforest beyond. Flickering torches lined the perimeter, their golden flames casting soft, dancing shadows across the polished wooden stage. Overhead, the sky had deepened to a velvety indigo, scattered with stars that shimmered like spilled diamonds across the horizon. A half-moon hung low, silver and watching.

The air was rich with scent—sea salt, frangipani, and jasmine—all carried on a soft, salt-kissed breeze that whispered through the palms. Somewhere in the distance, the ocean murmured against the shore, its steady rhythm echoing like a heartbeat beneath the growing anticipation.

As Rachel stepped backstage, a familiar current of energy wrapped around her—electric, urgent, alive. It buzzed through the performers as they stretched and checked their marks, through the stagehands as they gave cues and double-checked lighting positions. Laughter and nervous chatter mingled with the final notes of the pre-show playlist, the melodies drifting out toward the crowd like a promise.

She moved easily through the space, her bare feet soundless against the worn wooden boards. Her sapphire costume shimmered with each step, catching the torchlight and throwing tiny flecks of silver onto the darkened curtains around her.

"Hi, Sam! How was your day?" she asked, sliding one last pin into place at the nape of her neck, securing her sleek bun with practiced precision.

Sam glanced over, grinning as he adjusted the cuff of his sleeve. "Not bad. Spent most of it baking on the beach while you were off being mysterious."

Rachel laughed. "Mysterious is part of my charm."

He arched a brow. "Is that what we're calling it now?"

Sam was as solid as they came—tall, broad-shouldered, with sun-kissed skin and a mop of blond hair that always looked just a bit too perfect. Guests loved him, and why wouldn't they? He was charming, graceful, and an incredible dancer. But for Rachel, he was more than that—he was her partner in every sense that mattered on stage. Reliable. Steady. In tune with her rhythms like he could hear her thoughts before she spoke them.

"You ready for a lively crowd?" he asked, rolling his shoulders as he glanced toward the curtains.

Rachel followed his gaze. Beyond the soft glow of lanterns and flickering candlelight, the theatre seats were filled. A full house. She could hear the clink of glasses, low conversations, occasional laughter—the unmistakable hum of an audience on the cusp of being swept away.

"Definitely," she said, her voice low with anticipation. "First-night energy is always the best."

Sam nodded. "Let's make them remember it."

She smiled at that. Because that was the part she loved most—not just the dancing or the applause, but the way the performance made people feel. How, for a moment, everything else disappeared. It was connection. Emotion. Escape.

Tonight's routine was a showpiece—an intoxicating blend of Latin fire, jazz precision, and the fluid elegance of contemporary dance. It was a celebration of movement, of chemistry, of control. Fast-paced, physical, intricate. It demanded more than just technique—it demanded trust.

And after months of performing together, she and Sam had it down to an art. Every glance was a cue, every breath a shared beat. They moved like twin flames— unpredictable yet always in sync.

As the final song on the pre-show playlist faded into silence, a hush settled over the crowd like a held breath.

The torches flared slightly in the breeze. The stage lights brightened, casting a warm golden glow across the floorboards. Shadows receded. The air thickened with anticipation.

Rachel closed her eyes for a beat and drew in a deep, grounding breath. Her heart was already dancing, every pulse in her body alive with the thrill of what was coming.

She stepped into the wings, her bare foot brushing the edge of the stage.

The silence grew deeper.

Then—the music began.

A pulsing rhythm. A heartbeat wrapped in melody. The world beyond the theatre slipped away.

Rachel opened her eyes.

Showtime.

The performance opened with a sultry, tango-inspired duet—an intimate conversation told through movement, full of tension, grace, and unspoken promises. The music was rich and evocative, its deep, pulsing rhythm underscoring each step, each glance, each breath. Rachel moved in perfect harmony with Sam, their bodies orbiting one another in fluid, magnetic circles.

His grip was firm yet fluid, guiding her through dramatic dips and sweeping turns. Their limbs brushed, their torsos aligned, their feet finding impossible synchronicity as they wove a story of desire and resistance. The flick of her wrist, the arch of her back, the calculated pause just before she leaned into his touch—none of it was accidental. They weren't just dancing. They were performing alchemy.

Then, as if the island itself exhaled, the music shifted—tempo quickening, melody brightening—and the tango's simmering heat gave way to the sun-drenched vibrancy of a fast-paced salsa. The audience clapped instinctively, drawn in by the infectious rhythm that reverberated through the open-air theatre like a living heartbeat.

Rachel's hips swayed in mesmerising sync with the beat, her feet gliding across the stage with barely a whisper of sound. Sam matched her with effortless precision, spinning her out and back again, his movements powerful but graceful. Laughter and gasps of delight rose from the crowd as the dance escalated, the chemistry between the pair igniting the stage like fire meeting oxygen.

The transitions between routines were seamless—styles blending and bleeding into one another like watercolour strokes. Latin merged into contemporary, tango giving way to lyrical expression, complex footwork melting into elegant lifts. At one point, Sam lifted Rachel high above his head, her body stretching into a perfect arc, back bowed, arms extended like wings. The audience collectively held their breath—then erupted into applause as she landed softly, her feet striking the floor with pinpoint control.

Energy surged through her veins like lightning. The music didn't just guide her—it possessed her. Each step was a release, each movement a surrender. And through it all, she was aware of the audience not as faces, but as one collective force—leaning forward, breathing with her, caught in the spell.

Between dance sequences, Rachel and Sam sang in harmony. His voice was deep and velvety, grounding; hers floated above it, clear and bright, with just a hint of huskiness that made the notes feel lived-in. They sang in English, Creole, and soft lilts of Spanish, blending languages as effortlessly as they blended rhythms.

The songs were chosen not just to entertain, but to evoke. To seduce. To make the audience feel something they didn't know they needed. Love, joy, longing, freedom.

And it worked.

Rachel could see it in their expressions—the way guests leaned in, their eyes wide, their fingers tapping unconsciously in time with the music. The way even the most jaded traveller allowed themselves to be pulled into the moment.

For this one hour, they belonged to her.

As the final notes swelled and the last crescendo rose, Rachel struck her closing pose—one leg extended, chest lifted, breath racing. Sam mirrored her perfectly beside her, his chest rising and falling in time with hers.

A split second of stillness.

Then the crowd exploded.

Thunderous applause rolled through the theatre like a wave, punctuated by whistles, cheers, and even a few whoops from guests now standing in ovation. The sound crashed over her, thrilling and overwhelming.

Adrenaline surged through her body, white-hot and euphoric. For a moment, everything else—the doubts, the ache of indecision, the cold weight of London—faded to nothing.

Here, under the lanterns strung like stars and the heat of the stage lights, with the scent of salt and sweat and wildflowers in the air, Rachel felt utterly alive.

This, she thought, is who I am.

At least… for now.

But as the applause rose, her gaze swept the audience—searching, almost without intention—and locked onto something unexpected.

Or rather… someone.

Chapter Three

A man sat alone at a front-row table, set slightly apart from the clusters of guests still clapping and chatting enthusiastically. He wasn't the type to draw attention—not in the way of loud laughter or flashy clothes. But somehow, he commanded the space around him.

He was still. Composed. Watching her.

Even in the low flicker of candlelight, he stood out. His dark hair was neat but not overly styled, a touch tousled as if he'd raked a hand through it earlier and forgotten to smooth it back. His features were striking—sharp cheekbones, a strong jaw, and a mouth that looked like it could curve into a devastating smile, though it didn't now.

But it was his eyes that caught her breath.

Deep. Focused. Disarming in their intensity.

He wasn't watching her like a tourist admiring a pretty performer.

He was studying her. Seeing her. Not just the dancer—but the woman beneath the sequins and spotlight.

Rachel was used to being watched. Admired. Even desired. She could spot flirtation from a hundred feet away. Could feel the heat of it on her skin like a second spotlight.

But this… this was different.

His gaze felt like a question. A challenge.

And she had no idea how to answer it.

For the briefest moment, her poise faltered. Not enough for the audience to notice—but she felt it. A ripple of something… unfamiliar.

She looked away.

The crowd was still applauding as she and Sam took their final bows, bowing low in unison before slipping offstage. Her heart still pounded, but the beat had changed. Not adrenaline. Not entirely.

Something else.

Something new.

As the curtains closed and the music faded into memory, Rachel exhaled deeply. She rolled her shoulders back, trying to release the tension that had crept in during those last few seconds. But it clung to her skin like humidity.

Not from the dance.

From him.

Backstage, voices swirled—praise, laughter, high-fives. But Rachel moved through it all in a daze, her mind lingering on the stranger with the unreadable expression and the eyes that saw far too much.

Sam appeared at her side in a heartbeat, practically buzzing with post-show energy, his skin still glowing under the backstage lights.

"Did you see the hunk in the front row?" he asked, eyes wide with mock scandal and mischief. "Front and centre. Smouldering. Silent. A total brooding god. I almost forgot my steps."

Rachel reached for a towel, dabbing at the light sheen of sweat along her collarbone, doing her best to maintain a nonchalant tone. "Yes, I noticed him."

Sam gave her a knowing side glance. "Noticed? Honey, he looked like he was ready to devour you with his eyes. I'm surprised the stage didn't catch fire."

Rachel let out a quiet huff of laughter, though her pulse still hadn't quite returned to normal. "Don't be ridiculous. He was watching both of us."

"Mmm," Sam drawled, unconvinced. He nudged her with his elbow, cocking a perfectly groomed brow. "No, babe. Trust me. I know when I'm being watched— and he wasn't watching me. He didn't blink the entire tango. I swear I could feel his eyes dragging over you like velvet."

Rachel rolled her eyes, but her mouth twitched at the corners.

"Maybe he just likes dance," she said, but her voice lacked conviction. Because even now, as she stood backstage, wrapped in a towel and sweat and the fading rush of applause, she could still feel the echo of that stranger's gaze. Not leering, not obvious. But focused. Intense. Curious.

And it had gotten under her skin in a way that no look ever had.

Sam waggled his brows dramatically. "I think you've got yourself an admirer, Rach. And not the usual honeymooner type, either. He had CEO energy. Mysterious. Reserved. And those hands? Whew. I would not mind being scandalous with him in a hammock."

Rachel barked a laugh, grateful for Sam's flair. "Well, according to the official resort handbook, fraternising with guests is strictly forbidden." She lifted her chin with mock seriousness. "So, he's out of luck."

Sam sighed, placing a hand over his heart. "Such a waste of good cheekbones."

"Go for it, lover boy," she teased. "Maybe he's into cheeky blondes with fast feet."

Sam winked. "If he's not, he should be."

Their laughter lingered in the air like the last note of a melody, easy and familiar. Rachel was grateful for Sam's presence, the way he always knew how to diffuse the swirl of thoughts she kept tightly coiled beneath the surface.

He tilted his head. "What are you doing now? Want to grab a drink? I need to ride this adrenaline high, or I won't sleep for hours."

Rachel hesitated.

Just for a second.

The weight of that stranger's stare was still there, like a phantom touch on the back of her neck. Her mind was trying to brush it off, but her body hadn't gotten the message. Her skin tingled. Her chest felt tight. It was ridiculous.

He was just a guest.

Just a pair of dark eyes and a sculpted jaw in a sea of passing faces.

And yet…

She cleared her throat and forced a smile. "Yeah, sure. Why not? Meet you out front when I get changed."

"Perfect," Sam said, giving her a peck on the cheek. "Don't keep me waiting, diva."

As he sauntered down the hallway, his towel slung dramatically over his shoulder, Rachel stayed where she was, fingers tightening around the cotton draped over hers.

She'd been performing on this island for months.

She'd danced for hundreds of strangers. Guests who came for a few nights, maybe a week. They watched, they applauded, they moved on.

None of them had ever left a mark.

None of them had ever made her feel seen in the way that one silent man had in a single, electrifying moment.

And that terrified her more than she was willing to admit.

Rachel made her way to the changing area, the muted sounds of applause and laughter still echoing faintly in her ears. Inside the private shower stall, she turned on the water and let the stream pour over her, rinsing away the glitter, sweat, and residual high of the performance. The water was warm, soothing, a gentle contrast to the adrenaline that had been buzzing in her limbs.

She tilted her head back and closed her eyes, letting the cascade work through the tension in her neck and shoulders. The tango, the lifts, the chorus—it had all gone perfectly. But even in the afterglow of the show, his gaze lingered.

The stranger.

It wasn't just the way he looked at her—it was the way she felt being seen. As if he wasn't just admiring her performance, but reading her, layer by layer.

Rachel exhaled sharply, as if she could steam the thought away with the heat of the water.

Focus.

She turned off the shower, wrapping herself in one of the thick resort towels. Moving to the mirror, she began undoing the pins from her hair, releasing the tight bun until soft waves tumbled down her back in a golden cascade. She shook her hair out gently, watching as it framed her face—sun-kissed, flushed from the performance, alive.

Reaching into her bag, she rummaged for something to wear, her fingers brushing over linen, silk, cotton—until they stilled on something unexpected.

She pulled it out slowly.

The burnt-orange dress.

She had packed it on a whim back in London, unsure why. It wasn't island wear—too fitted, too bold. It clung in all the right places and demanded a confidence she hadn't been sure she'd have.

Rachel hesitated, her eyes drifting to her reflection.

Why not?

She stepped into the dress and pulled it up over her hips, smoothing the fabric over her curves. The colour brought out the warmth in her skin, deepened by months under the sun, and the soft sheen of the fabric caught the low light as she moved.

She studied herself for a long moment.

The woman in the mirror wasn't the same woman who had landed here with tired eyes and the weight of too many questions. This woman stood taller. There was something lighter in her gaze, something quieter but stronger.

Not someone who had all the answers.

But someone who'd finally stopped being afraid of asking the questions.

She considered makeup, even reached for her lip gloss, but paused. Tonight wasn't about impressing anyone.

Except maybe… herself.

She slipped on a pair of delicate strappy sandals, grabbed her small clutch, and stepped out into the night.

The evening air wrapped around her like silk—warm, balmy, rich with the scent of salt and tropical blooms. Somewhere in the distance, laughter floated from the bar, along with the mellow hum of music and clinking glasses.

Sam was waiting by the entrance to the open-air bar, leaning casually against a wide wooden pillar, his white shirt rolled at the sleeves, collar open. His easy charm was impossible to miss—but it was the genuine grin he gave when he saw her that warmed her chest.

He let out a low whistle. "Well, damn. Haven't seen that dress before."

Rachel smoothed her hands self-consciously down the sides of the dress, suddenly second-guessing. "I forgot I packed it. It's not too much, is it?"

Sam straightened, giving her a slow once-over with theatrical reverence. "Nope. Not too much. Just the right amount of stunning."

She rolled her eyes but couldn't hide the smile tugging at her lips. "Flatterer."

"Only when I mean it," he said, his grin softening into something almost tender. "You look… beautiful, Rach."

Her smile faltered slightly, caught off-guard by the quiet sincerity in his tone.

But before the moment could turn, Sam swept into a playful bow and offered his arm. "Shall we, my lady?"

Laughing, she looped her arm through his. "Let's go before I change my mind and throw on a sarong."

"I'd still be impressed," he said easily as they began walking.

They strolled along the torch-lit path toward the bar, the tropical air humming with energy. Laughter drifted ahead of them, accompanied by soft live music—the lazy strum of a guitar, the occasional beat of a bongo drum.

But beneath the familiar rhythm of the night, Rachel felt something new—like the slow unfurling of something she hadn't realised had been wound tight inside her.

Tonight wasn't about the performance. It wasn't about Jeremy, or London, or the choices she wasn't ready to make.

Tonight was hers.

As they strolled down the sandy path, the night wrapped itself around them like a silk shawl—warm, fragrant, and thick with salt and the heavy perfume of blooming hibiscus and plumeria. The air shimmered with life. Glasses clinked in the distance, waves whispered softly against the shore, and laughter spilled from open-air lounges like champagne overflowing from a glass.

Music drifted on the breeze—low and rhythmic, the slow strum of acoustic strings beneath a steady percussive beat. It pulsed softly beneath the stars, a quiet heartbeat that belonged only to this island night.

Rachel let herself fall into the rhythm of it all—the sound of Sam's footsteps beside hers, the scent of the sea in her hair, the brush of warm air across her collarbone. Sam chatted easily about the show, the crowd, his own minor mishaps on stage, and she responded with light quips and easy smiles. It was familiar. Safe.

But beneath the surface, a current ran through her—low and constant. A flicker of something unshaped and elusive. Not nerves. Not exactly.

A restless kind of awareness.

Was it the afterglow of the performance? Or was it something else?

They reached the entrance to the bar, framed by strings of golden lanterns swaying lazily in the ocean breeze. The lights bathed the path in a soft amber glow, casting flickers of light across the sand like fireflies in flight.

Inside, the open-air space unfolded like a secret sanctuary—low, rustic beams overhead, carved wooden tables scattered throughout, flickering candles set in hurricane glass. The scent of spiced rum, roasted sugar, coconut, and citrus hung in the air like a welcome. Conversations overlapped in melodic waves, rising and falling, a murmur of joy and warmth that wrapped around the room like a favourite song.

Rachel's gaze swept the space, taking in the clusters of couples nestled in corners, groups of friends raising glasses, solo travellers writing in notebooks or gazing out at the night sea. It was vibrant, intimate—beautiful in its unstudied elegance.

And then—she saw him.

Near the back, half cloaked in the shadows cast by a tall palm tree and a flickering wall sconce, he sat with quiet, effortless composure. He didn't lean. He didn't lounge. He simply was—his presence settled like gravity.

The candlelight traced over his features, carving them in sharp relief. A clean, strong jawline. High cheekbones. The faintest furrow between his brows, as if deep in thought. His dark hair was neatly styled, though there was something unruly about it, like he'd been through a storm or run his hands through it a hundred times since sunset.

But it was his eyes that caught her. Stopped her cold.

Dark. Focused. Still. And locked entirely—unmistakably—on her.

He held a tumbler of something amber, his fingers resting lightly against the glass, one long finger circling the rim as though lost in absentminded thought. But there was nothing absent about his gaze.

He wasn't simply watching.

He was seeing.

And Rachel, for one fragile second, forgot how to breathe.

The air between them charged in an instant—silent but electric, like the atmosphere just before a summer storm. Her heartbeat kicked, a flutter in her chest, too sudden, too strong. A warm pressure bloomed low in her stomach. A flicker of something she hadn't felt in a long, long time.

Not desire.

Not exactly.

Recognition.

As if some part of her already knew him and had merely been waiting for their eyes to meet.

She should've looked away.

Should've laughed it off.

But she stood still, caught in the space between instinct and curiosity, held by something in that gaze that made her feel like the only thing in the room still moving.

He didn't smile. Didn't nod. Didn't look away.

And neither did she.

Then—

"Stop staring at lover boy," Sam whispered beside her, nudging her lightly with his elbow.

Rachel blinked, as if surfacing from a dream. She turned to him, a nervous laugh slipping past her lips. "I wasn't staring."

Sam's grin was full of amusement and mischief. "You definitely were."

She shook her head, trying to summon a sense of normalcy. "He's just another guest."

"Sure," Sam said, unconvinced. "And I'm just here for the snacks."

With a huff of reluctant laughter, she let him guide her toward the bar. But as they moved, Rachel could still feel the stranger's gaze at her back, like heat from a flame she wasn't ready to touch.

Her pulse hadn't slowed.

Her hands felt suddenly empty, restless.

And no matter how she tried to dismiss it, one thing was very clear:

Whoever he was, he had just stepped into her world like a question she didn't know how to answer.

Chapter Four

Darcy Williams sat at the back of the bar, his sharp gaze sweeping over the space as he nursed a glass of whiskey. He wasn't here to relax. He was here to observe—to analyse, to decide exactly what needed to change.

The eco-friendly resort had potential, but it was outdated. The aesthetics were charming, but the infrastructure needed work. Service was good, but not exceptional. The entertainment, while lively, could either be a standout feature or a forgettable addition. That was what he needed to determine. He hadn't bought this place just to keep it running—he intended to improve and modernise it, bringing it up to the high standards of his other properties.

At thirty-four, he was a self-made billionaire, a man who had built his empire from nothing. He now owned twenty boutique hotels and resorts around the world, each one carefully curated to be both luxurious and highly profitable. This resort was his latest acquisition, finalised only a week ago. He hadn't announced himself to the staff yet. Before making any sweeping changes, he wanted to experience the place as a guest, to see firsthand what worked and what didn't.

He had spent the past few days making mental notes—on the staff, the food, the facilities. But tonight, something unexpected had happened.

Tonight, he had watched the nightly entertainment, expecting something standard. He had seen countless resort performances before—some polished, some amateurish—but none that had truly held his attention. This time was different.

The show had been vibrant, polished, and engaging. But what had truly caught his attention was the lead female dancer.

She was captivating.

From the moment she stepped onto the stage, she owned it. Every movement was fluid yet precise, her presence magnetic. She wasn't just dancing—she was telling a story, drawing the audience into the rhythm, into the world she created with every step, every turn, every flick of her golden head.

And then she sang.

Her voice had stunned him. It was rich, velvety, full of depth and emotion. It wasn't just technical perfection—it was the way she infused every lyric with feeling, as if she wasn't just performing, but living the song. It sent a shiver through the audience, holding them spellbound. She was more than just a dancer. She was a performer in every sense of the word, someone who could command a stage with nothing but sheer talent and presence.

Darcy had seen some of the best performances in luxury hotels and world-class venues, yet none had made him sit up and take notice quite like this.

And then there was her.

She was stunning. That much was undeniable. But it wasn't just her beauty—it was the way she carried herself, the raw energy she exuded, the way she lost herself so completely in the music. She was utterly unselfconscious in her movements, not performing for attention, but because it was who she was. It intrigued him.

And now, she was here.

He had spotted her the moment she walked into the bar. She had changed out of her stage outfit, now dressed in a fitted burnt-orange dress that hugged her figure in a way that made it impossible not to notice. The fabric skimmed over her curves, accentuating the graceful lines of her body. Her long, wavy golden-blonde hair cascaded down to her waist, shimmering under the dim lighting of the bar. Without the stage makeup and the dazzling costumes, she was even more breathtaking— effortlessly stunning, with an air of confidence that made her stand out even in a crowded room.

She moved with the same effortless confidence she had on stage, but now, there was something different. Offstage, she wasn't performing. She was just herself.

And for some reason, he found himself wanting to know more.

Her gaze swept the room, casual but searching. And then their eyes met.

The moment their gazes locked, something shifted. It was a flicker of awareness, a silent pull, as if the air between them had suddenly thickened. He saw the moment she registered him—not just as another guest, but as someone who had been watching.

She didn't look away.

Neither did he.

Darcy wasn't a man who indulged in distractions.

Not in boardrooms. Not in business. Not in life.

He was here on the island for one reason: to evaluate a resort he'd just added to his growing portfolio of properties. It was business, pure and simple. He had an itinerary, a checklist, and a mental catalogue of inefficiencies already forming in his mind.

And yet—there he sat. Half-finished drink in hand. Not thinking about structural integrity or underwhelming spa menus.

He was watching her.

Across the bar, bathed in the low, golden flicker of lantern light, she was laughing with the tall blond dancer—her stage partner, the one who had lifted her like she weighed nothing, who had guided her through the tango as if they'd been dancing together for years.

Her laugh was effortless, open, musical.

Darcy's jaw tightened in spite of himself.

She moved through the room like she belonged to it. No—like it belonged to her. Each step had the same unconscious elegance as her dancing, as though the line between performance and real life blurred wherever she went. She drew glances, quiet stares, subtle admiration from others around the bar.

Darcy wasn't immune.

And he hated that.

He watched as the blond man leaned closer, said something that made her tilt her head and laugh harder, brushing her hand over her heart. Their ease with each other—her familiarity with him—irritated Darcy in a way he refused to examine.

It's irrelevant.

She was a performer. A staff member. A name he didn't even know, in a resort he now owned.

And yet… when she smiled, when she tucked a strand of gold-blonde hair behind her ear with a careless flick of her fingers, Darcy felt something shift inside him.

A slow pull.

Unfamiliar.

Unwanted.

But impossible to ignore.

For the first time in longer than he could remember, the spreadsheets, the projections, the business strategy receded from the front of his mind.

Because for the first time in a long while—

Work wasn't the most interesting thing in the room.

Then came the interruption.

Another man approached—young, tanned, and radiating the kind of confidence that came from years of being told yes. He wore a linen shirt unbuttoned too far, a grin too smooth. Darcy didn't need to hear the exchange to know the type.

The young man said something, gestured toward the dance floor, already assuming she'd agree.

Darcy's eyes narrowed.

Sam, the dancer, stepped aside with a knowing grin, offering no interference. But she—Darcy's dancer, as some treacherous part of him kept calling her—simply tilted her head. Calm. Amused. Unmoved.

Then she lifted her hand.

The motion was subtle. A soft, almost apologetic smile. A flash of a delicate gold band on her ring finger.

Engaged.

Darcy's stomach dropped, then twisted. Not in disappointment—he refused to call it that—but in something closer to unease. Something sharp and sour he hadn't expected.

The young man blinked, recovered, and gave a good-natured shrug before drifting off into the crowd, brushing off rejection like it was nothing. Sam leaned back in with a teasing look, nudging her side. She laughed again, brushing her fingers over the ring in an unconscious gesture. Protective. Possessive.

Darcy exhaled slowly, his grip tightening around his glass.

It shouldn't matter.

It didn't matter.

And yet.

He rolled the whiskey between his palms, staring into the amber swirl. His reflection shimmered faintly on the surface—cool, composed, detached. All the things he was known for.

So why couldn't he look away?

He'd spent his adult life surrounded by beautiful women—effortlessly polished socialites, poised entrepreneurs, actresses with practiced charm. They came into his world like art pieces: exquisite, admired, and ultimately interchangeable.

But this woman…

She was different.

There was no artifice. No pretence.

Just presence.

And power.

Maybe it was the way she danced. Or the sound of her voice. Or the fact that, despite everything, he still hadn't figured her out—and he was a man who prided himself on knowing everything.

This is ridiculous.

Up close, she'd lose some of that allure. He'd built her up in his mind—crafted her out of stage lights and island heat. She was a moment, not a reality.

Only one way to find out.

Darcy set his glass down with quiet finality and rose from his seat.

He moved through the tables with unhurried purpose, every step deliberate, his expression unreadable.

He wasn't headed for her.

Not really.

He just needed another drink.

Or so he told himself.

But as he reached the bar, he found himself angling closer to her. Close enough to hear the soft cadence of her voice, to catch the subtle scent of her skin—coconut, vanilla, something clean and sun-warmed.

Close enough to see the fine golden freckles that dusted her shoulders. The gentle slope of her collarbone. The way her lips curved when she smiled, slow and genuine.

And close enough to realise, with a mix of awe and reluctant frustration, that she was even more captivating offstage than on it.

He turned to face the bar, signalling the bartender with a flick of his fingers. But his focus didn't shift from her.

Not really.

Because for all his control, all his rules, all his reasons for being here—

He couldn't deny it anymore.

He wanted to know her.

Chapter Five

"Watch out, Rach. Lover boy's headed this way," Sam murmured under his breath, barely concealing his amusement.

Rachel didn't flinch. Didn't turn. She kept her gaze on the rim of her glass, swirling the contents slowly. "He's just getting a drink," she said, voice low and even. "You're reading too much into it."

Sam snorted. "No, I'm reading it exactly right. That man is not wandering. He's on a mission—and I'm fairly certain the mission has something to do with you."

She rolled her eyes, but her fingers betrayed her—tightening ever so slightly around the cool stem of her glass.

And then she felt it.

That quiet weight of his gaze. Heavy and still. Like a hand pressed lightly against her spine.

She didn't have to look to know it was him.

Her pulse jumped, that stubborn thump of awareness beating against her ribs like a warning.

She didn't know him. Didn't know his name, where he was from, what he wanted. He was just another guest—one of dozens she'd performed for over the past three months. A stranger, passing through.

And yet…

There was something about him. Something that made her skin tighten, her breath catch. He hadn't even spoken to her, and already, he occupied space in her mind like a man she'd known for years.

She lifted her drink to her lips, took a long, measured sip. The cold liquid did little to cool the flicker of heat curling in her stomach. An ache born of pure awareness. It was maddening—uninvited, unwelcome, and entirely out of her control.

You're engaged; she reminded herself.

This wasn't anything.

It couldn't be.

Behind the bar, the bartender reached for a familiar bottle and poured with practiced ease. A glass slid across the polished wood.

"Another whiskey?"

A pause.

Then came the reply. Deep. Steady.

"Yes."

Her breath stilled.

That voice…

It was smooth, but with an undercurrent of gravel. Polished and masculine, laced with quiet command. It wasn't loud, yet it cut clean through the noise of the bar, through the chatter, music, and laughter. The kind of voice people turned toward—not because it demanded attention, but because it already had it.

Rachel blinked, her fingers tightening on her glass. Something inside her dipped, unsteady.

What is wrong with you?

She didn't turn.

She wouldn't.

And then—of course—Sam did exactly what she'd been praying he wouldn't do.

"Hello," he said brightly, spinning slightly on his stool toward the man in question.

Rachel closed her eyes and exhaled through her nose. She barely resisted the urge to elbow him.

Subtlety was not Sam's strong suit.

There was a moment of silence. A stretch of breathless stillness. Then the stranger spoke.

"Evening."

Simple.

Unhurried.

His tone wasn't flirtatious. Wasn't aggressive. It was composed, calm, but with that same undercurrent of control Rachel had felt from him across the room.

The air between them shifted—denser somehow, like the moment before a storm rolled in.

She turned, slowly, carefully, as if giving her body time to brace itself.

And when their eyes met, the world tilted.

Up close, he was even more striking. His features were sharply defined—strong jaw, straight nose, eyes so dark they seemed to draw the light from around them. He was dressed in a simple charcoal button-down and slate trousers, tailored perfectly to his lean, powerful frame. Understated. Elegant. Lethal.

And his eyes—God, his eyes. Steady. Watchful. As if he was trying to figure her out in real time and didn't plan to stop until he had.

She held his gaze, refusing to flinch—even though something in her chest tightened under the weight of it.

"Hi," she said smoothly, though her voice felt a touch too steady. Controlled. She wasn't sure if she was trying to keep him at arm's length—or keep herself from slipping.

"You two were the dancers in the entertainment tonight, right?"

Rachel nodded, mustering a polite smile. Light. Professional. Detached. He was just another guest—nothing more, nothing less.

"Yes, we were. I hope you enjoyed it?" She replied, her voice soft but clear.

His gaze didn't waver. Didn't roam. He looked at her like he saw her—not just the performer from the stage, but the woman behind it. And that was what made her pulse skip.

"I did," he said, his lips curving into a slow, deliberate smile. "Very much."

There was something in his tone—something that wrapped around her like warm silk, unspoken but undeniable.

Then, with quiet confidence, he extended his hand. "I'm Darcy."

She hesitated only a beat before reaching for it.

The moment their palms met, something sharp and electric jolted through her—an unexpected surge of heat that travelled from her hand up her arm and straight to her core. Her breath caught, subtle but real, and her fingers instinctively curled into his before she forced herself to pull back.

She hoped he hadn't noticed the way her skin flushed or the way her stomach fluttered like a traitor.

"Rachel," she said, tucking a loose strand of hair behind her ear in a half-conscious attempt to anchor herself. "And this is Sam."

Sam, blissfully unaware of the tension thickening between them, gave Darcy a firm handshake. "Nice to meet you, Darcy. You here alone?"

"Yeah," Darcy replied easily. His grip was firm, his voice even. "Just needed a break from the grind. This place seemed like a good spot to get away."

"It is that," Sam agreed with a grin, lifting his glass. "No better place to lose time and pretend the outside world doesn't exist."

Darcy's gaze flicked back to Rachel. "And you? You work here full-time?"

She shook her head, golden-blonde strands sliding over her shoulder in soft waves. "Just a short-term contract. Three months." Her voice turned quieter. "I leave next week."

Something subtle shifted in Darcy's expression. A brief flicker of… disappointment? Regret?

"Shame," he said quietly, more to himself than anyone else.

Rachel glanced at him from the corner of her eye. It was a simple word. A throwaway, really. But somehow, it lodged itself under her skin and stayed there.

"It is," Sam added, nudging her playfully. "I'm going to miss Rach around here."

Rachel rolled her eyes at him with a smile. "I'll miss you too. But you'll survive."

Darcy watched their easy exchange with measured interest. The way they joked, nudged, laughed—it hinted at closeness, but not the romantic kind. He saw the platonic rhythm in it, the lack of tension in their body language. That… was interesting.

His eyes returned to Rachel. "Why only three months?" he asked, his tone casual but layered with curiosity.

Rachel paused, then answered with a quiet honesty. "The resort needed a lead dancer for the season, and it felt like a good opportunity. A change. Something… different."

There was something wistful in her voice—faint, but unmistakable.

Darcy noted the way she ran her fingers along the condensation on her glass, as if drawing patterns she didn't realise she was making. Her gaze drifted briefly to the open air beyond the bar, to the shadows of palm trees swaying gently in the breeze.

She wasn't just passing through. She was escaping something.

She wore no makeup now, but she didn't need any. Her beauty was understated and striking all at once. Her grey eyes—cool and stormy—seemed both guarded and endlessly expressive. And those lips… full, soft, parted slightly as if they held something she wasn't ready to say.

His fingers tightened slightly around his glass, and an intrusive thought whispered through his mind before he could stop it:

Those are the kind of lips meant to be kissed.

He blinked once, sharply, and shifted in his seat, redirecting his attention back to the conversation.

"And after the contract ends?" he asked, lifting his drink. "Back home?"

Rachel nodded, brushing her fingers over the base of her glass. "Back to London," she said quietly. "Back to reality."

There was no warmth in her voice. No enthusiasm. Just resignation—soft, tired, and too heavy for someone who had just finished performing with such fire.

Darcy watched her carefully. "Not looking forward to it?"

A pause.

Then, her smile wavered. Just slightly. "It's complicated."

That again.

His eyes flicked briefly to her left hand. The ring.

Complicated.

He took a slow sip, letting the taste settle. He knew better than to ask. He didn't even know her. Didn't have a right.

But he wanted to.

And that, more than anything, was the problem.

"How long are you here for?" Sam asked, swirling the ice in his glass with a casual grin that masked the glint of mischief in his eyes.

Darcy leaned an elbow on the bar, the dim golden light brushing the edge of his jaw. "A couple of weeks," he replied smoothly, though his gaze remained anchored on Rachel. "Any recommendations on how I should spend my time?"

Rachel welcomed the change of topic with a small smile, grateful for the reprieve from the low hum of tension curling between her and the stranger who now had a name—and a voice she hadn't stopped hearing in her head since he spoke.

"The beaches are incredible," she offered, shifting slightly in her seat. "The water's warm, the sand's like powder, and if you're up early enough, the sunrise will ruin you for all others."

Before she could continue, Sam smirked into his drink. "Especially when Rachel's there," he added, elbowing her lightly. "She looks damn good in a bikini."

Rachel shot him a sharp look, her cheeks flushing instantly. "He's joking," she said quickly, her voice a little too bright. "Ignore him."

Darcy's lips twitched at the corners, not quite a smile—but close. His eyes flicked over her, slower than before, thoughtful. "I bet he's not," he said, voice low, just rough enough to make her breath catch.

It wasn't lewd. It wasn't crude. But it landed in the space between them like a dropped match.

Rachel shifted in her seat, fingers tightening around her glass. She was used to attention—admiring glances, flirtatious comments, the occasional overly confident guest who mistook her performance for an invitation. But Darcy's gaze wasn't like that. It didn't leer. It didn't linger too long.

It studied. It remembered.

And it made her feel… seen. In a way that went far beneath skin and sequins.

"Well," she said, folding her arms loosely across her chest in mock defiance, "if you're looking for something adventurous, there are hiking trails all over the island. Some are a little rough, but the views at the top are worth every scratch."

Darcy leaned in slightly, the warm shadows of the bar casting the hard planes of his face in soft contrast. "And do you guide these hikes personally?"

Rachel arched a brow, amusement curving one side of her mouth. "Only if you can keep up."

Sam let out a bark of laughter. "Careful, Darcy. She may be small, but she'll leave you for dead on the trail without blinking."

Darcy's smile widened—slow, deliberate, undeniably intrigued. "Now that sounds like a challenge."

Their eyes locked again, and the pulse of the bar—music, chatter, clinking glasses—dimmed around her like the volume had been turned down.

In that moment, Rachel wasn't thinking about London. She wasn't thinking about packed bags or wedding plans or the growing sense of disconnection that had been threading through every call with Jeremy for weeks now.

She wasn't thinking at all.

She was feeling—the heat of Darcy's attention, the coil of tension winding in her stomach, the way her body leaned toward his without meaning to. And the realisation hit with startling clarity.

She wanted to know what his laugh sounded like when he wasn't trying to hold it back.

She wanted to know if the heat in his gaze would feel different if he let it go completely.

She wanted to know him—and that was the most dangerous thing of all.

She caught herself, blinked once, and sat straighter. "There's also a hidden waterfall," she said lightly, trying to reel the conversation back to safer ground. "Hard to find unless you know where to look."

Darcy tilted his head, his eyes never leaving hers. "Sounds like I'm going to need a very good guide."

Rachel smiled, but this time, there was something softer beneath it. A thread of warning.

"Maybe," she said. "Or maybe you're better off exploring at your own pace."

Darcy lifted his drink, his voice low. "Where's the fun in that?"

Sam cleared his throat, grinning between them. "You two need a moment, or should I start narrating?"

Chapter Six

Rachel laughed at Sam's comment, grateful for the break in tension—grateful, but not ready for it.

Not entirely.

And that realisation curled through her like a warning.

"How often do you two perform?" Darcy asked, his tone deceptively casual, though his gaze never strayed far from her.

"Every night except Monday, Wednesday, and Friday," Sam replied, leaning back in his stool and swirling the melting ice in his glass.

Darcy took a slow sip of whiskey, nodding thoughtfully. "Is it the same routine each time?"

"Nope. We mix it up," Sam said with a grin. "Keeps things fresh. Right, Rach?"

Rachel let out another laugh, the sound lighter than she felt. Her nerves were buzzing—low and steady—like the hum of something coming alive beneath her skin. "I do," she teased.

Sam feigned offence, nudging her shoulder. "Excuse me? We're a team, remember?"

She rolled her eyes and nudged him back, her smile genuine despite the chaos stirring inside her.

Darcy's eyes remained on her. "And what do you do on the other nights?"

Rachel tucked a loose curl behind her ear, hoping he didn't notice how warm her cheeks had grown. "Wednesdays we teach a dance class for guests. Mondays and Fridays are our actual days off."

"No better way to spend your time than dancing," Darcy mused, voice dipping lower. "Good for the body. Better for the soul."

"You should join one of the classes," Sam offered with a smirk. "See if you've got any rhythm."

Rachel shot Sam a sideways glance. "You don't know he needs help."

Darcy lifted his brow, amused. "Oh, I do. That's why I don't dance in public."

Rachel tipped her glass toward him, smile sly. "A shame. Dancing's good for letting go. For finding freedom in the middle of chaos."

Darcy studied her as though the comment had a second meaning—and maybe it did. "Maybe I've just never had the right partner."

Her fingers tightened around her glass.

It wasn't just the words. It was the way he said them—soft, low, intimate. As if they were already dancing in the silence between them.

Sam grinned. "Sounds like he's angling for a private lesson, Rach."

Rachel tried to laugh, to deflect, but the tremor in her chest was too real. "Wednesday's our last class," she said, her voice a little too light. "We're teaching the tango."

Darcy's smile was slow, knowing. "Tango. Dangerous dance."

Rachel met his gaze. "Only if you do it right."

"I'll think about it," he said, voice velvet-smooth.

There was something unreadable in his eyes—curiosity, yes, but something more. Something that made her stomach dip.

"What do you do on your days off?" he asked after a moment, his tone turning softer, more personal.

Rachel hesitated, caught off guard by the shift in his voice. "I explore. I love finding the hidden places on the island. Beaches no one else goes to. I usually run the trails before sunrise—the jungle's beautiful when it's quiet, when it's still waking up."

Darcy pictured it: her bare feet on soft sand, hair loose and windblown, the early sun kissing her skin. Something pulled in his chest—unfamiliar and dangerous.

"I might have to see some of these hidden spots," he said. "They sound… unforgettable."

Sam chuckled. "Careful, Rach. He's working his way toward a private tour."

Rachel rolled her eyes, but her fingers kept fidgeting with the stem of her glass.

"I doubt he has time for that," she said, hoping her voice didn't betray her. "Didn't you say you were here to relax?"

Darcy's gaze didn't waver. "Maybe I just found the perfect way to do that."

Her breath caught.

Too much.

Too fast.

Too tempting.

Sam leaned back, his grin as easy as ever. "Well, well. Things just got interesting."

That was the tipping point.

Rachel stood abruptly, setting down her glass a little too hard. The quiet clink seemed louder than it should have been.

"I should go," she said, immediately wincing at how blunt it sounded. "I mean—nice meeting you, Darcy. Enjoy your stay."

He didn't move. Didn't press.

But his gaze held hers for a breath longer than necessary.

"You too," he said, his voice lower now. Slower. Like he wasn't just saying goodbye—but memorising her.

She turned to Sam, kissing his cheek quickly. "Enjoy your day off. See you Wednesday."

"Night, Rach," Sam said, his grin softening. "Text me if you need anything."

She nodded, then turned, walking toward the exit with measured steps. Calm on the outside.

Inside, her thoughts spun.

She felt his gaze on her the entire way out—like a hand trailing down her spine, like a question left unanswered.

And for the first time in a long time, the memory of Jeremy felt… distant.

Weightless.

Forgettable.

Darcy watched Rachel weave through the bar crowd and disappear into the warm, balmy night.

And Sam watched Darcy watching her.

"You've got no hope, mate," Sam said with a smirk, swirling the last of his drink.

Darcy's eyes didn't move from the doorway. "For what?" he asked smoothly, feigning innocence he knew wouldn't fly.

Sam chuckled, not buying it for a second. "Come on. Don't insult both of us. You've had your eyes locked on her since she stepped on that stage. Hell, I thought you were going to short-circuit when she said 'tango.'"

Darcy finally turned to face him, one brow lifting. "I was appreciating the performance."

Sam laughed. "Right. The performance. Listen, I've been working with Rachel for almost three months. She's smart, grounded… loyal to a fault. That girl's got steel in her spine and morals like a fortress."

Darcy said nothing, but the tightening of his jaw betrayed more interest than he let on.

"She's engaged," Sam went on with a shrug, his tone more thoughtful now. "Fiancé's back in London. Used to call her every day like clockwork, but lately?" He took a sip of his drink, then set the glass down with a soft clink. "Calls have gotten shorter. Less frequent. Feels like there's trouble brewing in paradise—if you catch my drift."

That caught Darcy's attention, but he kept his expression neutral.

"Not that it matters," Sam added. "I've seen guys hit on her daily—twice a day at least. Wealthy, charming, stupid-hot—you name it. She shuts them all down. Doesn't even dance with the guests outside our lessons."

Darcy leaned back slightly, nursing the last of his whiskey. "Is that a warning?"

"It's a friendly heads-up," Sam said, his grin easy but his tone edged with something more serious. "Rachel's not a game. Not a fling. She's the kind of woman who loves deeply and doesn't stray."

Darcy nodded slowly, his gaze drifting once more to the door she'd walked through. "Good to know."

Sam arched a brow. "You're not planning on proving me wrong, are you?"

Darcy's mouth curved slightly, but his answer came low and unreadable. "Let's just say… I'm reconsidering how I spend my Wednesday."

Sam groaned. "God help us. Tango night's never going to be the same."

Chapter Seven

The next morning, Darcy absolutely did not wake at the crack of dawn just to catch a glimpse of Rachel on her morning run.

That would be absurd.

He told himself that again—as he laced his shoes with more urgency than usual.

And again, as he stepped outside his bungalow and headed toward the trail that led to the quieter edge of the island, where the jungle met the sea.

This was simply research. A chance to observe the guest experience in the early hours. Morning operations, resort flow, natural noise levels—things a responsible owner would notice.

It had nothing to do with the dancer who'd been haunting his thoughts since last night.

That would be unprofessional.

He adjusted his pace, wandering the resort's network of raised boardwalks with fresh eyes. In the golden hush of morning, everything felt cleaner, calmer. The luxury here wasn't about marble floors or extravagant amenities. It was subtle—thoughtful. Intentional.

The bungalows, made of weathered teak and glass, peeked out from behind thick palms and wild hibiscus. Built on stilts and designed to disappear into the surroundings, they were elegant without being showy. A few sat perched over the surf, others tucked into the folds of jungle like secrets.

Solar panels caught the first light of day, gleaming like sleek armour above the canopies. Wooden walkways wound gently through the terrain, elevated just enough to preserve the land beneath them, as if the resort had been placed here with permission rather than force.

It impressed him more than he'd expected.

At the water's edge, the open-air restaurant stirred to life, soft clinks of breakfast prep echoing from the kitchen. A pair of guests sat barefoot at a table, sipping coffee as the sun spilled fire across the ocean.

Further down the shore, a yoga deck stretched out over the lapping tide, empty for now except for a single linen mat swaying in the breeze. In a few hours, the scent of lemongrass and warm coconut oil would carry across the sand. But for now, it was just the hush of the surf and the rustle of the jungle.

He passed the entertainment pavilion and paused.

Even without the crowd, the place had presence. The polished floor still bore the faint scuff marks from last night's performance. The thatched roof filtered soft light through its weave, casting a pattern of dancing shadows.

And then—he saw her.

Just ahead, running along the curve of the tide.

Rachel.

Her golden hair was pulled back into a low ponytail, swinging rhythmically with each stride as she jogged along one of the quieter, untouched stretches of the resort. The early morning sun poured like honey over the sand, gilding her skin in warm light and turning her into something out of a painting—earthy, fluid, alive.

She wasn't just exercising—she moved with fluid grace Her body worked in sync with the land, each stride measured and effortless, her breathing steady and calm. The island didn't resist her presence—it responded to it. The sand moulded to her steps. The breeze chased her like it had been waiting all night to catch up.

Darcy slowed.

So much for not looking for her.

He told himself he wasn't watching her. Not really. Just…noticing.

But then she stretched.

And whatever noble lie he'd been telling himself evaporated.

She stopped at the edge of the boardwalk, lifted her arms overhead, and tilted into a long side stretch, her limbs elongating like water pouring from a glass. The tank top clung to her in places where the breeze hadn't yet cooled her sweat-dampened skin. Her leggings hugged long, toned legs that flexed with quiet strength. It was the kind of body built from years of movement—not the gym, but the stage. A dancer's body.

It shouldn't have affected him.

But it did.

She's engaged, his brain repeated, like a broken alarm trying to go off. Again and again.

But his heart—and some unhelpful part of his gut—didn't seem to care. Not when she moved like she was born from sunlight and rhythm. Not when she looked so completely unaware of the spell she cast on everything around her.

She folded into a stretch, resting one foot against the railing and bending over her leg with slow, precise control. Her breath came out in a quiet exhale, and somehow, even that sounded intimate.

Darcy raked a hand through his hair, muttered something under his breath that sounded a lot like idiot, and prepared to turn away.

Too late.

She turned.

And their eyes met.

For a heartbeat, she stilled. He saw the flicker of surprise—the brief, visible pause— as though she hadn't expected to see him either. Her lips parted on a quiet inhale, but she recovered fast. Too fast.

"Morning," she said, voice smooth, composed. Almost too composed. Her grey eyes searched his face like she was trying to decide if this was a coincidence or something else.

Darcy shoved his hands into his pockets, a slow smirk curling his lips. "Morning. Didn't peg you for a late sleeper. Then again, I wasn't expecting to see you out this early either."

Rachel arched a brow, shifting her weight as she moved into another stretch. "I like to run before the resort wakes up. It's the only time the trails are mine."

His gaze followed the path winding into the trees. "Sounds peaceful."

"It is," she replied, wiping a bead of sweat from her brow. Her voice was even, but her eyes… her eyes hadn't stopped watching him.

"And you?" she asked, casually, but not without weight. "Out for a sunrise stroll— or were you looking for something?"

Darcy didn't answer right away. He tilted his head, let the silence settle for half a second longer than was necessary. Then: "Maybe I found it."

Rachel blinked, her lashes fluttering once. That moment—subtle, so fast you could miss it—was there. That shift. A crack in the calm.

She let out a quiet laugh, more breath than sound, and said, "Careful, Darcy. You're starting to sound like trouble."

He stepped closer, just enough to feel the warmth still radiating off her skin. "I've been told that before."

She smiled—just barely—and turned away. "I bet you have."

And just like that, she was running again.

Darcy watched her go, her silhouette dissolving into the trees, the flash of her ponytail vanishing with each stride. The jungle closed behind her, like it was swallowing her whole.

He stood still, his pulse ticking a little too fast for his liking.

He wanted to chase her. To match her step for step. To say something reckless just to make her stop and look at him again.

But he didn't.

She's engaged; he reminded himself. Again.

It should have been enough.

But it wasn't. Not when every time she looked at him like that—half-curious, half-daring—he didn't just want her.

He wanted to be the reason she stayed.

Darcy exhaled hard and turned toward the main building, dragging his thoughts with him like heavy luggage.

He needed a distraction. Something practical. Something professional. Something safe.

There were excursions he hadn't tried yet—reef diving, deep jungle hikes, a cooking class at noon. He could blend in as a guest, keep collecting notes, play the role he was here for.

And maybe, if he was lucky, the next time he saw Rachel... he'd remember how to look at her like she was just another member of staff.

Not like temptation in motion.

Rachel ran, her feet pounding against the dirt path in a steady, urgent rhythm—the slap of her soles slicing through the hush of dawn.

The jungle stirred around her, vibrant and alive. Leaves rustled overhead like whispers, dew clung to low-hanging branches, and the air was thick with the scent of earth, salt, and something sweet and elusive—frangipani, maybe, or hibiscus blooming deep in the underbrush. But she barely registered any of it.

The world blurred at the edges, reduced to sound, breath, and motion.

She wasn't running for fitness. Not for peace or clarity, either.

She was running to silence the noise in her head.

To burn away the ache in her chest.

To escape the truth she wasn't ready to say out loud.

She was running from a life she wasn't sure she wanted anymore—

And toward a man she had no business wanting at all.

No matter how fast she moved, the thoughts chased her—tenacious, invasive, clinging like brambles to bare skin.

Darcy.

Every time she saw him, her pulse betrayed her—jumping, fluttering, twisting itself into knots. Every glance he gave her felt weighted. Intentional. Like he wasn't just seeing her but seeing into her—through the polish and the smiles and the carefully curated façade.

And that terrified her.

Because a part of her wanted him to.

Stop it. You're engaged.

The words thundered through her mind, sharp and unrelenting. But they didn't stop the images from creeping in—

The low rasp of his voice when he teased her.

The way his gaze followed her, dark and steady, like he was memorising every inch of her.

The almost imperceptible pause before he smiled—like he was weighing something deeper.

The way her breath caught when he stepped closer.

The way her body leaned in before her mind could tell it to step away.

You're engaged.

To Jeremy.

The safe choice. The logical one.

The man she was supposed to marry.

He was stable. Steady. Predictable.

A future with him was mapped out in clean, careful lines. No sharp edges. No chaos. No surprises.

And no fire.

A hot prickle of shame slid down her spine, mixing with the sheen of sweat on her back. She pushed herself harder, legs stretching, lungs burning. She needed to outrun this.

But the truth—God, the truth—was too fast.

When she'd seen Darcy watching her stretch, something inside her had stilled. Not her body—her breath. Her thoughts. Her walls.

Their eyes had met. And something unspoken passed between them. Something bold and quiet and utterly, dangerously real.

She should've looked away.

Should've said something casual, dismissed it, turned the moment into nothing.

But she hadn't.

Instead, she'd stood there and let it happen. Let herself feel it. Let it coil low in her belly like heat she didn't know what to do with.

Darcy Williams was not hers to want.

He was a guest. A stranger. A complication she couldn't afford.

But she hadn't felt this alive in a long, long time.

And that, more than anything, scared her.

Did he know how much his presence affected her?

God, she hoped not.

She hoped the tension that coiled in her chest whenever he was near was just a trick of the heat—too much sun, too much island air, too little distance. A fleeting crush brought on by tropical illusion and proximity. Nothing real. Nothing lasting.

But she wasn't naïve.

And she knew better.

Darcy noticed things. He wasn't the type to miss subtle glances or quiet pauses. He moved through the world like a man who saw too much and said too little—and that made him dangerous. Not just because he was perceptive, but because when he looked at her, it felt like he understood her. Like he saw past the polished performer, past the curated smiles and graceful choreography, and glimpsed the woman beneath. The one she didn't show anyone.

And whatever this was between them—this simmering, unspoken tension that made her breath catch and her thoughts scatter—

…it wasn't one-sided.

She felt it in the space between words.

In the brush of silence after a glance held a beat too long.

In the way her skin warmed before he even spoke.

But it didn't matter.

It couldn't.

Because she was leaving.

Flying home on Saturday. Back to London. Back to her job. Her life. Her fiancé.

Jeremy.

The name landed in her chest like a stone—familiar, heavy, and oddly hollow.

Jeremy was her future.

Or at least, the version of the future she'd constructed—neatly, carefully—around safety. Around logic. Around what made sense. A life that looked good on paper and wouldn't scare her parents. A relationship built on predictability, not passion.

He was steady. Dependable.

The man who planned everything in tidy increments, who kept his shoes lined up by the door and his life in perfect order.

But he wasn't the man who made her heart race without touching her.

He wasn't the man whose voice could unravel her resolve with a single low-spoken word.

He wasn't the man who made her feel seen.

Darcy was.

And maybe that was the problem.

Because in the deepest part of her—the quiet corners she rarely visited, the ones she locked up behind practical choices and carefully drawn boundaries—she already knew the truth.

Jeremy wasn't her future anymore.

She didn't want a life that looked good in photographs but felt empty in motion. She didn't want to be the woman who smiled through quiet dissatisfaction because she was too afraid to rewrite her story.

She wanted more.

She wanted to feel alive.

Rachel pushed harder, her legs pumping faster, the burn in her calves rising with every pounding stride. Her lungs protested, her breath coming in sharp bursts. But she welcomed the pain. Needed it. Welcomed the ache in her muscles, the slap of her soles against the dirt. She needed something—anything—to hurt more than the guilt unfurling like wildfire inside her.

She wasn't a cheater.

She wouldn't let herself be that woman.

Not now. Not ever.

She would talk to Jeremy.

She would be honest.

She would end it face to face—with integrity and grace, and no loose ends.

Because deep down, she'd already crossed a line—maybe not with her body, but with her heart.

Because you already know it's over, don't you, Rachel?

And the moment you admit that—you're free.

The thought hit like a punch to the chest. Sudden. Merciless.

She stumbled slightly, breath catching, blinking against the sting in her eyes.

And for the first time in weeks, it wasn't the heat or the exhaustion that slowed her.

It was the truth.

Chapter Eight

After her run, Rachel headed straight for the shower, peeling off her damp clothes and stepping under the cool spray. The water cascaded over her heated skin, washing away the sweat, the tension in her muscles, and—at least for a moment—the thoughts she was trying so hard to ignore. She tilted her head back, eyes closed, letting the droplets drum against her face, willing them to drown out the memory of Darcy's gaze lingering on her that morning.

It didn't work.

By the time she finished, her mind was still tangled in things it shouldn't be, but at least she felt refreshed. She wrapped a towel around herself, squeezing the excess water from her hair before towelling it dry. It had lightened in the sun over the past few months, the salty air adding natural waves she rarely bothered to tame.

She reached for her bikini—bright teal, the colour of the ocean just beyond her bungalow—and slipped it on. The fabric hugged her skin, still cool from the shower, a welcome contrast to the heat outside. Denim shorts came next, frayed at the edges, well-worn from countless beach days. A cropped top completed the look, airy and light.

A day of swimming and sunbathing sounded perfect—exactly what she needed to clear her mind. She'd spend hours under the sun, let the waves carry her worries away.

Rachel grabbed her bag, tossing in a towel, sunscreen, and a bottle of water before slinging it over her shoulder. But before heading to the beach, she had one more thing to do. She wanted to book a tour for Thursday—her last day off before leaving the island.

The hiking tour on the far side of the island had been one of the first she'd taken when she arrived, and she still remembered how breathtaking it had been.

An open-air vehicle would take her through the winding jungle roads before dropping her at the trailhead. From there, she'd hike along the cliffs, where the world stretched open before her—nothing but sky and ocean, the water shifting between endless shades of blue. It was the perfect blend of adventure and serenity; the kind of beauty that made her feel small in the best possible way.

She'd known, even back then, that she wanted to do it one last time before leaving.

A perfect goodbye.

Decision made, she slipped on her sandals and stepped outside, the warm breeze stirring her hair as she made her way to reception.

The resort was quieter in the late morning, the usual hum of guest activity replaced by a soft, lazy stillness. Most vacationers were off enjoying breakfast on the terrace or scattered across excursions around the island. The air was rich with the scent of hibiscus and plumeria, sweet and thick from the sun, blending with the briny undertone of the sea that drifted in on a gentle breeze.

Rachel stepped through the open-air lobby, her sandals whispering over the smooth wooden floor. Sunlight filtered through the slatted roof above, casting dappled patterns on the reception desk.

Behind it, Daniel sat hunched over a clipboard, flipping through a thin stack of paperwork like it might suddenly offer him entertainment. He looked up, and his face lit with familiar mischief.

"Hey, Rach!" he called, tossing the clipboard aside with dramatic flair. "How's the morning treating you?"

She smiled, the kind that came easily with Daniel. "Hey yourself. It's good. Quiet. Peaceful. Perfect for running."

He leaned against the counter, arms folded as he grinned at her. "So… same routine—morning jog, mysterious brooding on the beach, followed by pretending not to notice every guest who stares at you?"

Rachel laughed, shaking her head. "You're ridiculous."

"I'm observant," he corrected, pointing a finger in mock offence. "Also: underpaid, overworked, and criminally good-looking."

She snorted. "Well, one out of four isn't bad."

Daniel clutched his chest. "Cruel. Just cruel."

Rachel rolled her eyes, resting her elbows on the counter. "Slow shift?"

"Painfully. I've refreshed the excursion list three times and restocked brochures no one reads. Honestly, I'm begging for a guest to lose a keycard or fake a lizard sighting in their room—anything for a little drama."

She grinned, then glanced over her shoulder at the path leading toward the water. "I was going to head to the beach for a bit. Make the most of my last week."

Daniel's expression shifted, the grin softening just slightly. "That's right… you finish up Friday."

The words hung in the air for a second longer than they should have.

"We're really going to miss you, you know," he said, quieter now. "It's been fun having you around."

Her chest tugged. Harder than she expected. She'd made real connections here—honest, easy friendships that didn't feel forced. Daniel had been one of the first people to welcome her when she arrived, all jokes and charm, but underneath that, a sincerity she'd grown to value more than she'd let on.

"That's sweet," she murmured, her voice softening. "I'll miss you guys too."

Then—true to form—Daniel grinned, his eyes twinkling with mischief. "So, real talk… when exactly are you dumping that fiancé of yours and marrying me instead?"

Rachel's jaw dropped in a burst of surprised laughter. "Daniel!"

He raised both brows innocently. "What? I've been waiting patiently for months. I figured now's the time to shoot my shot. You're leaving, I'm heartbroken—it's basically a rom-com setup."

She shook her head, still laughing. "You're impossible."

"Yeah, but charming. And house-trained. I make a killer coconut mojito. Just think about it."

Rachel gave him a playful shove across the counter. "You're ridiculous."

"Again, observant," he said with a wink. "But seriously, Rach. Whatever happens when you get back to London… I hope it's what you want. Not what's expected."

That caught her off guard. The playfulness faded for just a breath, and something real shimmered beneath the surface.

She nodded slowly. "Yeah. Me too."

Daniel smiled again, gentler now. "Alright, go soak up some sun before I get all weepy. But if you decide to elope with me at the last minute, I'll have a passport and a very snazzy white linen shirt ready."

Rachel laughed. "I'll keep that in mind."

Unnoticed in the corner of the open-air reception, Darcy pretended to study the tour brochures lined up on the low wooden shelf. His fingers flipped through them absently—sunset cruises, deep-sea diving, yoga retreats—but he wasn't taking in a word. Not really.

His attention was elsewhere.

It was on her.

On Rachel, leaning against the counter, golden hair catching the light as she spoke with easy warmth to the receptionist. On the soft note of nostalgia in her voice. On the fact that she sounded like someone preparing to say goodbye.

And then she said it—casually, like it meant nothing.

"I want to do the hiking tour on Thursday. The one on the far side of the island."

Darcy stilled.

She wasn't just booking an activity. She was drawing a line—closing a chapter.

His jaw flexed, the sensation sharper than it should have been. He hadn't expected that word—goodbye—to land like a punch.

Daniel typed a few things into the computer and nodded. "Good choice. You went on that one before, didn't you?"

"Yeah," she said, her voice softer now. "My first week here. The views were incredible. It feels like the perfect way to end it."

End it.

The words echoed louder than they should have.

Darcy looked down at the brochure still clutched in his hand, the one she'd just picked up—a full-day hike that wound through untouched jungle, up coastal cliffs, ending at a remote beach with views that looked like something from a postcard. It did sound like the perfect farewell.

But that wasn't why he stepped forward.

"I'll take a spot on that tour as well."

His voice was calm, casual—but there was a thread of intent woven through it.

Rachel's head turned at the sound, her eyes widening slightly. She hadn't seen him standing there. She hadn't expected him to speak.

"You're doing the hike?" she asked, guarded curiosity in her tone.

Darcy met her gaze without flinching. "Why not? It sounds like a view to remember. Might as well see what all the fuss is about."

The words came easily, but the truth behind them was harder to admit—even to himself. He wasn't thinking about panoramic views or challenging trails.

He was thinking about time.

Specifically, how little of it he might have left with her.

Daniel handed them both their confirmation slips. Rachel took hers with a nod of thanks, tucking it into the canvas bag slung over her shoulder. She shifted subtly, a quiet signal that she was about to leave.

But Darcy wasn't ready to let her walk away just yet.

"You know this place better than I do," he said, his tone easy, almost offhand. "What's the best beach around here?"

Rachel blinked, caught off guard. "That depends. Do you want quiet or postcard-perfect? Or something you won't find in a brochure?"

Darcy tilted his head slightly, the corner of his mouth lifting. "I want the one *you* would choose."

That gave her pause. Her fingers tightened slightly around the strap of her bag, and for a beat, she didn't answer.

It wasn't just a question about beaches. They both knew that.

A faint smile curved her lips, guarded but genuine. "That's a bold request."

He shrugged. "I've been told I'm persistent."

There was something between them now—unsaid, undeniable. The charged space that existed between what was appropriate and what felt inevitable. And still, he didn't push. He offered the opening and waited to see if she'd step through it.

She glanced out toward the sunlight streaming through the palm-framed entrance, then back at him. Let out a quiet breath.

"Alright," she said. "But just one."

A flicker of satisfaction moved through Darcy, though he buried it beneath a relaxed, unreadable smile.

"Lead the way," he said, his tone smooth. "But I just need to stop by my bungalow and grab a few things."

Rachel arched a brow, folding her arms with a teasing tilt of her head. "Don't forget a bottle of water. I'm not carrying you if you pass out."

He gave her a playful salute. "Understood. I'll bring snacks too just in case you get grumpy."

She smirked in spite of herself, but her heart beat just a little too fast for a casual walk to the beach.

As Darcy turned and headed off, Daniel—still behind the reception desk—let out a low chuckle, shaking his head like a man watching a predictable story unfold.

"He seems keen," he said, half under his breath.

Rachel rolled her eyes, even as something twisted beneath her ribs. "Not on me, I hope. I'm engaged, remember?"

Daniel's smile dimmed just slightly, though he covered it quickly. "Yeah. I haven't forgotten."

She knew he hadn't. During her first week at the resort, Daniel had asked her to dinner—not pushy, not sleazy. Just curious. Interested. She'd turned him down gently, explaining her situation. He'd laughed it off, claimed he understood. And maybe he did. But sometimes, like now, there was something unreadable in his eyes when the subject came up—some half-swallowed thought he kept to himself.

They drifted into safer conversation, the kind meant to fill the space without stirring anything deeper. The heat. A new shipment of towels. The karaoke night one of the other departments was organising for Friday. Harmless, easy things.

But Rachel felt the pulse of something else beneath it all.

A man who wasn't her fiancé had just invited himself along on her final hike—and she didn't object.

"We're due for rain soon," Daniel said, glancing at the horizon. The sky was still brilliant blue, streaked with the soft haze of distant clouds, but the weight of the air hinted at change.

Rachel adjusted the strap of her canvas bag. "I hope it holds off until I'm on the plane. It's been perfect ever since I got here."

Before Daniel could answer, her gaze was pulled—instinctively, involuntarily—toward the movement at the edge of the reception.

Darcy.

He was back, dressed for the hike in a faded charcoal tee and navy shorts, a slim backpack slung over one shoulder. His dark hair was tousled, wind touched. He looked like he belonged to the island and had never belonged to anything else.

His eyes found hers instantly—steady, deliberate.

"All set," he said, as if they hadn't just been suspended in weeks' worth of silent questions and unspoken what-ifs.

Rachel hesitated.

Just for a second.

But in that heartbeat lived everything she didn't want to name—doubt, temptation, a longing that stretched beyond reason. She should say no. She knew better.

But her feet didn't move away.

Instead, she nodded—small, silent—and turned without a word, the choice pressing heavily against her chest.

They stepped outside together, and sunlight spilled across the main boardwalk like melted gold. The wooden planks were warm beneath their feet, heat rising in lazy waves. The scent of salt mingled with the faint sweetness of frangipani and the subtle warmth of coconut oil still clinging to her skin.

Darcy fell into step beside her, close enough to feel, far enough to deny.

Neither of them spoke.

But the silence between them was anything but empty.

It thrummed—charged, magnetic, full of all the things they hadn't said and maybe never would.

Rachel stared ahead, eyes locked on the narrow trail that would lead them away from the resort, away from the safety of reception desks and neatly drawn lines.

A few guests passed with polite nods, laughter floating behind them like mist. But when they veered off onto the narrower trail that wound away from the resort, the world fell quiet. Too quiet.

Rachel felt it instantly. The shift.

The trail narrowed beneath a thick green canopy. The air turned heavy with the scent of damp earth and moss. Sunlight fractured through the trees in gold and shadow, brushing against her arms like fingers.

The jungle surrounded them—wild, quiet, and watching.

Every step she took felt like a choice. Every sound, every breath, pulled her deeper into the kind of silence where the truth could be heard too clearly.

And right behind her… was the man who made that silence feel dangerous.

"You're not taking me somewhere dangerous, are you?" Darcy teased, adjusting the strap of his bag as he stepped over an exposed root.

Rachel smirked without glancing back. "Not unless you consider a little effort dangerous."

The path sloped upward, winding through thick vegetation. Towering trees loomed on either side; their trunks wrapped in twisting vines. Bright bursts of colour dotted the greenery—clusters of hibiscus blooms, fiery red and golden yellow, peeking out between the leaves. The scent of salt became stronger as they climbed, mingling with the rich, sunbaked earth beneath their feet.

Occasionally, the foliage parted just enough to reveal glimpses of the ocean below— a vast stretch of endless turquoise, shimmering beneath the sun. Each time the view appeared; Darcy found his gaze lingering. It was breathtaking. Untouched. A kind of raw beauty that couldn't be replicated, no matter how many luxury resorts or private beaches he'd visited before.

Rachel set a steady pace, moving with the kind of ease that suggested she'd walked this trail countless times. Darcy followed without complaint, though he noted the way his pulse had picked up—not just from exertion but from something else. Something unnamed.

After a solid twenty minutes of walking, Rachel slowed as they reached the crest of a hill. She turned back to him, her expression unreadable except for the slight glint of mischief in her eyes.

"Almost there."

Darcy scanned their surroundings. Lush greenery stretched in every direction, thick and untamed. The ocean was visible in the distance, but there was no beach in sight.

"I don't see a beach," he said, arching a brow.

Rachel simply grinned, a knowing sort of smile that sent a flicker of intrigue through him. Without another word, she stepped forward, pushing through a narrow gap in the foliage.

Darcy followed—and then stopped dead in his tracks.

Chapter Nine

The cliffside sloped down into a secluded cove, where the world seemed to pause. Untouched white sand stretched along the shore, pristine and unmarred by footprints. The turquoise water lapped lazily at the beach, shifting between shades of sapphire and gold as the sunlight danced across its surface. A warm breeze stirred the palm fronds above, carrying the crisp scent of salt and sun-warmed earth.

For a long moment, neither of them spoke.

Rachel exhaled slowly, feeling the tension in her chest ease just slightly, as if the quiet beauty of the place had seeped into her bones. She had come here countless times, yet it never lost its magic. It was the kind of place that made the world feel bigger and smaller all at once—vast, endless, and yet intimately peaceful.

She stole a glance at Darcy.

He stood a few steps behind her, his gaze fixed on the cove below, but there was something different about his expression. Something quiet. Intense. His eyes had darkened, and his breath hitched just slightly, so small a shift that most people wouldn't have noticed.

Rachel did.

She looked away quickly.

"This," she said, her voice softer than she intended, "is the best beach on the island."

Darcy let out a low whistle, dragging a hand through his hair as his eyes swept the secluded cove. "You weren't kidding."

But it was the way he looked at her—not the ocean—that made her breath catch.

There was something in his expression. Something quiet and focused. Like he wasn't admiring the view at all but memorising her instead.

A shiver traced the length of her spine, and this time, it had nothing to do with the breeze.

This was a bad idea.

She was already in too deep, letting him get too close—not just to her body, but to the part of her she kept guarded. The part that was starving for connection and terrified of what it would mean to feel seen.

She should have turned away. Should have walked down to the sand and put distance—physical and emotional—between them.

But she didn't.

She stood there, pulse ticking in her throat, the weight of his presence wrapping around her like the humid air. And somewhere inside her, something dangerous stirred—a longing she couldn't afford, for a man she shouldn't want.

It wasn't just attraction anymore.

It was the beginning of a choice.

Darcy shook his head slightly, his gaze returning to the view. "How do more people not know about this?"

"They do," she admitted, trying to focus on the conversation instead of the awareness humming beneath her skin. "But it's a bit of a trek, and most guests don't want to bother when the main beach is right outside their bungalows."

She turned to look at him again, forcing herself to sound casual. "Worth the effort?"

Darcy met her gaze, and for a split second, something flickered in his expression— something unreadable, something that made the air between them feel charged in a way she didn't want to acknowledge.

His lips curved into a slow, knowing smile.

"Definitely."

For a moment, neither of them spoke. The air between them felt thick, charged with something unspoken, something neither of them wanted to acknowledge. The quiet intimacy of the secluded cove only amplified the tension, making it impossible to ignore. The rhythmic crash of waves against the shore and the rustling of the palm trees above were the only sounds, but between them, the silence hummed—alive, waiting.

Rachel forced herself to move, to break the spell stretching tight and silent between them. Her pulse still beat too loudly in her ears, and every inch of her skin felt too aware, too exposed—even though he hadn't touched her.

Clearing her throat, she turned away, toward the shade of the overhanging trees, pretending she was unaffected. Just another day. Just another beach.

She knelt beside her bag and pulled out her towel, giving it a brisk shake more for distraction than necessity. The fabric snapped in the air before settling onto the warm, sun-drenched sand.

Her fingers hesitated at the hem of her cropped top.

She could feel him behind her—close enough to sense, but not close enough to see. And somehow, that was worse. The not-knowing. The what-if of whether he was watching, whether he was thinking the same forbidden thoughts looping through her head.

This is nothing. Just a beach day. Just sun and water and silence.

She tugged her top over her head, her movements efficient, practiced—but her heart stuttered all the same. Then came the shorts, sliding down over tanned legs until she stood in nothing but a deep green bikini that suddenly felt much more revealing under the weight of imagined eyes.

She told herself she didn't care if he looked.

She told herself she didn't want him to.

Both were lies.

Behind her, Darcy shifted—subtle, restrained. But she didn't need to turn around to feel it: the sudden tension in the air, the deliberate rustle of fabric as he unfolded his towel a little too slowly.

Darcy looked away—too quickly, too deliberately. He busied his hands with smoothing the towel beside hers, but the effort was hollow.

Out of the corner of his eye, he caught glimpses of golden skin, the curve of her waist, the way her hair caught the sunlight like it had been dipped in fire. She moved like she belonged here—wild and effortless—and it made something primal stir low in his gut.

His jaw clenched, his fingers gripping the edge of his towel with too much force.

He hadn't touched her.

But God, he already felt the heat of her.

Rachel, seemingly unaware—or perhaps just choosing to ignore it—sat down and reached for her sunscreen. She squeezed some into her palm, smoothing it over her arms and legs with practiced ease. But when she reached behind her, fingers fumbling to reach the space between her shoulder blades, she hesitated.

A quiet sigh slipped past her lips. Then, after a moment's hesitation, she turned toward him, holding out the bottle.

"Would you mind?" she asked. Her voice was casual, but something about the way she said it—soft, uncertain—sent a jolt of awareness through him.

Darcy looked up, and the moment their eyes met, the air shifted. The simple request suddenly felt like something more, like a boundary neither of them should cross but both were dangerously close to stepping over.

His throat went dry. "Ah—yeah. Sure."

Taking the bottle, he poured a small amount into his palm, rubbing his hands together before pressing them gently to her back. Her skin was warm and soft beneath his touch—sun-kissed silk stretched over muscle—and for a moment, he forgot to breathe.

He smoothed the lotion over her shoulders, his fingers moving in slow, measured strokes, pretending he didn't feel the subtle hitch in her breath. But he did. Every inch of her stillness, the tension humming just beneath her skin, told him she felt it too.

Rachel inhaled—barely more than a breath—but it whispered straight to his gut. She didn't move, didn't pull away, as if she didn't trust herself to lean in.

Darcy clenched his jaw, keeping his touch light, clinical. Or at least, trying to. Because nothing about this felt impersonal. Not when the scent of her skin curled into his lungs. Not when the curve of her spine trembled faintly beneath his hands. Not when every cell in his body wanted more.

For a dangerous second, he imagined what it would be like to let go—to follow the path of his fingers with his mouth, to taste the salt on her neck, to feel her melt into him the way he knew she would.

He exhaled sharply, banishing the thought before it became something he couldn't undo.

"Done," he said, his voice lower than he intended, rougher. He pulled his hands back, his palms tingling with her warmth like a phantom touch.

Rachel turned her head just enough to glance over her shoulder. "Thanks."

Her voice was steady, but her eyes gave her away. They held a flicker of something—heat, hesitation, awareness—something that said she wasn't nearly as unaffected as she wanted to appear.

She looked away first.

Then, with deliberate casualness, she stood, brushing grains of sand from her thighs, her movements smooth but too practiced. "I'm going for a swim," she said, and without waiting for a reply, she walked toward the water.

Darcy smirked, masking the fact that he needed a distraction just as much as she did.

"I figured."

She walked toward the water, the sway of her hips completely unintentional—or maybe not. He watched as she waded in, the water lapping at her skin, glistening as she dove beneath the surface.

Darcy dragged a hand through his hair, exhaling slowly.

Coming here had either been a mistake—or the best damn decision he'd made since arriving.

The fire in his veins had nothing to do with the midday sun. He needed to cool off, now, before he did something he couldn't take back.

He grabbed the back of his shirt and pulled it over his head in one fluid motion, stuffing it into his bag before making his way toward the water. The sand was hot beneath his feet, but the moment he reached the shoreline, the cool waves rushed over his skin. Without hesitation, he dove in, the saltwater shocking the tension from his muscles.

For a few moments, he stayed under, letting the water mute the world above, willing his body to calm.

When he surfaced, Rachel was floating a few feet away, her face turned toward the sky, eyes closed, droplets of water clinging to her skin like diamonds in the sunlight.

She didn't acknowledge him, but she had to know he was there.

Darcy ran a hand over his face, pushing his wet hair back, then started swimming, keeping his strokes slow, measured. He refused to let himself look at her for too long, refused to let his mind wander to how she'd felt under his hands just minutes ago.

They swam in the same water, their movements echoing each other in the gentle rhythm of the tide. But neither spoke. Neither touched.

The silence wasn't just quiet; it crackled between them, heavy with unspoken thoughts. Charged. Dangerous.

Darcy forced himself to keep his distance. He needed more than just the water to cool his blood before he stepped back onto that beach.

Because the second he did, he wasn't sure how much longer he could pretend he didn't want her.

Rachel emerged from the water first, her body breaking through the glittering surface like a vision conjured by the sun itself. Droplets slid down her golden skin in slow rivulets, clinging to the curves he was doing a damn poor job of not staring at. She walked toward her towel with the kind of quiet confidence that made everything else around her blur.

Darcy's eyes followed her—helplessly, hungrily.

God, she had a body that could bring a man to his knees. Long, toned legs. A narrow waist. Hips that moved with an effortless, feminine rhythm that made it impossible not to look. Her deep green bikini clung to her like a secret meant only for him, and his jaw clenched hard enough to ache.

She bent slightly to retrieve her towel, water sliding off her in glistening streaks, and he swore under his breath, dragging a hand across his mouth.

And then there was her hair.

Thick, wild waves of golden blonde, darkened now with seawater, cascaded down her back in perfect disarray. He imagined it tangled in his fingers, spread across his chest, his pillow—his hands buried in it as he kissed his way down her body, coaxing soft, breathless sounds from her lips.

A sharp pulse of heat surged through him.

Darcy exhaled harshly, forcing himself to look away before he made a damn fool of himself. Get it together.

She's engaged.

The reminder did little to cool the fire burning beneath his skin.

He remained waist-deep in the water, grounding himself in the gentle pull of the tide, willing his pulse to steady. He couldn't go up there like this—not when every cell in his body was screaming to close the space between them, to drag her down into the sand and kiss her until she forgot her own name.

He had to wait.

So he did.

Until the pounding in his chest eased. Until the hunger in his blood dulled to something manageable. Until he could breathe without imagining what her skin would taste like.

Only then did he stride out of the sea, the water sliding off his body in shimmering rivulets, his every step deliberate.

By the time Darcy reached the shore, Rachel was already settled on her towel, sitting cross-legged as she wrung the water from her hair. Strands clung to her skin, glistening in the sunlight like threads of gold. She glanced up as he approached, her grey eyes shaded by damp lashes—but in them, something flickered.

Awareness.

Not just that he was there. Not just acknowledgment.

But a silent recognition of what was slowly unfurling between them.

Darcy met her gaze and let the silence stretch between them like a taut wire. He didn't know what was going to happen next—but he knew with a clarity that unnerved him that if he wasn't careful, he was going to cross a line neither of them could uncross.

And the worst part?

He wasn't entirely sure he wanted to stop himself.

Chapter Ten

Rachel shifted, stretching out on her towel, propping herself up on one elbow. She didn't look at him again—her eyes were fixed on the ocean, watching the waves roll toward the shore with a faraway expression. The way she stared at the horizon, like she was trying to memorise every shifting shade of blue before it slipped away, twisted something deep in his chest.

He grabbed his own towel, shook off the remaining seawater, and sat beside her—not too close, but close enough that the warmth radiating from her sun-kissed skin reached him. Close enough to hear her breathe.

"The water's nice," he said casually, his voice lower than intended.

She turned her head toward him, her smile soft but bright—and damn, it nearly levelled him. "Yeah," she said, her voice gentle. "It is."

They fell into a quiet rhythm, the silence between them filled with the rustle of palm leaves, the rhythmic hush of the tide, the distant call of birds. It wasn't uncomfortable. It felt… suspended. Like the world had tilted and time was stalling around them.

Darcy glanced at her again. "It's peaceful here."

"That's why I love it." Her tone was more wistful now, a thread of melancholy weaving through her words. She sighed and absently drew lines in the sand with her fingertip. "I'm really going to miss it."

His brow furrowed. "So don't leave. Extend your contract."

Rachel let out a dry laugh and lifted her left hand. The diamond on her ring finger caught the light and sparkled—a perfect, polished contradiction to the quiet uncertainty in her eyes.

"Jeremy would probably lose his mind," she said, giving the ring a wiggle. "He didn't even want me to take this job."

Darcy's jaw tensed, though his expression remained neutral. Classic. A man who didn't want her to leave—but also didn't want her to fly.

He leaned back on his hands and turned his gaze toward the waves. But he wasn't thinking about the sea anymore. He was thinking about the way she'd said it—like it was a reflex, a reason she didn't believe in anymore.

Like she was reminding herself why she should still care.

A slow, knowing smile tugged at his mouth. "If he didn't want you to come… why did you?"

Rachel's finger stilled in the sand. She didn't answer right away. When she finally did, her voice was quiet, almost reluctant.

"I needed space. To think."

He studied her—really studied her. The downturn of her lips. The thoughtful crease between her brows. The subtle weight in her posture, like she'd been holding something too long and was tired of carrying it.

Darcy could have pushed then. Asked what she was thinking about. Asked what she was running from.

But he didn't.

Instead, he met her halfway.

"And?" he asked, his voice soft. "Have you figured things out?"

Rachel turned to face him fully, her expression unreadable. But her eyes—they gave her away. Something raw flickered there. A crack in the armour she wore too well.

He didn't look away.

And for a moment, neither did she.

Then her gaze dropped to the sand, and she exhaled slowly, as if the truth had been pressing against her ribs and finally demanded to be set free.

"I think he's already figured it out for the both of us," she murmured.

Darcy didn't move. Didn't speak. But something delicate shifted in the space between them—a subtle but unmistakable change. The quiet tension they'd been circling for days stretched thinner, trembling on the edge of something neither of them had dared to name.

Not yet a confession.

But closer than either had come before.

He arched a brow, keeping his expression carefully neutral, though something sharp and restless stirred low in his gut. "Oh? What makes you say that?"

Rachel hesitated, then sat up slowly, pulling her knees to her chest. Her arms wrapped around them in a loose, almost protective way, like she was bracing herself. Once the words began, they spilled out with the quiet urgency of someone who'd been holding them in for too long.

"For the last month, every time I call, he's always too busy to talk," she said, her voice softer now, threaded with something brittle. "It didn't used to be like that. I used to smile when I saw his name on my screen. Now… every call feels like a task. Like we're just checking a box."

She stared at a distant point on the horizon, blinking against the light as if the sunlight itself was too much to look into. "He says he'll call me back but never does."

Darcy's brows drew together. "And when you do get a hold of him?"

She gave a dry, humourless laugh—thin and tired. "He sounds irritated—like I've interrupted something important. Like I'm the inconvenience now." She grimaced, shoulders lifting in a helpless shrug. "I don't know if I'm just overthinking it, but something feels… off."

Darcy stretched his legs out in front of him, bracing his hands behind him in the sand. He studied her in silence, weighing the flickers of vulnerability in her eyes. "Have you asked him about it?"

Rachel glanced sideways at him, her jaw tightening. "Every time." A beat passed before she added, "And all he ever says is, 'I'm busy, Rachel,' then practically hangs up."

Darcy exhaled slowly, his lips pressing into a line. He wasn't the kind of man to get involved in someone else's relationship. But this—this didn't sit right. Not when she was sitting next to him, the light in her dulled and her voice aching with doubt.

"That doesn't sound like someone who's happy to be engaged," he said carefully, his tone even—but laced with quiet honesty.

Rachel didn't respond right away. She bit her bottom lip and turned her gaze back to the waves, the sea breeze catching the ends of her damp hair. Her voice, when it came, was quiet. Measured. Almost like she was hearing the words for the first time herself.

"No," she murmured. "It doesn't."

Darcy's chest tightened. The way she said it—it wasn't defensive or uncertain. It was a quiet surrender to something she'd been trying to ignore. And it hit him harder than he expected.

Because it didn't just sound like the beginning of an ending.

It sounded like the beginning of something else entirely.

Something she wasn't ready to say…

And something he wasn't ready to walk away from.

Rachel let out a slow breath, dragging her fingers through the damp strands of her hair. "I have to talk to him," she admitted, her voice barely above a whisper. "I'm pretty sure it's over. But you know what upsets me more than that?" She turned her gaze back to the waves, watching them roll endlessly toward the shore in their steady, hypnotic rhythm. "It's the fact that I don't think I'd be heartbroken about it."

She braced for guilt—for that sharp sting of shame that should've come with admitting something so final, so indifferent. But it didn't come. What came instead was relief. Quiet and undeniable.

Darcy studied her, silent. She didn't flinch, didn't rush to fill the space. Her fingers toyed with the frayed edge of her towel, her shoulders curling in slightly, like the words had taken more out of her than she expected. He could see it happening in real time—the moment a woman let go of something she'd been clinging to out of obligation, not love.

"So why did you get engaged, then?" he asked, his tone soft. Curious. Not judgmental.

Rachel hesitated, chewing the inside of her cheek like she was debating how honest she wanted to be. "It happened so fast," she said finally. "Now that I really think about it, I'm not even sure why I said yes." A dry, humourless laugh escaped her. "God, that sounds awful, doesn't it?"

"No," Darcy said simply. "Not at all."

She shifted, drawing her knees tighter to her chest, arms folding around them like a shield. "Jeremy was my first real boyfriend. The first person who made me feel… seen. Wanted. Safe. And for a while, that was enough." Her lips quirked at the corners, but it wasn't a smile—it was something sadder. Smaller. "I kept telling myself love wasn't about fireworks or losing control—it was about choosing someone solid. Someone who fit."

Darcy arched a brow. "And now?"

Rachel exhaled, eyes tracking the path of a seabird drifting lazily across the horizon. "Now I feel like he's holding me back. I want to see the world, meet people, live a hundred lives before I settle into just one. He doesn't want that. He wants stability. Routine. A life with neat little lines and no messy edges." She paused, then glanced at him, her voice quieter. "Maybe I wanted to believe in it more than I actually felt it."

She looked at him then—really looked at him—like she was bracing for judgment. "That makes me sound like a terrible person, doesn't it?"

"No," he said without hesitation. "It makes you honest."

Something flickered behind her eyes. Gratitude, maybe. Or the bittersweet sting of being seen too clearly.

She looked away again. "Still… even if I know it's over, I can't do anything until I talk to him. I owe him that much. I could never do something behind his back. That's not me."

Darcy nodded slowly. That, he believed without question. Rachel had a code— quiet, firm, unshakeable. He respected the hell out of it. It didn't make things easier, but it made her who she was.

And yet…

Every time she glanced at him, every time her breath caught in that barely-there way, every time silence thickened between them and neither of them moved to break it—

He felt it.

And from the way she was avoiding his eyes now, carefully sipping from her water bottle like she needed something to hold on to, he knew she felt it too.

"Sorry," Rachel muttered. "I've said too much."

Darcy shook his head. "Sometimes talking to someone who's not involved helps," he said, his voice low and even. "Gives you clarity."

She held his gaze for a beat longer this time. Then nodded. "Yeah. You're right." A small smile tugged at the corner of her mouth—soft, grateful, a little tired. "Thanks for listening."

Darcy didn't answer right away. He just studied her—quiet, thoughtful. Something raw and real flickered between them again. Unspoken. Unwelcome.

And inevitable.

Rachel turned away, fixing her eyes on the ocean once more. "I guess I'll find out what's going to happen soon enough," she said softly. "I leave on Saturday."

The words landed with more weight than she probably meant them to. Darcy felt it settle in his chest like a slow pressure.

Saturday.

Three days.

He should've felt relieved. Detached. This whole thing—whatever it was—was temporary.

But instead, he felt the faint, unmistakable ache of something he didn't want to name.

And as he looked at her, with sunlight kissing her skin and the wind tugging at her hair, one thought echoed louder than the rest:

You don't want her to go.

The thought hit Darcy hard—unwelcome, uninvited, but impossible to ignore.

Before he could untangle the knot twisting in his chest, Rachel pushed herself to her feet, brushing sand from her legs with brisk, practiced sweeps. "Well, I don't know about you, but I'm starving," she said, her voice too bright, too casual. "Time to head back, I think."

The shift in tone was deliberate. He could hear it—the carefully constructed wall sliding back into place.

Darcy watched her for a beat longer, noting the way she kept her gaze fixed ahead, not on him. She was retreating, not physically, but emotionally. Pretending nothing had passed between them. Maybe she needed to. Maybe it was the only way to keep things from slipping further down a path they both knew was dangerous.

Still, it didn't erase the moment that had cracked open between them. That quiet truth neither of them had named, but both had clearly felt.

Wordlessly, he rose, brushing sand from his hands, and helped her gather their things. A towel. A bottle of water. A pair of sandals kicked carelessly into the shade. Every action felt heavier than it should have.

They walked back along the shoreline, the rhythm between them familiar now—easy, companionable. But there was something different in the silence. A new current beneath the surface. Quieter than before. But there.

By the time they reached the resort's beachfront restaurant, the sun had shifted overhead, casting dappled light across the wooden deck. They took a table beneath the shade of a wide umbrella, and the ocean breeze softened the edges of whatever they were trying not to say.

Lunch came, easy and unremarkable—grilled fish, fresh fruit, cold drinks. The kind of meal made for vacationers with nowhere to be.

Conversation drifted from light topics—places they'd travelled, embarrassing childhood stories—to playful sarcasm and shared laughter. On the surface, it was relaxed. But Darcy couldn't stop noticing the small things. The way Rachel tucked her hair behind her ear without y it. The way her lips curved when she tried not to smile. The way her fingers grazed the rim of her glass, slow and distracted, like her mind wasn't fully in the conversation anymore.

Neither was his.

And then, just as seamlessly as she'd slid into his company, she began to pull away.

"I think I'll head back to my bungalow for a bit," Rachel said, rising from her chair, stretching her arms overhead. Her tank top rode up slightly, revealing a sliver of golden skin before she smoothed it down. "I've got a book I've been meaning to finish."

Darcy nodded, masking the disappointment that rose in his chest. "Enjoy your reading," he said, his voice even.

She hesitated for half a heartbeat, her gaze flicking toward him—quick, uncertain, unguarded. And in that single glance, he saw it. The war inside her. The tug of something neither of them had named but both had stopped pretending to ignore.

But then it was gone. Her smile returned—small, composed, polite. "See you later."

And she turned and walked away, her sandals soft against the boardwalk, her ponytail swaying in the breeze like a punctuation mark at the end of a sentence neither of them had dared to write.

Darcy sat back in his chair, eyes tracking her until she disappeared around the corner.

And just like that, the sun didn't feel quite as warm. The ocean didn't seem quite as inviting. And the food in front of him might as well have been sand.

Because suddenly, he wasn't hungry anymore.

Wednesday afternoon, Darcy made his way to the open-air studio, the hum of distant music growing louder with each step.

It was just another part of his evaluation of the resort. A guest experience. Research. Nothing more.

At least, that's what he told himself.

Over and over.

But the tightening in his chest said otherwise.

So did the way he straightened his shirt and slowed his steps just before turning the corner.

The studio was already alive with the rhythm of the tango—its sensual, pulsing beat curling through the space like smoke. A few couples stood off to the side, watching the demonstration with hesitant fascination.

And then he saw her. Rachel.

Locked in a slow, hypnotic dance with Sam. His breath caught before he could stop it.

Chapter Eleven

Sam's hand rested low on her back, fingers splayed possessively as he guided her into a deep, sweeping step. Rachel followed, her body a study in control and surrender—each movement sharp, sensual, and impossibly fluid. Her fitted black dress clung to her every curve, the hem fluttering around her knees as she pivoted. Then, in one seamless motion, Sam dipped her low, her golden hair cascading like liquid sunlight over her shoulder.

Darcy's jaw tightened.

There was no mistaking the intimacy between them—the trust, the timing, the way their bodies moved like they'd been rehearsing for years. And maybe they had. But that didn't make it any easier to watch.

Rachel's head tilted back slightly as Sam pulled her upright, the movement exposing the curve of her neck. Her cheeks were flushed, her lips parted, her expression lit with the kind of joy that wasn't just about dance—it was about freedom. Energy. Passion.

She was stunning.

And she wasn't his.

Darcy folded his arms, planting himself just inside the studio, watching with a tightness coiling low in his gut. He shouldn't care. She was engaged. He had no claim to her.

But the way Sam's hand glided down her arm—the way their thighs brushed in the next slow, smouldering cross-step—set something primal off inside him.

He didn't see the others in the room anymore.

All he saw was Rachel.

And the man touching her like he'd earned the right to.

When Sam slid his hand lower again, fingers grazing the bare skin of her back before dipping her for the second time, Darcy's restraint snapped.

He stepped forward, his voice low but cutting clean through the music.

"Mind if I cut in?"

The music faltered.

Rachel and Sam froze mid-step. Rachel's eyes widened, breath caught halfway between a gasp and a protest. Sam straightened slowly, and a slow, knowing smirk tugged at the corner of his mouth.

"Well," he drawled, clearly amused, "someone's feeling brave."

Darcy held his gaze without flinching. "Be my guest," Sam added, with a mock bow, before stepping back with exaggerated flair.

Darcy didn't smile. He didn't speak.

He just extended his hand.

Rachel stared at it for a moment, a hundred thoughts flickering behind her eyes— confusion, caution, and something else entirely. Heat. Curiosity.

Then she took it.

Her fingers slid into his—warm, familiar, grounding in a way that stole her breath.

They had no right to feel that way. No right to feel like home.

Rachel arched a brow, schooling her features into something breezy. "I didn't think you danced in public."

Darcy met her gaze, his tone smooth, unreadable. "It's all coming back to me."

Before she could form a reply—or even protest—his hand slid around her waist, confident and unapologetic, drawing her in with practiced ease. The movement was sudden, fluid, and it sent a jolt through her—sharp, electric. She inhaled sharply, her other hand rising instinctively to his shoulder. Beneath the soft cotton of his shirt, muscle tensed under her fingertips—solid, steady, real.

Sam, unfazed by the shift in dynamic, turned to the single woman who'd been watching with wide eyes. "Looks like you just got lucky," he said with a charming grin, offering his hand. She giggled and accepted eagerly.

But Darcy wasn't paying attention to Sam anymore.

His focus was locked entirely on Rachel.

The music swelled again—deep, sultry, intoxicating. A tango with teeth. It wasn't a melody that asked for polite steps or awkward shuffling. It demanded closeness. Control. Connection. It was a dare set to rhythm.

And Darcy accepted.

He led her into the movement with stunning ease, and Rachel had no choice but to follow.

But it wasn't just following—it was falling.

Into the beat. Into him.

He moved with sharp precision, with deliberate force softened only by the heat in his gaze. This wasn't beginner-level dancing. This was something raw. Instinctive. Controlled. And impossibly intimate.

Rachel matched him, her training kicking in like muscle memory—but the rest of her, the woman beneath the performer, was unravelling fast. Every glide of his hand, every brush of their bodies, every perfectly timed pivot set her nerves on fire.

And still, she didn't pull away.

He spun her, and her skirt flared around them. When she returned to his chest, his hand found the small of her back again—firmer this time. Possessive. Anchoring. His fingers splayed just slightly, as if memorising the feel of her.

Her breath caught. Her resolve slipped another inch.

And then he dipped her.

The world fell away. For a suspended second, she was weightless, nothing but breath and heat and the overwhelming presence of him. His face hovered inches from hers, close enough to count the darker flecks in his hazel eyes. His breath brushed her cheek, and every nerve ending she had lit up in response.

Her pulse thundered in her ears.

"You dance better than I expected," she murmured, somehow keeping her voice even.

His lips curved—slow, deliberate. There was dark amusement in his eyes, but something else too. Hunger. "And you like being surprised, don't you?"

Rachel swallowed. She hated how well he read her. Hated how right it felt to be in his arms.

This wasn't just a dance.

It was a confession neither of them was ready to speak.

The song ended, and applause rippled softly through the small class. Darcy's grip loosened, but he didn't let go immediately. Their eyes met—too long, too loaded.

Dancing with him had felt like walking a razor's edge, the air between them thick with something unspoken. Her pulse had been erratic, her skin burning where he had touched her. And the way he had looked at her—like he knew exactly what he was doing to her—was enough to make her head spin.

So, she focused on her other partners, keeping her movements light and her smile effortless. She laughed at Sam's exaggerated flair, guided the nervous guests with patient encouragement, and kept herself busy.

Even when she turned away, she felt it—the weight of his gaze, tracking her like a silent promise. A challenge. A question she wasn't ready to answer.

And when the lesson finally ended, when she clapped politely and thanked the guests for their effort, she knew she needed to get out of there before she did something reckless.

Like let herself want him.

Her heart was still racing as she turned away, her skin tingling from where his hands had been. The warmth of his touch lingered, an invisible imprint she couldn't shake. She needed distance. Space to breathe, to remind herself why this—whatever this was—couldn't happen.

Without looking back, she murmured a quick excuse to the group and slipped away, weaving through the crowd. The open-air pavilion suddenly felt stifling, the weight of Darcy's gaze pressing against her back like a silent question.

She didn't dare turn around.

Darcy walked away from the dance lesson, his pulse unsteady, his body still humming with the imprint of her. Rachel had fit against him like she was made to be there, her every movement instinctive, seamless. She hadn't just followed his lead—she had matched him, challenged him, ignited something in him he hadn't felt in a long time.

And that was the problem.

He flexed his fingers, as if shaking off the ghost of her touch. It didn't work. The memory of her warmth, the way she'd looked at him—breathless, uncertain, tempted—clung to him, refusing to let go.

Damn it.

This wasn't supposed to happen. He had convinced himself that the pull between them was fleeting, something he could ignore. A momentary spark—nothing more.

But nothing about tonight had felt fleeting.

He had seen the hesitation in her eyes, the silent war she was fighting. She wanted to resist him. And maybe that should have been enough to make him walk away.

But it wasn't.

Instead, he found himself watching her disappear into the night, already anticipating the next time he could pull her back into his arms.

Thursday dawned with a sky streaked in soft grey, the sun hidden behind a veil of clouds. It wasn't stormy, just overcast, casting a muted glow over the island. The air was still warm, thick with the scent of salt and damp earth from the night's humidity.

Rachel stretched on the patio of her bungalow, taking a slow sip of her morning coffee. Today was supposed to be about adventure—about immersing herself in the beauty of the island. But instead of the usual excitement that came with exploring new places, a nervous energy coiled tight in her stomach.

Because Darcy would be there.

She had gone out of her way to avoid him after the dance lesson, retreating to her bungalow and ordering room service, unwilling to risk another encounter. The feelings he stirred in her—the heat, the breathlessness, the sheer pull of him— unnerved her. She had never reacted to anyone like this before. Not with Jeremy. Not with anyone.

All-consuming. Desperate. Dangerous.

But there was no avoiding him today.

By mid-morning, she made her way to the resort's front entrance, where a rugged open-air safari vehicle was parked beneath a sprawling palm tree. A local guide stood beside it, his sun-kissed skin and easy smile giving off the relaxed confidence of someone who knew the island like the back of his hand.

"Welcome, everyone," the guide greeted as Rachel approached. "I'm Leo. Today, we'll be hiking to one of the most secluded and breathtaking spots on the island. Expect stunning views, a few steep climbs, and maybe even some wildlife if we're lucky."

Rachel nodded, offering a polite smile as she took in the rest of the group. There was only one other couple—a pair of honeymooners who looked more like they belonged at the spa than on a rugged trail. The woman, dressed in pristine white linen, was already fanning herself, while her husband adjusted the straps of a brand-new backpack with an uncertain expression.

And then, as if she had summoned him with sheer thought alone, Darcy appeared.

He strode toward the group with effortless ease, dressed in a fitted black T-shirt and cargo shorts, a water bottle dangling from one hand. Rachel braced herself, but if he was affected by their dance yesterday, he didn't show it.

"Morning," he greeted, his gaze settling on her for half a beat longer than necessary.

Rachel forced herself to look away, focusing on the guide instead.

Leo clapped his hands together. "Alright, let's get going! It's about a thirty-minute drive to the trailhead, so hop in."

Rachel climbed into the open-air vehicle, sliding onto one of the bench seats. She was about to exhale in relief when the honeymooners settled onto the opposite bench, leaving only one available seat.

Right beside her.

Darcy stepped up onto the vehicle and, without hesitation, lowered himself onto the bench next to her. Their thighs brushed, just for a second, but it was enough to send a jolt of awareness up Rachel's spine.

She shifted, looking straight ahead as the engine rumbled to life and the vehicle rolled forward.

The drive was stunning—lush greenery framed the dirt road, the scent of tropical flowers drifting through the open sides. The island was alive with sound: the chirp of unseen birds, the distant rush of waves against the cliffs, the occasional chatter of monkeys in the trees.

Rachel focused on the scenery, determined not to acknowledge the heat of Darcy's body so close to hers.

Thirty minutes later, they reached the base of the trail—a narrow, winding path that disappeared into dense foliage.

Leo hopped out first. "Alright, folks! This hike is moderate, with some steep sections. We'll take breaks as needed but just let me know if you're struggling." He shot the honeymooners a knowing smile.

As they started up the trail, it quickly became clear that "moderate" was subjective. The incline was sharp, the ground uneven with tangled roots and scattered stones. Rachel loved it—the burn in her legs, the steady rhythm of her breathing, the way the jungle seemed to swallow them whole.

The honeymooners, however, weren't faring as well.

Ten minutes in, the woman groaned, stopping to lean against a tree. "Oh my god. I thought this was supposed to be leisurely."

Her husband wiped sweat from his brow. "Maybe we should've done the botanical garden tour instead."

Leo chuckled. "No worries, we'll take it slow." Then he glanced at Darcy and Rachel, noting their easy pace. "You two seem comfortable. If you want, you can go ahead—I'll stick with these two and catch up at the first rest stop."

Rachel hesitated, feeling Darcy's gaze on her. But the thought of standing around awkwardly while the honeymooners complained wasn't appealing.

"Sure," she said, adjusting the strap of her backpack. "We'll meet you up there."

Leo nodded, giving them quick directions to the first lookout point. "It's about thirty more minutes up. Just follow the path."

Rachel turned and started walking, Darcy falling into step behind her.

For the first few minutes, neither of them spoke. The only sounds were the rustling of leaves and the distant call of a tropical bird.

But the silence between them wasn't empty. It was thick. Charged.

Rachel kept her eyes on the trail ahead, but no matter how much distance the jungle placed between them and the world beyond, she was acutely aware of him.

Of the measured way he moved behind her.

Of the quiet power in every stride.

Of the silence they shared—thick, charged, alive.

And in that silence, there was no escaping him.

Not this time.

Chapter Twelve

The narrow path opened up suddenly, the dense foliage giving way to a sheer cliff. Rachel stepped to the edge, her breath catching—not from the hike, but from the sheer majesty stretching out before her.

The sea roared far below, crashing in wild bursts against black, jagged rock. Endless turquoise stretched toward the horizon where distant islands rose like mist-wrapped guardians.

She stood there, stunned, as if the wind itself had pressed pause on the world.

"Isn't it beautiful? So… majestic," she murmured, barely louder than the ocean's breath.

"Yes," came the low reply. "It is."

But when she turned slightly, Darcy wasn't looking at the view.

He was looking at her.

Heat bloomed in her chest, too sudden, too strong. She snapped her gaze back to the horizon, pretending not to notice the tension that now hummed between them like static.

Overhead, the sky had begun to shift—patches of blue giving way to roiling grey. Clouds gathered like an advancing army, swallowing the light in broad strokes.

A gust of wind whipped her hair across her face. The jungle behind them stilled, unnaturally quiet, as if holding its breath.

She stepped a little closer to the edge, heart thrumming. The earth squelched beneath her boots. A few loose clumps of dirt tumbled over the side and vanished into nothingness.

Then came the first fat drops—cool against her skin.

And then, the sky exploded.

The monsoon arrived like a beast unleashed—violent, unforgiving. Rain pounded down in torrents, soaking her in seconds. The wind shrieked, ripping through the trees, sending leaves and branches spinning through the air. Thunder cracked like cannon fire, shaking the ground beneath her feet.

"Rachel—move!" Darcy's voice was urgent, cutting through the storm.

She turned—just as the ground betrayed her.

There was a deafening crack. A rush of air. A terrifying sense of nothing.

The trail crumbled beneath her, the world vanishing in a blur of wet green and grey. She screamed as gravity yanked her down—but just before she slipped entirely into the abyss, her hand caught on a thick, gnarled root jutting from the cliffside.

Her body jerked violently. Her arms screamed in protest. She dangled over the churning sea, suspended by trembling fingers.

Below, waves exploded against rock. Foam and fury. Death and distance.

Rain lashed her skin. Her arms burned. Her grip was slipping.

"Rachel!" Darcy's voice was raw—closer now, desperate.

She looked up and saw him drop to his knees, rain pouring down his face, eyes locked on hers.

"I've got you," he growled, reaching. "Hold on."

She tried—but her fingers were numb, her strength draining. "I—I can't—" she gasped, blinking away the water.

"Yes, you can!" he barked. "Take my hand! Now!"

With one last breath, one last burst of terrified strength, she let go of the root—and lunged.

Their hands collided.

Fingers locked.

Darcy hauled her upward with a grunt, his muscles flexing, rain streaming down his arms. He dragged her over the edge with brute force, and they collapsed—mud and skin and breathless bodies tangled on the jungle floor.

For a moment, neither moved.

Only the storm breathed for them.

Then—Darcy surged upward, cupped her face in both hands, and crushed his mouth to hers.

It wasn't soft.

It wasn't slow.

It was raw—born of adrenaline and panic and something far more dangerous.

His kiss was unrelenting, bruising, and Rachel—drenched, shivering, shaken—kissed him back like he was the only thing keeping her tethered to this earth.

The heat of his mouth, the demand in his grip, the need in every second of that kiss—it tore through her like lightning. Her fingers clenched the front of his shirt, her body curving instinctively into his.

And just as quickly as it had begun, he pulled back—forehead pressed to hers, his breath ragged.

"Thank God you're okay," he whispered, his voice thick, shaken. "I thought I was going to lose you."

Her eyes burned. Her chest heaved. Her fingers still fisted in his shirt, holding onto him like she didn't dare let go.

The rain beat down, the wind howled, but in that one infinite moment—it didn't matter.

Only he did.

She should speak. Should move. Should say anything.

But when she looked into his storm-dark eyes, her own heart felt like the ocean—raging, wild, impossible to calm.

And all she could do was hold on.

The world around them was chaos—rain pounding the earth, wind howling through the trees, thunder rolling across the sky like the roar of an angry god. And yet, in this moment, none of it touched her. Only him. The feel of his body beneath hers, the heat of his breath mingling with hers, the intensity in his gaze that sent a shiver through her despite the warm, humid air.

Rachel broke the spell first. A shaky breath left her lips as she shifted, pressing her hands into the muddy ground to push herself up. But the moment she moved—

"Aaahh!" Pain shot through her ankle like a hot blade, sharp and immediate.

Darcy sat up instantly, his hands steadying her before she could collapse again. "What's wrong?" His voice was still rough from adrenaline, but concern had taken over.

"My ankle—" Rachel swallowed against the wave of pain, her fingers digging into the wet earth. "I think I twisted it when I fell."

Darcy's jaw tightened. "Let me see."

He didn't wait for permission. Gently, but with firm efficiency, he shifted so he could examine her ankle. Rachel bit her lip as he carefully lifted the fabric of her damp leggings, his fingers brushing against her bare skin. Even through the haze of discomfort, awareness sparked at his touch.

His brows furrowed as he ran his fingers lightly over the swelling joint, his touch both careful and confident. "It's already bruising," he muttered, his voice low. "You definitely sprained it."

Rachel let out a frustrated breath. "Perfect."

Darcy glanced up, his blue eyes locking onto hers. "Can you stand?"

"I don't know. I—" She shifted slightly, attempting to test her weight, but the moment she tried to move, pain flared, making her wince.

Darcy's expression darkened. "That's a no."

He sat back on his heels, running a hand through his rain-soaked hair, his jaw tightening as he looked around. The storm wasn't letting up. If anything, the rain was falling harder, turning the trail into a slick, muddy mess. The jungle around them felt more claustrophobic, the heavy wind sending leaves and branches whipping through the air.

"We need to find shelter," Darcy said, his voice all business now.

Rachel let out a short, humourless laugh. "Right. And how exactly am I supposed to walk on this?" She gestured at her ankle, which was already swelling beneath the mud and rain.

Darcy gave her a look—steady, unyielding. "You're not."

Before she could protest, he moved. In one swift motion, he scooped her into his arms, lifting her as if she weighed nothing.

"Darcy—"

"Save it," he cut in, his grip firm, secure. "I'm not leaving you here, and I doubt you want me to go find help and leave you alone in a storm. We can't go back down—the path's too dangerous now. Our best bet is to keep moving up, find higher ground." He adjusted his hold on her, his arms tightening. "Unless you have a better plan?"

Rachel sighed, knowing there was no point in arguing. "You're right," she muttered, reluctantly wrapping her arms around his neck as he started walking. Then, after a beat, she added, "But I'm too heavy."

Darcy huffed out something between a laugh and a scoff. "You weigh nothing."

Rachel rested her forehead against his shoulder, her breath uneven—not just from the pain, but from the way he held her so effortlessly, like she belonged there. Like protecting her was second nature.

The storm raged around them, wind howling, rain slashing against their skin. But in his arms, she felt something she hadn't expected.

Safe.

And that was almost more dangerous than the storm itself.

Darcy moved swiftly, his grip on Rachel unwavering as he carried her up the slick, treacherous path. Rain lashed against them, the storm intensifying with every step. The wind howled through the trees, bending branches, and sending leaves whipping through the air.

Rachel clung to him, her breath warm against his neck, but he barely noticed. His focus was on finding shelter—somewhere safe, somewhere dry.

Then, a jagged bolt of lightning slashed across the sky, turning the jungle into a stark, electric landscape.

For a split second, everything was illuminated—the twisted branches, the sheets of rain, the endless, churning dark. And just beyond the ridge, half-hidden by the dense foliage, he saw it.

A cabin.

Weathered but standing firm, its wooden walls slick with rain, tucked between the towering palms like a secret waiting to be found.

Darcy's pulse kicked up. His gaze swept the ridge again, desperate, searching— praying—for something, anything. The storm roared around them, wind howling like a living thing. Then, through the shifting veil of rain, the shape emerged once more, solid, and unmistakable.

Relief slammed into him. "There," he breathed, gripping Rachel tighter. "I see a cabin."

She lifted her head, blinking through the downpour. "Are you sure?"

"Positive." Determination surged through him as he adjusted his grip and quickened his pace. "Hold on. We're almost there."

Sure enough, the cabin stood just beyond the ridge, nestled between the towering palms. The rain pounded against the wooden walls, the wind howling through the gaps in the shutters. Without hesitation, Darcy shifted Rachel's weight in his arms and reached for the door. It creaked open under his touch, the hinges stiff with age.

Inside, the cabin was dim, the only light coming from occasional flashes of lightning seeping through the cracks in the shutters. Shadows danced along the wooden walls, making the space feel both intimate and eerily still. The air was thick with the scent of damp wood, mingled with something faintly metallic—perhaps from the storm. A battered lantern sat on a shelf, dust coating its glass, and a wool blanket lay folded at the foot of the cot, forgotten but promising warmth. The place felt abandoned, yet lived in, as if it had been waiting for them.

A modest stone fireplace stood against one wall; its hearth cold but stacked with firewood that looked dry enough to burn. A small, rough-hewn table and two mismatched chairs sat in the centre of the room. Against the far wall was a narrow cot, the blankets neatly folded, suggesting someone had been here recently— perhaps a ranger or a fisherman seeking shelter from storms like this.

Darcy carried Rachel straight to the cot, lowering her gently onto the thin mattress. "We should be safe here for now," he murmured, brushing wet strands of hair from her face.

Rachel shivered, her soaked clothes clinging to her skin, a chill seeping into her bones. She exhaled a shaky breath, glancing around their temporary refuge. "Looks like we're stuck here for a while."

Darcy met her gaze, his expression unreadable, his dark eyes lingering on her for a fraction too long. "Yeah," he said quietly. He ran a hand through his damp hair before nodding toward the stone fireplace in the corner. "I'll see if I can start a fire. We need to get warm."

Rachel forced a small smile, trying to make light of the situation. "Sorry, can't help you there. I think I'll just sit here and supervise."

Darcy huffed a laugh, shaking his head. "Of course you will."

Darcy got to work, gathering dry kindling from a small stack near the hearth. He struck a match, shielding the tiny flame from the lingering drafts before coaxing it to life against the wood. The fire crackled, sending flickering light dancing across the cabin walls, its warmth slowly chasing away the chill that had settled in Rachel's bones.

Outside, the storm still raged, rain hammering against the roof in relentless sheets, but the wind had started to ease. The worst of it was passing.

Darcy stood, rolling his shoulders before turning back to her. He pulled a chair closer to the cot where she sat, his gaze dropping to her ankle. "We need to get your shoe off," he said, his voice firm but gentle.

Rachel swallowed, eyeing the swollen joint. "Yeah. That's going to hurt."

Darcy's lips pressed into a thin line. "Probably. But leaving it on isn't an option."

She hesitated, then gave him a small nod. "Okay. Just… be careful."

A smirk ghosted across his face. "I'm always careful."

He crouched in front of her, his fingers working the sodden laces with meticulous precision, his touch surprisingly tender. Rachel winced as he eased the shoe off, her breath catching when pain shot up her leg.

Darcy glanced up; his brow furrowed. "Sorry."

She let out a shaky laugh. "Not your fault. Just—ow."

His hands lingered, hovering just above her ankle, his fingers barely brushing her skin. "It's already swelling a lot," he murmured, his voice lower now, almost to himself. "We need to keep it elevated."

Rachel bit her lip, trying to ignore the warmth that spread through her at his touch—warmth that had nothing to do with the fire crackling behind him. This was dangerous. This was wrong. She was engaged. But as Darcy's fingers brushed lightly over her skin, careful and deliberate, a traitorous part of her didn't want to pull away.

Chapter Thirteen

Darcy rummaged through the small kitchenette, opening cabinets, and checking the tiny icebox. He found a cloth and a bottle of water, the liquid inside still cold. It wasn't much, but it would do.

Returning to Rachel's side, he folded the cloth, poured the cool water over it, and gently pressed it against her swollen ankle. She tensed at the initial shock, but then exhaled, her body relaxing slightly.

"You're a good man to have around in a crisis," she murmured, offering him a tired but genuine smile. Her gaze softened. "Thank you, Darcy. You saved my life."

His hands stilled for half a second before he resumed his careful work, his jaw tightening as if the weight of her words unsettled him. He glanced up, meeting her eyes. Something flickered there—something unreadable, almost guarded.

"You don't have to thank me," he said, voice gruff but quieter this time. "I wasn't about to let anything happen to you."

For a moment, Rachel wondered if he meant it in the same way she felt it—that the thought of losing her, even in a storm, wasn't just about responsibility.

Something unspoken passed between them in the dim firelight. A flicker of something deeper. It hummed in the air between them, fragile yet undeniable.

Rachel felt it—the shift in him—not just in his hands, which lingered a heartbeat too long, but in the tight line of his jaw, the flicker of restraint in his eyes.

He was holding something back.

So was she.

She wanted to speak—to break the silence, to say something that might ease the pressure coiling between them—but the words caught in her throat, tangled in the storm still echoing inside her.

Darcy cleared his throat and shifted his focus back to her ankle, his touch now measured and methodical, as if anchoring himself in the practical was the only way to keep from unravelling. As if tending to her injury was safer than looking her in the eye.

But he wasn't thinking about her ankle.

He was thinking about the moment she slipped—that sickening second when the ground vanished beneath her and she disappeared from his reach. That image had burned itself into his mind, more terrifying than any storm. For a moment, everything inside him had gone still, seized by a raw, primal fear.

He'd moved without thinking, heart pounding, instincts overriding logic. And when he'd pulled her back, when he'd felt her body in his arms again, breathing, alive—he hadn't just been relieved. He'd been undone.

Now, even with her sitting there, safe, his heart still hadn't slowed.

He swallowed hard, forcing his attention back to the makeshift bandage. "You scared the hell out of me back there," he said, his voice low and rough, as if the words scraped their way out.

Rachel blinked, the quiet sincerity catching her off guard. "I didn't mean to," she whispered.

"I know." He dragged a hand down his face, rain still dripping from his hair, his lashes. Then he met her eyes again, something unguarded flickering beneath the surface. "But I still saw you fall. And I—" He broke off, jaw tightening. "Doesn't matter."

But it did. It mattered more than he could admit.

Rachel studied him, her chest tightening with something she didn't want to name. His words weren't just about the fall. They were about her. About something neither of them had said aloud but both of them felt. And for the first time since the sky cracked open, it wasn't the cold or fear that made her shiver.

It was him.

Darcy finished wrapping her ankle, tying the cloth in a neat, firm knot. His fingers paused—just for a moment—on her skin, warm and grounding. "There," he murmured. "That should help."

She shifted slightly, testing the pressure. It stung, but it was stable. "Yeah. Thank you."

She glanced toward the window carved into the side of the emergency hut. Outside, the storm had softened, the thunder reduced to a distant growl. Rain no longer slammed the jungle—just misted gently, as though the sky had spent itself.

"The rain's stopped," she said softly.

Darcy followed her gaze. "Yeah," he agreed. "But the ground's unstable. We're not risking a hike in the dark."

She nodded, her shoulders relaxing slightly. "They'll come looking for us when it's safe."

He glanced at her, and for a moment something close to amusement tugged at the edge of his mouth. "I'll give you this—you're not one of those women who panics in a crisis."

Rachel let out a quiet huff. "Trust me, I'm panicking. Just doing it very discreetly."

His mouth quirked into a faint smile, one that softened him in a way that undid her. "Well, you wear it well."

A hush settled between them—no longer awkward, but dense with something unspoken. The kind of silence that said too much. The kind that hovered like a held breath.

The fire crackled softly in the centre of the hut, casting shadows on the wooden walls and bathing them in flickering warmth. Outside, the jungle exhaled.

Inside, Rachel's heart beat unevenly, a quiet drum of questions she wasn't ready to ask. Because the storm outside may have passed…

But the one inside her?

That was only just beginning.

Darcy pushed to his feet, stretching out the tension in his shoulders. His eyes flicked toward the small kitchenette. "There's a kettle we can hang over the fire. And some tea in the cupboard if you want some?"

Rachel shook her head. "Not much of a tea drinker."

His mouth quirked. "Coffee more your taste?"

"Definitely. What about you?"

Darcy let out a low laugh, running a hand through his damp hair. "Right now? I could do with a whiskey, to be honest."

She huffed out a soft chuckle. "Same."

For a moment, the quiet settled again, comfortable but edged with something unspoken. Rachel shifted slightly, adjusting her injured ankle before glancing up at him. "I really don't know much about you," she admitted. "Where are you from?"

Darcy hesitated, just for a fraction of a second. Then he leaned back against the table, arms crossing over his chest. "New York," he said, his voice lighter than the shadow that passed through his eyes.

He thought about how she still had no idea who he really was—that he wasn't just another guest at the resort. That the place they were stranded in? He owned it.

And it wasn't something he could just drop into casual conversation.

Not here.

Not now.

What would be the point?

She'd be gone soon. And after that, their paths would never cross again.

Probably.

Rachel was watching him, a trace of curiosity in her expression, like she could sense there was something more beneath the surface.

"You got any family?" she asked, her voice quiet but direct.

Darcy's lips pressed into a thin line before he answered. "A sister. Eleanor." His tone was even, clipped. Then, as if he realised he'd given too much away, he smirked, deflecting. "What about you? Where's home?"

"London." Her voice softened a fraction, the word weighted with something unspoken. "No family. My mother passed two years ago."

The smirk vanished from his face. "I'm sorry."

Rachel gave a small shrug, but it was practiced—automatic. Her eyes, however, told the real story. They darkened with the kind of grief that didn't fade with time, just settled deeper into your bones. "She did everything for me. It was just the two of us for as long as I can remember."

Darcy hesitated. "What about your dad?"

Her entire expression changed—tightened. "No father."

The air shifted.

She exhaled, slow and deliberate, like she was weighing what to reveal. "I know who he was. He's gone now."

Darcy said nothing, letting her speak. He could feel something sharp coiling beneath her words, and he didn't want to interrupt whatever truth she was trying to find.

"My mother worked for him," Rachel continued, her voice thinner now, edged with something brittle. "He promised her the world, but when she got pregnant, he vanished. Just like that." She gave a short, bitter laugh. "Rich men always think they can do whatever they want."

Darcy's jaw tightened. "Not all of them are like that."

She scoffed, eyes flashing. "I don't care to find out. One was enough."

"Did you ever meet him?"

"Oh, I met him." Her mouth twisted, not quite a smile. "And he told me—on the one and only time I showed up at his door—that my mother should've kept her legs closed. Said she only opened them to try and get his money."

The words hung between them, vile and heavy. Darcy's hands curled into fists in his lap.

"I was seventeen," she added softly. "Seventeen when he said that to my face."

He exhaled through his nose, voice low and dark. "Charmer."

Rachel rolled her eyes, but the pain still flickered behind them. "Oh yeah. Real prince."

There was a long pause.

"You know the worst part?" she asked, quieter now. "My mother loved him. Even after everything. Never married. Never looked at anyone else. She gave her heart to a man who didn't deserve to hold it for a second."

Darcy's throat worked. "She deserved better."

Rachel nodded faintly. "Yeah. She did."

Her gaze drifted to the fire, the flames reflected in her eyes. "Love makes people do stupid things, doesn't it?"

He didn't answer right away. But something in his chest pulled taut—like the truth of it had struck a chord far too close to his own guarded past.

Finally, he murmured, "Yeah. It does."

Rachel exhaled and looked over at him, her expression softer now, more searching than before. "I don't know why I tell you everything," she admitted. "First Jeremy. Now this." She paused, as if surprised by her own openness. "There's just something about you. I think it's because you actually listen. That's rare."

Darcy let out a quiet laugh, trying to shake off the ache in his chest. "You're the first woman to ever say that to me."

She raised an eyebrow. "Really? You don't usually listen?"

"I listen," he said with a crooked grin. "I'm just not sure anyone's ever noticed."

"Well," she said, giving him a look that was equal parts fond and exasperated, "I do. And I appreciate it."

Something shifted in his expression—just for a moment. Then, before the air between them could grow too heavy again, he pushed off the table and stood. "Tea might not cut it," he said, glancing toward a battered cupboard. "I saw a bottle of something in there earlier. Want to risk it?"

Rachel leaned back, smiling for the first time in a while. "That depends. Are you trying to get me drunk, Darcy?"

He looked over his shoulder and flashed her a grin. "Depends. Would you tell me more if I did?"

She threw her head back and laughed, the sound rich and warm and alive. "Probably."

They spent the rest of the night sipping bad liquor and talking about everything and nothing—movies from their childhoods, disastrous travel stories, the worst food they'd ever had. Somewhere between the second and third glass, the firelight started to feel softer, the world outside quieter.

Rachel stopped caring that the drink burned on the way down. It was warm.

So was the company.

Eventually, she yawned, stretching her legs out on the cot.

Darcy noticed and nodded toward the pile of blankets. "You should get some sleep."

She blinked drowsily at him. "What about you?"

"I'm fine."

"No, there's room here for you." She patted the space beside her.

He hesitated, jaw tightening. "I don't think that's a good idea."

She smirked, the alcohol making her bolder. "Don't you trust me, Darcy? You think I'll take advantage of you?"

His lips twitched, something flickering in his eyes—sharp, amused, but wary. "No."

Rachel tilted her head, grinning. "We're adults, Darcy. I'm sure we can resist each other."

He exhaled, rubbing the back of his neck. "Go to sleep, Rachel."

"Don't be ridiculous. I insist." She tugged on his wrist lightly. "You can't sit up all night just to be noble."

Darcy sighed, but finally relented, lowering himself onto the cot with obvious reluctance. "Fine. But you face that way, and I'll face this way."

She chuckled, shifting to her side. "Deal."

He draped a blanket over both of them, the space between them barely enough. His body was tense, as if bracing against something invisible.

"Goodnight, Rachel," he murmured.

"Night, Darcy."

Silence settled, but the awareness between them remained, heavy in the dim firelight. Neither of them moved, each acutely aware of the other's presence—the warmth, the steady rise and fall of breath. It took a long time before sleep finally claimed them, and even then, it was restless.

Chapter Fourteen

Rachel woke with a start the next morning. For a moment, she didn't remember where she was—only that she was warm, cocooned in soft heat. Then she felt it— the steady rise and fall of his breath, warm against her skin. The solid weight of his arm, heavy, unmoving, anchoring her in place.

Her eyes fluttered open. Darcy was in front of her, still asleep.

She should move. She should pull away. But she didn't.

Instead, she let herself stay there, just for a moment longer. It was the safest she had felt in a long time. His arm around her wasn't confining—it was steady, reassuring. Protective.

Her gaze drifted over his face, tracing the strong lines of his jaw, the faint shadow of stubble that darkened his skin, the way his lashes—longer than any man's had a right to be—rested against his cheek. He looked different in sleep. Softer. Less guarded. Peaceful in a way he never allowed himself to be when awake.

God, he was beautiful.

Too beautiful.

Rachel swallowed hard, her breath catching as the realisation of just how close they were settled over her. His arm was still around her waist, anchoring her to him beneath the warmth of the blanket. All she had to do was lift her hand and she could touch him—run her fingers down the line of his jaw, trace the curve of his mouth.

Her fingers twitched, as if they might.

Then—like he felt her watching—Darcy stirred. His brow furrowed slightly, lashes fluttering open. His eyes, still hazy with sleep, blinked slowly before locking onto hers.

He didn't move.

Didn't speak.

And he didn't let go.

Rachel froze, breath caught in her throat, her heart thudding painfully loud in the quiet. She should say something. A joke, a quip—anything to break the spell that had stretched taut between them. But her mouth refused to move. So did his.

Then, slowly, deliberately, Darcy lifted a hand. His fingertips grazed a stray strand of damp hair from her cheek. The touch was light—barely there—but it sent a shiver down her spine, heat flaring where his skin met hers.

His gaze dropped to her lips.

Rachel's breath stuttered. She knew what that look meant. She should turn away. She should remind him—remind herself—that this was wrong.

She didn't.

His fingers slid lower, tracing the edge of her jaw, tilting her face toward his. And then—

He kissed her.

It started soft, almost hesitant—his lips brushing against hers like a question. But when she didn't pull away—when her body melted into his, her mouth parting in a breathless invitation—he answered.

The kiss deepened.

It turned slow and aching, his mouth moving against hers with a hunger held carefully in check. One hand threaded into her hair, angling her closer. The other pressed against her lower back, pulling her into him, heat sparking where their bodies met.

Rachel sighed into him, her fingers curling into the front of his shirt, anchoring herself to something real. Her mind was blank—no worries, no doubts, just the sensation of his mouth claiming hers. And when his tongue slid against hers in a lazy stroke, coaxing, exploring, she arched toward him, the fire in her belly flaring white-hot.

Darcy shifted, half-covering her body with his, his weight warm and solid, anchoring her to the moment. His hand skimmed down her side, slow and reverent, fingertips ghosting over the curve of her waist before settling on her hip.

She gasped softly at the contact, and he took the sound as invitation—his mouth trailing kisses along her jaw, down the curve of her neck. His breath was hot against her skin, his lips lingering just beneath her ear, where he whispered something she couldn't hear but felt in her bones.

Her hands found his shoulders, the hard lines of muscle beneath the fabric of his shirt and then slid up into his hair. She scraped her nails gently against his scalp, drawing a low, guttural sound from his throat.

His hand tightened at her hip—just once, a grounding grip—before he pulled back, just enough to rest his forehead against hers.

Their breaths mingled, ragged and uneven. Her skin tingled. Her lips were swollen. Her heart pounded so violently it was a wonder he couldn't feel it.

Darcy didn't say a word.

He didn't have to.

Rachel stared up at him, her thoughts slowly catching up to her body. Guilt twisted in her gut, cold and sharp. Her hand—still tangled in his shirt—began to tremble.

She was engaged.

And this wasn't just a kiss.

It was the beginning of something she couldn't take back.

Darcy watched her, his dark eyes searching her face for something—permission, apology, maybe even regret. But he said nothing, as if letting her decide where this would go next.

She didn't move.

Didn't speak.

And yet... they both knew something had changed. Something real. Something dangerous.

Eventually, she drew in a shaky breath and lowered her gaze. Her fingers loosened their grip on his shirt, falling away.

Darcy shifted back slightly, his expression unreadable now—but his hand lingered at her hip, thumb tracing slow, absent circles against her skin, as if even he didn't want to let go.

The air around them stayed thick, charged with everything they hadn't said.

And neither of them reached for the blanket.

His fingers were still resting on her hip, his breath still mingling with hers. She could feel the rapid thrum of his heart beneath her palm—steady, strong, mirroring the wild rhythm of her own. For one suspended moment, everything inside her screamed to close the gap again. To chase the fire, to drown in it.

But reality hit hard.

Cold.

Unforgiving.

With a sharp inhale, Rachel turned her face away, the movement small but final. "We shouldn't have done that," she whispered, and even as the words left her mouth, they rang hollow. A lie dressed as logic.

Darcy didn't flinch, didn't protest. But she felt it—the retreat. The slow draw of his hand from her waist. The way tension pulled through his body like piano wire, tight and silent. He let out a breath, low and rough. "I know."

Silence pooled between them—thick, echoing with everything they hadn't said, with everything they'd let slip between their lips in that kiss.

Rachel sat up, clutching the blanket like armour, wrapping it tight around her as though it could erase what had just happened. "It was just—" Her voice faltered. There were no easy words, no tidy ending. "I'm sorry."

Darcy's hand ran through his hair, fingers scraping back damp strands with a restless motion. "You don't have to apologise." But his tone had changed. No longer warm, no longer teasing. Quieter now. Cautious.

She glanced at him, stealing a look she wasn't sure she had the right to. His jaw was set tight; his eyes fixed on the dimming fire as if he could force the moment out of existence.

And just like that, the space between them—once charged with electricity—felt cavernous.

It hurt.

Because as much as her head screamed for distance, her heart rebelled. Part of her wanted to reach for him again, to pull him close and pretend the ring on her finger didn't exist. Pretend this island, this man, was all that mattered.

But she couldn't.

Darcy's gaze flicked toward her and then away, his expression unreadable. "I should stoke the fire," he murmured.

She nodded, though he wasn't looking at her. He stood and crossed the room, crouching in front of the hearth. Rachel curled her legs beneath her, burying deeper into the blanket, the silence pressing in on all sides.

She watched him in the flickering firelight, his movements efficient, practiced. But the tension in his shoulders gave him away. He was just as wrecked by this as she was.

And she couldn't let it end like this. Not in silence. Not with the weight of that kiss hanging between them like a noose.

"I need to say something," she murmured.

Darcy turned, the glow of the fire lighting one side of his face, the shadows clinging to the other. His expression was blank—but alert. Listening.

Rachel inhaled slowly. "I'm attracted to you," she said, her voice shaky but clear. "More than I should be. More than I want to be." Her eyes lifted to meet his, steady now. "But I can't do this. I can't cheat on Jeremy."

A flicker of pain crossed his face—quick, but undeniable. His jaw worked for a second before he gave a single nod. "I know."

"I just…" she hesitated, searching for the words. "I didn't want you to think that kiss meant nothing. Because it did."

Darcy's fingers curled into a fist at his side, then flexed again. "It meant something to me too." His voice was low, almost raw. "I want you, Rachel. And if things were different…"

She closed her eyes. The ache in his voice tore through her like glass. "But they're not."

He nodded again, slower this time, like it cost him something. "No. They're not."

Silence followed, heavy with unsaid truths. They sat across from one another—two people on opposite sides of a line neither could cross, even though their hearts already had.

Rachel looked down at her hand, at the diamond glinting in the firelight. "I've been here three months and never once thought about going against my morals," she said quietly. "Not until you."

Darcy let out a breath, something fractured in it. "You're not wrong for wanting more than safe, Rachel. You're just brave enough to admit it."

Her eyes met his, something fragile and broken in her chest beginning to unravel. "You think I'm brave?"

"I think," he said carefully, "you're trying not to break anyone's heart. Even your own."

Her throat tightened. She swallowed hard.

Darcy watched her for a beat longer, then leaned back against the table, looking at the fire like it held answers he didn't have. "Whoever you end up with," he said quietly, "he'll be lucky."

Her breath hitched at the finality in his tone. She forced a small smile, her heart aching beneath it. "Thanks, Darcy."

His gaze lifted to hers one last time, dark and steady. "You don't owe me anything. Just… don't lie to yourself. That's all I'll say."

She nodded once, fingers tightening around the blanket, then turned her face away.

The fire crackled softly. The rain outside had stopped.

But inside her, the storm hadn't moved on.

He lingered for a second longer before turning away, retreating toward the fire as if needing the distance.

Rachel lay back down, staring at the ceiling, listening to the crackling flames and the steady rhythm of her own heartbeat. The fire warmed the small cabin, but the space beside her felt colder than ever.

And yet, no matter how hard she tried, she could still feel him—his touch, his lips, the unspoken tension still humming between them.

She closed her eyes, willing herself to sleep. But even in the quiet, the truth remained.

She was falling for him. And there wasn't a damn thing she could do about it.

Rachel and Darcy kept their distance for the remainder of their time in the cabin. The unspoken tension between them lingered, thick as the humid air, but neither addressed it. Instead, they stuck to safe topics—small talk about the storm, the resort, anything that didn't touch the charged moment they had shared.

By the time rescue arrived early Saturday morning, the trails were still slick with mud, treacherous in some areas. The guides helped Rachel carefully navigate the path, her ankle still swollen and sore but slightly better. Darcy stayed close, watchful, but he didn't touch her. Didn't offer to carry her, though she had no doubt he would have in an instant if she let him.

They returned to the resort in silence, the weight of what had happened—and what hadn't—settling between them like a storm that had passed but left destruction in its wake. The world around them had resumed as if nothing had changed, but Rachel felt different. Everything felt different.

She had missed her flight, but the resort had kindly rebooked it for her for Sunday. It gave her a day to rest, to try and process the mess of emotions tangled inside her. But no amount of time would have been enough.

Chapter Fifteen

On Sunday morning, with the help of crutches and more willpower than she cared to admit, Rachel made her way down the winding path to the wharf. The early sun shimmered on the water, casting a golden haze across the lagoon, but the beauty of it barely touched her. The lull of the waves—usually soothing—only stirred the ache inside her deeper.

Sam and Daniel were already there, waiting by the edge of the dock. Their presence, their smiles, felt like a thread pulling her back to the present.

"You sure you have to leave?" Daniel asked as he pulled her into a hug, his voice low, almost hopeful.

Rachel nodded, resting her chin on his shoulder for a brief second. "Yeah," she murmured. "I think it's time."

He stepped back, eyes lingering on her like he was trying to memorise her face. "We'll miss you around here."

Before she could respond, Sam stepped in and kissed her cheek, then wrapped her in a careful but tight hug. "We'll miss you, trouble," he whispered.

And then, just as he pulled back, his mouth lowered to her ear. "Lover boy is here."

Rachel stiffened.

She didn't have to ask who he meant.

Slowly, almost against her will, she turned—and there he was.

Darcy.

Walking toward her with slow, measured strides, his expression unreadable. But his eyes… those gave him away. There was something in them. Something sharp, searching, and raw.

Sam and Daniel exchanged a silent glance and drifted away, leaving her alone to face him.

The silence between them stretched, taut and frayed. The wind stirred the hem of her dress and lifted strands of her hair, as if even the breeze didn't know what to do with the weight of the moment.

"Have a safe trip home," Darcy said finally, his voice low but steady.

But Rachel heard what he didn't say—the strain beneath the calm, the crack just under the surface. Her fingers tightened around the crutches.

There were so many things she wanted to say.

And he… he wanted to say one thing.

Stay.

But he didn't.

Because she wasn't his to ask.

She forced herself to smile. "Thank you, Darcy. For everything."

His throat worked. "You don't need to—"

"No," she interrupted gently, holding his gaze. "I do. You saved my life. And I'll never forget that."

He opened his mouth again—maybe to protest, maybe to confess—but the words didn't come. And in the quiet that followed, she took a step closer, close enough to feel the heat radiating off him, close enough to feel the tension vibrating in the air between them.

"I want you to be happy," she said softly. "I wish you all the happiness in the world."

And then, without waiting, without thinking too long or giving herself a chance to hesitate—she leaned up and pressed her lips to his.

It was meant to be a goodbye. A thank-you. One last taste of something she would never allow herself to keep.

But the moment her mouth touched his, the world tilted.

Darcy went still. Just for a beat.

Then his hands found her waist, and everything inside him shattered.

He kissed her back—fierce, unrestrained, desperate. One hand cradled her back as if to keep her from slipping away again. The other found the nape of her neck, holding her there, holding her still, as if this kiss was the only thing anchoring him.

And maybe it was.

It wasn't slow. It wasn't careful.

It was a collision.

Of all the words they hadn't said.

Of the moments they hadn't taken.

Of the ache of wanting and the agony of letting go.

When they broke apart, they were both breathless, both trembling.

Darcy's hand lingered at her waist, and his eyes burned into hers—hungry, searching, memorising.

Rachel swallowed hard, blinking up at him. For one impossible second, she thought he might stop her. That he might ask. That she might say yes.

But he didn't.

And she couldn't.

With a shaky breath, she stepped back—slowly, carefully—putting inches between them that felt like miles.

"Goodbye, Darcy," she whispered, the words catching in her throat.

He didn't speak.

He just nodded once, and the look in his eyes nearly undid her.

She turned before she could crumble, her fingers clutching the crutches tighter as she made her way down the narrow dock. Each step felt heavier than the last, every footfall echoing through her like a warning.

She didn't look back.

Not when the crew helped her aboard.

Not when the boat pushed away from the dock.

Not even when the island began to fade, swallowed by distance and salt spray.

Rachel kept her gaze locked on the horizon, her chest aching with every beat. She had made her choice. She was going home.

But it felt like she'd left something behind on that island.

No—not something.

Someone.

And as the water stretched wide and endless before her, the kiss still clinging to her lips like a ghost, Rachel couldn't help but wonder…

What if she had stayed?

Darcy stood at the edge of the dock, the wind tugging at his shirt, the sun climbing higher behind him. He didn't move, didn't speak—just stared at the shrinking outline of the boat carving through the water, carrying her away.

His hands were clenched at his sides, his knuckles tight, as if by sheer force of will he could hold her there. Keep her from disappearing.

But it was too late.

She was gone.

For now.

The ache in his chest was unexpected. Unwelcome. But undeniable.

He told himself this wasn't the end. That she'd come back. That she had to. That whatever existed between them—whatever that kiss had meant—it hadn't been one-sided. He could still feel her in his arms, still taste the goodbye on his lips.

But he also knew the next move wasn't his to make.

Rachel had to choose.

Not between two men. But between the life she had built around expectations… and the one waiting for her if she was brave enough to reach for it.

She needed space. Time. Clarity. And she needed all of it without his voice in her head. Without pressure. Without him chasing her across the world like some cliché romantic hero.

It had to be her choice.

Made on her own terms.

And God, that was the hardest part—standing there, watching the woman who'd turned his world inside out drift farther and farther away, knowing that he could do nothing but wait. Hope. Pray.

Every instinct in him screamed to go after her. To pull her back. To fight.

To tell her she didn't have to figure it out alone.

That he was right there.

Ready.

But he didn't move.

Because loving someone meant giving them room to decide what they really wanted.

Even if it killed you.

He let out a sharp breath and raked a hand through his hair, frustration and longing knotted tight in his chest. The resort behind him was quiet, still recovering from the storm. But the storm inside him had only just begun.

If she came back—if she chose him—there was still one more obstacle between them. One last truth standing like a wall between everything they could be.

He wasn't just another guest.

He was the man who owned the island beneath her feet.

A billionaire.

The kind of man she'd spent her whole life resenting.

Because of her past. Because of the father who abandoned her mother. Because wealth, in her world, had always come with cruelty. With betrayal. With silence and shame.

And he hadn't told her.

Not because he wanted to lie.

But because once he saw her... really saw her... he wanted to be a man she could trust. Not the man who signed her paycheck. Not the man who had power over her. Just a man.

A man who was falling for her—hard.

Now, that truth threatened everything.

Would she see it as manipulation? Another man with too much money and too many secrets? Would it confirm every fear she had about people like him?

Would it make her hate him?

Darcy's jaw clenched as the last sliver of the boat disappeared into the horizon, swallowed by distance and time. The silence that followed was absolute. Deafening.

He stood there long after she was gone, the dock empty, the breeze brushing against his skin like a whisper he couldn't decipher.

If she came back—if she chose him—he would tell her everything.

Every truth.

Every reason.

Every hope.

And then he would pray—to whatever god might be listening—that it wouldn't be too late.

That she would still believe in the man behind the fortune.

That she'd believe in them.

The London air was crisp—damp, familiar, unforgiving. A fine mist drifted down from the endless grey sky, clinging to Rachel's skin as she stepped out of the cab and onto the rain-slick pavement. The scent of wet concrete and cold metal wrapped around her, a stark contrast to the salt-laced breeze and golden heat she'd left behind on the island.

She stared up at her flat. Modest. Safe. Home—at least, it used to be.

Rachel adjusted the strap of her shoulder bag, wincing slightly as she shifted her weight to accommodate her crutches. The injury wasn't serious, but it served as a physical reminder of everything that had happened. Of everything she couldn't stop thinking about.

She unlocked the door, stepped inside, and stood in silence.

Nothing had changed.

The same soft throw draped over the back of the couch. The same flickering scent of vanilla and amber from the candles on the windowsill. Her shoes neatly lined by the entryway, her books stacked on the coffee table just as she'd left them. Everything was in its place.

Except her.

She wasn't the same woman who had walked out the door three months ago. Not even close.

Rachel wheeled her suitcase into the corner and set her crutches beside the wall. She took one steadying breath, and then another—but the stillness of the room pressed in, heavy and hollow.

Then came a knock.

Her heart skipped. For a fleeting, reckless second, she imagined it might be him. That somehow, impossibly, Darcy had followed her. That he couldn't bear to let her go.

She reached the door.

It wasn't Darcy.

It was Jeremy.

Her fiancé.

Or… her ex-fiancé.

He stood in the drizzle, his dark blond hair damp, a nervous crease between his brows. His posture was familiar—hands shoved in his coat pockets, shoulders slightly hunched—but his expression wasn't. This wasn't the Jeremy who'd always had a plan, always had the right words. This was a man who had come to say something he didn't want to say.

"Rachel," he said quietly. "Can I come in?"

She hesitated, then nodded, stepping aside to let him pass.

He walked into the flat like he still knew it. Like his memories hadn't faded—but hers had. Rachel leaned against the arm of the sofa, arms folded, waiting.

He turned to face her. "I wanted to talk to you in person. I owe you that."

"Then talk."

Jeremy ran a hand through his hair, exhaling. "I didn't mean for it to happen. I never wanted to hurt you. But while you were away… I started seeing Sophie again."

Rachel blinked once. Just once. But inside, something loosened. She should have felt a sting, anger, betrayal.

Instead, all she felt was… clarity.

Sophie. The woman who had hovered at the edges of their relationship for years. The woman Jeremy always swore he was 'just friends' with.

Jeremy looked at her, guilt clouding his expression. "It made me realise I never really let her go. I tried to ignore it for a long time. But when I was with her… it felt like I was finally being honest. And it wouldn't be fair to keep pretending with you."

Rachel nodded slowly, the ache in her chest dull and distant. "Thank you for telling me."

Jeremy blinked. "That's it?"

She gave a faint, almost wistful smile. "I think we both knew something was missing. We just didn't want to admit it. You love Sophie. And I… I want more than this." She glanced around the flat, her voice softer now. "More than what we were."

A beat passed. Then Jeremy said, "You're incredible, Rachel. I hope you know that."

She reached for her hand. Slid the engagement ring off her finger. And gently pressed it into his palm.

"Good luck, Jeremy. Truly."

He nodded, eyes shining with something like regret—or maybe just the weight of goodbye. He stepped back toward the door, paused, then left.

The door clicked shut behind him, and silence returned.

Rachel stared down at her bare hand. The ring was gone. The life she'd carefully built—the one she thought she was supposed to want—was gone with it.

And yet, she didn't feel empty.

She felt… free.

Her thoughts drifted back to Darcy. To the way he had looked at her on that dock, like he was memorising her. To the way his lips had tasted like rain and heartbreak and everything she hadn't known she needed. The way his voice had wrapped around her like something solid, something she could hold onto.

Jeremy had loved someone else.

But so had she.

She'd just been too afraid to admit it.

Now, staring out at the city she once called home, Rachel knew the truth she hadn't wanted to face until now:

She had never belonged in the life she left behind.

Because somewhere on a sun-drenched island, a man she couldn't stop thinking about.

Chapter Sixteen

Rachel had always been good at adapting, at slipping back into the routine of her life no matter how much it had changed. But this time, it was different. London felt colder, greyer, as if the vibrancy of the island had spoiled her for the dullness of her old world.

A week had passed since she left Silhouette, and each day had been a test of endurance. She filled her time with work, taking up a job as a singer at a cozy bar in the city. It wasn't much, but it kept her busy, kept her from thinking too much about things—or at least, that was what she told herself.

But at night, when the city quieted and she lay in bed staring at the ceiling, her mind betrayed her. It was always Darcy who crept in. Darcy, with his intense gaze and quiet strength. Darcy, who kissed her like he was afraid of what it meant, yet unwilling to stop. Darcy, who she thought had been nothing more than another resort guest.

She still didn't understand why it hurt so much to leave him behind. She barely knew him, yet she missed him as if he had been a part of her life for years.

Then, just as she was beginning to think she could move on, everything changed.

Rachel was on her way to work, humming a song under her breath, when she stepped out of her apartment building and was immediately blinded by flashing lights.

A wall of paparazzi surged toward her, cameras clicking, voices shouting over one another.

"Rachel! Rachel, over here! How long have you and Darcy Williams been seeing each other?"

"What's it like dating a billionaire?"

"Are you moving in with him? Are you engaged?"

Rachel's heart slammed against her ribs. "What?" she stammered, completely thrown off. "You've got the wrong person. I don't know any billionaires."

A reporter shoved a newspaper in front of her face. "Then explain these."

She glanced down at the front page, and her stomach dropped.

There, in full colour, was a photo of her and Darcy—locked in that heartbreaking, desperate kiss at the dock. The caption read:

Mysterious Woman Steals the Heart of Reclusive Billionaire Darcy Williams.

Rachel's breath caught. This had to be a mistake. Darcy… a billionaire? No. That wasn't possible. He had been just a guest. Just a man with rough hands and a quiet smile. A man who had carried her when she couldn't walk, who had held her in the dark, who—

The cameras flashed again. Questions flew at her from every direction. Did you know? Are you together? Did you plan it?

A cold weight settled in her stomach.

Darcy had never told her who he really was. And she had walked away without ever knowing the truth.

Rachel barely slept that night. She told herself that by morning, the frenzy would die down. That the press would move on.

But as soon as she stepped outside, the flashbulbs exploded again, brighter than before. The questions hit her like a barrage of bullets.

"Rachel! How long have you and Darcy been together?"

"Is it true he flew you home on his private jet?"

The words blurred together—nonsense, until one reporter's voice cut through the noise.

"Did you know who he was the whole time?"

The breath whooshed from her lungs. A sharp pang of betrayal cut through her, but there was no time to dwell on it.

She spun on her heel, shoving past the flashing cameras and desperate voices, and stumbled onto the street. With a frantic wave, she flagged down a cab. The reporters' shouts followed her even as the door slammed shut behind her.

Her heart was still hammering by the time she reached the bar where she worked. She pushed through the door, her breath coming too fast, too shallow. The familiar scent of spilled beer and citrus cleaner did nothing to ground her.

She barely registered her coworkers' curious glances as she headed straight for the back room.

"Rachel?" Mia, the bartender on shift, called after her. "What the hell? You're all over the news!"

Rachel ignored her, yanking off her coat with trembling fingers. Her mind spun in circles, trying to make sense of the past twenty-four hours. The headlines. The flashing cameras. The ugly accusations she couldn't even begin to process.

Manipulative. Gold-digger. Seductress.

The words clung to her like a stain she couldn't scrub away.

All because she'd spent two storm-ridden days stranded with a man she thought was just another guest. A man with a crooked smile and steady hands. A man who made her feel seen in a way she hadn't felt in years.

But it had all been a lie.

Darcy hadn't told her he was the billionaire owner of the resort. He hadn't corrected her assumptions. He had let her believe he was just passing through, just another traveller. And somehow, that hurt more than if he'd outright lied.

Because he had let her fall for a version of him that wasn't real.

Rachel gripped the edge of the bar counter, the cool surface grounding her, but doing nothing to quiet the storm inside her. She felt foolish. Worse—betrayed.

She had seen this story before. Different names. Different lies. Same ending.

She thought of her mother—of the way she used to sit at the kitchen table late at night, eviction notice in one hand, a crumpled love letter in the other. Of the quiet strength it took to raise a daughter alone after the man who'd promised forever disappeared the moment things became inconvenient.

Rachel had spent her whole life vowing not to become her.

And now, she was standing in the exact same place.

Worse—she had let herself fall anyway. Despite the warnings, despite the ring she had worn, despite everything. She had let her heart get involved. She had let herself hope.

She would have let herself love him.

And then she saw the photo.

A friend had sent it without context—just a blurry tabloid shot from a charity gala two months ago. Darcy in a tuxedo, hand in his pocket, laughing with someone off camera. Effortlessly elegant. Effortlessly powerful.

Not the man who had kissed her on a cliffside in the middle of a storm. Not the man who had tucked a blanket around her shoulders and made her laugh over bad liquor in a forgotten cabin.

That man had never existed.

He'd been a dream. A lie wrapped in warmth and firelight and stolen moments.

Rachel had told herself she could forget. She'd gone home, returned to her life, and closed the door on Silhouette. But now the world refused to forget her.

And on the fourth day, her phone rang.

Jeremy.

She stared at the screen for a long moment before answering. Her voice was flat. "Hello, Jeremy."

"Rachel," he said, voice clipped.

"How are you?"

There was a pause. Then came the blow.

"I feel like a fool. Now I know why you were so calm when I told you about Sophie," he snapped. "It's because you were already sleeping with the billionaire."

Her fingers tightened around the phone. "I wasn't."

Jeremy let out a bitter laugh. "Oh, really? So that's not you in the photo kissing him on the wharf like some tragic love story?"

Rachel closed her eyes. Her voice was quiet but firm. "I didn't sleep with him, Jeremy."

A silence crackled between them, brittle and sharp.

"I kissed him goodbye. That's all it was."

"That's all it was," he repeated, voice dripping with sarcasm. "Right. Just a goodbye kiss to a man you barely knew."

Her jaw tightened. "Don't twist this. You had already chosen Sophie. You walked away. Don't pretend now that you get to be outraged."

"I wasn't the one kissing someone else while still wearing an engagement ring," he shot back.

Rachel flinched. Not from guilt—but from the truth she hadn't wanted to admit until now.

"I made a mistake," she said softly. "It was only a kiss. I didn't sleep with him."

He didn't respond. She heard the silence shift on his end—something duller, maybe regret, maybe just defeat.

"I hope she makes you happy," Rachel said, quieter now. "Truly. I hope you found what I couldn't give you."

Another pause. Then Jeremy exhaled. "You did love me, didn't you?"

She didn't answer right away. When she finally did, her voice was honest. "Yes. But not in the way you deserved."

And with that, she ended the call.

Rachel set the phone down and pressed her palms against the counter again. Her reflection in the window stared back at her—older, wiser, heartbreak blooming in her chest like a bruise.

She wasn't crying.

She wasn't breaking.

But something inside her had changed.

And for the first time since she'd left the island, she asked herself the one question she had been avoiding:

What if it wasn't just a lie?

What if Darcy was the only real thing in the entire story?

By the fifth day, the relentless harassment had started to wear her down. The whispers. The stares. The way people at work hesitated a second too long before speaking to her, like they weren't sure whether to offer sympathy or ask for details.

When she stepped into the bar that afternoon, the exhaustion pressed down on her like a weight she couldn't shake.

"Rachel." Mia's voice was softer than usual, her concern unmistakable. "Are you okay?"

Rachel let out a breathless, bitter laugh. "Do I look okay?"

Mia hesitated, her fingers tightening around the phone in her hand. "Rach…" She glanced at the screen, then bit her lip.

Rachel's stomach coiled. "What?"

Mia sighed and turned the phone toward her. "You should see this."

Rachel stiffened. "No. I don't want to."

"You should." Mia stepped closer, setting the phone on the bar. "Because Darcy Williams just made a statement."

Rachel's pulse stuttered. Against her better judgment, her gaze dropped to the glowing screen.

And there, in bold, merciless black letters, was the headline that sent ice rushing through her veins.

Billionaire Darcy Williams Defends Mystery Woman:

Rachel let out a hollow, humourless laugh and shook her head. "That's nice of him, isn't it?" The words dripped with sarcasm, bitter and sharp on her tongue.

Mia winced. "Rachel…"

But Rachel was already turning away. Nice? No. It wasn't nice. It was damage control. A carefully crafted PR move. A last-minute attempt to fix what couldn't be undone.

She shoved the phone back at Mia and focused on getting ready for her set. If she could lose herself in the music, even for just a few minutes, maybe she could silence the storm raging inside her.

But as soon as she stepped out into the lounge, reality crashed back in.

A tidal wave of flashing lights.

Cameras clicking.

Voices shouting her name.

The reporters had found her.

Rachel's stomach twisted into a hard knot as the theatre manager's panicked whisper hit her ears— "They're out front. Cameras. Asking for you by name."

No. No, no, no.

Her chest tightened. Without a word, she turned on her heel and strode toward the dressing rooms, her heels clacking sharply against the backstage tiles. She barely paused to yank off her costume, tugging the sequinned fabric over her head with shaking hands.

She needed to get out. Now.

Her breath came fast and shallow as she threw on a dress and her long-hooded coat. She stuffed her stage clothes into her bag without folding them and pushed through the back door into the alley.

The cold hit her like a slap. Rain slicked the pavement, and the distant hum of traffic mixed with the metallic stink of the city. She yanked her hood up, keeping her head down, her pace fast.

She didn't stop to look around. Didn't dare.

But then—a shift.

A presence.

A shadow peeled away from the darkness ahead, stepping into her path. Tall. Broad-shouldered. Silent.

She skidded to a halt.

Before she could spin, a hand gripped her arm—firm, gloved, immovable.

"Miss Roberts," a deep voice said, low and calm. "Come with me."

Her heart slammed into her ribs.

"What? No—who the hell are you? Let me go!" She tried to pull free, twisting her arm, but his grip didn't budge. Panic spiked, hot and dizzying.

Then a black limousine glided up to the curb, ghostlike and silent on the wet asphalt.

Its back door opened.

Rachel froze. The leather interior yawned like a mouth ready to swallow her whole.

"I said let go," she snapped, trying again to wrench away. But the man didn't fight her. He didn't speak. He simply turned her gently, like she was weightless, and guided her toward the open door with a calm authority that made her pulse spike.

And before she could shout, before she could think—

She was inside.

The door clicked shut behind her with a finality that stole the breath from her lungs.

The world outside vanished.

Inside, the cabin was dimly lit, quiet. The scent of leather and expensive cologne hung faintly in the air.

Rachel's breath hitched.

Then she turned.

And saw him.

Darcy.

Sitting across from her in the shadows, his long frame folded into the seat, his expression unreadable. His hazel eyes locked on hers with something stormy and still.

He looked exactly as she remembered him—and nothing like she remembered at all. Gone was the man in worn T-shirts and sand-slicked boots. This man wore a dark suit, open at the collar, with quiet command stitched into every line of his body.

She couldn't breathe.

"Hello, Rachel," he said, his voice low and level.

Chapter Seventeen

Rachel stared at him, her breath catching somewhere between disbelief and fury.

Darcy.

Sitting there in a tailored suit, calm as ever, like he hadn't just shattered her world with quiet precision. Like she wasn't being hunted by paparazzi because of him. Like she hadn't bled emotions in a jungle cabin for a man who had never told her the truth.

A sharp, bitter laugh clawed its way out of her throat. It sounded brittle—too tight, too close to the edge. "Of course," she muttered, shaking her head. "Of course it's you."

Darcy's eyes softened. "Rachel—"

"No." The word was a blade. Her voice trembled, but the edge was sharp, controlled. "You don't get to say my name like that. Not anymore."

Her hands curled into fists in her lap, nails digging into her palms as she fought to stay composed. She couldn't afford to fall apart—not now. Not in front of him.

"I'm not here to fight," he said, quietly, like he actually believed that mattered.

She let out a hollow laugh, her shoulders shaking. "Then what are you here for? Closure? A clean conscience?" Her eyes flared. "Because last I checked, you let me walk away. You didn't stop me. You didn't say anything. And now, because of you, my name's in tabloids next to headlines like 'The Dancer and the Billionaire.'" Her voice cracked. "My phone hasn't stopped. My agent dropped me. My life— my actual life—is a goddamn mess."

Darcy exhaled slowly, as if trying to contain something. "I never wanted that for you."

"But you let it happen," she snapped. "You stood there, in that cabin, letting me believe you were just another guest. Just some charming guy with too many secrets and a good mouth. You let me—" Her voice faltered, the rest sticking like glass in her throat.

You let me fall for you.

She blinked hard, her throat tight. The inside of the limousine felt too still, too silent—like the calm before a storm she couldn't brace for.

Darcy's jaw tightened. "I never lied to you."

Rachel stared at him, then laughed—a low, raw sound. "Don't split hairs, Darcy. You didn't tell me the truth. That's the same thing. You knew how I felt about wealth. Power. You knew my story. My mother's. You knew. And you let me open up to you anyway."

His voice was quiet, but rough-edged. "I didn't tell you because I didn't want to be that guy. I didn't want you to see him. I wanted you to see me."

"And you didn't think I had a right to choose?" Her voice cracked again, and this time she didn't hide it. "You think I wouldn't have kissed you if I knew who you were? That I wouldn't have let myself want you? That's the problem, Darcy. You never gave me the chance."

She reached for the door handle, her body screaming to flee before the tears spilled.

And then—

Flashes. A sudden burst of white-hot light lit up the car. Voices. Screams. A wall of shouting pressed against the glass.

"Rachel! Over here!"

"Miss Roberts, how long were you involved with Darcy Williams?"

"Are you still together?"

She froze, her hand still on the door. The limo rocked slightly as more bodies crowded against it. A camera flash stuttered through the tinted glass, and another question was hurled like a stone.

Rachel's breath hitched. Her throat closed. She buried her face in her hands, trembling—not with fear, but with fury. Shame. Exhaustion.

There was no slipping away unnoticed. No clean break. She had stepped into something so much bigger than herself, and there was no getting out of it now.

Darcy moved—not toward her, but stillness evaporated from his frame like steam rising off boiling water. Tension thrummed in the air.

"I can make them go away," he said quietly, watching her hands tremble.

Rachel lifted her head slowly, her eyes rimmed with fire and hurt.

"You already did this," she whispered. "Now you want to play the hero?"

Darcy didn't answer.

Because there was no right answer.

Not anymore.

Rachel reached for the door handle again.

And again, his hand stopped her.

Not rough. Not forceful. Just there—a steady, grounding presence that made her freeze.

"Don't," he said, barely above a whisper.

She jerked her hand back like he'd burned her. "You don't get to tell me what to do, Darcy."

"I'm not letting you walk away like this." His voice cracked at the edges—lower than before, closer to pleading. "Not without hearing me out."

Rachel let out a dry, bitter laugh, swiping at her eyes. "A little late for that, don't you think?"

He raked a hand through his hair, his composure fraying. "Just… come with me. Let me explain. Everything."

She narrowed her eyes. "Explain what? That you played me? Let me pour my heart out while you sat there knowing damn well I hated everything you are?"

"I didn't play you." His voice turned sharp, desperate. "I just—I didn't know how to tell you without ruining what we had. Without making you see me like… him."

Rachel flinched. Because he was right. He had reminded her of her father—the charm, the power, the money. And that terrified her more than anything else.

Her silence stretched.

It was all he needed.

Darcy reached forward and tapped the partition. It slid down silently, exposing the driver.

"Drive," he said, his voice clipped.

The limo eased into motion before Rachel could react, the city lights blurring through the tinted glass like streaks of gold and neon.

Her heart slammed against her ribs.

She turned to him, voice sharp. "Where are we going?"

Darcy met her gaze without flinching. "My apartment."

Her breath caught. "Pull over. Now."

His jaw tensed, but his voice remained calm. "Not until I've said what I need to say."

Rachel's hands balled into fists in her lap, her chest heaving as the car turned another corner.

She could hate him. She should hate him.

But beneath the anger—beneath the betrayal, the exhaustion, the pain—was something far more dangerous.

Hope.

And it was that hope—the wild, stupid, traitorous hope—that made her stay in the car.

Silent.

Shaking.

And still desperately wanting to hear what came next.

She clenched her jaw, forcing her voice to stay steady. "This is only making it worse, Darcy. Now that they've seen us together—"

"I know." His voice was quiet. Steady. He didn't argue, didn't try to justify. He just watched her with that same unreadable look, something like regret flickering in his eyes.

She wanted to hate him for it. For being so composed when her world was falling apart.

The ride passed in tense silence until the limousine finally pulled into an underground garage. The driver stepped out, opening her door, but Rachel didn't move.

Her whole body felt taut, wired with too many emotions to name.

Darcy stepped out first, then turned to her, waiting.

She should have run. Should have stayed in that car and demanded the driver take her home. But somehow, she found herself stepping onto the cold concrete floor, her legs unsteady beneath her.

He led her to a private lift, the doors sliding shut behind them with a soft click. The ride up was suffocating, silence stretching thick between them. Rachel stared at the floor, arms wrapped tightly around herself, her breath shallow and uneven.

By the time they reached the penthouse, her entire body was shaking. She wasn't even sure if it was from anger anymore—or the sheer weight of everything crashing down on her at once.

Tears burned hot against her cheeks, sliding down before she could stop them.

She turned to him, her voice raw, barely above a whisper. "Why did you bring me here, Darcy?"

His expression was unreadable, but his voice was firm. "We need to talk."

Rachel let out a hollow laugh, swiping at the tears on her cheeks. "Talk?" Her voice cracked. "About what? How you must have been laughing at me this whole time? How ridiculous it must have seemed—me, thinking a man like you could actually be interested in someone like me?"

Darcy's jaw tightened, his entire body tensing. "Is that what you think?"

She scoffed, shaking her head. "What else am I supposed to think? You let me believe you were just a normal everyday traveller. You stood there, smiling, while I—" She stopped herself, choking on the words.

While I fell for you.

She clenched her fists, her nails biting into her palms. "You knew exactly what you were doing, Darcy. You let me believe in something that wasn't real."

Darcy took a step closer, his voice rough with something she couldn't name. "Rachel, it was real."

She let out a shuddering breath, blinking hard against the tears threatening to fall again. "Then why didn't you tell me?"

Darcy exhaled, raking a hand through his hair. "I wanted to. I just didn't know how."

Rachel let out a sharp, bitter laugh. "Oh, come on, Darcy. It's not that complicated." Her voice dripped with sarcasm. "'Hey, Rachel, just so you know, I'm not just some random guest. I own the resort. And about two dozen more. Oh, and don't forget my private jet and the fleet of limousines.'" She threw her hands up. "See? That wasn't so hard."

Darcy's expression darkened, but he didn't rise to the bait. "It wasn't like that."

Rachel shook her head, wrapping her arms around herself as if that could hold her together. "Then what was it like? Because from where I'm standing, it feels like a game I never knew I was playing."

Darcy stepped closer, his hands settling gently on her shoulders, his touch warm despite the cold knot in Rachel's chest. "It wasn't a game, Rachel. It was real. You were real. I have feelings for you."

Rachel let out a sharp, disbelieving laugh and shrugged off his touch, her shoulders tight with frustration. "Don't do that," she snapped, blinking back the burn in her eyes. "Don't stand there and feed me pretty words like they mean something." Her voice cracked, and she hated how vulnerable it made her sound—but she pushed on. "You were just slumming it for a while, playing the part of a normal guy. How can you have feelings for me? I'm a nobody."

Darcy's jaw clenched, a muscle ticking beneath the surface. "Don't say that." His voice was quiet, but every word was laced with something almost desperate. "You're somebody to me, Rachel. You always were."

She scoffed, arms wrapping tighter around her frame as if she could contain the storm inside her. "I now know what sort of women you date, Darcy. Models. Socialites. Heiresses. I'm none of those things."

He took a step closer, his voice lower now. "No. You're more real than any woman I've ever met."

Rachel shook her head slowly, her breath unsteady, her thoughts a tangled mess of emotion and disbelief. "I can't believe this," she whispered. "I don't even know what to think or feel."

Darcy held still, the tension in his frame almost palpable. When he finally spoke, his voice was steady—but beneath the surface, it was raw. Unfiltered. "Believe that I care."

She stared at him, wide-eyed, disoriented by the sincerity in his words. Then a breathless, bitter laugh escaped her lips. "Care?" she echoed, her voice rising. She looked up at him, eyes brimming with disbelief. "Then tell me this—why were you checked in as just another guest? You own the damn place."

"I was there to assess the resort," he said, his gaze never leaving hers. "To see what needed upgrading or replacing. I wanted to see it for myself before making any changes."

Rachel stared at him incredulously. "And lying about who you were just made that easier?"

Darcy exhaled, rubbing a hand across the back of his neck. "That morning at the wharf—the day you left—I knew I was going to see you again. I just didn't know how or when. But I had to let you deal with Jeremy in your own time." His voice softened. "So, I stayed on the island. I didn't know someone recognised me, took that photo, and sold it to the papers. It was a fortnight before I even knew any of this was happening."

Rachel's stomach twisted. A part of her wanted to believe him. Wanted to believe this wasn't all some cruel, elaborate joke. But the ache in her chest—the one that had been there since she first saw the headlines—refused to ease.

Darcy ran a hand through his hair, exhaling heavily. "And to be honest, it was nice to be treated like a man instead of a bank balance for once."

Rachel let out a shaky breath, her voice laced with bitter disbelief. "Well, congratulations. You got to play at being normal while I got my life torn apart." Her eyes burned as she shook her head. "The press thinks I'm a gold digger. They think I knew who you were and abducted you."

Darcy's jaw tightened. "I know. That's why I'm trying to fix this."

"Fix it?" A sharp, humourless laugh escaped her. "You can't fix this, Darcy. My name is everywhere. People are calling me a manipulative liar, a nobody who tricked her way into your bed." She swallowed hard, her throat tight. "You don't know what it's like to have your entire life reduced to a scandalous headline."

Then, to her own disbelief, a laugh broke from her lips—bitter and hollow. She wiped at her damp cheeks, her fingers trembling, and shook her head. "The irony, huh?" she murmured. "I didn't even sleep with you, and yet the whole world thinks I did." Her voice cracked with disbelief, then sharpened with scorn. "The joke's on them, right?"

Darcy flinched, the words landing like a slap. His expression shifted—guilt, anger, frustration—flashing across his face in quick succession. "Rachel—"

She held up a hand, silencing him before he could speak. "Don't. Just… don't." Her voice wavered, heavy with fatigue. "I guess I'm famous now. Infamous, really. And somewhere along the way, I lost my dignity."

Her hands curled into fists in her lap. "Even Jeremy called me." She laughed again, a sharp sound with no humour in it. "Jeremy."

Darcy's brow furrowed. "Why would he—"

"He said he understands now," she snapped, her laugh curdling into something cold. "Said it all makes sense—why I was so calm when he told me about Sophie. Because apparently, I was the one cheating the whole time." She looked away, her jaw clenched. "Even when I wasn't."

Darcy's eyes darkened, his jaw tight. "He was cheating on you?"

"Yeah," she said, her voice quieter now. "For months." She gave a helpless shrug. "Ironic, isn't it? He was lying to me while I was trying to save a relationship that didn't deserve to be saved. While I was faithful…" Her voice caught, thick with emotion. "Until I met you."

The words hung in the air—soft but devastating.

She sank onto the sofa, the weight of the past few weeks pressing down on her like wet cement. Her shoulders curled inward, as if she could fold herself small enough to escape everything. The scandal. The betrayal. The heartbreak.

The truth.

She buried her face in her hands, her breaths coming shallow and uneven. "I kept trying to be the person who stayed. Who forgave. Who made it work. And for what?"

Darcy stood frozen for a beat, then quietly moved to sit beside her—close, but not too close. He didn't reach for her this time. He just sat with her in the silence, the air thick with everything they couldn't undo.

And everything they still hadn't said.

"I'm really sorry, Rachel," he said quietly. "I never wanted any of this to happen. Not to you."

His voice was soft—too soft—and when she turned to look at him, she found no arrogance, no charm, no shield of indifference. Just a man who had messed up. Who was trying, in his own way, to make something right.

And in his eyes, she saw it: regret. Real and raw.

A small, tired smile ghosted across her lips. "I believe you." She exhaled slowly, the fight draining from her shoulders. "I just don't know what to do about any of this."

Darcy's grip on her hand tightened slightly, his gaze unwavering. "I want to see you, Rachel. I want us to start dating."

She let out a sharp breath, staring at him like he'd lost his mind. Dating? After everything?

"You can't be serious." Her voice was quiet, disbelieving. She loved him—God help her, she loved him—but they were from two different worlds. His life was headlines and high society, while hers was barely keeping afloat.

Darcy didn't flinch. "I've never been more serious about anything."

"I told you in that cabin that I wanted you," Darcy said, his voice low, unwavering. "I wasn't lying then, and I'm not lying now. I still want you—more than anyone I have ever known."

Chapter Eighteen

Darcy lifted his hand slowly, his fingers trembling slightly as he brushed his thumb over Rachel's bottom lip. The simple touch felt electric, sending a shiver through her. Her breath hitched, her body frozen in the moment, as if time had stopped.

"Rachel—" His voice was thick with longing, low and raw, like a quiet plea.

She lifted her gaze to meet his, her heart pounding in her chest, caught between everything she had been trying to resist and the overwhelming pull of the man before her.

"You told me in the cabin that you wanted me too," Darcy said, his voice hushed, as if the weight of the question pressed against them both. "Was that the truth? Or has that changed?"

A tightness coiled in her chest, stealing her breath, the words stuck in her throat. She wanted to say everything—that her feelings hadn't changed, that they'd only grown stronger. But all that escaped was a breathless whisper, "It hasn't changed."

"I'm the same man you got to know," Darcy said, his voice low, almost a whisper. He moved closer, his breath mingling with hers, the space between them narrowing. "Are you the same woman?"

A rush of heat surged through her, her breath turning shallow as the intensity in his eyes held her captive. She met his gaze, unable to look away. "Yes," she murmured, mesmerised by him, her body swaying slightly towards him, drawn in by the magnetic pull of his presence.

Darcy's voice dropped even lower, thick with longing. "Can I kiss you, Rachel?" His words were a raw, desperate plea. "I'm going out of my mind not being able to kiss you."

Her lips parted, a breath escaping her, a soft, shaky whisper of a "yes" slipping from her lips before she could stop herself.

In an instant, his lips were on hers, a soft, gentle caress at first, like he was savouring the moment, feeling the warmth of her against him. But then, as if the restraint of everything he'd been holding back snapped, he deepened the kiss, pulling her closer with an intensity that left her breathless. The kiss became more urgent, more desperate—his hands tracing the curve of her back, his fingers threading into her hair as he tugged her impossibly closer.

Rachel responded eagerly, her hands exploring his chest, feeling the heat of his skin beneath his shirt. With a soft gasp, she tugged him closer, until the world around them seemed to fade away, leaving only the two of them, locked together in a kiss that spoke of everything they had yet to say.

Darcy pulled back for a moment, his forehead resting against hers as they both caught their breath, their chests rising and falling in unison. He looked at her with such raw emotion in his eyes that it made Rachel's heart ache.

"Rachel," he whispered, his voice thick with need. "I need you."

She shivered, her pulse thrumming. "I need you too… more than I should."

Desire overruled hesitation as she pushed him back against the sofa. She straddled him without a word, her dress sliding up her thighs, her fingers cradling his face before she kissed him—deep, desperate, searing.

Darcy responded instantly, groaning into her mouth as his hands gripped her waist, sliding up the curve of her back. His touch was rough with need, reverent with restraint. Their tongues tangled, hungry, reckless, chasing the fire neither of them could ignore any longer.

She ground herself against him, the friction sending a bolt of heat through her that left her gasping. He let out a low, guttural sound, his grip tightening, his body rising to meet hers.

The air between them pulsed with urgency.

Rachel slid off his lap, her fingers moving with single-minded intent—unfastening his belt, popping the button of his pants, easing the zipper down inch by torturous inch. His body tensed beneath her touch, his breath shuddering out of him.

"Rachel…" he rasped, his voice rough, barely holding on.

She met his gaze, eyes dark with promise, and pressed a finger to his lips. "Shh… you talk too much."

Then, with agonising slowness, she lowered herself. Her tongue flicked over him—soft, slow, deliberate. His entire body jerked, his hands fisting in her hair as a groan ripped from his throat.

"God, Rachel—" His voice fractured, drowning in the pleasure she drew from him with every stroke of her mouth, every flick of her tongue. She took her time, working him with maddening precision, watching him unravel—completely at her mercy.

His thighs tensed. His breath turned ragged.

"Rachel… please…" His voice was hoarse, broken by need. "Stop. I can't— I need to be inside you. Now."

A shiver coursed through her at the urgency in his tone. She rose gracefully, sliding her underwear down her legs before climbing back onto his lap. Her fingers moved swiftly, unbuttoning his shirt, revealing the hard, sculpted planes of his chest. He helped her, tugging her dress over her head and tossing it aside, his gaze dark with hunger.

"You're so beautiful," he murmured, his hands cupping her breasts, his thumbs circling and teasing, sending jolts of pleasure through her.

She arched into his touch, a moan spilling from her lips as he lowered his head, capturing one taut peak in his hot mouth.

"Darcy," she breathed, her fingers threading through his hair.

He moved to the other, licking, sucking, his tongue driving her higher, until she could take no more.

Desperate, aching, she braced herself and reached for him, guiding him to her entrance. Their eyes never left each other as she slowly, torturously, sank down onto him. The sensation stole the breath from both of them.

A simultaneous groan escaped as she moved, setting a slow, intoxicating rhythm. His mouth found her breasts again, his lips and tongue worshipping her as their bodies entwined in a perfect, primal dance.

She rose, then sank again, harder this time, and all coherent thought dissolved.

Need took over, raw and consuming, their rhythm building—faster, wilder—until there was nothing left but sensation, the desperate friction of skin against skin, the delicious pressure coiling tighter and tighter—

Until finally, the tension snapped, pleasure crashing over them in waves, their bodies trembling, shuddering, as they shattered together.

They clung to each other, breathless, hearts pounding in unison, lost in the aftermath of something deeper than just pleasure.

For a long moment, they simply breathed, lost in the remnants of ecstasy. Then, with a firm yet gentle hold, Darcy stood, lifting her effortlessly into his arms. She wrapped her arms around his neck, their lips brushing in a lingering, tender kiss as he carried her to the bedroom.

The door clicked shut behind them, the dim light casting soft shadows across the room.

Darcy lowered her onto the bed, joining her, his fingers tracing slow, reverent patterns over her skin, as if memorising every inch of her. His touch sent shivers down her spine, a fire rekindling in its wake.

Their second time was different—slower, deeper. Each movement was deliberate, as if savouring not just the feel of each other but the emotion woven into every touch. His lips travelled a path over her body, worshipping, claiming, until she was gasping beneath him.

"I want you again," he murmured against her skin.

She answered him not with words, but with the press of her lips against his, with the way her body arched into his. When they finally joined again, it was more than passion—it was a confession, a surrender neither dared name.

They moved together in a rhythm unhurried yet devastating, each caress, each kiss, igniting a deeper hunger. His hands roamed over her, reverent and possessive, while hers traced the hard lines of his jaw, his chest, as if she could never have enough of him.

And when release claimed them once more, it was nothing short of earth-shattering—a breaking and a becoming, leaving them utterly undone in each other's arms.

Afterwards, they lay tangled in the sheets, their bodies pressed close, the remnants of their passion still thick in the air. Their breathing slowly evened out, but neither of them spoke, as if words might shatter the intimacy of the moment.

Rachel rested her head against Darcy's chest, her fingers idly tracing the hard lines of his torso. The steady rhythm of his heartbeat was a soothing lullaby, grounding her in the moment. His warmth enveloped her, his scent—clean, masculine, utterly intoxicating—lingering on her skin.

For a while, they simply stayed like that, wrapped in each other. But then, Darcy shifted, pressing a kiss to her forehead before slipping out of bed. Before she could protest, he scooped her into his arms.

"Darcy—" she gasped, but he silenced her with a smirk.

"We need a shower." His voice was hoarse, teasing, but his eyes burned with something deeper.

The bathroom was dimly lit, steam already curling in the air as he turned on the shower. The sound of rushing water filled the space, and before she could take a step, he pulled her under the warm spray with him.

His hands moved over her body with slow, deliberate intent, his fingers tracing over every curve, washing away the remnants of their lovemaking. But the soft, tender gestures quickly turned into something more.

Rachel let out a small whimper as his touch lingered, his palms gliding over her hips, down her thighs, before sliding back up to cup her breasts. Heat coiled low in her belly, need reigniting as he pressed his lips to the sensitive spot just beneath her ear.

"Darcy…" she breathed, her nails digging into his shoulders.

"God, I can't get enough of you," he rasped against her throat.

With a growl of hunger, he gripped her thighs and lifted her effortlessly. She wrapped her legs around his waist, gasping as her back met the cool tile.

And then he took her—hard, fast, desperate.

There was nothing gentle about it this time. It was raw, unrestrained, a collision of need and desire. The contrast of the hot water cascading over their bodies and the cold tile against her skin only heightened the intensity.

Rachel clung to him, her fingers fisting in his wet hair as he thrust into her, every movement claiming, possessing, until all she could do was hold on.

Pleasure built swiftly, spiralling higher and higher, until it consumed them both in a blinding, white-hot release.

As the aftershocks pulsed through her, she slumped against him, breathless, boneless, utterly undone. Darcy held her close, his forehead resting against hers, his ragged breathing mingling with hers.

Neither of them spoke. They didn't need to.

He simply kissed her—slow this time, deep and lingering—as if trying to etch this moment into his very soul.

He washed her again, his touch slow and reverent, as if memorising every inch of her. When the water finally ran clear of steam and soap, he reached for a plush towel, drying himself off before wrapping her in its warmth.

Without a word, he lifted her into his arms and carried her back to bed, laying her down as if she were something precious, something fragile. His gaze lingered on her, dark with an emotion she couldn't name before he slipped beneath the sheets and pulled her into his embrace.

The night air was cool against their damp skin, but wrapped in his arms, she felt nothing but warmth. He drew the sheet over their bodies, tucking her close, his lips brushing the crown of her head.

Slowly, her eyes fluttered shut, her mind sinking into a blissful haze, lulled by the steady rise and fall of his chest, the rhythmic beat of his heart.

But sleep did not hold them for long.

The quiet stretched between them, thick with an unspoken promise, a need neither of them could deny.

Before long, their bodies sought each other out again. And again.

They made love twice more, each time more desperate, more unrestrained, as though trying to etch the feel of each other into their very souls. The hunger between them was insatiable, the need to stay connected overwhelming.

It was as if the world outside didn't exist—only the heat of their touch, the softness of their whispered names, the shuddering breaths, and trembling limbs as they lost themselves completely in one another.

And when exhaustion finally won, when their bodies could take no more, they remained tangled together, unwilling to let go. Even in sleep, their fingers remained laced, their hearts still beating in tandem.

Rachel woke slowly, the soft morning light filtering through the curtains. She stretched, reaching out instinctively for Darcy, but the bed was empty. Her gaze drifted to the pillow where he had slept—there, nestled against the soft linen, was a single rose. Its petals were delicate, almost translucent, and the deep red colour stood out starkly against the white of the pillow. A quiet smile tugged at her lips, but it didn't quite reach her eyes. Darcy's presence lingered in the room, though he was no longer there.

She pushed herself up, the warmth of the bed still clinging to her skin and padded to the bathroom. The cool tiles felt refreshing under her feet as she stepped into the shower, letting the water cascade over her. She washed her hair slowly, feeling the warm streams of water ease the tension in her muscles. Afterward, she wrapped a towel around her head to keep her damp hair in place and dried herself off, enjoying the soft feel of the plush towel against her skin.

She reached for the robe hanging on the back of the door. It was too large for her, the sleeves falling past her hands, but it was soft and warm, a comforting embrace after the whirlwind of the night. She tied the belt loosely around her waist, the fabric pooling around her feet, and wandered out into the kitchen. Her footsteps were soft against the cool floor, the apartment quiet except for the gentle hum of the morning light creeping in.

Darcy was standing at the kitchen bench, his back to her as he poured himself a cup of coffee. The morning light illuminated his silhouette, making him seem even more effortlessly handsome.

"Morning," Rachel said softly, her voice still carrying the remnants of sleep.

Darcy turned at the sound of her voice, his face lighting up with a smile that made her heart skip a beat. It was effortless for him, the way he moved toward her, the way he kissed her like it was the most natural thing in the world.

But was it? Was she just another woman caught up in his orbit, another fleeting connection in the kind of life he lived? A tightness crept into her chest. She wanted to believe this was real. *But could she?*

"Morning," he murmured, his lips brushing against hers. "I hope you slept well."

Rachel chuckled lightly, the warmth of his kiss still lingering on her lips. She tilted her head, a playful smirk tugging at the corners of her mouth. "I don't remember much sleep happening," she teased, her voice a mix of humour and satisfaction.

"Are you complaining?" Darcy raised an eyebrow, his lips curling into a mischievous grin.

She leaned against the counter, crossing her arms. "Do you think I'm mad?" she asked, her tone laced with mock incredulity.

Darcy stepped closer, his hand sliding around her waist. His eyes gleamed, lips curving into a teasing smile. "Mad for me I hope?" His voice dropped, the warmth of his breath skimming her skin.

Rachel's heart skipped a beat. She chuckled softly, her fingers tracing the edge of his shirt. "Mmm, maybe," she teased, lifting her eyes to meet his, her smile playful yet full of something deeper.

Before she could say another word, Darcy kissed her, his lips warm and insistent. The kiss was tender at first, but as it deepened, the world outside seemed to fade away. He pulled back just enough to look at her, his gaze still intense.

"What do you want to do today?" he asked, his tone a perfect mix of care and curiosity. "Anything, just name it." His fingers traced the outline of her jaw, waiting for her answer, as if he were ready to fulfil any wish she had.

Rachel smiled, her stomach giving an involuntary rumble as she looked up at him. "Well, breakfast would be good. I'm starving," she said with a soft laugh. "I didn't have dinner last night."

Darcy raised an eyebrow, his lips twitching into a smile. "What would you like? I'll make anything you want."

She gave him a small, teasing smile, a playful spark in her eyes. "Toast will be fine," she replied, her tone light but with a hint of mischief.

He chuckled, the sound warm and genuine, before stepping back and heading to the kitchen counter. "Toast it is then. But you're not getting away with something so simple. I'll make sure it's the best toast you've ever had."

Rachel leaned against the doorframe, fingers drumming absently against her arm as her heart still raced. The heat between them lingered in the air, a quiet hum that wouldn't go away.

As Darcy moved effortlessly around the kitchen, preparing breakfast with a kind of quiet confidence that drew her in, Rachel let her gaze linger on him. Barefoot, tousled, and entirely at ease, he looked nothing like the man the world saw in magazine spreads or polished headlines.

It was almost impossible to reconcile this man—who now buttered toast with precise care—with the one who had touched her with such unrestrained hunger just hours earlier. A man who had kissed her like she was the only thing keeping him grounded. Who had held her through the night like he wasn't ready to let go.

And maybe, she wasn't either.

But beneath the warmth of the moment, a knot of uncertainty curled in her chest. The way he moved around her, so natural, so unguarded—it chipped away at her defences, made her want to believe in something more. In him. In this.

But could she?

Her mind still circled the truth he had hidden, the life he had kept from her, however unintentionally. Trust didn't come easily to her—not when she'd spent a lifetime watching her mother give her heart to the wrong man. Not when she'd nearly done the same with Jeremy.

She blinked and pushed the thought aside, watching as Darcy flipped a slice of toast with practiced ease. He looked up, caught her staring, and smiled—lazy, charming, warm. A smile that made her stomach flutter… and her pulse trip.

But it also stirred something quieter, more hesitant.

What if I'm just another distraction? Another fleeting thrill in a life built on movement, power, and polished exits. *What happens when reality catches up to the fantasy?*

Still, when his eyes met hers again, softer now—unguarded—something in her steadied.

Maybe she was overthinking. Maybe she wasn't the only one standing on the edge, unsure whether to jump.

"Best toast, huh?" she said, her voice light with challenge, masking the emotion tangled just beneath the surface. "You've set some high expectations now."

Darcy smirked, sliding the plate toward her with exaggerated flair. "I always deliver."

She smiled, but this time, it reached her eyes. Because as ridiculous as it sounded, toast with him—this morning with him—felt more intimate than almost anything that had come before. And as she reached for her a piece of toast, brushing his fingers in the process, one thought echoed quietly in her mind.

Maybe this isn't the end of something.

Maybe it's the start.

Chapter Nineteen

Rachel and Darcy went out to lunch, slipping into a quiet, sunlit café tucked away from the busiest streets. Darcy had insisted on it, reasoning that if they behaved like any other couple—normal, mundane, unscandalous—the press would eventually lose interest.

"They thrive on drama," he told her, his fingers lacing through hers as they walked inside. "If we give them nothing to sink their teeth into, they'll move on soon enough."

Rachel wasn't so sure. The relentless swarm of reporters, the flashing cameras, the whispered speculations—none of it felt normal to her. But she trusted him, so she nodded, letting him guide her to a cozy corner table by the window.

Of course, they were followed. The moment they sat down, a cluster of paparazzi gathered outside, cameras pressed against the glass, snapping endless photos. A few diners sneaked glances at them, whispering behind their hands.

Rachel's stomach twisted. She had never wanted this kind of attention.

Darcy, on the other hand, looked completely unfazed. He picked up a menu, scanning it leisurely before glancing up at her. "Try the pasta," he said casually, as if they weren't being watched like zoo animals. "You'll love it."

She forced a smile, determined to play along. "Fine. But only if you order dessert so I can steal some."

His lips quirked in amusement. "Deal."

They ordered, talked, and ate as if nothing was out of the ordinary. Rachel tried to ignore the flashing lights outside, tried to match Darcy's effortless nonchalance. It was easier when he looked at her like that—like she was the only thing in the world that mattered.

But when a particularly bold reporter shouted her name through the glass, asking if she had trapped Darcy into a relationship, her grip on her fork tightened.

Darcy reached across the table, covering her hand with his. "Ignore them," he murmured, his thumb brushing soothing circles over her skin. "They want a reaction. Don't give them one."

She inhaled deeply, exhaled slowly.

For the rest of the meal, she focused on him—on the way he spoke, the way he listened, the way his presence grounded her even in the chaos. And slowly, just a little, the noise around them began to fade.

Darcy had been right. The paparazzi presence began to dwindle after a few days of them spending as much time in public together as possible. At first, Rachel struggled with the constant attention, but over time, she started to forget they were even there.

One afternoon, as they strolled through the park, she instinctively leaned in and kissed him. Darcy responded eagerly, as he always did, his hand curling around her waist, pulling her closer. But then, reality crashed back—she remembered the cameras, the eyes watching them. She pulled away, murmuring an apology.

Darcy frowned slightly, brushing his fingers over her cheek. "Don't apologise for being yourself," he said firmly. "I don't want you to change. You're perfect the way you are."

Warmth spread through her chest at his words, and she couldn't help but beam up at him.

A mischievous glint sparked in his eyes as he leaned down, his lips just a breath away from hers. "In fact," he whispered, "let's give them something to really talk about."

Her laugh barely had time to escape before his mouth crashed into hers, stealing her breath, stealing her thoughts—until there was nothing left but him.

They spent nearly every spare moment together over the next two weeks, their days blending into a seamless rhythm of quiet intimacy and effortless joy. From early morning strolls along the Thames to shared cups of coffee on her tiny balcony, laughter came easily, silences felt like comfort, and their chemistry was undeniable.

And yet… neither of them said it.

The words hovered like a breath between them—*I love you.* Unspoken, but ever present. They lived in the glances that lingered just a second too long. In the way Darcy would absentmindedly brush his fingers over the small of Rachel's back, like he couldn't quite stop touching her. In the way she would turn toward him in bed and simply stare, drinking him in like he might vanish if she blinked.

He thought about saying it almost every night. The words burned at the tip of his tongue whenever she looked up at him with those storm-grey eyes, wide open and unguarded. But something always stopped him. What if it's too much, too fast? What if she doesn't feel the same?

And Rachel—she'd caught herself nearly blurting it out at least a dozen times. Usually in the quiet hours, when they were tangled up on the couch watching terrible TV or laughing at something that wasn't really that funny. But every time she opened her mouth, something else came out. Because what if this version of him—this version of them—was temporary? What if she let herself fall completely, only to find out she wasn't enough after all?

So instead, they let the silence say it for them. Let their bodies and their time and their everyday moments whisper the truth they were too afraid to speak aloud.

Despite the difference in their worlds, Darcy never seemed out of place in Rachel's small apartment. She'd worried at first that he might find it too modest, too ordinary. But he proved her wrong at every turn. He made coffee like he'd been doing it there for years. Took conference calls sitting cross-legged on her threadbare rug. Fell asleep with his head in her lap as if her lap was his favourite place on earth.

He was never impatient. Never distant. Never once made her feel like she didn't belong beside him.

And when the cameras did show up, when a lingering paparazzo snapped a shot from across the street or a gossip column speculated about their relationship, Rachel surprised herself by not caring. Not really.

Because for the first time in her life, she felt chosen. Not for show, not for convenience—but for her.

One evening, as the soft glow of streetlights shimmered beyond the balcony railing, Darcy reached for her hand and twined their fingers together. The air was cool, but his touch was warm and certain.

"I have to leave for a few days," he said quietly.

Rachel's stomach dipped, but she kept her expression calm. "Where to?"

"Singapore," he replied, his thumb stroking over her knuckles. "Meetings, investors… the usual chaos." He hesitated, then turned to face her fully. "But when I get back… I want you to meet my sister."

Darcy nodded, a small, almost hesitant smile tugging at his lips. "She's the only family I have left, and she means a lot to me." He paused, squeezing her hand. "I want her to meet you."

Rachel's brows lifted. She had never seen or heard anything about his sister in the media. "She's never in the press," she said, curiosity lacing her voice.

Darcy chuckled. "That's by design. Eleanor's fiercely private—happily avoiding the spotlight while I get dragged through it." His expression softened. "She hates all the attention that comes with my name, so she's built a life far away from it. But she's my anchor, the one person who's been with me through everything."

Warmth bloomed in Rachel's chest, but so did a small flutter of uncertainty. Meeting family—especially someone as important as his sister—felt like a step toward something bigger. Something real.

"You're sure she wants to meet me?" she asked, unable to keep the hesitation from her voice.

Darcy's grip on her hand tightened slightly. "She's already been asking about you," he admitted with a small smile. "She can't wait."

Rachel let out a breath, her lips curving into a smile. "Then I'd love to meet her."

Darcy grinned, bringing her hand to his lips, and brushing a kiss against her knuckles. "Good. Because she's dying to meet the woman who's been keeping me up at night."

Rachel laughed, swatting at his arm, but her heart was racing. Not just from his teasing, but from the quiet, thrilling realisation that this—whatever they had—was becoming everything.

Darcy looked at her, his gaze tender. "I'll call you every chance I get."

Rachel smiled, though her heart already ached. "I'll look forward to when you're back."

What she didn't say—what neither of them could say—was I love you.

It sat there, just beneath the surface, beating in time with her pulse, echoing in the way he brushed her hair from her eyes before he kissed her goodnight.

She would have said it as he pulled away from the curb the next morning. He would have said it when she waved from the balcony, silhouetted against the morning light.

But both held back.

Not because they didn't feel it.

But because once it was said—truly said—everything would change.

And neither of them was ready for the fall.

Not yet.

The paparazzi were still lurking outside her apartment, their interest in her relationship with Darcy simmering just beneath the surface. A few had grown bored and drifted off, but others remained—persistent, waiting for a story to break. Rachel tried to ignore them. She focused on work, tried to find normalcy in routine, and counted down the days until Darcy returned from Singapore.

But the countdown stopped abruptly.

Because the day after he left, everything changed.

It started like any other morning—rain misting the pavement, the city still half-asleep. Rachel stepped out of her building, coat pulled tight, her headphones in. She didn't see them until it was too late.

A wall of bodies swarmed.

A burst of flashing bulbs exploded in her face—cameras, microphones, reporters shouting over each other, their questions slicing through the chilled air like blades.

"Rachel, have you and Darcy broken up?"

"Who's the other woman?"

She staggered back a step, blinking against the blinding flashes. "What are you talking about?"

They didn't answer.

They didn't need to.

Someone thrust a tabloid into her hands—its glossy front page already damp from the drizzle. There he was.

Darcy.

Arms wrapped tightly around a woman Rachel didn't recognise.

Elegant. Tall. Beautiful. Their bodies pressed together with a familiarity that made Rachel's stomach turn. Her heart hammered against her ribs as her eyes locked on the headline:

Billionaire Betrayal: Williams' Secret Romance Exposed

The world tilted.

No.

No, this couldn't be real.

Her hands trembled, crumpling the paper as she stared at the photo. Her Darcy—smiling at another woman, his head bent close to hers, whispering something into her ear.

Her lungs tightened. Tears blurred her vision.

It didn't make sense. Just days ago, he'd kissed her like he couldn't bear to let her go. Promised phone calls. Introduced the idea of family.

Promised something real.

And now this?

"Are you crying?" a voice called out, eager, cutting.

"Did he break your heart, Rachel?"

"Was it all just a game to him?"

Rachel's throat closed. She tried to move, to push through the crowd, but the voices multiplied, cruel and relentless. Her chest rose and fell in shallow gasps. The pressure of the crowd, the headlines, the lies—all of it was too much.

"You really thought someone like him would choose you?"

The words cut like a blade.

The sidewalk spun beneath her. Her vision tunnelled.

She needed air.

She needed to get away.

Panic surged through her as she turned—too fast, too blindly—and stepped off the curb.

A horn blared. Tyres screamed. Someone shouted her name.

Then came the impact. A sickening thud. A burst of pain, sharp and consuming.

And then—

Nothing.

Darcy stepped off the jet, the sharp heat of the tarmac hitting him like a slap. He rolled his shoulders, trying to work out the stiffness from the long flight, but the ache behind his eyes refused to ease.

Singapore had been productive. Profitable, even.

But none of it mattered now.

He needed to see Rachel.

Two days. That was all. And still, the hollow in his chest had grown with every hour, every mile between them.

"I can't wait to meet Rachel," Eleanor said as she descended the steps beside him, her tone light with curiosity.

He glanced over, forcing a tired smile. "She's looking forward to meeting you too."

Eleanor gave him a knowing look, amusement dancing behind her sharp blue eyes. "You really missed her, didn't you?"

Darcy didn't even try to deflect. "Yes," he said quietly. "Very much."

They stepped into the VIP terminal, the air-conditioned hush of luxury closing around them. A familiar cocoon of privilege. Still, Darcy felt oddly exposed—restless. Like something was just… off.

Then his phone buzzed. Once. Twice. Then a stream of vibrations that didn't stop.

He frowned, pulling it from his pocket. His screen was flooded—calls, texts, news alerts. Dozens of them. A pulse of unease bloomed in his chest.

Before he could say a word, Philip appeared at a near-run, eyes dark and jaw clenched. "Darcy—you need to see this. Now."

Darcy's blood turned cold.

Philip gestured toward the wall-mounted television in the lounge. The news was muted, but the footage needed no sound.

A chaotic crowd. Flashes of cameras. A woman trapped in the middle.

Rachel.

Eleanor gasped beside him. "Oh God… that's Rachel."

Darcy stepped closer, his breath caught somewhere between his ribs.

Onscreen, Rachel stood frozen outside her apartment, surrounded by reporters. She looked small. Pale. Her hands shook as microphones crowded in, flashes exploding in her face. And then the camera zoomed in—on the newspaper she held, the headline clear:

Billionaire Betrayal: Williams' Secret Romance Exposed

The image beneath it—him with Eleanor. Mid-embrace. Captured at the worst possible angle.

"No," Darcy whispered, his voice hollow.

Not her.

Not like this.

"Rachel, have you and Darcy broken up?"

"Who's the other woman?"

That wasn't another woman. That was his sister.

"My God," Eleanor breathed. "They're making her believe I'm your lover."

The video kept rolling.

Then came the worst part.

The reporters circled Rachel like vultures, their voices sharp, relentless.

"Rachel, are you crying?"

"Did he break your heart?"

"Was it all just a game to him?"

"You really thought someone like him would choose you?"

Darcy saw the exact moment her resolve broke.

The glisten of tears carving down her cheeks. The tremble in her lips. The way her breath hitched like her lungs couldn't keep up.

Then she turned—blinded by the chaos, the camera flashes searing her like lightning—and stepped back.

Right into the street.

The footage jolted. A blur of movement. The screech of brakes.

Then the sound that would haunt him.

A sickening thud.

Screams. Sirens. Chaos.

And then—static.

Darcy's stomach dropped.

Philip's voice came from far away, grim and clipped. "She was hit by a car. She's in the hospital."

For a heartbeat, Darcy couldn't breathe. The world tilted, sound warping around him like he'd been thrown into deep water.

"God," he rasped, "please tell me she's alive."

Eleanor's hand gripped his shoulder, anchoring him. But even her steady touch couldn't reach the storm inside him.

Philip hesitated. "Last I heard… yes. She was alive when they brought her in."

That was all Darcy needed.

His phone was already in his hand, fingers moving on instinct. He paced the lounge like a caged animal, jaw clenched, heart pounding with each unanswered ring.

"Come on. Come on," he muttered, eyes burning.

Finally, Helen picked up. "Sir—"

"I need to know where she is," he snapped. "Now. Which hospital. Room. Condition. Everything."

His voice was hoarse, ragged with panic. Controlled chaos barely held together.

He didn't care about the headlines. Didn't care about reputations or misinterpreted photos or the vultures waiting to tear them apart.

None of it mattered.

Only one thing did.

Rachel.

Chapter Twenty

As soon as Darcy and Eleanor stepped outside the terminal, chaos descended.

Reporters surged forward, microphones thrust out like weapons, cameras flashing like a barrage of gunfire.

"Is this your new lover, Darcy?"

"Did you know Rachel's in the hospital?"

"Did you break her heart?"

The questions hit him like shrapnel.

Darcy's jaw clenched, fury pulsing beneath his skin. He didn't answer. He couldn't. If he opened his mouth, he wouldn't be able to hold back the explosion building inside him.

He kept walking, fists clenched, his body a coiled spring.

They were just steps from the limousine when Eleanor suddenly stopped. She turned on the crowd, her voice sharp and furious.

"I'm his sister, you vultures!" she snapped, her eyes blazing. "And you—all of you—are part of the reason she's in the hospital. You hounded her. Shoved that lie in her face like it was entertainment. You should be ashamed."

Gasps and flashes followed her words, but she didn't wait for a reply. She stormed toward the car and climbed in, slamming the door shut behind her.

Darcy followed, his silence a pressure-cooker about to blow. He yanked the door shut as the limousine peeled away, reporters shouting into the dust behind them.

Inside, Eleanor exhaled hard. "Sorry. I couldn't help myself."

Darcy didn't respond. He stared out the tinted window, his knuckles white against his knees.

"That's okay," he said at last, voice low and brittle. "I didn't say anything because if I had—I would've hit someone."

Eleanor studied him, her anger fading into concern. "This isn't your fault."

But he wasn't listening.

Darcy leaned forward, elbows braced on his knees and buried his face in his hands. His whole body thrummed with tension, tight with guilt, fear, and fury.

"God," he whispered. "Please let her be okay."

The image of Rachel—frightened, tear-streaked, stumbling back into the street—flashed behind his eyelids again. Over and over. Like a punishment.

"This is my fault," he said hoarsely. "She was already hurting, and then that photo—those lies… They cornered her. Pushed her. And I wasn't there."

His hands curled into fists, trembling with helpless rage. "She wouldn't have been there if not for me."

Eleanor reached over, placing a firm hand on his shoulder. "She's strong, Darcy. She's going to fight."

Darcy lifted his head. His eyes were storm-dark, full of grief and something colder: resolve.

"God, I hope so," he said. "But first—I need to see her."

The limousine sped toward the hospital, but for Darcy, it wasn't fast enough.

The limousine barely rolled to a stop before Darcy shoved the door open and stepped out, his heart pounding like a war drum.

Flashes exploded around him. A chaotic swarm of paparazzi had already gathered outside the hospital, their cameras clicking furiously.

"Darcy, is Rachel awake?"

"Do you blame yourself for what happened?"

"Is it true she ran into traffic because of you?"

"Are you here with your new lover?"

Darcy's jaw tightened, fury coiling in his chest. Eleanor stepped out behind him, shielding her eyes from the relentless flashes.

"For God's sake," she muttered.

Darcy didn't break stride. He pushed forward, his focus razor-sharp. He had no time for these vultures.

Security guards surged forward, forming a protective wall between Darcy and the swarm of reporters shouting his name.

Just beyond the chaos, Helen stood waiting, composed but visibly tense. Her tablet was tucked under one arm, her other hand fidgeting with the edge of her blazer—a rare crack in her usual calm.

"Mr. Williams," she said as he reached her, stepping into his path, "I've been monitoring everything here."

"Thank you, Helen," he replied, his voice clipped and low. "I need to see her. Now."

She nodded briskly. "I'll alert the staff."

Without another word, she turned and strode toward the nurse's station. Darcy and Eleanor followed her into the hospital, the automatic doors hissing closed behind them.

The noise of the paparazzi faded—but the pressure in Darcy's chest didn't.

If anything, it grew worse.

Eleanor stepped up beside him, arms folded tightly, her voice soft. "She's going to be okay."

It sounded more like a prayer than a fact.

Darcy didn't answer. He couldn't. His breath felt too shallow, his skin too tight. His thoughts were a blur of images—Rachel's face twisted in panic, her body collapsing onto the street, the blood…

A doctor approached from the hallway. White coat. Clipboard. Calm eyes. But the lack of urgency didn't soothe him—it terrified him.

"Mr. Williams?" the doctor asked, glancing between him and Eleanor.

"Yes." Darcy's throat was dry. "How is she?"

The doctor paused—just long enough to make Darcy's heart stutter. "She sustained contusions, a concussion, and mild internal bruising. But the main concern is that she still hasn't regained consciousness."

Darcy's stomach dropped.

"It's been twenty-four hours since the accident," the doctor continued, voice steady but cautious. "At this stage, we consider it prolonged. It's possible her body is prioritising healing. But if she doesn't wake soon, we'll need to perform further scans to rule out neurological damage."

Darcy's hands clenched at his sides. The control he'd fought so hard to maintain slipped another inch.

He had come here ready to explain everything—to fight for her.

Now he could only hope she'd open her eyes.

"Can we see her?" Eleanor asked, her voice quiet, respectful.

The doctor nodded. "Yes. She's stable. But keep it calm. She needs rest—no distress, no stimulation."

Darcy nodded mutely, but inside, every nerve was screaming.

Please, Rachel. Wake up. Just let me see your eyes.

Darcy followed the doctor down the corridor, each step a silent battle against the panic coiling tighter around his chest. The sterile scent of antiseptic and quiet hum of machines only made it worse—too clean, too quiet, too cold.

When they reached her door, he hesitated for a heartbeat, then stepped inside.

The world narrowed.

Rachel lay motionless in the hospital bed, her skin pale against the stark whiteness of the sheets. Faint bruises bloomed along her temple and jaw, a cruel contrast to the soft rise and fall of her chest beneath the blankets.

She looked so small. So breakable.

Nothing like the woman who had once faced him with stubbornness in her voice and fire in her eyes.

Darcy's breath caught. He moved to her side, every inch of him aching.

"Rachel," he whispered, his voice raw and low. "I'm here."

No response.

Just the rhythmic beep of the heart monitor, steady and impersonal. Each sound landed like a blow—proof of life, but no sign of her.

He reached for her hand, brushing his thumb gently across her knuckles. Her skin was warm, but there was no movement. No squeeze. No flicker of lashes. Just stillness.

He bent down, pressing a kiss to her forehead, letting it linger. "You need to fight, sweetheart," he murmured, his voice breaking. "Please… come back to me."

Behind him, Eleanor hovered near the doorway, her arms wrapped tightly around herself, her expression stricken but silent.

Darcy straightened slowly, dragging a hand through his hair. Grief and guilt churned in his gut like acid.

"She doesn't deserve this," he said, the words scraping out of him. "She was just trying to live her life. None of this should've happened."

Eleanor stepped forward, placing a gentle hand on his arm. "She's strong, Darcy. You said it yourself. She's a fighter."

He nodded, but it didn't ease the tightness in his throat.

"I just need her to open her eyes," he whispered. "I need her to look at me and know I didn't betray her."

A sharp noise outside the room made Eleanor turn. She stepped toward the door, peering through the narrow window—and froze.

Flashes. Movement. The unmistakable blur of camera lenses.

"Jesus," she muttered. "They're in the hospital now?"

Darcy stiffened. His jaw clenched as he followed her gaze. Paparazzi. Inside.

They'd bribed someone, no doubt. There was no other way they could've slipped past security. But that didn't matter now.

They were here, hunting for their next headline—hoping to snap a photo of Rachel unconscious in a hospital bed, to plaster her pain across the world with no thought for the damage it would cause.

Darcy's grip on her hand tightened protectively.

He wasn't going to let them turn her into a spectacle. Not again. Not like this.

Before he could speak, Eleanor turned to Helen, her voice like a blade. "Get security. Now. I want those vultures out of this hospital, and private guards posted at this door. No one gets in unless we say so."

Helen didn't hesitate. "On it." She spun on her heel, her shoes clacking down the hallway as she vanished around the corner.

Within minutes, the corridor erupted into controlled chaos. Hospital security surged in, backed by Darcy's own team. Reporters were dragged out protesting, their shouts echoing off the walls. Two of Darcy's private guards took position outside Rachel's door, their expressions stone cold.

Inside the room, Darcy didn't move.

He barely registered the noise.

His focus remained locked on Rachel, his fingers curled gently around hers, desperate for even the slightest sign of life.

He sank into the chair beside her, the monitor's steady beeping beating in time with the ache in his chest.

"I should've been here," he murmured, his voice barely audible. "I should've protected her."

Eleanor sat across from him, her voice calm but firm. "Darcy, this isn't your fault. She was ambushed by the press. That's on them."

He let out a bitter breath, shaking his head. "No. It started with me. The photo. The lies. She was already hurting. And then they pushed her until she—" His voice cracked. "Until she panicked and stepped into traffic."

Eleanor leaned forward, her hand resting on his arm. "She's going to wake up. And when she does, she's going to need you steady. Don't give in to the guilt. Be here. For her."

Darcy swallowed hard, nodding.

Please… come back to me.

Then—a flicker. A twitch beneath his thumb.

His breath caught.

"Rachel?"

Eleanor bolted upright. "Did she move?"

Darcy leaned in, heart pounding, eyes fixed on her hand. "Sweetheart, if you can hear me, squeeze my hand. Just once."

The silence stretched long and thin.

Then—faint. Subtle. But real.

A gentle pressure closed around his fingers.

Relief crashed into him, sharp and overwhelming. His shoulders slumped, eyes stinging with emotion.

"She's fighting," he whispered, a smile breaking through the anguish. "She's still fighting."

Eleanor pressed a hand to her chest, blinking hard. "I'll get the doctor."

Darcy didn't move. He didn't even look away.

He kept holding Rachel's hand, steady and warm, willing her to stay with him.

"I'm right here," he whispered. "I never left."

Eleanor returned with the doctor—a middle-aged man with sharp, perceptive eyes and the calm presence of someone who'd walked through countless crises. A nurse followed closely, already moving to check the monitors as he stepped up to Rachel's bedside.

"You said she moved her fingers?" the doctor asked, pulling a small penlight from his pocket.

"Yes," Darcy answered quickly, leaning forward. "She squeezed my hand when I asked her to."

The doctor nodded, his expression focused. He gently lifted one of Rachel's eyelids and flashed the light across her pupil. It was slow—but there was movement.

"That's a good sign," he murmured. "She's still unconscious, but she's responding. It suggests she's aware, at some level. Her brain's trying to bridge that gap."

He checked her vitals with practiced efficiency, his eyes scanning the monitors, then turned back to Darcy and Eleanor.

"She's stable. That's important. These small reactions—blinking, twitching, slight muscle responses—can be early signs of regaining consciousness. It might not happen all at once, but her body is fighting to wake up."

Darcy let out a shaky breath, some of the tightness in his chest loosening—but only slightly.

"How long could it take?" he asked, his voice raw.

The doctor exhaled slowly. "It varies. Hours, maybe days. The concussion and trauma have pushed her system into a protective state. Right now, rest is the best medicine. And voices can help. Familiar ones. Talk to her. Let her know she's safe."

Darcy nodded, his throat too thick for words. He didn't need instruction.

He wasn't leaving.

The doctor gave him a reassuring pat on the shoulder. "You're doing the right thing. I'll check in again soon. If you notice anything new—movement, sound, changes in breathing—press the call button."

With a final glance at the monitors, the doctor stepped back. The nurse followed, silent and efficient.

Darcy remained where he was, his fingers still wrapped around Rachel's, his eyes locked on her face.

"She's fighting," he whispered again, more to himself than anyone else. "And I'm not letting go."

Darcy barely registered the doctor leaving. His world had narrowed to the stillness of the woman in front of him.

Rachel looked impossibly small against the sterile white of the hospital bed. Pale. Bruised. Fragile in a way he'd never seen her.

But she'd responded. However faint, it was a thread of hope—and he was holding on with everything he had.

Eleanor rested a gentle hand on his back. "I can stay," she offered quietly. "If you need a break."

Darcy shook his head. "I'm not leaving her." His fingers tightened around Rachel's, grounding himself in the feel of her warmth. "She wouldn't leave me."

Eleanor gave a soft, understanding smile. "I'll make sure you're not disturbed."

She slipped out of the room, the door clicking softly shut behind her.

Darcy leaned closer, brushing his thumb slowly across Rachel's knuckles. "I'm here, sweetheart," he murmured. "And I'm not going anywhere. So, whenever you're ready… come back to me."

A heartbeat passed. Then another.

And then—barely perceptible—the faintest flutter of lashes. A flicker. Fragile but real.

His breath caught.

She was fighting her way back.

And he would wait—no matter how long it took.

Chapter Twenty-One

Darcy stayed by Rachel's side for hours, his voice a quiet anchor in the sterile hush of the hospital room. He spoke to her in soft, steady tones—telling her she had to fight, that he needed her, that he wasn't going anywhere.

That he loved her—even if she couldn't hear it yet.

Eleanor sat with him on and off, offering quiet companionship, her presence grounding without demanding anything from him.

Eventually, she broke the silence.

"You love her, don't you?"

Darcy didn't even blink. "Yes." The word left him stripped bare. "I think I fell in love with her the first night I saw her dance."

Eleanor studied him—really studied him. His usual polished composure had fractured, leaving only truth and heartbreak behind. And she'd never seen her brother look more human.

"She doesn't know, does she?" she asked gently.

Darcy's exhale was rough, like it scraped its way out of his lungs. His fingers never left Rachel's.

"No," he admitted. "And after everything that's happened... I don't know if she ever will. She thinks I lied to her. That I was just another rich asshole playing games."

Eleanor nodded slowly. "Well... you did hide who you were."

"I wanted her to see me," he said quietly. "Not the brand. Not the money. Just me."

He looked at Rachel, his gaze softening. His thumb brushed over the back of her hand like it was something precious. "And she did. For the first time in my life, I felt... seen."

Eleanor's eyes softened. "Then don't let her walk away from that."

Darcy swallowed hard. "I won't."

He paused, his voice dropping to a whisper. "But right now, I just need her to wake up. I need her to open those beautiful eyes and look at me… even if it's just once."

As if summoned by his desperation, Rachel's fingers twitched in his grasp.

Darcy froze.

"Darcy," Eleanor breathed, eyes wide. "She moved."

His heart slammed against his ribs. "Rachel?" he whispered, leaning in, hope surging through his veins. "Sweetheart, can you hear me?"

Her lashes fluttered. A faint crease formed between her brows, as if she were trying to push through fog.

Darcy leaned closer, his hand trembling as he cupped her cheek. "It's me. I'm here."

A soft sound escaped her lips—fragile and thin—but it was something. She was coming back to him.

Relief hit him like a tidal wave. "Get the doctor!" he barked, eyes still locked on Rachel's face.

Eleanor spun and sprinted into the hallway, shouting for help.

Rachel's eyes cracked open. Just a sliver of grey beneath heavy lids—dazed, unfocused. But alive.

Darcy's chest nearly caved in. "Hey, sweetheart," he said softly, brushing her cheek with his knuckles. "You scared the hell out of me."

Her lips moved, barely forming the shape of his name. "Darcy?"

A broken laugh slipped from him, half relief, half wreckage. "Yeah, baby. I'm here."

She blinked slowly, fighting to focus. "W-what… happened?"

"You were in an accident," he said, voice tight. "But you're safe now. You're okay."

Her brow furrowed again, confusion clouding her gaze—until something shifted.

Wary.

Distant.

Her fingers twitched weakly in his, subtly pulling away. The movement was slight, but it gutted him.

Darcy felt the change in her before she even spoke. The space she was already placing between them.

Her voice was little more than a rasp. "You were with… someone."

He stilled, the words like ice in his blood.

He shook his head, the denial spilling out immediately. "No. Rachel, no. That's not what it looked like—"

Her eyes shimmered, not from tears, but from something quieter. Deeper. Hurt.

"Why?" she whispered, and that one word held more weight than any accusation could.

Before he could answer, the door burst open. Eleanor returned with a doctor and nurse, the flurry of motion breaking the moment apart, their brisk movements slicing through the fragile silence like a scalpel.

Darcy stayed where he was, his heart cracking open in his chest, her question still hanging in the space between them like a blade.

The doctor stepped forward, his smile calm and reassuring. "Well, hello, Rachel. It's good to see you back with us."

He flipped briefly through her chart before setting it aside and turning his attention to her. As he checked her vitals, the nurse moved efficiently to adjust monitors and record the readings.

"You gave us quite a scare," the doctor added gently, shining a penlight into Rachel's eyes. "But your reflexes are improving. That's a very good sign."

Rachel tried to speak, but her throat caught on the effort. A rasp, nothing more.

The nurse immediately offered her a cup with a straw. She sipped carefully, the cool water easing the rawness in her throat. Her eyes fluttered shut for a moment, then reopened—clearer now but guarded.

Darcy leaned forward slightly, his voice quiet but strained. "She's been in and out a few times—trying to say things. Is that normal?"

The doctor nodded as he listened to her heartbeat, his expression calm. "Completely. With the concussion and trauma, it's expected. What matters is that she's awake, aware, and responsive. From here, it's about rest and careful monitoring."

Darcy nodded, but his eyes never left Rachel.

Neither of them had forgotten what she'd asked.

Neither of them had moved past it.

And though the doctor's words were reassuring, all Darcy could think about was that moment—stolen, broken—and the ache in Rachel's gaze when she looked at him like a stranger.

After the doctor left, silence settled like dust over the room.

Rachel, still groggy and disoriented, turned her head slightly. Her gaze drifted to Eleanor, confusion clouding her bruised features.

"Who…?" she whispered, the word dry and strained.

Then her eyes found Darcy.

The confusion gave way to something far more fragile.

Hurt.

"Why?" she breathed.

Darcy saw it—the thoughts racing through her mind, the puzzle pieces rearranging themselves into the worst possible picture. The betrayal. The heartbreak. The photo.

He leaned in, speaking quickly but gently. "This is my sister."

Rachel flinched, her breath catching audibly. "Eleanor?"

Eleanor stepped closer, her expression soft and open. "It's probably not the best way to meet," she said, her voice laced with warmth and a touch of humour, "but I'm really glad we finally are."

Rachel blinked, her eyes darting between them, uncertainty still written across her face. "I… I don't understand."

Darcy's thumb moved in slow, soothing circles over the back of her hand. "It's okay," he murmured. "You don't have to understand everything right now. Just breathe."

But Rachel shook her head, wincing with the effort. "No. I need to…" Her gaze slid back to Eleanor, her voice raspy and raw. "You're really his sister?"

Eleanor nodded gently. "I am."

Rachel swallowed, her throat working visibly. "And you're here because…?"

A quick glance passed between Eleanor and Darcy before Eleanor stepped forward again.

"I came to meet you," she said honestly. "My brother hasn't stopped talking about you since you two met. He's been here since he heard what happened. Wouldn't leave your side. Not for a second."

Her words landed with a soft weight.

Rachel stared at Darcy, her heart thudding in her chest—not from fear now, but from something far more vulnerable. Her eyes searched his face, and in his expression, she found no deflection, no defence.

Just emotion. Raw. Honest. Unfiltered.

"The reporters…" she whispered. The memories began pressing in again—flashes of flashing bulbs, cruel headlines, that photo.

Darcy immediately shook his head, his voice low but firm. "Don't think about them. They got it wrong, all of it. That photo—Rachel, it was taken out of context. She's my sister. That's all."

Her fingers tightened weakly around his.

She wanted to believe him. And deep down, she already had.

Because no one held you like he did and lied to you.

No one looked at you like he did without meaning it.

Her voice trembled—not from fear, but from something far more fragile. "Darcy, I—"

Her throat closed up before the words could come.

But Darcy heard them anyway—in the way she whispered his name, in the way her fingers clung to his like they were the only solid thing left in her world.

Rachel exhaled shakily, the weight of the moment pressing down on her chest. Everything still felt unreal—the accident, waking to Darcy's voice, the revelation that the woman in the photo was his sister.

Her body ached, hollow with exhaustion. Her limbs felt heavy, her mind fogged. Slowly, her eyes drifted shut.

Chapter Twenty-Two

When she opened them again, the light in the room had shifted, softer now, the shadows longer. A calm stillness lingered in the air, broken only by the quiet beep of the monitor beside her.

Eleanor sat at her bedside, a gentle smile tugging at her lips.

"Hello, sleepyhead," she said lightly. "Darcy just went to get some coffee. Against his will, I might add."

Rachel tried to return the smile. "You and Darcy should get some rest," she rasped. "You look as tired as I feel."

Eleanor chuckled. "Good luck convincing him. He's not going anywhere."

A flicker of warmth stirred in Rachel's chest. Even through the fog, she could feel it—Darcy's devotion. Quiet. Steadfast. Unshakeable.

"You should tell him," she murmured, her voice barely above a whisper. "I don't want him worrying."

Eleanor tilted her head slightly, studying her with eyes far more perceptive than her easy smile let on. "You really care about my brother."

Rachel didn't flinch. "I love him," she said simply, truth ringing in every syllable.

Eleanor's expression shifted—softening, deepening. Something like respect flickered in her gaze. But before she could speak, her eyes moved past Rachel, toward the door.

And then—his voice.

Low. Rough. Unmistakable.

"Do you?"

The question cut through the air, sending a shiver down Rachel's spine.

She turned her head slowly toward the doorway.

Darcy stood just inside the room, a cup of coffee in one hand, but his focus was entirely on her. His eyes were dark with something unreadable—hope and hurt and everything in between.

Rachel's heart gave a fragile, trembling beat.

This was the moment she'd feared.

And the one she'd been aching for.

Her breath caught, chest rising in a shallow gasp as she took him in—Darcy standing just inside the doorway, like nothing and everything had changed.

His face was unreadable. But his eyes…

They were raw. Intense. Wide open.

And the emotion in them—naked, unguarded—hit her like a wave.

Neither of them moved.

The silence between them stretched, thick with everything they hadn't said. It hung there like a tension wound tight between them, threatening to snap with one wrong word.

Eleanor rose from her chair, her expression gentle, knowing. She touched Rachel's hand briefly—warmth and reassurance in a single squeeze.

"I think I'll leave you two to talk," she murmured, offering Rachel a small, supportive smile.

As she passed Darcy, she placed a hand on his arm. Just a touch. Just enough.

Then she slipped from the room, the soft click of the door leaving them alone in the quiet.

Rachel swallowed hard, her throat suddenly dry, the words she'd spoken only minutes ago echoing in her mind.

Darcy moved slowly, setting the cup down on the table beside her. His gaze never left her.

"Say it again," he said, his voice low and rough, every syllable scraped from the raw edges of his heart.

Rachel's fingers tightened around the blanket.

"Darcy—"

"Please." The word was broken. A plea. His hands clenched at his sides, as though holding himself back from reaching for her. "Just once more. I need to hear it."

Rachel swallowed hard, the weight of everything—the misunderstanding, the fear, the love she'd held back for too long—tightening in her chest like a vice.

"I… I didn't know you were there," she whispered. "In the room. I didn't know."

Darcy's expression flickered—something fragile and unguarded breaking through. "Rachel…"

But she couldn't hold it in anymore.

"I love you," she blurted, voice trembling with truth. "I've loved you since the beginning. Since the first moment you looked at me like I was more than just a girl on a stage." She let out a shaky breath. "I'm sorry—I couldn't stop it. I didn't want to."

Darcy exhaled, the sound rough and disbelieving—a breathless laugh laced with relief. And then he moved.

He crossed the space between them in one heartbeat, his hands lifting to frame her face as he kissed her—hard, desperate, full of everything he'd never said. His love. His regret. His longing.

She melted into him, her fingers gripping the front of his shirt, holding on like she was afraid the moment might dissolve if she let go.

When he finally pulled back, his forehead rested gently against hers. His voice was low, reverent.

"Sorry?" he echoed, brushing a thumb over her cheek. His eyes shone with emotion. "Rachel, why would you ever be sorry for loving me?"

She couldn't answer—not with words.

But he didn't need them.

"I love you," he said, fiercer now. Steadier. "More than anything. More than I knew I could love anyone."

Her lips trembled. "Darcy… you have my heart. My body. My soul. If you want them."

His eyes darkened, not with doubt—but with certainty. With the kind of love that anchored, that promised, that never left.

"I want them," he whispered, his voice raw. "Because you already have mine. You've had it from the beginning."

He pressed a kiss to her forehead, his hands cradling her face with a tenderness that made her eyes sting. "And I'm never letting you go."

Rachel let out a soft, breathless laugh, her chest swelling with more than love—peace, trust, joy.

"Good," she whispered, tilting her face up to his. "Because I don't want you to."

Darcy exhaled softly, then kissed her again—slower this time. Tender. Deep.

The kind of kiss that said everything words couldn't.

His lips moved against hers with reverence, sealing every promise between them, wrapping her in warmth, in certainty. A quiet shiver coursed through her, not from doubt, but from the aching truth of how much she needed him—of how deeply she was already his.

Minutes passed in a haze of whispered words and lingering touches. Rachel traced the line of his jaw with her fingertips, memorising him—the shape of him, the feel of him, like she might wake up and find this all a dream.

Darcy brushed a strand of hair from her face, his thumb gliding over the curve of her cheek. His gaze held hers, steady and full of something quietly fierce.

"I should've told you sooner," he murmured, voice rough with regret. "Before I left. I wanted to. I was going to. But… I got scared."

Rachel shook her head gently, her fingers tightening around his. "You're here now," she whispered. "That's what matters."

He swallowed, emotion thick in his throat. "When I saw that footage—when I saw you on the ground, not moving—I thought I was going to lose you. And it felt like the world just… stopped."

"I'm okay," she soothed, brushing her fingertips across his hand. "It was an accident. I was overwhelmed—I wasn't paying attention."

His jaw tightened. "No. It wasn't your fault. It was theirs. The press, the pressure, the lies… You shouldn't have to live like that."

He paused, searching her face.

"Promise me," he said softly, but with unshakable intensity. "If you ever see something again—anything—don't believe it. Not until you've talked to me. Not until you hear it from me."

Rachel met his gaze, her eyes luminous with understanding. "I promise," she said. "I know now how easy it is for the truth to be twisted. And how much damage it can do."

A quiet beat passed.

Then Darcy asked the question that had haunted him most.

"Will you be able to live with it?" he asked. "The constant attention. The scrutiny. The spotlight that comes with being in my world?"

Rachel didn't hesitate.

A soft smile touched her lips, full of calm certainty. "If I'm with you, nothing else matters."

Darcy let out a breath he hadn't even known he was holding, his eyes shining with emotion.

"Thank God," he whispered, his voice low and rough. "Because I don't just want you in my life, Rachel. I want everything. I want you by my side every day. I want to raise a family with you. Wake up next to you. Fall asleep holding you. Grow old with you."

He cupped her face with both hands, his thumbs brushing away the tears she didn't even realise she'd let fall.

"Rachel," he said, his voice steady now, anchored by everything he felt. "Will you marry me?"

Her breath caught. Her heart pounded like it was trying to break free from her chest. She searched his face—every line, every shadow—and found only love. Deep, steady, unwavering love.

"Darcy…" Her voice trembled, thick with emotion. Her fingers curled tighter around his.

"I mean it," he whispered, his grip firm, his eyes never leaving hers. "I don't want a future without you. Not just for a season. Not just until it's hard. Forever." He leaned in, resting his forehead against hers, his voice barely a breath. "Be my wife."

Tears welled in her eyes, shimmering with something bright and undeniable. A shaky laugh slipped past her lips. "You really mean that?"

Darcy exhaled, his hands cradling her face with the gentlest reverence. "With everything I am. I love you, Rachel. I want you. Always."

One tear slipped down her cheek—this time not from pain or fear, but from joy. Full. Fierce. Unstoppable.

A smile broke across her face, radiant and certain. "Yes," she whispered. Then, stronger, more sure— "Yes. I'll marry you."

Darcy let out a breath that sounded like the first one he'd taken in days, then crushed his lips to hers—soft, desperate, full of every vow he hadn't yet spoken.

When he finally pulled back, he kissed her forehead and brushed his fingers along her jaw like she was something precious. Sacred.

"You're going to be the most beautiful bride," he murmured, awe threaded through his voice. "Just... don't make me wait too long."

Rachel laughed softly, her fingers sliding into his hair. "I don't want to wait either."

A slow smile curved his lips—deep, satisfied, a man who knew he'd just found everything he'd ever wanted.

But before he could respond, a sharp knock echoed at the door.

A second later, Eleanor stuck her head in, her expression hovering between amusement and exasperation. "I figured I'd give you two a moment, but it's been nearly twenty minutes." She arched a brow at her brother. "Are you planning on letting her rest at some point, or should I have a nurse come in to pry you off her?"

Darcy groaned but didn't let go of Rachel's hand. "Eleanor, do you ever knock?"

Eleanor smirked, leaning casually against the doorframe. "I did knock, and I gave you twenty minutes. Consider it a kindness."

Darcy laughed. "Go away, Eleanor."

Eleanor chuckled. "I see your charm is still intact." Then her gaze softened as she looked at Rachel. "You look happy."

Rachel's smile grew, warmth blooming in her chest. "I am."

Darcy glanced at his sister, his expression full of quiet certainty. "Rachel has agreed to marry me. Soon."

Eleanor's eyes widened before a genuine grin spread across her face. "That's wonderful." She pulled them both into a quick but heartfelt hug, pressing a kiss to Rachel's cheek. Stepping back, she shot Darcy an amused look. "Good. Because, honestly, I don't think I could've handled my lovesick brother much longer."

Darcy rolled his eyes, but Rachel just laughed, the sound light, free, and filled with something she hadn't felt in a long time—pure, undeniable happiness.

Epilogue

Darcy lay half-draped over Rachel on the plush sofa in the sunlit living room of their London penthouse, their bodies tangled in a haze of warmth and satisfaction. The silk throw beneath them was rumpled, forgotten, just like the world outside their windows.

Their skin still glistened from the intensity of their lovemaking—an intimacy that had only deepened with time. He braced himself slightly on one arm, careful not to shift too far, keeping their bodies joined, his other hand cradling the curve of her waist.

His gaze met hers, dark and burning with that same hunger that had once stolen her breath in a bungalow by the sea.

"Can you believe," he murmured, his voice husky, threaded with awe, "that after five years of marriage, I still can't wait to have you? I can't even make it to our bedroom a few metres away."

Rachel laughed softly, the sound low and affectionate as she traced the line of his cheek with feather-light fingers. "I'm not complaining…" Her smile turned teasing. "But maybe try to restrain yourself when Alexander and Megan are here."

Darcy's grin was devilish as he dipped his head and kissed her again—slow, deep, reverent. "Luckily, they adore their Aunt Eleanor, which means we get the entire day to ourselves. Anniversary rules: no interruptions. No guilt."

Rachel hummed contentedly, her fingers sliding up into his hair. "You're lucky I love you more than coffee and uninterrupted naps."

"Even more than wine?" he teased.

"Dangerously close," she whispered against his mouth.

They had married quietly just two weeks after his hospital proposal—a simple ceremony at a London registry office with Eleanor and a handful of close friends. There'd been no designer gown, no lavish venue, no press frenzy. And Rachel hadn't wanted any of it.

All she had ever wanted was him.

Darcy had asked her a dozen times over the years if she regretted not having a grand wedding, some sweeping fairytale affair. Each time, she gave him the same answer, soft and unwavering:

"Why would I? I didn't marry a fantasy. I married you. That was always the dream."

The media storm that once threatened to tear them apart had faded, like noise retreating behind closed doors. The paparazzi moved on when it became clear there was no scandal, no secrets to uncover—just a fiercely devoted man protecting the woman he adored, and later, the children they are raising with quiet joy.

Their son, Alexander, had arrived a year into their marriage—curious, fearless, and the centre of Rachel's universe. Megan followed just over a year later, her laughter bright enough to light a room, her eyes the same grey as her mother's.

Now, as Darcy gazed down at the woman who had changed his life forever, he slid his thumb along the curve of her lower lip, feeling the soft puff of her breath against his skin. That same love—the one that had knocked him off his axis from the moment she danced beneath tropical stars—surged through him like a current. Fierce. Permanent.

"Happy anniversary, Mrs. Williams," he murmured, his voice rough with emotion.

Rachel's eyes shone, their grey depths lit with a thousand memories. She reached up, cupping his face with a tenderness that still stole his breath, her fingers grazing the light stubble along his jaw. Her smile was soft, radiant.

"Happy anniversary, my love," she whispered, her voice catching on the last word.

Darcy exhaled, drawing slow, lazy circles on her bare shoulder. "You still haven't told me what you want to do today," he said. "It's your day too. Anything you want."

Rachel's eyes sparkled with something mischievous and intimate.

"Well," she said, drawing her fingers down his chest, "we already started the day off exactly the way I wanted…"

Darcy's brow lifted, amused. "That so?"

She leaned in, her lips brushing his ear. "But I wouldn't mind a repeat performance… after breakfast."

He laughed—full and low—the sound reverberating through her like a favourite song. Warm. Familiar. Unshakeably hers.

"I love the way you think," he murmured, before claiming her mouth again in a kiss that felt timeless. Like the first one. Like the last. Like every kiss between them had led to this one, and still, it wasn't enough.

When he finally pulled back, Rachel tilted her head, a teasing glint dancing in her grey eyes. "Do you remember that day on the island in Seychelles? When we danced the tango?"

Darcy's smirk was immediate. "How could I forget? You were smiling at me like you already knew I'd never recover. I almost made love to you right there and then."

Rachel's lips curved in wicked delight. Her voice dipped into a sultry whisper as she leaned in close. "That's what I want today. To dance with you the way we did back then… bodies pressed together, your hands on me, heat building between us—until we can't take it anymore. And then I want to come back here and make love to you until the sun comes up."

Darcy's low groan made her pulse flutter. His fingers tangled through her tousled hair, and he dropped his forehead to hers, his voice thick with want. "That might be the sexiest anniversary request I've ever received."

Then, reluctantly, he pulled away with a playful groan, reaching for his jeans and dragging them on.

Rachel sat up, watching him with amusement as she reached for her silk robe—the one he'd so eagerly discarded earlier—and slipped it around her shoulders. She cinched the sash loosely and leaned back against the cushions, her bare legs tucked beneath her. Her smile was pure mischief.

She arched a brow. "And what exactly are you up to now, Mr. Williams?"

Darcy shot her a smouldering look as he reached into his pocket. "You'll see, Mrs. Williams."

He pulled out a small silver key and held it out to her.

Rachel blinked, curiosity flaring as she took it and turned it over in her palm. "What does this belong to?"

His smile deepened, softer this time. "Do you remember that old stone house in the country you fell in love with a couple months ago?"

Her breath caught, and the key trembled slightly in her hand. "Darcy... you didn't."

"I did," he said, his voice thick with affection. "It's ours now."

She stared at him, stunned.

"You said you wanted the kids to have a backyard. Now they have five acres of woods, a garden, a treehouse I'm already planning with Alexander, and space to run until they wear themselves out. And you, my love, have the sunroom you adored, the orchard, and that old library with the fireplace you couldn't stop talking about."

A delighted gasp escaped her as her eyes filled with emotion. Then, without another word, she launched herself into his arms, wrapping her limbs around him and burying her face in his neck.

"Darcy!" she laughed, breathless, planting a string of giddy kisses along his jaw. "I can't believe you—this is... God, this is everything."

He held her close, the sound of her joy sinking into his chest like sunlight. He kissed her temple, smiling against her skin.

When she finally pulled back, still draped across his lap, she looked up at him through lashes damp with happy tears, her smile wide and playful. "I mean, I got you a Rolex," she said, laughing. "And you got me a house. This feels a little... unbalanced."

She narrowed her eyes playfully, tipping her head. "So, tell me, Mr. Williams— what exactly do you get out of this arrangement?"

Darcy cupped her face in his hands, his thumb brushing along her cheekbone, his gaze suddenly serious—deep, steady, soul-deep.

"You," he said simply. "Your laughter. Your love. The look on your face right now. That's what I get."

He leaned in, his lips brushing hers in a kiss that was soft, unhurried, full of reverence.

"I love you, Mrs. Rachel Williams," he whispered against her mouth. "You have my heart. You always have. You always will."

Rachel's smile trembled as emotion swelled in her chest. She kissed him back, slow and sure, anchoring herself to the man who had become her home.

"Then I'm the richest woman in the world," she whispered.

Darcy grinned. "And don't you forget it."

The End

Reckless Hearts

Alison Reid

A complete standalone romance

Previously published individually

Chapter One

The Hale Industries penthouse office was a blend of glass, marble, and carefully curated silence. Perched like a crown atop one of Manhattan's most exclusive high-rises, it overlooked the city with a kind of detached majesty—cold, commanding, and utterly untouchable. Everything in the space gleamed: from the crystal decanter of whiskey on the sideboard to the chrome-edged furniture arranged with mathematical precision. It wasn't designed for comfort. It was meant to impress. To intimidate.

The man who owned it, Alec Hale, was much the same.

Brad Allen stood near the floor-to-ceiling windows, his silhouette cut clean against the cityscape, sharp as the glass beneath his fingertips. He didn't move, didn't fidget—stillness came naturally to him, like it does to men who had learned early how to wait, to watch, to act only when it mattered most. The late afternoon sun carved a blade of gold along his jaw, catching in the tousled waves of his dark brown hair. A faint shadow of stubble darkened his chin and jawline—the permanent five o'clock scruff that suited him better than any polished clean shave ever could.

He was tall, broad-shouldered, and carried himself like a man who was always aware of the exits. A man who could break bones with precision but rarely needed to—because his presence alone shifted the atmosphere of any room he entered. He didn't demand attention; it found him. A quiet, authoritative kind of gravity. His charcoal-grey suit fit him like it had been tailored by someone who understood how to dress power, understated but unmistakably expensive. Like everything about him.

Brad's eyes, a piercing steel-blue, tracked the skyline as if scanning for threats—or memories. He saw patterns most people didn't. It was second nature, built into him from a decade in the military and refined through years running his own private security firm. Allen Strategic Risk Solutions wasn't just a name on a glossy card; it was one of the most elite personal protection agencies in the world. Fortune 500 CEOs, foreign diplomats, royalty—they all came to him when discretion, loyalty, and results mattered more than price.

The business had made him a multi-millionaire, though he rarely acted like one. He didn't care for yachts or champagne-soaked parties. His wealth lived in precision: the high-performance vehicles in his private garage, the black-card retainer clients who called his direct line at 3 a.m., the tech-laced safe house outside of Zurich that only five people in the world even knew existed.

But money had never interested him.

What drove Brad Allen—what built his empire—was control. Order. The quiet satisfaction of solving problems before they exploded, of protecting people who never even knew how close they'd come to danger.

There was a rugged handsomeness to him, undeniable and effortless, but it was paired with a kind of emotional distance that seemed carved into his very bones. He was the kind of man women noticed—and the kind he never stayed for. Relationships were liabilities. Emotions, distractions. He didn't do long-term. He didn't do attachment. What he did was protect. Solve problems. Get out clean.

His jaw ticked, just once, before he finally turned his attention to the man behind the desk.

"I'm asking as a friend, Brad," Alec said, voice low but resolute. "Not as a client."

Brad turned from the window, slowly, his expression unreadable. "That's exactly the problem."

His voice was calm, but underneath it ran the familiar edge of controlled friction. Personal and professional never mixed well—not in his world. Brad didn't take favours lightly, especially not from men like Alec Hale. There was always a cost, even if no one said it aloud.

"I run a full-service protection firm, Alec," Brad said, folding his arms across his chest. "I don't tail people anymore. I haven't in years. I hire operatives. I review reports. I write contracts. You want surveillance, I've got a dozen men and women who can shadow your sister across Europe without ever being seen."

Alec shook his head, jaw tightening. "This isn't about the job, Brad. It's about trust."

Brad let out a quiet, humourless breath. "You mean it's about control. You don't want someone watching Scarlett. You want someone you trust watching her."

Alec didn't deny it.

Brad's gaze narrowed. "Why me? Why now?"

"Because she's vulnerable," Alec said simply. "And because you're the only person I know who won't lie to me about what he sees."

Brad tilted his head, sceptical. "You don't need me. You need a therapist, a guilt coach, and maybe a family mediator."

Alec gave a tight smile that didn't reach his eyes. "That too. But right now, I need you."

Brad looked at him for a long moment, jaw flexing, every instinct telling him to say no. He didn't babysit billionaires spoilt sisters. He didn't follow socialites through cobblestone streets and cocktail bars in foreign countries. That wasn't his work anymore. He handled real threats. Real risk.

But Alec had once pulled Brad from a burning Humvee after an ambush in Kandahar. Had kept him alive with his bare hands. Brad owed him his life.

And Brad wasn't the kind of man who forgot a debt.

Alec leaned forward across the sleek glass desk, fingers laced, sharp green eyes fixed on him. "I wouldn't ask if it weren't important."

Brad exhaled and crossed his arms. "Your sister's twenty-four. She's not a child."

"No," Alec said tightly. "She's reckless. She always has been."

Brad didn't respond immediately. He knew Alec well—well enough to know that beneath the polished billionaire exterior, the man was wound tight with guilt and responsibility. They had shared more than a battlefield overseas. But this—this wasn't a battlefield. This was Europe. And this was about Scarlett.

Scarlett Hale.

The name alone stirred something unsteady in Brad's mind—half a memory, half a question mark.

He had only met her once. Years ago. She'd been fourteen then, all legs and laughter, with a shock of wild red hair that refused to be tamed and a mouth that didn't know how to filter a single thought. There'd been something electric about her even then—too much life crammed into one fragile frame, like she didn't know how to be quiet or small. Not in those sterile Hamptons hallways, not in the shadow of her powerful family. She hadn't fit, not even a little.

He remembered her laughter most. Sharp, unfiltered, and unbothered by pretence. She had called him "Soldier Boy" after overhearing Alec mention his rank. Then she'd spent the entire weekend needling him with questions about snipers and stealth tactics—barefoot in the garden, sipping lemonade like a southern belle in a war film.

He'd found her amusing. Unsettling, too. Like a flash of colour in a greyscale world.

That was before the crash.

Before the Hale family jet went down somewhere over the Atlantic and took both of their parents with it. Before the light behind Scarlett's eyes—so Alec had told him—dimmed to something quieter. Angrier. More careful.

Before the silence.

Whatever bond had existed between the Hale siblings fractured that day, not loudly, but completely. Brad had watched from a distance as Alec buried himself in Hale Industries, and Scarlett disappeared into the kind of grief that didn't make headlines.

"She's going to Italy," Alec said, breaking the silence between them. "Then Greece. Maybe the south of France."

Brad blinked, dragged back to the present.

Alec frowned. "She wouldn't give me an exact itinerary."

Brad arched a brow. "And that's where your concern lies?"

Alec's jaw clenched, his voice low and sharp. "That, and the man she's travelling with. Jeff Bozeman."

Brad's brow furrowed. "The boyfriend?"

"Friend," Alec corrected, though the word sounded like it left a bad taste in his mouth. "At least, that's what she says. They met in college. I barely know the guy— he's never spent more than ten minutes in the same room with me, and that was years ago."

Brad raised a brow. "So, what's the concern?"

Alec exhaled hard through his nose. "Ever since our parents died, Scarlett's had partial access to the family trust. Enough to live comfortably. But on her twenty-fifth birthday next month, she inherits everything—the remainder of the estate, stocks, international assets, property, you name it. No restrictions. No oversight. Overnight, she'll become a multimillionaire in her own right."

Brad whistled low under his breath. "Hell of a birthday present."

"Hell of a target," Alec muttered.

Brad crossed the room slowly, his steps silent on the polished floors. "And you think Jeff's playing the long game."

"I think," Alec said carefully, "that I can't afford to be wrong. If he's a good guy, fine—I'll eat my words. But if he's using her? Manipulating her? I want to know before my sister ends up heartbroken, or worse—married to a man who sees her as a walking bank account."

The room went still, tension hanging between them like a held breath.

Brad turned his gaze back to the skyline, the late-afternoon light casting a soft amber glow across the city. Below, Manhattan buzzed with its usual symphony of motion and noise, though none of it could pierce the insulated glass.

He didn't like this.

Brad hated assignments tangled in personal history and emotional landmines. Family made things messy. Women made them dangerous.

Brad didn't trust women. Not in any lasting sense. In his experience, they always wanted more than he was willing—or able—to give. More time. More openness. More heart.

Things he'd long since learned to lock away.

It wasn't bitterness. Just survival. The kind learned the hard way—when you realised love had a longer half-life than the truth. He'd seen what happened when emotions got involved. Messy breakups, blurred boundaries, expectations that crept in and grew teeth. He didn't do attachments. He didn't do forever. He did clean exits, controlled outcomes, and zero complications.

He felt like Scarlett Hale would have complication written all over her.

But loyalty was a complicated thing. Brad knew all about carrying debts that didn't come with an expiration date. And Alec—Alec had never let him down. Not once.

He drew in a slow breath. "What exactly are you asking me to do?"

Alec's eyes didn't waver. "Shadow her. Stay close. Keep her safe. Keep Jeff honest."

Brad's shoulders stiffened. "Does she know you're sending someone?"

Alec shook his head. "No. And I want it to stay that way. If she finds out I'm interfering, it'll just push her further away."

Brad's jaw worked silently as he weighed the ask. He didn't like it. But he already knew what his answer would be.

Alec's voice was quieter now. Not colder—sadder. "I wasn't there for her when our parents died. I should've been, but I couldn't look at her without seeing the crash. The guilt." He looked down at his desk, then back up. "I'm trying now. It may be late, but I'm trying."

Brad didn't speak. The part of him that had shut down years ago wanted to walk away. But the part of him that owed Alec—really owed him—remained.

"How long?"

"Ten days, two weeks at the most. I'll cover your expenses, of course—private flights, accommodations, whatever you need."

Brad rolled his neck once and nodded slowly. "You get me a name for her hotel in Rome. I'll take the next flight."

Alec rose from behind the desk and extended a hand. "Thank you, Brad."

Brad took it without hesitation—grip firm, steady, professional—but his expression remained unreadable. There was no smile. No nod of reassurance. Just the quiet acceptance of a favour that carried more weight than either of them was willing to acknowledge.

Alec reached for a slim black envelope resting on the edge of his desk and handed it over. "Everything's in here—background on Jeff Bozeman, travel itinerary where available, and some recent photos of Scarlett."

Brad accepted the envelope with a nod, his fingers brushing against the smooth paper. It was heavier than it looked. Or maybe it just felt that way.

He didn't open it. Not yet. He simply slipped it inside the inner pocket of his jacket, as if delaying the moment, he'd have to see Scarlett's face again—older now, but likely still wearing that same fire behind her eyes.

"She doesn't know you're doing this?" he asked, a final note of confirmation.

"No," Alec said. "And if you can help it—she never should."

Brad gave a short nod, then turned for the door, his voice cool but quiet. "Understood."

But as he reached for the handle, Alec's voice stopped him.

"And Brad—"

He paused, glancing back.

"Be careful with her," Alec said. His expression was unreadable now. "She's not who she used to be."

Brad didn't respond. He just held Alec's gaze for a long beat, then opened the door and walked out, the envelope tucked against his chest like a sealed promise.

Chapter Two

The wheels of the sleek private jet touched down at Leonardo da Vinci International Airport with a gentle thud, and Scarlett Hale exhaled a breath she hadn't realised she'd been holding.

She was in Rome.

After nearly nine hours of white-glove service, vintage champagne, and plush first-class comfort, she should have felt relaxed. Instead, there was a restless kind of energy humming beneath her skin—part nerves, part anticipation.

She glanced out the window as the runway rolled beneath them, the late morning sun casting long shadows over the tarmac. Rome was real now. No longer a fantasy scribbled in the margins of her journal, or a dream discussed over too much wine with Jeff. It was here. It was happening.

For the first time in years, she wasn't on anyone's schedule. She wasn't required to smile for cameras or make polite conversation with business associates twice her age. She wasn't "the Hale heiress."

She was just Scarlett.

Not a headline. Not a legacy. Not the carefully manicured public image the world expected her to uphold.

And for the next ten days, she planned to remember exactly what that meant.

Not in a boardroom, where her last name opened doors, she hadn't asked to walk through. Not at some black-tie charity gala, draped in couture and paraded like a symbol of resilience—the Hale family's polished, surviving daughter.

She wouldn't have to smile through another cloying cocktail party or nod politely while someone offered hollow condolences wrapped in curiosity.

No. After years of living on autopilot, she was just Scarlett. Passport in hand. Luggage in tow. Her heels clicking against foreign pavement, her decisions entirely her own. No handlers. No agenda. No older brother watching from a distance with that quietly judgmental gaze.

From beside her, Jeff leaned closer, elbow brushing hers, his grin bright and unapologetic. "You look like someone who just broke out of prison."

Scarlett's lips curved slowly, a rare genuine smile blooming. "That's not far off."

The truth was that this trip had been a long time coming.

For three years, she'd stayed anchored in New York. Some days out of obligation. Most days out of fear.

After the crash, everything had collapsed in slow motion. Her world had shrunk— once sprawling and vibrant, it had narrowed to penthouse walls and carefully filtered air. The media had been relentless. So had the grief.

The world kept spinning. Alec buried himself in Hale Industries. And Scarlett? She stood still, emotionally marooned in the wreckage of that awful day.

She had lost her parents, yes. But she had also lost Alec—her big brother, her compass. He had become someone else entirely. Colder. Distant. A man of steel and silence.

And then, three weeks ago, she had woken up, stumbled into the bathroom, and caught her reflection in the mirror.

And she didn't recognise the woman staring back.

The girl who used to dance barefoot on summer lawns was gone.

In her place stood a woman—taller, quieter, sharper around the edges.

Her once-fiery red hair had deepened into a polished auburn, still catching the light with hints of copper, but more refined now. Sophisticated. Controlled. She sometimes missed the wildness of her younger self—the girl who didn't care if her hair tangled in the wind or if her laugh was too loud for polite society.

Her freckles, once scattered across her face like a constellation, had faded with time and caution, leaving only a faint dusting across the bridge of her nose—ghosts of the innocence she'd long outgrown.

She was beautiful. She knew that. Objectively, at least.

Men noticed. They always had. Even when she didn't want them to.

Sean had noticed.

Sean had chased.

And even now, he was still trying—sending texts that bordered on poetic and desperate, messages she hadn't answered in weeks. He'd been a comfort once, in those first hollow months after the crash. Familiar arms. A place to hide. But love had never truly lived there, not the kind that could survive grief and guilt.

That ship had sailed—drifted far beyond the horizon, and she had no interest in turning the wheel back.

Scarlett stood tall—taller than most women, and a fair number of men—but it suited her. She didn't shrink herself anymore. She moved with a quiet confidence and an elegance that didn't ask for attention but often commanded it anyway. Her legs—long, shapely, purposeful—carried her forward like she had somewhere important to be, even when she didn't.

But her real armour wasn't physical.

It was silence. Distance. Control.

The kind of emotional armour you forge when you've lost too much too young.

She wasn't that barefoot girl anymore. And she wasn't broken, either.

Not anymore.

Rome was chaos wrapped in poetry.

Vespa engines buzzed like hornets between narrow cobblestone streets, weaving between pedestrians and centuries-old fountains with reckless grace. Laughter spilled from open-air cafés where locals sipped espresso like it was holy, and tourists paused every few feet to capture the beauty on their phones. The air was thick with the scent of fresh ground coffee, warm bread, motor oil, and blooming jasmine—heady, intoxicating, alive.

It was overwhelming. It was loud. It was beautifully imperfect.

And it was perfect.

"Welcome to the good life, *mia cara*," Jeff declared with theatrical flair, lifting his designer sunglasses and spinning in a slow, dramatic circle. His linen shirt fluttered like a sail in the breeze, and he grinned like he'd just been cast as the lead in a Netflix series about sun-drenched European escapism.

Scarlett laughed—actually laughed—as she trailed behind him, her carry-on rolling over uneven stones and threatening to topple every time she hit a groove. "People are staring," she murmured, amused.

"They're admiring," Jeff corrected with a toss of his perfectly styled hair. "Let them bask. Rome wasn't built in a day, but this outfit was."

Scarlett rolled her eyes but felt a warmth bloom in her chest.

Jeff had been her one unshakable constant since college—the friend who didn't flinch when her world imploded, who didn't treat her like porcelain or a headline. He never offered pity, only presence. When she told him she needed to disappear for a while, he hadn't hesitated. He declared himself her "international emotional support human," complete with an itinerary of wine, food, and unapologetic indulgence.

He didn't ask questions. He just showed up.

And that meant more to her than she could ever say.

Their hotel was a sun-drenched boutique oasis tucked into a quiet side street just off the Piazza Navona, shielded from the crowds by flowering vines and wrought-iron balconies. The concierge greeted them like old friends, switching seamlessly between Italian and English as he handed over their suite keycard and offered to send up complimentary prosecco.

Scarlett barely heard him.

Because the moment she stepped inside the room, something shifted.

Warm light spilled through tall arched windows onto crisp white sheets and pale terracotta tile. The soft breeze rustled sheer curtains like whispers, and beyond the balcony railing, she could see a sliver of the piazza—golden in the afternoon sun, alive with artists, laughter, and the music of another life.

Scarlett dropped her suitcase by the door and walked to the window. Her hand found the iron railing, cool beneath her fingers.

And for the first time in a very, very long time—she felt it.

Not grief.

Not expectation.

Not the weight of being the Hale daughter.

But something else.

Freedom.

It came not as a scream or a sob, but a quiet, steady beat beneath her ribs. She didn't know what this trip would bring. She didn't know what she was looking for. But finally, she was looking.

And that was enough.

Their suite was beautiful—understated luxury with just the right amount of charm. Two bedrooms, high arched windows, gauzy white curtains billowing in the warm Roman breeze. Crisp linen sheets, polished floors, and a private balcony draped in cascading bougainvillea that painted the air with a subtle, sweet fragrance.

Scarlett dropped her suitcase just inside the doorway and stepped out onto the balcony, drawn like a magnet to the sunlight and the symphony of life below.

Rome unfolded before her in shades of terra cotta and gold, a city alive with history, heartbreak, and beauty. Rooftops stacked like puzzle pieces stretched into the distance, their edges softened by ivy and age. Domes punctuated the skyline. Church bells echoed faintly in the distance.

She leaned against the wrought-iron railing, the metal warm beneath her fingertips, and closed her eyes. The sun kissed her face. Her chest rose slowly as she took in her first true breath of freedom in years.

"I miss them," she whispered, more to herself than anyone else. She hadn't meant to say it out loud.

But Jeff was already there.

He moved beside her with quiet grace, setting down his sunglasses on the small café table beside them. His presence didn't startle her—it never did. He'd always had an uncanny ability to show up exactly when she needed him.

"I know," he said gently.

Scarlett kept her eyes closed. "I miss my mother's laugh. I miss the way my dad always burned the pancakes but insisted they were gourmet. I miss Sunday mornings in pyjamas and messy hair and feeling like… like the world was still intact." Her voice caught, a soft hitch in her throat. "And I miss Alec. Or at least the version of him who used to make me feel safe."

Jeff didn't respond right away. Instead, he reached for her hand, lacing his fingers through hers with quiet tenderness. Then, without a word, he pulled her into a hug—full, warm, protective. The kind of hug that said you don't have to be strong right now.

Scarlett didn't resist. She folded into him, letting her cheek rest against his chest.

To anyone watching, they might have looked like lovers. They weren't—but the intimacy they shared was its own kind of rare. Fierce. Loyal. Unshakeable.

"He's still in there," Jeff murmured, stroking her back once. "Your brother. Buried under the guilt and the responsibility and the corporate suit of armour. He hasn't disappeared. He's just… hiding."

"Maybe," Scarlett said quietly, pulling back just enough to look up at him. "But I don't think he sees me anymore. Not the way he used to. Not since the crash. I think all he sees now is the wreckage."

The silence stretched between them, filled only by the low hum of the city and the distant toll of a bell tower. But it wasn't uncomfortable.

Finally, Jeff bumped her gently with his hip and flashed a smile that was pure sunshine. "Okay. Enough emotional devastation for one day. You, my gorgeous Amazon of a best friend, are in the Eternal City. That means it's time for three things: absurd amounts of pasta, copious Aperol spritzes, and reckless flirting with devastatingly charming men named Lorenzo."

Scarlett let out a laugh, wiping a stray tear with the back of her hand. "Deal," she said, the word tasting like relief.

She didn't know what this trip would become. She had no itinerary, no expectations, no plan beyond living in the moment and trying—really trying—to feel something again.

To remember what it was like to be alive.

What she didn't know—what she couldn't know—was that she was already being watched.

Across the street, beneath a striped café awning dappled in sunlight, a man in a crisp white shirt stirred his espresso slowly. He sat with the effortless ease of someone used to blending in—just another tourist with a newspaper and a quiet drink.

But his eyes—steel blue and razor sharp—flicked upward just once.

Just long enough to catch a flash of auburn hair dancing in the breeze.

Chapter Three

Brad arrived in Rome under cover of darkness.

The private jet had touched down just after midnight, the city stretched out below him like a labyrinth of secrets and soft golden light. He cleared customs quickly, travelling light as always, and flagged a black car waiting on the tarmac. No luggage carousel. No lines. No questions.

The driver dropped him at the boutique hotel off Piazza Navona—quiet, discreet, elegant in that European way that didn't need to flaunt wealth to prove it existed. The same hotel Alec had confirmed Scarlett would be checking into the following morning. Brad didn't ask how Alec knew. He didn't want to know.

The clerk barely glanced up when Brad handed over the forged reservation under the name Brad Jenkins. Just another guest. Just another passport. The alias held, as always. Without fanfare, he was handed a key and escorted up a narrow marble staircase to the third floor. The suite at the end of the hall was quiet, discreet, and— he noted with a flicker of dry amusement—a mirror image of the one booked under Scarlett Hale's name. Of course it was.

When the door clicked shut behind him, Brad finally exhaled. Not out of fatigue— he rarely allowed himself that luxury—but out of necessity. He removed his jacket, rolled up his sleeves, and retrieved the slim black envelope from the inner pocket where it had sat, unopened, for nearly twenty-four hours.

He stared at it for a beat. Then broke the seal.

Inside were two slim dossiers and a short note in Alec Hale's handwriting:

I trust you. Keep her safe.

Brad flipped first to Jeff Bozeman's file. Education: Columbia. Political science. Minor in Italian. No criminal record, no suspicious financial activity, no red flags— at least not the kind that would show up in a standard dig. Socially well-connected. Well-liked.

And good-looking. Of course.

Blond hair, hazel eyes, sharp cheekbones. One of those tall, lean guys who probably wore vintage sweaters and cologne that smelled like money. In the photo, he had an arm casually draped around Scarlett, both of them laughing at something off-camera. Natural. Familiar. Close.

Too close?

Brad set the dossier down and picked up the next one.

Scarlett Hale.

Five photographs, all clipped neatly to the inside flap.

The first was from a charity gala—she stood in a midnight-blue gown, posture flawless, a champagne flute held delicately in her hand. Her expression was poised, serene. Unapproachable.

The second was from a fashion week event. The third from some tech investor luncheon. Each one carefully staged, professionally lit. She was breathtaking. Objectively stunning. Auburn hair swept into elegant chignons. Emerald eyes sharp and unyielding. Porcelain skin with just the faint trace of freckles that hinted at a girl she might once have been.

And yet—there was a chill to her. A polished frost that seemed to coat every photograph. She looked like every other trust fund princess Brad had spent his career protecting from themselves. Self-involved. Emotionally vacant. Probably just another pampered, out-of-touch heiress who thought Europe was a personal playground and people like him were paid wallpaper.

He closed the file and tossed it on the table.

He didn't sleep that night. He rarely did when he was on assignment—especially ones that required proximity to people who could ruin everything just by smiling the wrong way.

The next morning, he had eyes on her before breakfast.

From a quiet corner of the hotel café, his espresso cooling at his elbow, Brad watched her, and Jeff arrive—no handlers, no fanfare. Just the two of them wheeling matching luggage through the ivy-lined entrance, laughing about something he couldn't hear.

Scarlett Hale looked… different.

Not polished. Not cold.

She wore linen pants and a loose white blouse, sunglasses perched in her hair, her skin flushed from the flight and something else—excitement, maybe. Wonder. She wasn't guarded. She was radiant. There was no entourage. No arrogance. No expectation that the world should revolve around her.

Brad's brow furrowed slightly.

That wasn't the girl from the photos.

They spent the day weaving through the heart of the city—Piazza Navona, Campo de' Fiori, Trastevere. Brad stayed close but unseen, blending in with the crowds, watching from across cobblestone alleys and through mirrored shop windows. And every time he thought he understood her, she did something that didn't fit.

She helped an elderly woman carry groceries up three uneven steps. She stopped to pet a stray cat stretched across a sun-warmed stoop. She asked questions of the locals—in hesitant but passable Italian—and laughed when she got the words wrong.

She didn't act like royalty slumming it in Europe.

She acted like someone trying to remember how to breathe.

Jeff stayed close, never straying far from Scarlett's side. Protective, but not overbearing. They moved together with the ease of old familiarity—like people who had shared more than just years, but memories, secrets… maybe a bed. It was hard to ignore the intimacy between them. The way he touched the small of her back without hesitation. The way she leaned into his shoulder when she laughed. The low, private tones exchanged between them that seemed to shut out the rest of the world.

Brad watched them closely, analysing every gesture, every look. Body language didn't lie—not usually. And what he saw was connection. Deep and personal. A kind of closeness that didn't have to announce itself to be understood.

Lovers. That was the obvious conclusion.

And yet… something didn't sit right.

Jeff was affectionate, yes—loudly so. But not in a possessive way. More… indulgent. He was the one to reach for her hand when she drifted, to slide an arm around her waist when she paused too long in front of a memorial, to lean in and murmur something that made her laugh when her eyes began to shine at the Pantheon.

Brad's jaw tightened.

Whatever they were, it didn't look temporary.

And for reasons he couldn't—or wouldn't—name, he didn't like that. Not one damn bit.

That evening, he followed them back to the hotel. They dined at a corner trattoria tucked between crumbling stone walls and ivy-laced balconies, beneath a canopy of fairy lights that blinked like stars strung too low. The table was small, the wine plentiful, and they laughed like locals—sharing forkfuls of carbonara, clinking mismatched glasses, tasting everything with the delight of people who hadn't yet decided where tomorrow would take them.

Scarlett's laughter floated into the street more than once—bright, warm, entirely unguarded. It surprised him.

So did the quiet, fleeting moments in between.

Like the way her gaze sometimes drifted—just for a second—far past the candlelit table and out into the dark. Or the way she tucked her hair behind one ear, over and over, as if trying to steady herself. Or how her smile, when it faltered, slipped just slightly off-centre, like it had forgotten how to hold itself in place.

From across the street, Brad watched from the shadows of a tiny café, his back to the warm stucco wall, a bitter black coffee cooling beside a folded newspaper he hadn't turned the page on in nearly an hour. He was half-hidden beneath the striped awning, blending into the shadows like just another tourist lingering over an espresso.

From this distance, he could almost pretend it was routine. Detached. Professional.

But it wasn't.

Because he noticed.

Too much.

The soft curve of Scarlett's bare shoulder beneath the fluttering sleeve of her sundress when she leaned into Jeff's laugh. The way her fingers curled absently around the stem of her wineglass, as if it anchored her to the moment. The sound of her laugh—unguarded, golden—rising like a melody above the hum of clinking silverware and Italian chatter. And the flicker of something else, too. A shadow behind her eyes. Fleeting, but unmistakable. Not enough to dim her spark completely—just enough to remind him that joy, for her, came with weight.

He hated this part.

The noticing.

The way it slipped in, quiet and uninvited, dismantling the professional wall he was trained to keep. This wasn't supposed to be about her. She was a subject. A surveillance target. A job.

She wasn't the kind of woman you could forget. No matter how hard you tried.

And that was quickly becoming a problem.

Jeff excused himself from the table, ducking inside the trattoria with a parting joke that made Scarlett laugh again, tossing her head slightly as she reached for her water. Alone now, she shifted in her seat, legs crossed, posture relaxed but alert. A breeze lifted a lock of auburn hair from her collarbone, and she tucked it behind one ear— an unconscious gesture Brad had seen her repeat all day.

That was when he saw the man.

Mid-thirties, tan, tailored navy blazer over a crisp white shirt, Italian to his core— wealth practically stitched into his cuffs. He was handsome in the polished, practiced way of men who knew their reflection too well. And he moved like someone used to getting what he wanted.

He approached Scarlett with a casual confidence, stopping just beside her table. Said something—charming, clearly. She glanced up, startled, then smiled politely, her body language neutral but not dismissive.

Brad's jaw tightened.

The man leaned closer, gesturing toward her wine with a grin that was a blend of suggestion. Flirtation poured from him like cologne—slick and calculated. Scarlett tilted her head, listening, amused. But not interested. Brad could read it in the angle of her shoulders, the small polite nods, the smile that didn't quite reach her eyes.

Still, the man lingered.

Brad shifted forward in his seat, newspaper forgotten. His eyes narrowed as the Italian touched the back of Scarlett's chair—light, familiar, too bold for someone who'd just introduced himself. Brad's pulse kicked up, slow and steady, a conditioned response. His gaze flicked toward the trattoria door. Jeff was still inside.

Scarlett, to her credit, handled it with grace. A few words, firm but pleasant. A shake of her head. Another faint smile. She didn't shrink, didn't look uncomfortable—just effortlessly dismissed him like a woman who'd been fending off unwanted attention her entire life.

And still, Brad didn't relax.

When Jeff returned, the man made a quick, charming exit, tipping his head in farewell before vanishing into the crowd.

Brad leaned back, exhaling through his nose. He picked up his coffee but didn't drink it.

This was supposed to be a simple job.

Watch the girl. Protect the asset. Report back.

But Scarlett wasn't just another heiress sipping her way through Europe with a bodyguard-shaped shadow behind her. She wasn't spoiled or naïve. She was smart, observant, kind in a way that didn't feel rehearsed. She laughed easily but carried sorrow like it had shaped her. Like she knew how quickly the ground could vanish beneath your feet.

She was becoming dangerous to him.

Not because of what she did.

But because of what he felt when he watched her.

And Brad Allen didn't like that at all.

Chapter Four

The suite was quiet except for the distant hum of Rome outside the balcony doors—Vespa engines whining, laughter echoing in the alley below, the occasional clink of silverware from a rooftop terrace.

Brad sat at the small desk near the window, his laptop open, a glass of scotch sweating beside it. Surveillance photos were pulled up—nothing invasive, just street-level shots he'd taken discreetly with his phone: Scarlett laughing in front of the Trevi Fountain, Jeff with his arm around her shoulders outside a gelato stand, the two of them sitting close at the trattoria that evening, heads tilted toward one another.

He was cataloguing the day's patterns, just like he was trained to. Movements. Stops. Expressions.

And yet, he'd hovered too long on a shot of Scarlett staring out over the Spanish Steps, her expression unreadable. Not sad. Not happy. Something in between.

His burner phone buzzed on the desk. The screen lit with one word: Alec.

Brad picked it up, jaw already tight. "Yeah."

"Update," Alec said without preamble. "How is she?"

Brad leaned back in the chair, eyes still on the screen. "She's fine. Settled in. No signs of trouble."

"And Jeff?"

Brad hesitated, watching a paused frame of Jeff holding out a camera, coaxing Scarlett into a photo. "Charming. Attentive. Maybe a little too polished for my taste, but nothing overtly suspicious."

Alec's voice sharpened. "But?"

"But," Brad said slowly, "he's not making a move. No manipulation, no possessiveness. If anything, she leads the rhythm between them. He follows."

There was a pause on the other end. Then, "So it's more than just friendship?"

Brad's jaw flexed. "They act like it, yeah. But—" he hesitated, unsure why he was even defending the guy, "there's no physical chemistry. Not the kind that reads romantic. Close friends. Familiar. But that's it."

Alec let out a low exhale. "You're sure?"

"I've been doing this a long time, Alec. I know when someone's angling. Jeff's not. If anything, he seems more interested in making her laugh than getting in her will."

Another pause.

Brad could hear the gears turning in Alec's mind—doubt, relief, the stubborn kind of guilt that didn't admit itself out loud.

"Is she… okay?" Alec asked finally, quieter now. "I mean—really okay?"

Brad looked toward the balcony, where the breeze ruffled the white curtains like a whisper.

"She smiles a lot," he said. "Laughs even more. But sometimes—when she's not talking, when she thinks no one's looking…" He stopped, unsure how to explain the weight he saw in her silences.

"She's not fine," he said finally. "She's surviving. And she's trying."

Alec said nothing for a long time. Brad could picture him—back in the penthouse, probably still in a suit, jaw tight, emotions buried under strategy and steel.

"She said she misses your mom's laugh," Brad added, unprompted. "Your dad's bad pancakes. And you."

He didn't know why he said it. Maybe Alec needed to hear it. Maybe he did too.

Alec's voice was rough when it came. "She said that?"

"Not to me," Brad said. "To Jeff. But I was close enough."

There was a pause on the other end of the line. Then Alec's voice came, low and edged with something unreadable. "So, they're… together."

Brad's jaw flexed. "They act like it, yeah." He hesitated, unsure why the words felt so reluctant. "There's no kissing. No overt affection. But there's familiarity. A lot of it. They touch often. Sit close. He's always looking out for her."

Alec exhaled, a sound that was half resignation, half frustration. "So, they might be sleeping together."

Brad's grip tightened around the phone. He didn't want to speculate—but he knew what Alec was really asking. Knew what it meant coming from a man who'd spent years holding everyone at arm's length, only to suddenly find himself shut out.

"…Yeah," Brad said finally. "It's possible."

Another silence.

Brad could feel it through the line—the slow churn of guilt and worry grinding through Alec's carefully guarded armour. The kind of protective panic that only showed up when it was already too late to undo the distance.

He leaned back in the hotel chair, the leather creaking under his weight. "I've been doing this a long time, Alec," he said evenly. "I know the signs. If Jeff were using her, I'd see it. But he's not. The guy's not a leech, he's not angling for a payout."

There was a beat of silence. Then Alec spoke, quieter this time. "She used to laugh all the time. Before."

Brad didn't respond. He couldn't.

"Stay with her," Alec said after a moment. "Don't let her know you're there, but… stay close."

"I know the job," Brad replied.

A pause. Then, more quietly, Alec added, "Yeah. I just don't know if I still know her."

Brad stared at the empty glass on the table beside him, the weight of that confession sitting heavier than the scotch he hadn't poured yet.

He didn't answer. There was nothing to say.

He hung up, set the phone down with more care than necessary, and finally reached for the decanter. The scotch burned on the way down, but it didn't settle the tension curled low in his chest.

Outside, Rome buzzed beneath the stars—laughter rising from the street, music spilling from a distant café.

And for the first time in years, Brad Allen wasn't sure where the lines of the mission ended… or where Scarlett Hale began.

The second day was more of the same—if "the same" meant unfiltered joy wrapped in sunlight.

They wandered through Rome with no agenda. Scarlett fed pigeons near the Trevi Fountain and made Jeff pose for selfies with a crooked gelato cone. She danced—actually danced—to a street violinist playing Vivaldi in the square, her laughter ringing out, clear as the bell tower two streets over.

She wasn't who Brad expected.

Not even close.

By sunset, he was alone on the rooftop terrace of the hotel, bourbon sweating in a short glass beside him. Below, Rome glowed in shades of rose and gold, the city humming softly like a lullaby. The bougainvillea rustled in the breeze, petals brushing against his arm.

He should've been drafting a report. Reviewing footage. Calling it in.

Instead, he pulled out the photo again—the one from the gala. Scarlett Hale, poised and frosted like a museum piece. Beautiful. Impeccable. Remote.

He glanced down into the courtyard below.

Her voice floated up. Clear. Warm. Unmistakable.

She was barefoot, her heels in one hand, her hair a little wind-tossed from the day. Jeff said something, and she mock shoved him, laughing as she sank into a cushioned bench. Brad leaned on the railing, watching.

Just for a moment.

Then the moment shifted.

A shadow crossed the courtyard.

Brad tensed.

A man approached—tall, confident, with the kind of swagger that belonged to someone who never questioned whether he was welcome. Designer jacket, expensive watch, practiced smirk. He leaned in like he belonged there.

Scarlett froze.

Only for a breath—but Brad saw it. She blinked once. Smiled tightly.

Jeff straightened, his entire body bristling in one subtle move.

Brad couldn't make out every word, but he caught the sharp edge in Jeff's voice—low, tense—as he muttered, "What the hell is he doing here?"

Scarlett rose, calm as ever. If she was rattled, it didn't show. She greeted Sean with a kiss on the cheek, all European polish. Polite. Distant. A masterclass in civility.

Sean didn't take the hint. He lingered, clearly expecting something. A seat. A welcome. Maybe even a second chance.

Jeff stepped in. "She's not interested, Sean."

Scarlett touched Jeff's arm—gently, a calming pressure. "It's fine," she said, not taking her eyes off Sean. "He was just leaving."

Sean's smile was polished, too smooth to be sincere. "Still as graceful as ever, Scar."

Scarlett didn't miss a beat. "And you're still not listening," she said, voice even, almost bored. "It's over, Sean."

From his vantage point above, Brad took in every detail—the tightness around her mouth, the flicker of tension in her shoulders. Jeff, standing beside her now, looked like he was barely restraining himself, jaw clenched, hands curled into loose fists. Scarlett, by contrast, stayed composed. Unshaken.

But Brad caught it—the subtle twitch of her fingers against her thigh. Small. Telling.

A single crack in the otherwise perfect armour.

Finally, Sean gave a tight nod, offered some throwaway line about catching up, and turned back into the night, ego slightly bruised.

Scarlett sat down slowly, blowing out a breath.

Jeff muttered something and passed her a wineglass.

Brad exhaled too, sharp, and quiet—only then realising how tight his grip had been on the railing.

This wasn't in the dossier.

This woman wasn't cold or aloof. She wasn't reckless or naive. She was careful. Controlled. Kind. And strong enough to look her past in the eye without flinching.

He took one last sip of his drink, then slipped the gala photo back into its envelope and walked inside.

Whatever this job had started as—it wasn't simple anymore.

Not even close.

Chapter Five

The morning market in Trastevere was already alive with colour and chaos. Sunlight spilled over canvas awnings, catching on the glint of ripe pomegranates, silver trinkets, and the occasional bottle of limoncello. The scent of citrus and freshly baked bread clung to the warm Roman air.

Brad moved through the crowd like smoke. Invisible by design.

He was only meant to watch.

But then he saw her—standing near a fruit vendor with a lopsided basket of peaches in one arm and a crooked smile on her lips as she bartered, in broken Italian, for a better price. Her hair was tied in a loose knot at the nape of her neck, wisps escaping to kiss her cheeks. She laughed when the old vendor playfully swatted her hand away from the scale.

Brad didn't mean to move closer.

But he did.

A few steps. A slight pivot.

And then—

"Sorry—" His shoulder brushed hers just enough to be felt, not enough to alarm.

She turned. Quick. Alert.

Bright green eyes met his. Curious. A flicker of wariness behind them, but nothing she couldn't smile through. "Oh—no worries," she said, adjusting her bag on her shoulder. "Markets are dangerous places."

Brad returned the smile, easy and casual. "Especially if you're standing between a Roman nonna and her tomatoes."

That earned him a laugh. Light, spontaneous. She shook her head. "No kidding. I almost lost a finger over a bunch of basil."

Brad glanced at her basket. "Worth it?"

She held up a peach like a trophy. "You have no idea."

A voice called from behind—Jeff, returning with two iced coffees and a canvas tote slung over one shoulder. He froze when he saw Brad, instantly on guard.

Scarlett gestured between them. "Jeff—this is…?"

Brad offered a hand. "Brad. Just here for the espresso and overpriced antiques."

Jeff didn't take it immediately, but after a beat, he gave a polite shake. "Nice to meet you."

Brad turned back to Scarlett, his tone light. "Didn't mean to interrupt."

"You didn't," she said before Jeff could interject. She studied Brad with a curiosity that made something shift in his chest. "Are you sightseeing?"

"Trying to," he said. "I've been circling this piazza for twenty minutes. I think it's conspiring against my sense of direction."

She grinned, amused. "Well, we were heading to Castel Sant'Angelo. If you don't mind sharing the road with two painfully American tourists…"

Jeff shot her a sideways look, but she didn't seem to notice.

Brad hesitated. Just for effect.

"Sure," he said, slipping his hands into his pockets. "I could use a local guide."

Scarlett laughed. "We're not locals."

"You know more Italian than I do," he countered. "That makes you qualified."

They walked on—Scarlett in the middle, Jeff still a little stiff at her side, eyes flicking toward Brad every few paces. Scarlett, oblivious or simply unbothered, chattered on, pointing out buildings with half-remembered facts from a walking tour app, her gestures animated, her eyes bright with that particular kind of wonder Rome inspired.

Brad hung back half a step, not because he was trying to be subtle—but because he wanted to see her.

Really see her.

It was supposed to be surveillance. Keep her in sight. Stay close without being obvious.

But the more she talked, the more he felt the lines blur—between the assignment and the woman, the job, and the spark.

Scarlett Hale didn't recognise him. Not from the weekend he'd spent at their family's Hampton estate when she was fourteen and too young to care about the quiet man in the background.

To her, he was just a stranger in a sunlit market.

And somehow, that made it worse.

Because Brad was already lying.

They crossed the Tiber at Ponte Sisto, sunlight filtering through the balustrades in broken gold. Scarlett stopped mid-bridge, turning to snap a photo of the river, her hair catching the light in loose waves. Brad offered a quiet comment about the stonework—factual, neutral—but something in the way she turned toward him, genuinely interested, made it feel like more.

Jeff lingered behind them at first, arms crossed, keeping a careful eye on their dynamic. But gradually, as the morning wore on and Brad never once stepped over a line—never flirted, never tried to dominate the moment—Jeff began to loosen.

It helped that Brad noticed things.

Like how Scarlett's sandals kept slipping on uneven stone, and he subtly adjusted his pace so she could lean into him without even realising it. Or the way he offered her his water bottle without a word when she started to fan herself from the heat. Nothing overt. Just thoughtful. Natural.

At Castel Sant'Angelo, Brad handed Jeff a five-euro coin without being asked when they came up short for entry. Jeff hesitated—then gave a nod that wasn't quite gratitude, but wasn't not, either.

Scarlett caught the exchange. Her eyes lingered on Brad a second longer than they should have.

They explored the castle slowly, winding through ancient corridors and sun-drenched terraces. Scarlett paused to trace her fingers along weathered stone, asking questions that didn't always have answers. Brad offered what history he knew—not much, but enough to keep her interested.

At one point, she slipped on a narrow stair, and Brad caught her elbow instinctively.

"Thanks," she said, a little breathless.

"Careful," he replied, voice low. "These old places have teeth."

She smiled at that. Not polite. Not distant. Just… real.

Jeff watched the moment unfold with narrowed eyes. But whatever he was looking for, he didn't seem to find it. Because when they sat down at a café afterward, ordering granita and espresso, he offered Brad the seat across from him without prompting.

"You always travelling alone?" Jeff asked, casual.

Brad sipped his coffee. "Most of the time. Easier that way."

Scarlett cocked her head. "Easier for what?"

He looked at her then, really looked. "Figuring out where you belong."

She blinked, clearly not expecting the honesty.

Jeff tilted his head. "What do you do, exactly?"

Brad smiled. "A little bit of everything. Logistics. Private contracts. Mostly security these days."

Scarlett raised an eyebrow. "Military?"

"Once," Brad admitted. "Long time ago."

That answer seemed to land gently between them—respectable, if vague. Jeff nodded, more approving this time.

Scarlett leaned back in her chair, sipping her granita, watching Brad over the rim of her glass like she was still deciding what to make of him.

Brad knew what she saw: a quiet man in a neutral shirt, with steady hands and sharp eyes. Nothing flashy. Nothing memorable.

Just enough truth to pass.

But the lie still sat heavy behind his ribs.

Because she didn't know who he was. Not really.

Not that he'd been hired by her brother. Not that he'd been following her since the moment she landed in Rome. Not that he knew things about her no stranger should—like the way her smile tilted when it was real, or how her fingers trembled slightly when she was tired.

And he couldn't shake the feeling that the truth would ruin everything.

Because the longer he stayed, the more he wasn't sure this was just a job anymore.

The day began to wind down the way perfect days in Rome always did—slowly, lazily, like the city didn't want to let them go. They lingered over one last gelato near the Piazza Navona, the light turning molten around them, painting Scarlett's skin in rose-gold and fire.

"We should head back," Jeff said eventually, checking his watch. "Dinner later?"

"Always," Scarlett replied, licking pistachio off her thumb. "But somewhere with air-conditioning this time. I love ambiance, but I'm melting."

She turned to Brad, her expression open—curious, but unreadable. "Where are you staying, anyway?"

Brad hesitated for half a beat. Then said, as casually as he could, "That boutique place just off the Piazza. The one with all the ivy around the entrance."

Scarlett blinked. "You're at our hotel?"

Jeff's brows lifted. "Seriously?"

Brad shrugged, trying not to make too much of it. "Booked it last minute. Seemed quiet. Convenient."

Scarlett let out a soft, surprised laugh. "Well, that's… unexpected."

Jeff studied him for a moment—eyes narrowed like he was still deciding something. Then, with a half-smile that wasn't quite reluctant, he said, "You should join us for dinner."

Brad glanced between them. "I don't want to intrude."

"You won't," Scarlett said easily, already turning toward the street. "We've spent all day together. Feels weird to stop now."

Jeff gave a nod, less casual but no less sincere. "Besides, you're interesting. And Scarlett hasn't grilled you nearly enough."

Brad smirked. "Guess I'll take that as a compliment."

As they walked back toward the hotel, the sky dimming overhead and Roman lanterns flickering to life along the stone path, Brad felt it settle in his chest—the weight of what he was doing, and the pull of what he couldn't seem to stop.

He wasn't just following her anymore.

He was falling into something he couldn't name.

And if he wasn't careful, he wasn't sure he'd find his way back out.

Chapter Six

The restaurant was tucked down a narrow side street just off the Piazza Navona, its ivy-draped terrace lit by tiny gold lanterns strung between crooked iron poles. Candlelight flickered in mismatched jars on each table, casting soft shadows that moved like whispers across the stone walls.

Scarlett picked the place—no reservations, no fanfare, just instinct. The hostess recognised her from the previous night and led them to a quiet corner, far enough from the bustle to feel private.

Brad took the seat across from her, Jeff to her right. For a moment, the only sound was the clinking of glasses and the distant clatter of a Vespa engine zipping past the alley.

"Okay," Scarlett said, folding her napkin with flair. "Rules of the evening: no politics, no work talk, and no photos of food unless it's truly artistic."

Brad raised an eyebrow. "Artistic food photography. Got it. What if it's just a really photogenic pizza?"

"Then I'll allow it," she said, grinning. "Barely."

Jeff chuckled, more relaxed now than Brad had seen him all day. The tension that had threaded through his shoulders during their walk had mostly loosened, and he even nodded in agreement when Brad suggested the Barolo.

Dinner arrived slowly, in courses they didn't rush—plates of burrata with charred figs, handmade pici tossed in pecorino, lamb that practically fell apart under a fork. Scarlett reached across the table more than once to steal from Jeff's plate, and once—boldly—from Brad's. He let her. Of course he let her.

Conversation wandered—from travel stories to the worst hotel rooms they'd ever endured. Scarlett's hands moved when she spoke, her eyes lighting up with each new story. Every now and then, Brad felt the warmth of her gaze land on him—brief, thoughtful, then gone again before he could place it.

She excused herself after dessert, weaving between tables toward the restroom.

And for the first time that evening, it was just the two of them.

Brad leaned back in his chair. Jeff watched Scarlett disappear into the hallway, then turned his focus to the man across from him.

"You're hard to read," Jeff said simply. Not accusing. Just honest.

Brad met his gaze. "So are you."

Jeff smiled faintly. "Yeah. I get that a lot."

Silence fell for a moment, not heavy, just watchful.

Then Jeff set down his wineglass with deliberate care, eyes steady across the table. "Look," he said, voice quieter now, "I don't know what your story is—and honestly, I'm not asking. But if you're planning to stick around, even for a couple of days… there's something you should understand."

Brad didn't respond. He waited.

Jeff leaned forward slightly, his tone dipping lower. "Scarlett's had a rough few years. Family losses. A personal hit that should've crushed her—but didn't. And some other personal stuff that…" He paused, running a hand over the back of his neck, choosing his next words with care. "Her ex—Sean—saw an opening. She was vulnerable. Trusted the wrong people. And she paid for that trust in ways most people never see."

Brad's expression stayed still. But his eyes… sharpened.

Jeff continued, slower now. "She looks like she's fine—laughing, smiling, charming the room without trying. But that's armour. She's proud. She refuses to be seen as broken. But don't mistake that for invincibility."

A beat passed.

Brad gave a single nod. "I won't."

Jeff studied him, something measured flickering behind his gaze. "Good. Because if you're going to be in her orbit… just don't be another guy who sees what he wants and takes something from her without giving anything back."

Brad met his eyes without blinking. "That's not why I'm here."

Jeff leaned back slowly, the edge in his shoulders loosening—not quite trust, but something close. "Alright then."

Scarlett returned a moment later, cheeks pink from the heat, her curls slightly mussed from the breeze. She dropped into her seat and offered a mock glare at the half-eaten lemon tart between them.

"You two better not have finished the good part."

Brad offered her the last bite without a word. She took it, smiling as she did.

Later, when they walked back toward the hotel under a sky full of stars and soft Roman shadows, Scarlett laughed at something Jeff said and looped her arm through his.

Brad walked beside them, silent but steady, his mind replaying Jeff's words.

He hadn't come to Rome to fall for anyone. He'd come to do a job.

But now… the lines were blurring more with every step.

The hotel lobby was hushed, wrapped in the soft hush of late evening. Warm light spilled from sconces along the walls, casting long shadows across the marble floor as the three of them made their way toward the elevator.

Scarlett let out a satisfied sigh. "That lemon tart nearly ruined me."

"You say that like it's a bad thing," Jeff said, chuckling as he punched the button.

Brad stood beside them, hands in his pockets, saying nothing. But he was listening. Watching. Cataloguing every glance, every small touch between them like a man who couldn't stop tracing lines he wasn't supposed to follow.

When the elevator arrived, they stepped inside in silence. Scarlett leaned lightly against the mirrored wall, her shoes dangling from her fingers. "I forgot how much Rome steals from you. Your time, your feet… your restraint."

Jeff laughed. "You've never had restraint."

She didn't deny it.

The elevator chimed softly as it stopped on the third floor. They stepped out together, but Scarlett paused after a few steps, glancing over her shoulder at Brad.

"You're on this floor too?"

Brad nodded once. "End of the hall."

Her brows rose. "Huh. Small world."

Jeff gave a soft, almost wary laugh. "Or well-reviewed hotel."

They moved as a trio again, feet muffled by the carpet runner, the quiet weight of the evening settling between them. Scarlett's laughter had faded to a calm stillness, that low hum of contentment that only came from a full day well spent.

As they neared their suite, Brad clocked the subtle shift—the way Jeff's hand slipped to the small of Scarlett's back. Light. Familiar. Protective.

It was nothing inappropriate.

And yet Brad felt it like a pressure behind the ribs.

Scarlett didn't seem to notice—or if she did, she didn't react. She simply reached into her bag for the keycard, offering them both a drowsy smile. "Well… thanks for not ditching us halfway through the heat stroke."

Brad met her gaze. "Thanks for letting me tag along."

"Anytime," she said.

Jeff added a nod. "Catch you tomorrow, maybe?"

Brad hesitated. Just for a moment. "Yeah. Maybe."

They disappeared inside a moment later, the door shutting with a soft click.

Brad stood in the hallway for a beat longer than necessary. The silence pressed in, broken only by the distant hum of city life leaking through the window at the corridor's end.

Same floor. Same hotel. Same mission.

But suddenly, everything felt different.

He exhaled, slow and controlled, and turned toward his suite.

And for the first time since arriving in Rome, Brad Allen realised he wasn't sure if he was still watching Scarlett Hale… or falling for her.

Brad slipped his keycard into the door, the lock blinking green with a soft click. The suite greeted him with silence—cool, dim, impersonal as ever. The faint hum of Rome drifted through the open balcony doors: distant conversation, a single Vespa whining down a side street, the clink of dishes being cleared at a nearby café.

He loosened the buttons of his shirt as he stepped inside, rolled his shoulders once, and tossed the keycard onto the marble-topped desk.

His phone buzzed.

Alec.

Of course.

Brad stared at the screen for a second longer than necessary before answering. "Yeah."

"Status?" Alec's voice was clipped. Straight to the point, as always.

Brad crossed to the mini bar, retrieved a bottle of water, and twisted the cap. "Quiet day."

Alec didn't respond right away. "That's it?"

Brad took a sip, eyes narrowing toward the balcony, where the soft breeze fluttered the edge of the curtain. He could still picture Scarlett's laugh echoing down the hallway. The way she tilted her head when she was curious. The feel of her shoulder brushing his arm at the market.

He cleared his throat. "They did the tourist thing. Markets, Castel Sant'Angelo, some cafés. Nothing out of the ordinary."

"Jeff still attached at the hip?" Alec asked.

Brad's jaw tightened. "Yeah."

"You see anything to worry about?"

Brad leaned against the edge of the desk, staring down at the grainy surveillance photo still half-tucked under the edge of his laptop—Scarlett, laughing in the sunlight, totally unguarded.

"No," he said finally, the lie tasting like gravel. "Nothing interesting."

There was a pause on the other end of the line. Alec's silence carried weight, but he didn't push.

"Alright," he said. "Keep a low profile."

"Always do."

Alec hung up without another word.

Brad stood there for a moment, the bottle of water still in his hand, the lie echoing in his head.

Nothing interesting.

Except the way her voice stayed with him.

Except the weight in Jeff's warning.

Except the way Scarlett Hale looked at him like he wasn't a stranger.

He twisted the cap back on and set the bottle down.

Then crossed to the balcony, hands braced on the railing and looked out over the city that was fast becoming a complication.

And for the first time in years, Brad wasn't sure who he was protecting her from—others… or himself.

Chapter Seven

Sunlight spilled through the gauzy curtains of the suite, warming the marble floor and casting gold across the rumpled couch where Scarlett had tossed her scarf the night before.

She stirred slowly in the bedroom, blinking against the light, a sleepy smile curving her lips as she stretched. The city was already alive beyond the windows—she could hear the hum of Vespas and the faint clatter of plates from the café below. It smelled like morning. Like promise.

She slipped on a robe and padded barefoot into the living area—only to stop short.

Jeff stood near the kitchenette, one hand braced against the counter, his other pressed to his temple. His face was pale, almost grey, and the skin beneath his eyes was drawn tight.

Scarlett's smile dropped in an instant.

"Jeff," she said, voice soft but sharp with concern. "What is it?"

He winced slightly at the sound. "Just a migraine," he muttered, blinking as though the light hurt. "It hit around four. I thought I could sleep through it."

Scarlett was already crossing the room, hand reaching for his arm. "Why didn't you wake me?"

He shook his head, carefully, like even that was too much movement. "You were dead asleep. And I've had worse. I just need to crash in a dark room for a few hours."

"You look like death," she said gently, brushing her knuckles against his forehead. "I'm not leaving you like this."

Jeff offered a tired, crooked smile. "Scar… you'll just hover and drive me crazy."

"I'm allowed to hover," she argued, trying to keep it light, but the worry in her voice betrayed her.

He turned, catching her hand briefly before she could pull away. "I promise, I'm just going to sleep. Close the curtains, shut out the world, and resurface when I'm human again. You should go out. Enjoy the city. You've been so happy these last couple days… don't waste today because of my skull drama."

Scarlett hesitated, frowning, thumb brushing over his knuckles. "You swear you'll rest? No phone, no pretending to be okay?"

"I swear," he said. "Scout's honour."

She raised a brow. "You were never a scout."

"Exactly. So, you know I'm serious."

Despite herself, she huffed a soft laugh. "Okay. But you call me the second you feel worse. Or better. Or bored."

Jeff nodded, already moving toward the bedroom with deliberate slowness. "Go soak up some sun, Scar. Maybe run into your new friend again."

She paused in the doorway, watching him with knit brows. "I don't know what you're talking about."

"Mmm," Jeff said, not looking back. "You really do."

He disappeared into the shadows of the suite, and Scarlett stood in the quiet that followed, her worry lingering like mist.

Still… he needed rest.

And maybe, she admitted to herself, she needed a little space too—just enough to clear her head and shake the way Brad Jenkins's eyes had stayed with her all night.

She turned toward the bathroom to get dressed, her thoughts already wandering toward the cobblestones and sunlight waiting outside.

The hotel's ground-floor restaurant was a quiet hum of soft jazz, polished cutlery, and the scent of espresso and warm croissants. Brad sat near the window, half-shadowed by sheer curtains, a black coffee in front of him and a newspaper spread across the table that he wasn't really reading.

He wasn't expecting her.

But when the door opened and Scarlett Hale stepped inside, the whole space seemed to shift. She wore sunglasses and a loose linen dress, her hair twisted into a lazy knot, a single curl falling loose near her temple. Effortless. Elegant. She scanned the room, spotted him, and didn't hesitate.

"Good morning," she said as she reached his table, sliding her glasses up into her hair.

Brad stood slightly out of habit—old training—and nodded. "Morning."

"Mind if I sit?"

He gestured to the empty chair. "Please."

Scarlett settled across from him, her fingers lightly trailing the edge of the napkin as she glanced toward the breakfast bar. "You always eat in shadows like some noir detective, or is that just a today thing?"

Brad gave a faint smile. "Habit. Less foot traffic near the windows."

She narrowed her eyes playfully. "Strategic seating. Of course."

The waiter appeared, and Scarlett ordered a cappuccino and something light—fruit, and a pastry—then turned her attention back to Brad, studying him in that quiet, observant way that always seemed to make him feel more seen than he liked.

"You're up early," she said. "Touristing again?"

"Something like that," Brad replied. Then, after a pause: "No Jeff today?"

Scarlett's smile softened, her fingers curling around the edge of her water glass. "Migraine. One of the bad ones. He's sleeping it off with blackout curtains and two noise machines. I offered to stay, but he insisted I get out for a bit."

Brad nodded slowly, filing away the concern in her voice, the gentle wrinkle that formed between her brows. "That happen often?"

"Often enough," she said. "They're awful. He won't admit it, but they take a toll."

Brad leaned back in his chair, unreadable, but quietly watching her. "You're close."

Her eyes flicked to his, steady. "He's family. Maybe not by blood, but definitely by life."

The silence between them was comfortable, laced with something unspoken—familiarity, maybe. Curiosity. A question they were both pretending not to ask.

Scarlett tilted her head. "What about you? Plans for the day?"

Brad's mouth curved slightly. "I hadn't decided. Rome's full of distractions."

Her cappuccino arrived—fragrant and delicate, the foam dusted with just enough cocoa to feel like a quiet indulgence. Scarlett wrapped her hands around the cup, drawing in the warmth like a small comfort.

Brad watched her for a moment, then said, casually but not without weight, "I was thinking of heading up into the hills today. Take a ride. Get out of the city for a bit."

She looked up, surprised—but pleasantly so.

"Would you like to come?"

Her smile came easily. Soft. Genuine.

"I'd love to."

They left midmorning, the sun already gilding the cobbled streets with a warmth that promised another golden Roman day.

Brad had arranged the scooter through the concierge—sleek, dark, and built for two. When Scarlett saw it waiting outside the hotel, her eyebrows lifted in amusement.

"Tell me you know how to drive that thing."

He handed her a helmet. "Better than I know how to parallel park."

She laughed, slipping it on. "Well, that's reassuring."

The streets narrowed as they weaved out of the city centre, the din of tourists fading behind them. Brad handled the curves with ease, his movements sure and smooth, as if he'd done this a hundred times before. Scarlett sat behind him, her hands resting lightly at first, then curling a little more securely around his waist as they climbed higher, past terraces draped in bougainvillea and sun-bleached walls etched with time.

They didn't speak much during the ride. They didn't need to.

The city fell away into open hills, cypress trees lining the winding roads like quiet sentries. Below them, Rome stretched wide and golden in the distance, the dome of St. Peter's glinting faintly through the haze.

Brad pulled over near a quiet overlook—just a patch of gravel and wild grass at the edge of a breathtaking view. He cut the engine. Silence settled in, broken only by the whisper of wind through olive branches.

Scarlett climbed off first, pulling off her helmet and shaking out her hair. "Okay," she said, breathless from the ride or the view—or both. "This is definitely not in the guidebook."

Brad smiled faintly as he joined her at the edge. "Good."

They stood there for a long moment, the breeze tugging at their clothes, Rome sprawled out like a painting below them.

Scarlett glanced sideways at him. "So… was this part of the plan, or just your way of making sure I fall in love with Rome?"

He didn't answer right away. Just looked at her—really looked at her.

"Maybe a little of both," he said quietly.

She held his gaze, something unreadable flickering in her eyes—curiosity, maybe, or something softer. But she didn't look away. Didn't retreat behind a joke or polite distance.

Instead, she turned back to the view, the breeze tugging loose strands of hair across her cheek.

Brad watched her in the quiet. The way the sunlight caught in her lashes. The ease in her shoulders. The stillness that wasn't empty, but full—of thought, of memory, of something he couldn't name.

And before he could stop himself, the words slipped out—low, unguarded.

"You're beautiful."

She blinked, startled, her head turning toward him. "What?"

Brad froze for a beat, caught between instinct and honesty. But there was no taking it back. So, he held her gaze this time.

"I mean it."

Scarlett didn't speak right away. She just looked at him—really looked. Not like he was a stranger in a market or a fellow tourist tagging along. But like she was seeing something she hadn't quite let herself see before.

Her voice, when it came, was softer than usual. "Thank you."

Not flirtatious. Not coy.

Just… real.

And that, somehow, made his chest tighten more than anything else she could've said.

Chapter Eight

They rode back in silence.

Not the awkward kind. Not filled with questions or tension. But the quiet that settles when something real has been said—something neither of them quite knew what to do with yet.

Scarlett held onto Brad more securely this time. Not just for balance, but because she wanted to. Her hands rested against his chest, the steady thump of his heartbeat grounding her as the road wound its way back toward the city.

The hills gave way to terracotta rooftops and narrow, sun-drenched streets. Rome buzzed with life again—horns blaring, footsteps echoing off stone, open-air cafés spilling laughter and espresso into the air. But the spell hadn't broken.

Not entirely.

Brad eased the scooter to a stop beside a narrow alley lined with market stalls—leather bags, silk scarves, silver jewellery that winked in the sunlight like scattered stars.

They wandered through the stalls at an unhurried pace. Brad lingered a few steps behind, hands in his pockets, pretending not to watch the way Scarlett's fingers skimmed across everything with quiet reverence.

She paused at a corner table stacked with handmade journals—the leather soft, the stitching delicate and precise. One caught her eye, deep chestnut with a weathered clasp. She picked it up, thumb brushing the seam.

"Beautiful hands," a voice murmured behind her.

Scarlett turned, surprised.

The man was too close.

Italian. Mid-thirties. Tailored navy blazer, sunglasses pushed into dark hair, confidence slick as oil. His smile was smooth—too smooth.

"American?" he asked, eyes sweeping over her. "You have the look. Curious. Hungry."

Scarlett offered a polite smile and stepped back a fraction. "Just browsing."

He followed, like her retreat was an invitation. "Let me buy you something. Or a drink, maybe?"

"I don't think so," she said, cool but firm.

He stepped in anyway, fingers closing lightly around her elbow as he leaned closer, his voice dropping to a whisper. "You're very beautiful."

She didn't flinch.

Scarlett Hale wasn't easily rattled.

But before she could speak, a hand snapped around the man's wrist—fast, unrelenting.

Brad.

He stepped between them like a drawn line, gaze sharp and voice low. "Let go."

The man blinked, caught off guard. His expression shifted—surprise, then irritation, then something colder. But Brad didn't move. Didn't blink.

The Italian raised both hands and backed away, muttering in clipped Italian before vanishing into the flow of foot traffic.

Scarlett stared after him, her heart kicking once, hard—then looked at Brad.

He was calm. Steady. Like he hadn't just nearly broken someone's wrist in the middle of a tourist market.

Like this was just another Tuesday.

But even as he stepped back, hands loose at his sides, Brad knew he'd moved too fast.

Too close.

And Scarlett had noticed.

"Are you always this protective of strangers?" she asked, tone casual—but her eyes were sharp. Curious. Wary. Measuring him now in a different light.

Brad offered a faint smile, but it didn't quite reach his eyes. "You're not a stranger," he said, trying to keep it light.

But the words hung there, suspended between them—too easy to say, too close to the truth.

Brad felt it—the shift. The quiet tightening of the air. So, he broke it, the way he always did when something threatened to dig too deep.

He nodded toward the journal still in her hand. "You like that one?"

Scarlett blinked, caught off guard by the pivot. Then she huffed a quiet laugh, tension loosening from her shoulders.

"Yeah," she said, still watching him closely. Still wary.

Brad gave a small, easy smile. "Better pay for it before someone thinks you're planning a getaway."

She rolled her eyes but stepped toward the stall, the ghost of a smile tugging at her lips despite herself.

And just like that, the moment passed.

But not completely.

Brad felt it—the crack in the rhythm, the shift in her gaze.

He'd moved too fast. Too protective. Too personal.

He'd come dangerously close to blowing his cover—and he knew it.

Next time, he'd have to be more careful.

Back at the hotel, Brad parked the scooter beside a row of mopeds near the entrance. He helped her off, steadying her hand as she stepped down, though she barely needed it.

"Thanks for the ride," she said, smoothing her dress with one hand, the helmet tucked under her arm. "And the view."

He gave her a look—quiet, unreadable. "You're welcome."

They moved through the lobby side by side, not touching, not speaking—but still tethered by the weight of what hadn't been said since the markets.

At the elevator, she reached for the call button. Brad stood beside her, his shoulder inches from hers, hands loose at his sides.

"I didn't mean to make things uncomfortable," he said, voice low.

She looked up at him, eyes still shadowed by whatever thoughts had taken root since the markets.

"You didn't," she said honestly. "You surprised me. That's not the same."

The elevator doors opened, and they stepped inside. The ride up was short—silent except for the soft hum of motion and the press of something electric between them. When the doors slid open on their floor, Scarlett paused just outside.

"Want to come in for a bit?" she asked, the words casual, but her expression anything but.

Brad studied her face. Not just the smile she gave the world, but the edges beneath it—the flicker of hesitation, the subtle vulnerability behind the question.

"I'd like that," he said.

But when they reached her suite, she paused again, hand hovering over the keycard. "Just coffee," she added with a half-smile. "And maybe to check if Jeff's still alive."

Brad returned the smile. "Fair enough."

She opened the door quietly, peeking inside. The lights were dim, the bedroom door still closed. No sound from within.

Scarlett slipped off her sandals and moved softly through the space. "Still resting," she said, glancing back.

Brad followed her into the small sitting area. She went to the kitchenette, setting the helmets down and flipping the switch on the electric kettle.

He watched her for a moment, the way she moved—calm, barefoot, still carrying the hush of the hills in the soft swing of her dress.

"Scarlett," he said, and she turned slightly.

He hesitated, then added, "Earlier… what I said on the hills… it wasn't about the view. Or the sunlight."

She didn't look away this time. "I know."

A beat of silence passed—quiet, but full.

Then she turned back to the kettle, opening a cabinet for mugs. "How do you take your coffee?"

Brad smiled faintly. "However you make it."

The suite was quiet, softened by the filtered light of late morning. Outside, Rome moved at its usual tempo—Vespas whining, cutlery clinking in cafés, life humming on. But inside, everything felt still.

Scarlett sat curled on the sofa, bare feet tucked beneath her. She held a warm mug of coffee close to her chest, as if it might anchor her. Across from her, Brad sat in the armchair, one hand around his own mug, his eyes steady on her.

She hadn't meant to say anything. But the silence was soft, safe. And when she finally spoke, her voice was quiet. Controlled.

"My parents died three years ago."

Brad didn't move. Just listened.

"Private jet. Bad weather. Mechanical failure." She stared into her coffee, lashes lowered. "They were flying back from a board meeting in Zurich. They never made it past the Alps."

Brad's knuckles tightened slightly around his cup.

Scarlett kept going, her voice calm, but stripped of her usual polish. "I was in L.A., stuck in traffic when I got the call. Alec—my brother—sounded like a stranger. Like someone trying not to fall apart."

She looked up, eyes distant. "We were close once. All of us. But after the crash, Alec just... shut down. He buried himself in work. In the company. It was like grief turned him into a machine."

Brad spoke quietly. "And you?"

She gave a soft, mirthless laugh. "I smiled for the press. Hosted the memorial. Took interviews I don't remember giving. And when it was over... I realised I'd lost everything. My parents. My brother. My sense of home. All in a single day."

Her hands trembled slightly as she set the mug down. "People think grief is loud. But it's not. It's quiet. It lingers in the things you don't say, the rooms you don't walk into. The way your phone never rings with the voice you want to hear."

Brad leaned forward, elbows on his knees, his voice steady. "You're not alone in that."

Scarlett looked at him—really looked. "No. I'm just tired of pretending I am."

A long silence settled between them—not awkward, not heavy. Just real.

Scarlett's fingers traced the rim of her coffee mug as she let out a breath. "I don't usually talk about it. Definitely not with people I've just met." She paused, eyes drifting toward the closed bedroom door. "Jeff's the only one who's really stood by me. After the crash, after everything… a lot of people saw an opening. And they took advantage."

Brad's gaze remained steady. "Like your ex. Sean?"

She blinked, startled. "How did you—" Her eyes flicked again toward Jeff's room, her voice softening. "He said something?"

"He did."

Scarlett's jaw tensed for a moment. "He hates Sean. Always has. Said he got a bad feeling from the beginning… and he was right."

Brad said nothing, giving her space.

She looked down, her voice quiet. "Sean was charming. Confident. He made me feel like I was standing on solid ground again. But it was a blend of smoke. Manipulation dressed as affection."

Brad's voice was low, almost reluctant. "Some people are good at that."

"Too good," she murmured. "And the worst part is… I thought I was a better judge of character. I used to be."

Brad leaned forward slightly. "You still are."

Scarlett looked up at him, searching his expression. "You don't know that."

"I don't have to," he said quietly. "I can see it."

She held his gaze—uncertain, vulnerable, but steady.

"Three weeks ago," she said softly, "I woke up and realised I hadn't just lost my family… I was starting to lose myself. The grief, the pressure, the pretending I was fine—it all just… blurred who I used to be."

She paused, the words hanging between them like something fragile.

"That's when I booked this trip. I didn't even think it through. I just needed to breathe. To feel something different. And these last couple of days…" A small smile ghosted across her lips. "I've laughed more than I have in three years. It feels good. Strange—but good."

Brad's voice was quiet, thoughtful. "It's good that you can laugh again. You have a beautiful laugh."

She raised an eyebrow, though there was no real bite behind it. "You should stop that."

He tilted his head. "Stop what?"

"Complimenting me like that," she said, a flicker of a smile tugging at her lips. "I'll end up with a massive ego."

Brad smiled, slow and easy. "Somehow, I don't think that's your style."

She looked at him for a beat longer, then shook her head with a soft laugh—real, unguarded, full of something lighter than she'd carried in a long time.

"You wouldn't say that if you'd seen some of the photos, they've taken of me at galas and fundraisers," she said, her voice wry. "Chin high, eyes cold—like I'm staring down a boardroom instead of a camera lens."

Brad's brow lifted slightly. "You don't strike me as cold."

She gave a small, almost sad smile. "When I broke things off with Sean, he called me an ice queen."

There was no bitterness in her tone—just a trace of old hurt, worn down to resignation.

Brad's gaze didn't leave hers. "Then he never really saw you."

Her eyes softened, but she didn't answer right away. Instead, she looked past him toward the hills, the quiet settling between them again—still honest. Still safe.

Brad watched her laugh—soft, unfiltered, the kind that curled at the corners of her mouth and lit her eyes before it ever reached her lips.

God, she was beautiful.

Not just the kind of beautiful that made strangers turn their heads in passing. That part was obvious. Anyone could see it—the elegant lines, the effortless poise, the way she moved like the world had once taught her to perform but she'd since outgrown the need.

But it wasn't that.

It was the way she leaned in when someone spoke. The way her brows furrowed when she cared—really cared. The warmth in her voice when she talked about Jeff. The quiet sadness she tried to hide when she spoke of her parents. The honesty she offered even when it cost her a piece of herself.

She was warm. She was real.

She felt everything—deeply. And maybe she'd learned to tuck that away, to armour it behind charm and grace and perfectly timed laughter. But it was there.

And he saw it.

The way she reached for connection in a world that had taken too much from her.

The way she made him feel like maybe he wasn't just some man with a job to do—but someone who mattered, if only for a moment.

Brad's hand curled tighter around his coffee cup, anchoring himself before the thought could spiral any further.

This wasn't supposed to happen. He was supposed to keep his distance. Blend in. Watch.

But every minute with her made the lines blur.

And the truth hit him harder than he was ready for:

Scarlett Hale wasn't just beautiful.

She was becoming dangerous.

Because caring about her…

That changed everything.

Chapter Nine

Brad almost stood too quickly.

"I better go," he said, the words more abrupt than he meant them to be.

Scarlett blinked, clearly caught off guard. "Oh… okay." There was a flicker of something in her voice—surprise, maybe a little disappointment—but she covered it with a small, polite smile as she stood with him.

He set his empty cup on the coffee table, trying to ignore the tight pull in his chest. The air between them had shifted—too intimate, too real—and it was starting to get under his skin in ways he hadn't prepared for.

She walked with him to the door, fingers brushing the handle as she pulled it open. The quiet stretch of hallway waited beyond, cool, and impersonal.

Brad stepped past her—almost. But then she leaned in, just slightly, just enough.

Her lips pressed gently against his cheek.

"Thank you for today," she said softly, close enough that he could feel her breath.

He froze.

Not from shock, not really—but from the sheer gravity of that small moment. It wasn't a kiss meant to tease or flirt. It was sincere. Warm. Grateful.

He turned to look at her, their faces suddenly close, the space between them too small and too charged.

Scarlett held his gaze—open, honest, unguarded.

And Brad felt it all at once: the pull, the conflict, the way she was beginning to undo him in quiet, irreversible ways.

He didn't say anything—not yet.

But he didn't step back, either.

For a moment, the world felt suspended in the space between them—still, weighted, full of something that hadn't quite taken shape.

Then, softer than he meant to, barely more than a breath, he whispered,

"Have a good night, Scarlett."

Her eyes searched his, something quiet and unreadable flickering there.

"You too, Brad," she murmured.

And then she gently closed the door.

Scarlett picked up the mugs from the coffee table, still warm from the coffee she and Brad had shared and carried them to the kitchenette. She rinsed them under the tap, the water hissing softly in the quiet.

Behind her, the bedroom door creaked open.

"I thought he would never leave," Jeff said with a huge grin, leaning against the doorway in pyjama pants and a worn T-shirt.

Scarlett glanced over her shoulder, startled. "You're up?"

"I was up halfway through your soulful confessions," he said, stepping into the room, "but I didn't want to ruin the moment."

She rolled her eyes, smiling despite herself. "Jeff."

"What?" He shrugged, unapologetic. "It was cute."

She turned off the tap, shaking the last droplets from the mugs before setting them on the rack. "Are you feeling better?"

"Much," he said, padding barefoot across the room and flopping onto the couch. "Migraine fog is mostly gone. And apparently emotional eavesdropping is great for recovery."

She narrowed her eyes at him. "You're impossible."

Jeff just grinned wider. Then his gaze shifted toward the door Brad had just walked through, and his smile took on a knowing tilt. "So… you like him?"

Scarlett froze for a beat, her hand still resting on the counter.

Then, quietly, "Yeah. I do."

Jeff didn't tease. He just nodded, his voice gentler now. "Good. You deserve something that feels real again."

Scarlett said nothing, but the way her fingers curled around the edge of the bench said everything she couldn't quite put into words.

Brad walked into his suite and let the door shut behind him with a quiet thud. The room was dim, the heavy curtains still drawn against the morning sun, but he didn't bother turning on the lights.

He stopped in the middle of the room, hands on his hips, his breath a little uneven—still carrying the faint scent of Scarlett's perfume. Still feeling the soft, unexpected press of her lips against his cheek.

"What the hell are you doing," he muttered aloud, dragging a hand through his hair.

He wasn't supposed to let it get this far.

This wasn't the plan. He was supposed to be a shadow—quiet, unseen, forgettable. Watch her, protect her, report back to Alec.

But now? Now she looked at him like he was someone who mattered. Trusted him with things no one else had heard. Kissed him like he'd given her something she didn't even know she needed.

And he let her.

"Damn it," he muttered, dragging a hand through his hair as he paced the length of the suite.

This was already messy.

And it was only going to get worse.

He hadn't meant for this to happen. He was supposed to observe. Protect. Keep his distance.

But distance was becoming impossible. Every time she looked at him—unguarded, trusting—it took another piece out of the wall he'd built. Every quiet moment between them felt less like a job and more like something dangerous.

He stripped off his shirt and headed for the shower, hoping the water might drown out the noise in his head.

It didn't.

All he could think about was Scarlett—her laugh, her mouth, the way she leaned into him on the scooter like she belonged there. The way she looked at him when she was telling the truth, raw and real, like she wasn't afraid of what he might see.

He wanted her.

Not just physically, though that pull was undeniable. It was something deeper. Something slower, more dangerous. A compulsion he couldn't name, couldn't shake. And it was growing.

Steam curled around him, but the heat did nothing to burn her out of his thoughts.

Maybe it was time to pull out.

He could call Alec. Say the situation was under control. That she was safe. Jeff was there—loyal, protective, trustworthy. Brad had seen it firsthand. If anyone would throw themselves in front of a threat for Scarlett, it was him.

Were they lovers?

He still didn't know.

But it was getting harder to care about the answer—for all the wrong reasons.

Brad leaned forward, bracing his hands against the cool tile, water pounding against the back of his neck.

He needed to get his head on straight.

Or he was going to make a mistake he couldn't walk away from.

Brad stepped out of the shower, water still clinging to his skin as he towelled off in silence. The suite was dim, curtains drawn, but the world outside pulsed on—traffic, lights, voices carried faintly on the Roman breeze.

He moved through the room like a man half-possessed, muscles tense, jaw set. He grabbed a T-shirt, pulled it over his head, then reached for his phone on the desk.

He stared at it for a long moment.

This was the right call.

Scarlett was safe. Jeff was solid. The trip was doing her good—she was laughing again, living again. Alec didn't need him there anymore.

He couldn't do it.

He had tried. He really had. But Scarlett wasn't just a name on a file or a responsibility to check off. Not anymore.

And the more time he spent near her, the harder it was to pretend this was just another job.

He unlocked his phone and pulled up Alec's number, thumb hovering over the call button.

"Come on," he muttered to himself. "Just say it. Just walk away."

But before he could press it, his screen lit up—Alec Hale calling.

Brad stared at the name as it rang, his stomach tightening.

Shit.

He hesitated for a heartbeat, then answered, voice low and even. "Alec."

"Brad," Alec said, all clipped control, like always. "Update."

Brad's mouth opened—but nothing came out at first.

He glanced at the door. Thought about Scarlett's voice, her kiss on his cheek, the way she'd looked at him like he was something steady in a world that had betrayed her too many times.

He swallowed hard.

"Yeah," he said quietly. "There's something you should know."

Okay, Brad told himself. This is it. Tell him. Scarlett's safe. She doesn't need you. Walk away.

He braced a hand on the desk, staring at the floor like it might offer courage.

But Alec's voice came through the line again, impatient. "Well?"

Brad's throat tightened.

Then, without meaning to, without planning it—

"Sean turned up."

There was a pause.

A long one.

Then Alec's voice came sharp, cutting through the static like a blade. "That leech."

Brad exhaled slowly, raking a hand through his damp hair. "Yeah. He made contact late last night—showed up while they were having dinner. Jeff stepped in, told him she wasn't interested."

Alec's voice sharpened. "And Scarlett? How'd she handle it?"

"She was calm. Graceful. Told him it was over." Brad paused, jaw tightening. "But I don't think he's going to take no for an answer."

A beat of silence stretched on the other end of the line. He could almost hear Alec weighing the implications.

"Well," Alec said finally, voice clipped, "good thing you're still there. I don't care what Jeff thinks of Sean. If that bastard's sniffing around, I want eyes on her. At all times. Understood?"

Brad's gaze drifted to the open balcony doors, the soft Roman breeze pushing in like a ghost. The space still felt touched by her—by her laugh, by the soft press of her lips on his cheek.

This wasn't supposed to be personal.

But it was.

And he was in too deep to pretend otherwise.

Still, when he answered, his voice was steady.

"Understood."

He hung up.

Silence reclaimed the room.

Coward, he thought.

He could lie to Alec.

Hell, he could even lie to Scarlett.

But not to himself.

Not anymore.

He was supposed to be the one watching her back—nothing more.

No feelings. No complications. No blurred lines.

But somehow, somewhere between the laughter, the quiet moments, and the way she looked at him like he was more than a shadow…

He'd let the lines disappear completely.

And no matter how he tried to justify it—duty, timing, proximity—

he couldn't lie to himself anymore.

He wanted Scarlett Hale.

Not casually.

Not in passing.

He wanted her with a desperation that was starting to feel dangerous.

Chapter Ten

The sun had just started to warm the stone corridor outside the suites when Brad stepped out of his room, the door clicking softly shut behind him. He paused, rolling his shoulders, trying to ease the tightness there. The sea air was crisp, tinged with salt and the scent of sun-warmed jasmine.

Down the hall, another door opened.

Scarlett stepped out, sunglasses in hand, her dress swaying as she walked. Jeff followed, yawning as he tugged his fingers through his hair. They were laughing quietly—easy, familiar, untouched by the weight Brad was carrying like armour.

Brad cleared his throat lightly. "Morning."

Scarlett's head turned. Her smile was immediate and soft. "Morning."

Jeff offered a lazy wave. "Hey, man. You're up early."

"Habit," Brad said with a faint nod. His eyes flicked to Scarlett for a second longer than they should have—just long enough to catch the echo of something in her expression. It passed quickly. He looked to Jeff instead. "You look better today. Migraine's gone?"

Jeff stretched his arms overhead. "Completely. I feel human again. Might even attempt real food."

Brad smirked. "Ambitious."

Jeff grinned. "We're heading to that café Scarlett found—the one with the cliffside view and insane pastries. You should come."

Brad hesitated. A beat too long.

Scarlett tilted her head slightly. "You don't have to," she said gently, almost as if giving him an out.

But Brad just nodded, slipping his hands into his pockets. "I'd like to."

Jeff clapped him on the shoulder. "Great. Apricot croissants all around."

As they walked down the hallway together, the sun spilling in through the high arched windows, Brad kept his gaze ahead—but he could feel her beside him. The quiet gravity of her presence. The soft brush of her dress as it shifted with her steps.

He hadn't told Alec yet.

Hadn't admitted what was already starting to show.

But as her laughter drifted beside him, low and warm and completely unguarded, Brad knew exactly what the problem was.

He was in trouble.

And the worst part was—he didn't want to get out of it.

The café clung to the edge of the cliff like it had grown there—whitewashed walls, cobalt shutters, and tables shaded by a canopy of flowering vines. From the terrace, the sea stretched out endlessly, a mirror of light and sky.

They took a table overlooking the water. Jeff ordered enough food for three people, and Scarlett laughed when the waiter raised an eyebrow but didn't question it.

Brad had never been a morning person. But this morning? With her laughter drifting across the table like sunlight—it felt different.

Scarlett's laughter was contagious—unfiltered and full-bodied, rising like music over the gentle clink of cutlery and the hum of the waking island. She tilted her face toward the sun between sips of coffee, eyes crinkling at the corners, hair catching gold in the light.

Brad watched her from across the table, his coffee cooling in his hands, the corners of his mouth tugging upward without him meaning to.

"You know," he said, "your name suits you."

Scarlett glanced up, amused. "Does it?"

He nodded. "It fits. Strong. Classic. A little dramatic, but in the best way."

She arched an eyebrow. "Dramatic?"

Jeff smirked. "He's not wrong."

Scarlett laughed again, shaking her head. "Well, if anyone's to blame, it's my mother. She was obsessed with Gone with the Wind. Read it every year like it was gospel. Watched the movie religiously."

Jeff groaned. "And quoted it. Constantly."

Scarlett nodded. "She wanted to name me Scarlett from the moment she found out I existed. I'm honestly shocked she didn't name Alec Rhett."

Brad's smile didn't falter, but something tightened in his chest.

She said it so casually—my brother.

She had no idea Brad already knew her brother. No idea that her brother was the one who'd hired him. That Brad was supposed to be a quiet shadow, nothing more.

Not someone laughing over breakfast with her.

Not someone falling for her.

"Your parents were clearly passionate about storytelling," he said, his voice easy, careful.

Scarlett smiled. "My mother definitely was. She believed in love stories, even the tragic ones. She used to say there was strength in women who could love fiercely and walk away when they had to."

Brad studied her, his gaze steady. "Sounds like you take after her."

Scarlett glanced down at her coffee, the corners of her mouth lifting just a little. "Maybe. I like to think so."

Brad couldn't look away. There was something in the way she said it—not pride, but quiet resilience. It hit him harder than it should have.

Jeff stretched out in his chair. "Well, whatever the name means—you've clearly grown into it. The drama, the heartache, the attitude. All very Southern belle meets European wine tour."

Scarlett tossed a grape at him. "Watch it, or I'll reenact the scene where she throws the vase."

Brad laughed, then leaned in slightly. "Just give me a heads-up before you start flinging glass."

She looked at him, her expression softening. "I'll try."

And despite everything he wasn't supposed to feel…

Brad couldn't help but think that Scarlett—the name, the woman, the quiet fire behind her smile—fit her perfectly.

The moment stretched between them, unspoken and electric, until Jeff cleared his throat with exaggerated timing and turned to Brad.

"Well," he said brightly, "we're off to the Colosseum today. Care to join?"

Brad lifted a brow. "Only if I'm not crashing the party."

Jeff waved a hand. "Please. The more the merrier."

Scarlett's lips curved. "Well then… that's settled."

The car ride to the Colosseum was filled with sunlight and the sound of Rome waking up—bustling streets, the occasional honk of a Vespa, and the rhythmic echo of footsteps against ancient stone. Their driver took the scenic route, winding through narrow lanes shaded by crumbling ochre buildings, past flower-draped balconies, and sunlit piazzas.

Scarlett sat between Jeff and Brad in the backseat of the black town car, her sunglasses pushed up in her hair, laughing at something Jeff had just muttered about a street performer juggling flaming torches outside a café.

"I swear," Jeff said with mock indignation, "the man nearly set his moustache on fire, and no one batted an eye."

Scarlett giggled, her head tipping back slightly. Brad, seated quietly on her other side, allowed himself a small smile, but his gaze was fixed out the window.

Jeff leaned in, his voice dropping just enough for Scarlett to hear over the quiet hum of the engine. "You know he likes you, right?"

Scarlett blinked. "Who?"

Jeff tilted his head, clearly amused. "Brad. Who else?"

She glanced subtly at Brad—stoic, unreadable, but entirely too close not to feel. "You're imagining things."

Jeff grinned like a man who knew better. "Sweetheart, please. I have eyes. I've seen the way he looks at you. Like he's trying not to want you."

Scarlett frowned, unsure. "I mean, we've talked, but… I don't know. Maybe he's just being kind."

Jeff scoffed. "Trust me. Brad Jenkins is not wasting that brooding intensity on 'just being kind.'" Then, more playfully, "Want me to prove it?"

Scarlett arched a brow. "How?"

Jeff's grin widened.

By the time they arrived at the Colosseum and stepped out into the morning sun, the street already buzzing with tourists and vendors, Jeff had a plan—and a flair for the dramatic.

He slipped his arm around Scarlett's shoulders as they walked, leaning in close to whisper something that made her laugh.

Then, as Brad joined them, Jeff upped the ante—resting his chin briefly on her shoulder, brushing a hand down her arm as if he couldn't help but touch her.

Scarlett gave him a sideways glance. "Subtle."

Jeff winked. "Just watch."

Brad, walking a few paces behind, caught it all.

He didn't say a word—but his silence spoke volumes.

His jaw was tight, his shoulders rigid. And when Jeff tucked a strand of hair behind Scarlett's ear, Brad's gaze sharpened—his expression unreadable, but the flicker of something dark moved through it.

Scarlett felt the shift before she turned to look. She caught the tension in Brad's frame, the way he looked everywhere but at her.

Her smile faltered just slightly.

Jeff, ever perceptive, caught it too. His voice dropped low, meant only for her. "Well, that worked."

Scarlett gave him a sideways glance. "Jeff..."

He grinned unapologetically, then patted her arm. "I'll make myself scarce for a little while. Let you two enjoy the ruins without my sparkling commentary."

Before she could respond, he veered toward a souvenir stand, calling over his shoulder, "Don't do anything I wouldn't do."

Chapter Eleven

Scarlett laughed, shaking her head—but her gaze drifted back to Brad, drawn to the quiet pull in his eyes.

He'd fallen quiet, more than usual. Brooding. Watching the ancient stonework like it might answer the questions storming behind his eyes.

She stepped a little closer, her voice gentle. "You okay?"

Brad glanced at her. His expression softened, but something still flickered beneath the surface—quiet, unresolved.

"I'm fine," he said.

But she didn't quite believe him.

They wandered the curved paths of the Colosseum, the air warm and still, history pressing close around them. Tourists moved in scattered clusters, but eventually they found a quiet spot—an alcove tucked between weathered stone and shadow, half-hidden from the rest of the world.

Scarlett stopped and turned to face him.

"Brad?"

He looked at her, brows slightly raised. "Yeah?"

She hesitated, then asked softly, "Would you be offended if I kissed you?"

His breath caught—visibly.

"What about Jeff?"

"What about him?"

Brad blinked. "Aren't you two…?"

Scarlett stared at him for a heartbeat. Then—

A burst of laughter escaped her, bright and unfiltered. She swatted his arm lightly. "Jeff? Oh my God—Brad, he's gay."

Brad froze. "He's—wait. Seriously?"

Her laughter doubled, spilling into the ancient stone like sunlight. "Yes. Seriously. You thought—?"

"I wasn't sure," he muttered, rubbing the back of his neck. "You're close. Protective. He sleeps in your suite…"

"In the other room," she said, still smiling. "We've been best friends since college. He's the one who held my hair back after too many tequila shots and told me I deserved better than every guy I ever dated. Jeff's not a boyfriend. He's family."

Brad exhaled, slow and stunned. "Good to know."

Scarlett looked at him then—really looked. Her expression softened, open, waiting.

And Brad couldn't hold back anymore.

He stepped forward, closing the last inches between them. His hand found the curve of her waist, the other sliding gently into her hair, like he'd imagined it a hundred times.

"In that case," he murmured, his voice low and rough with want, "I need to kiss you the way I've wanted to since the moment I met you."

And then he did.

His mouth met hers with aching precision—deep, deliberate, unhurried. It was the kind of kiss that didn't ask permission but gave everything. It unfolded like a promise, like a confession he didn't have words for. His lips moved over hers slowly, savouring the shape, the warmth, the way she tasted of wine and sun and something he hadn't known he needed.

Scarlett melted into him with a soft gasp, her hands sliding up to his shoulders, then his neck, anchoring herself to him like gravity had shifted. Her body curved into his, her mouth answering his with just as much hunger—fierce, breathless, sure.

He deepened the kiss, hand cradling her jaw, thumb brushing across her cheek. His mouth slanted over hers again—this time hungrier, needier. Tongues tangled, breath quickened. Her fingers curled in his shirt, dragging him impossibly closer.

There was fire, yes—but more than that, there was want. Real want. The kind that reached deeper than desire and burned slower than lust. A pull that felt inevitable.

He kissed her like he was claiming something he never thought he'd deserve.

She kissed him like she'd been waiting all this time for this exact moment.

When they finally broke apart, they stayed pressed together—chests rising and falling in tandem, foreheads nearly touching. Her lips were kiss-bruised, parted. Her eyes shimmered, dark, and unreadable.

And Brad—for the first time in a long time—didn't feel like he was pretending.

Scarlett's smile bloomed—slow, radiant, lighting up her whole face.

"That was… nice," she said, a teasing glint in her eyes.

Brad lifted a brow. "Nice?"

She nodded, lips twitching. "Mmm-hmm."

He pulled her closer, voice low, playful. "Then I'll just have to do better."

And before she could reply, he kissed her again.

This time there was no hesitation. No restraint. Just heat and want and the kind of hunger that came from waiting too long. His mouth captured hers, deeper, fuller— his hands anchoring her waist as she pulled him closer, kissing him back with just as much fire.

They didn't hear the footsteps. Didn't notice the shadow stretching across the ancient stone until—

"About time," Jeff said flatly behind them.

Scarlett broke the kiss with a startled laugh, hiding her face in Brad's shoulder as Brad let out a quiet curse under his breath.

Jeff stood a few steps away, arms crossed, and one brow raised. "I mean, I've been carrying this sexual tension for both of you for days. You're welcome."

Scarlett groaned. "Jeff…"

Brad just shook his head, trying not to smile.

Jeff grinned. "Don't mind me. Continue. Just pretend I'm a tour guide who saw nothing."

He turned on his heel and strolled toward the next archway, whistling as if he hadn't just walked in on a moment days in the making.

Scarlett looked up at Brad, still laughing. "He's never going to let this go."

Brad's eyes were softer now, the tension that had gripped him earlier dissolved in the warmth of her gaze. "Let him talk," he murmured, brushing a strand of hair from her face. "We've got ruins to explore."

They moved through the ancient amphitheatre hand in hand, the morning light slanting through fractured stone and casting long, golden shadows across the floor. Scarlett asked questions—about the structure, the gladiators, the history—and Brad, ever the quiet observer, surprised her with how much he knew.

"Did you always want to be in security?" she asked as they paused in a sunlit corridor where ivy spilled down the cracked walls.

Brad gave a small shrug; fingers still tangled in hers. "I liked the idea of protecting people. Still do." He glanced at her then, more serious. "Some people are worth protecting."

Scarlett looked up at him, heart stuttering just a little, but before she could speak, Jeff's voice echoed from the next chamber. "Scarlett! They've got a scale model of the Colosseum with tiny plastic gladiators!"

She laughed, resting her forehead against Brad's chest. "He's such a nerd."

Brad leaned down, his lips brushing the top of her head. "He's also giving us space. Let's not waste it."

They kissed again—deeper this time, unhurried. The kind of kiss that made the centuries feel like background noise. When they pulled apart, their fingers remained laced as they continued through the ancient stone maze.

Later that afternoon, they made their way through the winding cobbled streets toward the Pantheon. The sun was higher now, heat shimmering off stone and iron, but the energy of the city only seemed to pulse brighter. Street musicians played near the fountains, and vendors sold fresh lemons and handmade leather journals.

Scarlett bought a flower crown from a girl on the corner and placed it on Jeff's head with a flourish. He posed dramatically before handing it to her, and she wore it like a queen the rest of the walk.

As they stepped beneath the vast portico of the Pantheon, Brad reached for her hand again. She smiled up at him—no teasing, no hesitation—and let their fingers intertwine.

Inside, the cool hush of the ancient temple wrapped around them. Rays of sunlight spilled through the oculus in the domed ceiling, casting a perfect circle of gold on the marbled floor.

They moved in quiet awe through the space, Jeff veering off to examine an inscription. When Scarlett paused near a column, Brad stepped in close behind her.

"No Jeff to interrupt us this time," he murmured, his voice a low hum against her ear.

Scarlett turned, eyes bright. "What a shame."

Brad kissed her again, slower this time, reverent. It wasn't a kiss stolen in the dark. It was one given in the light—witnessed only by the centuries.

They broke apart just before Jeff reappeared, stuffing a brochure into his back pocket.

"Found the gift shop," he said. "Try not to make out on any sacred altars, yeah?"

Scarlett rolled her eyes but leaned into Brad as they walked toward the exit, her hand still warm in his.

And Brad—who wasn't supposed to feel anything, wasn't supposed to want anything—held on just a little tighter.

Because he realised, he didn't want to let go.

Chapter Twelve

That evening, the golden light of Rome softened into twilight as the trio returned to the hotel, the quiet hum of the city trailing behind them.

Scarlett felt lighter than she had in years.

She was glowing—and she knew it. Not because she'd spent the day beneath Roman sun or had laughed more in one afternoon than she had in months, but because of Brad.

She liked him. Really liked him.

He was steady, funny in a quiet way, and protective—not in the smothering, watchful kind of way she was used to—but in a way that made her feel safe. Valued. Like she wasn't walking through life alone.

As the elevator climbed toward their floor, Jeff stood beside her, hands in his pockets, whistling softly. Brad was on her other side, his pinkie brushing hers now and then, like even that small touch had become habit.

When the elevator doors slid open, the three of them stepped into the hall. Scarlett turned toward her suite but lingered as Brad slowed beside her.

"So," she said, reluctant to break the moment, "meet you in the lobby in an hour?"

Brad's smile was soft, a little crooked. "Yeah. An hour."

Their hands brushed—then held, fingers curling instinctively. Just for a moment. Neither of them seemed quite ready to let go.

Eventually, Brad gave a gentle squeeze before stepping away toward his room down the hall.

Scarlett stood there a beat longer, then turned and slipped into the suite she shared with Jeff.

As the door closed behind her, Jeff dropped his key card on the table and turned to face her, arms crossed, and eyebrows raised.

"That," he said, "was adorable."

Scarlett rolled her eyes, but she was still smiling. She couldn't seem to stop. "Don't start."

Jeff stepped closer, his expression softening. "No, really. It's good to see you like this. It's been a while since you looked… I don't know. Light."

She met his gaze, her voice quiet but sure. "I feel light."

Jeff grinned, watching her like he already knew every answer she hadn't said aloud. "He really likes you."

Scarlett's lips curved. "I know."

"And you…" He tilted his head. "You like him."

She didn't even try to hide it. The smile that bloomed was quiet, radiant, full of something that felt dangerously close to hope.

Jeff gave a single, approving nod. "Good. Because—I like him too."

Scarlett blinked. "Wait. Seriously?"

Jeff chuckled. "I know. Shocking, right? I've hated all your past boyfriends. Every last one of them."

"That's not true," she said, though she was already laughing.

He raised an eyebrow. "Scarlett, I once referred to that guy from New York as a sentient haircut."

She snorted. "Okay—fair."

"But Brad?" Jeff's voice softened. "He's different. He sees you. And he doesn't flinch."

Scarlett's smile faltered for just a moment—because Jeff was right. Brad didn't flinch. Not from her past, not from her scars, not from her softness or her fire.

She took a breath, full and steady. "Yeah. He really does."

Jeff gave her a meaningful look. "It's good to see you let someone in again."

Scarlett nodded slowly, her voice almost a whisper. "It's good to want to."

And for the first time in years… she wasn't bracing for heartbreak.

She was leaning into something real.

Brad stepped into his suite and let the door click quietly shut behind him. The room was dim, cool against the lingering heat of the day, but his skin still burned from where Scarlett had touched him. From where she had kissed him.

He stood for a moment, motionless, staring at nothing—just trying to breathe around the storm in his chest.

He'd never felt like this before.

Not for anyone.

Not like this.

He only had to look at her and it ached. Like something deep and rooted had cracked open inside him. The sound of her laugh, the way her hand fit into his, the kiss that had turned him inside out—it all lived under his skin now, impossible to shake.

And when she'd laughed and told him Jeff was gay?

The relief had hit like a physical wave. He hadn't realised just how tightly he'd been wound, how hard he'd tried to keep his distance, until that moment. One simple truth, and everything shifted.

But she didn't know the full story. Not yet.

She didn't know why he'd really been there. That it hadn't started with some chance meeting or summer whim. That her brother—Alec Hale—had hired him. To watch her. To keep her safe.

And God, at first, that's all it had been. A job.

But not anymore.

He crossed the room, slow and steady, tension still humming in his muscles. The setting sun bled gold through the curtains, casting the space in soft shadows. He looked out toward the sea and let the silence settle.

He wasn't going to take Alec's money.

Couldn't.

Not when every part of him knew this was no longer business. This was personal. This was real.

He wasn't guarding her out of duty now—he was doing it because he wanted to. Because he needed to. Because somewhere between watching and wanting, he'd stopped seeing Scarlett Hale as a client's sister and started seeing her as the only thing that felt real in a world he'd kept at arm's length for years.

Brad exhaled, ran a hand down his face, and let himself lean into it—for once not fighting what he felt.

This wasn't just a job.

This was her.

And he was going to embrace every second.

Scarlett stepped out of her room, the soft click of her heels tapping against the marble floor as she crossed the suite.

Jeff looked up from where he was lounging on the couch, drink in hand—and immediately let out a low, appreciative whistle. "Well, hello, sexy."

Scarlett paused, smoothing a hand down the front of her dress. It was slinky, midnight blue, the fabric hugging her curves in all the right ways. Her hair was soft around her shoulders, makeup subtle but striking.

Still… her brow furrowed. "Is it too much?"

Jeff sat up straighter, eyes wide with mock offense. "Too much? Scarlett, please. You look like a Bond girl and a Greek goddess had a baby. It's perfect."

She laughed, but there was a flicker of nerves in her expression. "I don't want to overdo it. I mean… it's just dinner."

"With a man who's been looking at you like you're the last star in the sky?" Jeff stood and crossed the room, gently taking her shoulders. "Scarlett. You've spent years hiding pieces of yourself. Tonight, you're not hiding. You're glowing. And you're allowed to."

Her smile turned softer. "You think he'll like it?"

Jeff grinned, stepping back to admire her like a proud stylist. "Oh, honey. He's going to forget how to speak."

Scarlett laughed again, more genuine this time. "Okay. I'll take that."

"Good. Now go knock him flat," Jeff said, giving her an approving once-over. "But not too flat—I still need him conscious enough to pick up the check."

Scarlett laughed. "Wait… aren't you coming?"

Jeff raised a brow, grabbing the remote and flopping back onto the couch. "Absolutely not. You two need some time together."

She hesitated. "But—"

"No but, Scarlett." His voice softened, a rare note of seriousness threading through the tease. "Go. Have a great time. I'll see you in the morning."

Scarlett narrowed her eyes at him, smiling. "You must like him. You'd never leave me alone with someone you didn't trust."

Jeff smirked but didn't deny it. "Maybe I'm growing. Maybe he's not a total idiot." He winked. "Or maybe I just know when something's right."

Scarlett rolled her eyes but couldn't stop the blush creeping into her cheeks. She blew him a kiss and reached for her clutch, her pulse quickening—not with doubt, but anticipation.

Tonight, she didn't just feel beautiful.

She felt brave.

And more than that—she felt ready.

Brad stood near the edge of the hotel's marble-floored lobby, nursing a drink he hadn't really tasted. He'd arrived early—too early—but patience wasn't exactly his strong suit tonight. He kept glancing toward the lift, expecting Jeff to appear with Scarlett in tow.

But when the doors finally slid open, he forgot everything.

He stopped breathing.

Scarlett stepped out alone.

And in that instant, the world narrowed.

He knew she was beautiful—he'd known that the moment he saw her. But this? This was something else. She didn't just turn heads—she stopped time. The soft curve of her dress skimmed over her like it had been made with her in mind, the colour catching the light in a way that made her glow. Her hair was swept back just enough to show off the elegant line of her neck, and the subtle glint of earrings that sparkled as she walked.

But it wasn't just how she looked. It was her. The quiet confidence in her step. The way she held herself like she knew exactly who she was and didn't need anyone's permission to shine.

Brad felt it—an ache deep in his chest, pulling him toward her like gravity.

She hadn't seen him yet. And for a moment, he just let himself look. At the woman who had upended every rule, blurred every line. The woman who'd made him forget that this was supposed to be a job.

When her eyes finally found his, her smile lit up the space between them.

And he knew.

He was already gone.

Scarlett crossed the lobby with slow, confident steps, her heels clicking softly against the marble floor. The low murmur of conversation and clinking glass faded into nothing as she reached him.

She smiled, a little uncertain now under the weight of his silence. "I hope you don't mind," she said gently. "It's only me. Jeff wanted a night in."

Still, he didn't speak.

Just looked at her—like the air had been knocked out of him.

She tilted her head slightly. "Brad?"

He shook his head slowly, as if trying to clear it. Then, finally—finally—his voice came, low and rough with feeling.

"I don't mind."

Scarlett's smile returned, softer now, touched with something warm and vulnerable. She reached out and slipped her hand into his, and that simple contact—skin to skin—snapped him out of whatever trance he'd fallen into.

He lifted their joined hands and brushed his lips lightly over her knuckles.

"No distractions," he murmured. "Just you."

And tonight, that was exactly what he wanted.

The restaurant was tucked into a quiet corner of the old city, hidden behind ivy-draped stone, and lit by strings of golden lights that glowed like fireflies in the dusk. Brad had found it—said he'd passed it earlier in the week and made a mental note to bring her here.

Scarlett understood why the moment they stepped inside.

The atmosphere was effortlessly intimate—candlelit tables, soft music drifting from a nearby guitarist, the faint aroma of garlic and wine curling through the air. It felt like a secret place carved out just for them.

They were led to a table on the small terrace, overlooking a sliver of moonlit rooftops and the gentle hum of evening Rome. The city murmured beneath them, alive but not overwhelming.

Scarlett was already smiling as they sat down, and it didn't fade.

Brad sat across from her, more relaxed than she'd ever seen him—his sleeves rolled up, jacket hung over the back of his chair, a half-smile playing at his lips as he teased her about her dramatic ordering of dessert before even looking at entrées.

"I like to plan for the important things first," she said with a wink.

He chuckled. "Clearly."

She laughed, that easy, unguarded kind of laughter that made his chest feel too tight. And when she wasn't looking, he couldn't help watching her—like she was something he didn't quite believe he got to have.

Between the shared wine and stolen glances, Brad reached across the table and took her hand in his. She didn't hesitate—just laced her fingers through his like it was the most natural thing in the world.

He brushed his thumb over her knuckles, slow, thoughtful. "You always laugh like that?" he asked, voice low, teasing.

"Like what?"

"Like it's the first time someone's made you feel safe."

Her smile softened. "Maybe it is."

The moment stretched, quiet and golden, the soft clink of plates around them like background noise to something that felt suddenly bigger than just dinner.

And when their food finally arrived, neither of them let go.

Not for a second.

Chapter Thirteen

Eating with Scarlett was… fun.

Brad never expected that.

He'd had dinners with women before—some pleasant, some awkward, most forgettable. But never fun. Never like this.

She made everything light. Effortless. She didn't just sit across from him and smile politely; she leaned into conversation, teased him without fear, laughed with her whole body, and—without warning—stole from his plate like it was the most natural thing in the world.

"Hey," he said as she pinched a roasted tomato from his dish.

She grinned, completely unrepentant. "It looked lonely."

Brad shook his head, amused. "You know you have your own, right?"

"Yes, but yours tastes better."

She followed it up by spearing a bite of her own risotto, holding it out toward him on her fork.

"Try this," she said. "You'll thank me."

He hesitated for half a second—and then leaned in, letting her feed it to him.

The bite was rich and warm, but the way she watched him—playful, expectant, completely unguarded—was even more intoxicating.

"Worth it?" she asked, smiling as she set her fork down.

Brad swallowed, not just the food, but the tension curling low in his stomach. "Very."

She tilted her head, eyes dancing. "Told you."

He chuckled and shook his head, but he didn't pull away. He didn't want to.

No woman had ever made him feel like this—off guard in the best way. Relaxed. Real. Like he could let his guard down and still be wanted.

Like maybe this wasn't just dinner.

Maybe it was the beginning of something he hadn't even known he was missing.

Dinner had ended in laughter and lingering glances. The night air was warm but laced with a breeze that danced through the narrow Roman streets like it carried centuries of secrets.

Brad held the door open as Scarlett stepped out of the restaurant, her heels clicking softly on the cobblestones. The street glowed gold beneath lamplight, the city alive with quiet music and distant voices.

He looked at her, his voice low. "Would you like to walk for a bit?"

Scarlett didn't hesitate. "I'd love that."

He offered his hand, and she took it—fingers slipping easily between his, like they belonged there.

They walked slowly, their footsteps unhurried. The buzz of the city faded into a gentle hum, and neither felt the need to fill the quiet with words. Rome wrapped around them, romantic and timeless—its beauty unfolding with every turn.

Brad led them through a narrow alleyway that opened onto a piazza where artists were sketching lovers under lamplight. Scarlett paused to admire a charcoal portrait, and Brad watched her instead—the way her eyes sparkled when she smiled, the way she seemed lit from within.

"You've been here before?" she asked as they continued.

"Years ago. Briefly." He looked ahead, then over at her. "But this… feels different."

Scarlett squeezed his hand gently, her heart tugging.

A few more turns, and the soft sound of rushing water met their ears.

Scarlett's eyes widened as they stepped into the open, moonlight spilling across pale marble. The Trevi Fountain stood before them—glorious and grand, its cascading water catching the light like crystal rain.

"Oh," she breathed. "It's beautiful."

Brad didn't say anything. He was too busy watching her.

She walked forward, eyes fixed on the sculptures, the water, the magic of it all. He joined her at the edge, and for a long moment, they just stood there, letting the sound surround them, letting the moment settle.

"Do you believe in wishes?" she asked, half teasing.

Brad smiled faintly. "I believe in things worth fighting for."

She turned to him, caught by the seriousness in his tone.

"And you?"

Scarlett reached into her clutch and pulled out a coin. She looked down at it, then at the fountain, then back at him.

"I don't know if I believe in magic," she said softly. "But I believe in timing. In second chances."

She kissed the coin, closed her eyes for a beat, then turned and tossed it over her shoulder into the fountain.

Brad watched her the entire time, something catching in his throat.

"You going to throw one in?" she asked, turning to him with a smile.

"I already got what I wished for," he said, voice rougher than he meant.

Scarlett's breath hitched—just slightly. Then, quietly, she reached for his hand again.

Brad didn't hesitate. He slid his arm around her waist, pulling her gently against his side. Scarlett leaned in without a word, resting her head on his shoulder, her hand still tucked in his.

They stood there like that—two souls suspended in a moment, the roar of the fountain behind them, the stars scattered above like a silent blessing.

Brad closed his eyes for a beat, breathing her in. The warmth of her body, the steady rhythm of her breath, the softness of her hair brushing his jaw—it all wrapped around him like a truth he hadn't wanted to admit until now.

He'd tried not to feel it. Tried to keep lines clear, to remember why he was here. But it was too late for all that.

He'd fallen for her.

Hard.

And standing there, holding her beneath the Roman sky, Brad knew one thing with absolute clarity—

He didn't want to fall carefully.

He wanted to fall completely.

They walked back through the quiet streets of Rome, the city's golden glow settling into something softer, dreamlike. The night had deepened, the air cooler now, laced with jasmine and the faint hum of far-off traffic.

At the hotel, Brad followed Scarlett to her suite. Neither spoke much. They didn't need to. Their silence was comfortable—charged only by the closeness between them, by what hadn't yet been said, but lingered in every glance and touch.

At her door, Scarlett turned, her hand on the knob. "Thank you for dinner," she said, voice low and sincere.

Brad's gaze held hers. "You're welcome."

She leaned back slightly against the doorframe, her expression open and unguarded, her lips tilting into a smile.

Brad stepped in, closing the small space between them. He reached up, his fingers brushing a strand of hair from her cheek. Then, slowly—almost like a question— he bent his head.

And kissed her.

It was tender at first—soft and searching, the kind of kiss that lingered with intention. But the moment her hand slid to his chest, the kiss deepened. He pressed her gently against the door, one arm braced beside her, the other curving around her waist.

Scarlett's fingers curled into the front of his shirt, holding him there. The world faded—no hotel, no hallway, no rules.

Just him. Just her.

When they finally parted, breathless and quiet, her forehead rested lightly against his.

Brad didn't move. Didn't speak.

Because in that moment—standing at her door, holding her close—Brad wasn't thinking about what he was supposed to do.

Only what he wanted.

Her.

He pressed one last kiss to her forehead, gentle and lingering, as if it held everything he couldn't say.

"Goodnight, Scarlett," he murmured, his voice rough with restraint.

She looked up at him, her eyes soft, glowing in the low hallway light. "Goodnight, Brad."

Their hands parted slowly, reluctantly, fingers slipping free like a promise left hanging in the space between them.

And as she stepped inside, the door clicking softly shut behind her, Brad stood there for a moment longer.

Smiling.

Already aching to see her again.

As Scarlett stepped quietly into the suite, closing the door behind her, Jeff turned from his spot on the couch, one brow arching as he took her in.

"What are you doing here?" he asked, eyes narrowing in mock suspicion.

Scarlett blinked. "What do you mean?"

Jeff sat up straighter, setting aside his drink. "Why aren't you with lover boy?"

She sighed, walking past him to place her clutch on the side table. "He walked me to my door."

"A gentleman." Jeff nodded but didn't look convinced. "Still, that doesn't explain why you're standing in this suite instead of in his arms, preferably in his suite."

"Jeff," she warned, turning to give him a look.

He grinned unrepentantly. "What? I'm just saying—there was a whole vibe today. That man looked at you like you were made of stars."

Scarlett rolled her eyes, but she couldn't suppress the soft smile on her lips.

"He did kiss me," she admitted, voice quieter. "At the door. It was… really nice."

Jeff's expression melted into something softer, less teasing. "You like him."

She nodded, her fingers trailing the edge of the counter absently. "I do. A lot."

He studied her for a beat, then said gently, "So why are you here?"

Scarlett glanced toward the door, then back at Jeff, uncertainty flickering in her eyes.

"I can't go to him… can I?"

Jeff stood without hesitation and crossed the room to her. His voice was gentle, but sure.

"Of course you can."

She looked up at him, torn. "But—"

"No buts," he said firmly. "Scarlett, you deserve a little happiness in your life. Real happiness. Not the kind you fake for everyone else's comfort."

Her eyes shimmered with something between hope and fear. "I might never see him again after we leave for Greece in a couple of days."

Jeff nodded, a soft, understanding smile tugging at his mouth.

"That's the point, sweetie. Enjoy yourself while you can. Don't overthink it. Don't protect yourself from something that might actually be good."

Scarlett swallowed hard, her heart thudding in her chest.

"You're allowed to want this," he added. "You're allowed to have this."

She let out a breath—shaky, full of nerves and longing. Then she straightened, lifting her chin slightly as her eyes drifted once more to the door.

And this time, she didn't hesitate.

As she opened it, one hand already on the handle, she glanced back over her shoulder with a flicker of a smile.

"Don't wait up."

Jeff grinned from the couch, raising his glass.

"I won't."

His laugh followed her into the hallway—light, warm, and full of quiet triumph.

Chapter Fourteen

Brad was in the bedroom, fingers at the buttons of his shirt, the soft fabric slipping open one by one as he tried—and failed—to shake the feel of her from his skin. The taste of her kiss still lingered, and his heart hadn't stopped its quiet thrum since he'd walked away.

Then—

A knock.

Sharp. Sure.

He froze.

For a moment, he just stood there, heartbeat pulsing in his throat. Then he moved, slow but certain, walking back into the main room and crossing to the door.

He opened it—and there she was.

Scarlett.

Framed in the hallway light, breathless and wide-eyed, her dress hugging every curve, her hair slightly tousled from the breeze outside. Her lips were parted, her eyes unreadable. But one thing was clear—she hadn't come to say goodnight.

"Scarlett—" he started.

She didn't let him finish.

She stepped forward, cupped his face, and kissed him.

Soft at first—but sure. Like she'd made up her mind and couldn't wait another second.

Brad froze for half a breath, stunned—then the world snapped into motion.

He reached back and flicked the door shut behind her with one hand. The other arm wrapped around her waist, pulling her flush against him. And then he kissed her back—deep and certain, all restraint forgotten.

There were no words. No explanations.

Only heat.

Only want.

Only them.

Scarlett's arms wrapped around his neck, pulling him closer as her body pressed flush against his. The kiss turned fierce—hungry, hot, full of need that had simmered for days, maybe longer.

Brad groaned softly against her mouth, one hand splaying across her lower back as the other slid down, firm, and sure, gripping the curve of her thighs. In one smooth motion, he lifted her, and she wrapped her legs around him without hesitation.

He carried her easily, their mouths never parting for long, stumbling toward the bedroom like gravity itself demanded they stay fused together. Her fingers threaded through his hair as his lips left hers and found the delicate skin of her neck, kissing, tasting, breathing her in.

Scarlett let out a breathless sound—half gasp, half moan—as he pressed her back against the wall for just a moment, anchoring her there. His hands roamed her sides, memorising every inch through the sleek fabric of her dress, his mouth trailing lower to the hollow beneath her jaw.

Her head tipped back, giving him more. Wanting more.

And Brad—

He didn't think. He didn't hesitate.

Because he'd never wanted anything more in his life.

Her legs tightened around him, drawing him impossibly closer. Brad groaned against her throat, the sound low and raw, his breath hot on her skin.

"God, Scarlett," he rasped, his voice wrecked with need. "You're driving me crazy."

Her fingers tangled in his hair, her mouth brushing his ear as she whispered, "I want you."

That did it. His grip on her tightened, his lips finding hers again—fierce, claiming, desperate.

"God, I want you too," he breathed between kisses, each word laced with a hunger he couldn't hold back anymore.

And in that moment, there was no past, no future.

Just this.

Just them.

He lifted her from the wall with ease, her legs still locked around his waist, their lips never parting for more than a breath. The feel of her, the taste of her—it was undoing him by the second.

He carried her through the soft-lit suite to the bedroom, the city outside forgotten. Sitting on the edge of the bed, he kept her straddled across his lap, her fingers buried in his hair, her breath warm against his cheek.

His hands roamed her back, slow, and deliberate, finding the zipper of her dress. With one long, drawn-out motion, he slid it down. The sound of it—soft, promising—was nearly drowned out by the way she sighed against his lips.

The dress gave way, slipping from her shoulders and pooling at her waist, revealing a midnight lace bra that made his breath catch.

He kissed a trail along her collarbone, reverent and hungry all at once, and with a deft flick, he unhooked the bra. It fell away, forgotten.

Brad drew back just enough to look at her—really look at her—and the words left him in a rough, stunned whisper.

"Jesus, Scarlett… you're more beautiful than I ever imagined."

His head dipped, lips trailing lower until his mouth closed over her breast. The moment his tongue touched her taut nipple, a strangled cry slipped from her lips, her fingers tightening in his hair.

She shifted against him instinctively, grinding against the heat of his arousal, and he groaned—deep and raw—against her skin.

Without breaking contact, he stood, still holding her tightly wrapped around him. Her breath hitched as he turned and gently laid her down across the middle of the bed, her hips near the edge, her eyes wide and wanting.

He kissed a path along her chest, licking and teasing each breast until she was gasping beneath him. Slowly, with deliberate care, he slid the rest of her dress down over her hips, taking her underwear with it—baring her completely to him.

Brad drew back just enough to take her in, his voice a reverent whisper against her skin.

"Scarlett… you're incredible."

And then his mouth was on her again—his hands and lips exploring every inch like a man lost and found all at once.

Brad dropped to his knees at the edge of the bed, his hands gliding slowly down the length of Scarlett's thighs. He kissed her inner knee, then the soft skin higher up, each touch deliberate—measured like a vow.

He gently hooked her legs over his shoulders, drawing her closer to the edge. Their eyes met for a heartbeat—hers wide, breathless, trusting—and then he lowered his head.

His mouth found her with aching precision, tongue sliding slowly through her slick heat. Scarlett's back arched as a gasp caught in her throat, her fingers flying to the sheets, to his hair, to anything she could hold on to.

Brad moved with focus, with reverence—each flick of his tongue a promise, each stroke drawing out another helpless sound from her lips. Her thighs trembled against him, and he gripped her hips to steady her, anchoring her to him as he lost himself in the taste and rhythm of her.

She was beautiful like this—open, unguarded, falling apart for him.

And God, he never wanted to stop.

When she shattered, it was music to his ears.

Scarlett cried out his name—raw, breathless, like a prayer whispered into the night. Her body arched, trembling, her fingers fisting in the sheets as wave after wave rolled through her.

Brad held her through it, anchored her as her world broke open around him. And the sound of his name on her lips—desperate, unfiltered, sacred—was something he knew he'd never forget.

Because in that moment, it wasn't just pleasure.

It was trust.

It was her giving him everything.

And he'd never wanted anything more.

He stood, his breath heavy, heart pounding as he stripped off the last of his clothes with practiced, efficient movements. Scarlett lay where he'd left her—flushed, breathless, the barest sheen of sweat glistening on her skin. Her thighs parted, still trembling, still open for him.

God, she was beautiful.

Brad stepped between her legs, the heat of her body drawing him in like a magnet. He reached down, guiding himself to her slick entrance, the head of him pressing against her as he looked into her eyes—dark with need, dazed with pleasure.

"Tell me you want me," he said, his voice low, hoarse, barely holding on.

Scarlett's gaze didn't waver. Her hands slid to his hips, her legs tightening around him again as she whispered, "I want you. Please. Now."

And that was what he needed.

Brad pressed forward, guiding himself into her with slow, deliberate care. His eyes never left hers—watching every flutter of her lashes, every breath she took as he slid deep inside.

It felt like nothing he'd ever known—like being let into something sacred. He was still standing his arms braced on the bed either side of her.

Scarlett gasped, her hands clutching at his shoulders, her body arching to take more of him. He stilled for a beat, letting the moment burn into memory—then withdrew almost completely before driving back in, harder this time.

She moaned, her head tipping back, and that sound undid him.

He set a rhythm—measured, consuming, each movement pulling a response from her lips, from her body, from his soul. It wasn't just heat. It wasn't just want.

It was everything.

Brad kept the rhythm steady, each thrust a tether between them, building her higher until she broke apart again—shattering around him with a cry that he caught with his mouth. He kissed her through it, grounding her as her body trembled against his.

Then, with a gentleness that contrasted the heat between them, he slipped free and gathered her into his arms. Scarlett clung to him, breathless, pliant. He laid onto the bed, taking her with him, his hands guiding her effortlessly as she straddled his hips.

She reached down, taking him in again, her body welcoming him with ease. She began to move—slow at first, hips rolling in a rhythm that made him groan aloud. Her palms pressed to his chest, grounding herself as soft moans spilled from her lips.

"Oh, God…" she whispered, head falling back as her movements grew more frantic, more desperate.

When she shattered again, her cry like music in the dark, Brad gripped her hips and took over—meeting her pace with his own, rougher now, raw, and real. He surged up into her, chasing the end he could no longer hold back.

And when it came, when he finally followed her over that edge, it was like falling into something vast and consuming—into her, into everything he hadn't known he needed until now.

His body tensed, breath catching in his throat, and then—release. A deep, raw surrender that left him shaking as he buried his face in her neck.

She collapsed onto his chest, breathless and trembling, her skin still flushed with the aftershock.

His arms came around her instantly, wrapping her close like he didn't know how to let go—and had no intention of trying.

Neither of them spoke. There was no need.

She rested there, listening to the steady thud of his heart beneath her cheek, and for the first time in what felt like forever, she felt completely… safe.

And he?

He held her like she was something sacred.

Because to him, she was.

Chapter Fifteen

Scarlett had fallen asleep on top of him, her breath slow and even, cheek pressed against his chest. Her body was still draped across his, bare skin warm against his, her legs tangled with his beneath the sheets.

Brad lay there, unmoving except for the hand that continued its slow, rhythmic strokes down the length of her spine. Over and over, soft, and sure. He wasn't trying to wake her—he just couldn't stop touching her. Couldn't stop memorising the feel of her like this. Peaceful. Unburdened. His.

He shifted slightly, careful not to disturb her, pressing a kiss to her temple as she murmured something incoherent against his skin. He smiled faintly, brushing a lock of hair from her cheek.

"You're killing me, Scarlett," he whispered, voice low and rough with emotion.

Gently, he slid his arms around her and rolled to his side, easing her down beside him. She stirred, eyes fluttering open just long enough to register the movement before settling again with a soft sigh, curling instinctively into him.

Brad pulled the sheet up around her shoulders and wrapped his arms around her once more, tucking her close. His thumb brushed slow, lazy circles along the curve of her back as her breathing evened out again.

He stared at the ceiling for a long moment, the soft glow of Rome filtering through the curtains. And for the first time in years, maybe ever, he felt something settle inside him.

Like coming home.

He closed his eyes, the scent of her in his lungs, the weight of her heart against his, and let himself drift.

Not away from her.

But deeper into her.

The first light of dawn filtered softly through the curtains, casting a pale glow across the room. Brad stirred slowly, eyelids fluttering open to find Scarlett curled against his side, her hair splayed like a halo on his chest.

He smiled before he even fully woke, the warmth of her body against him grounding and real. His hand instinctively reached out, fingers tracing the delicate curve of her cheek, lingering where the softest skin met the hollow of her jaw.

Scarlett's eyes cracked open, heavy-lidded, and warm. She blinked up at him, a slow smile blooming across her lips that made his heart skip.

"Morning," she whispered, voice husky from sleep.

"Morning," Brad replied, voice rough and low. He pressed a gentle kiss to her forehead, then to the tip of her nose.

They lay like that for a moment—breathing each other in, the quiet hum of the city beginning to stir beyond the windows.

Scarlett shifted slightly, nestling closer, her hand finding his and squeezing it softly.

"No regrets?" she murmured, playful but sincere.

Brad's grin was soft but certain. "None. Not a one."

Her smile deepened, eyes sparkling with something new—hope, maybe, or something tender and bright.

For a while, they just stayed tangled together, letting the morning wrap around them like a promise.

Outside, the world was waking. Inside, there was only this—this quiet, perfect beginning.

"I'm starving," he said, breaking the comfortable silence.

She wiggled closer, a mischievous glint in her eyes. "So am I. Not only for food."

He smiled down at her, amused. "You're wicked."

"Do you mind?" she teased.

"Hell no." He rolled her onto her back, their laughter mingling in the quiet morning light.

There was no rush this time—no urgency, no frenzy. Just a slow, sweet unravelling.

They made love like it meant something. Like every kiss was a question and every touch an answer. His hands mapped her body with reverence, relearning the lines he'd already memorised. Her fingers slid through his hair, over his shoulders, anchoring herself to him like she never wanted to let go.

They moved in perfect rhythm—savouring every moan, every whispered name, every soft gasp that filled the space between them. The world outside faded, and all that remained was the warmth of skin on skin, breath shared, hearts in sync.

It was tenderness wrapped in heat. Passion laced with affection.

And when they finally stilled, limbs tangled and breaths unsteady, it wasn't just satisfaction that lingered between them—

It was something deeper.

Something real.

"Now I need food," Scarlett laughed, breathless and warm against the pillows.

Brad sat up, grinning, and stretched his arm toward her. "You'll survive another few minutes."

Before she could protest, he was out of bed and scooping her effortlessly into his arms.

Scarlett squealed, delighted, wrapping her arms around his neck. "Brad! What are you doing?"

He looked down at her, his grin soft but sure. "Looking after you."

He carried her through the suite and into the bathroom, the early sunlight streaming across the tiles. He reached in and turned on the shower, waiting until the water was warm before stepping inside with her still in his arms. Steam rose around them as he set her gently on her feet.

Scarlett's laughter faded into a soft sound of surprise as he reached for a washcloth, lathered it slowly with soap, and began to run it over her skin in slow, careful circles.

The cloth traced the curve of her shoulder, down her arm, then across her back— each stroke patient, reverent.

She let out a quiet moan, her eyes fluttering shut.

"Brad…"

"Just let me take care of you," he murmured, voice husky.

And she did—melting beneath his touch, under the warmth of the water and the intimacy of something so simple, so tender.

Because in that moment, it wasn't just about want.

It was about care.

After Brad washed her with slow, attentive care—each stroke of the cloth a quiet declaration—he rinsed the suds from her skin, then turned the spray onto himself. Scarlett watched him, heart thudding in that strange, tender way that had nothing to do with lust and everything to do with him.

When he was done, he stepped out and reached for a thick, white towel. Without a word, he wrapped it around her, pulling her close as he gently dried her skin. His hands moved over her like he was memorising her all over again—reverent, protective.

He knelt slightly, rubbing the towel over her legs, then straightened, cupping her damp hair in the fabric, patting it gently.

Scarlett studied him, quiet, full of something she hadn't expected to feel so soon. Something that felt suspiciously like falling.

"I didn't realise…" she murmured, just above the hum of the still-running shower.

Brad looked at her, eyes steady. "What?"

She smiled—a slow, almost shy thing that didn't match the confidence she usually wore. "That you're so sweet."

His brows lifted, surprise flickering in his expression before a grin curved his mouth.

"Don't tell anyone," he said, mock-serious. "You'll ruin my image."

Scarlett laughed, leaning forward to press a kiss to his chest, right over his heart.

"Too late," she whispered.

Scarlett slipped back into her dress from the night before, smoothing the fabric down as she glanced at the clock. Her heels dangled from her fingers, and her hair, still slightly damp from the shower, curled at her shoulders.

Brad leaned against the doorframe, shirtless, watching her with that quiet, unreadable gaze that made her pulse skip.

She turned to him with a small, apologetic smile. "I need to go get changed."

He nodded, pushing off the frame and walking over to her. "I'll meet you and Jeff in the lobby in thirty minutes."

"Okay," she said, reaching up to kiss him—just a soft brush of her lips against his. "See you soon."

She turned toward the door, her hand just brushing the handle—when Brad caught her other hand and spun her around, pulling her straight into his arms.

Before she could catch her breath, he kissed her—deep, sure, and lingering.

The kind of kiss that made time stop.

Her heels clattered softly to the floor as she clutched his shoulders, kissing him back with everything she had left. When they finally pulled apart, both slightly breathless, he rested his forehead against hers.

"I just…" he murmured, his voice low, "wasn't ready to let you go yet."

Her lips curved into a smile. "Then don't."

But after a heartbeat, she gently stepped back, slipping her fingers through his once before picking up her shoes.

"I'll see you soon."

This time, when she walked out, she didn't look back.

She didn't have to.

She could still feel him everywhere.

As the door clicked softly shut behind Scarlett, Brad stood there for a moment, staring at the space she'd just left. The scent of her perfume lingered in the air—floral, warm, unmistakably her.

Eventually, he turned, crossing the room to the desk where he'd tossed his phone the night before. He'd silenced it before dinner, not wanting any interruptions. Not from work. Not from Alec. Not from anyone.

The screen lit up as he picked it up—three missed calls.

All from Alec.

Brad muttered a curse under his breath. "Damn it."

He pressed the name and lifted the phone to his ear.

The line didn't even ring once.

"Where the hell have you been?" Alec barked.

Brad didn't flinch. "Busy."

"Busy?" Alec snapped. "You were supposed to check in last night. I've been calling for hours."

"I turned off my phone," Brad said evenly, walking to the window and pulling back the curtain. Morning sunlight spilled across the rooftops of Rome, casting the city in a golden glow that felt too beautiful to match the tension creeping into his chest.

"Why?" Alec's voice crackled through the line. "How's Scarlett?"

"She's fine," Brad replied, his tone clipped but calm. He paused, raking a hand through his hair. "Look, Alec, it's obvious you have nothing to worry about. Jeff is nothing but a good friend to your sister."

Alec didn't respond right away.

Brad added, more pointedly, "He's gay, anyway."

A beat of silence. Then, Alec's voice, sceptical. "How do you know that?"

Brad stared out the window, jaw tight.

He lied. "It's obvious."

Another pause.

Alec exhaled, but not in relief—more like frustration. "That doesn't mean Scarlett isn't still too trusting. You know how she is."

Brad's grip on the phone tightened. "She's not a child, Alec."

"No, but she's still my responsibility."

Brad's jaw clenched. He kept his voice steady. "Then trust her judgment."

"I need you to stay on her," Alec said firmly. "It's important, Brad."

He sighed, rubbing the back of his neck as guilt pressed heavier on his shoulders. "Okay. But I can't always answer when they're close. I'll call you if there's any problem—but if I don't, it means all is well."

There was a pause, then Alec exhaled on the other end. "Okay. But Brad, just… keep an eye on her. I'm trusting you with the most important thing in my life."

Brad closed his eyes for a moment, guilt twisting deep in his gut. "Understood."

He ended the call and lowered the phone slowly, his chest aching.

He hated lying to his friend.

But worse…

He hated not telling Scarlett the whole truth.

Chapter Sixteen

Scarlett stepped quietly into her suite, the door clicking softly behind her. Jeff was waiting in the living room, perched on the edge of the couch, eyes bright with curiosity and a teasing grin tugging at his lips.

"So?" he asked, barely able to contain himself. "Tell me everything. How was it?"

Scarlett smiled, setting her clutch down and kicking off her heels. She leaned against the doorframe, the warmth of the evening still lingering in her cheeks.

"It was perfect," she said softly, her voice almost dreamy.

Jeff raised an eyebrow, clearly unimpressed with the vague answer. "Perfect how? Come on, spill."

She laughed, stepping fully into the room and closing the door behind her. Her eyes sparkled with something new—something bright and alive.

"More than perfect," she admitted, then paused, her smile deepening. "It was like everything I didn't know I wanted all at once. No pretences, no games. Just… real."

Jeff's grin widened. "Sounds like someone's smitten."

Scarlett rolled her eyes playfully but didn't deny it. "Maybe a little."

"But come on, tell me how he was?"

"Jeff…"

"Stop stalling."

She laughed softly, shaking her head. "He was… the best. And that's all I'm saying."

He whistled low, clearly impressed. "The best, huh? Now I really want details."

"No. I need to change. We're meeting in the lobby in twenty minutes."

He laughed. "Of course we are."

Scarlett quickly changed into a fresh sundress—something light and breezy that still felt effortlessly chic—and joined Jeff in the suite's sitting room. He gave her a quick once-over and a wink.

"Back to being the picture of innocence," he teased.

"Shut up," she said, swatting his arm, though the smile on her face was impossible to hide.

They rode the elevator down and stepped into the grand marble lobby, filled with soft morning light and the quiet hum of guests checking out and bellhops moving luggage.

"I'm going to ask the concierge about dinner reservations for tomorrow," Jeff said, already turning away. "Don't wander off and fall in love again."

She rolled her eyes with a soft laugh as he walked off.

Left alone, Scarlett drifted toward a small alcove off the main corridor, where a striking piece of modern art caught her attention. Bold, swirling colours in hues of red and gold painted a kind of chaotic romance across the canvas. She tilted her head slightly, studying the strokes, her fingers absentmindedly brushing the strap of her purse.

Behind her, a man's voice—smooth, low, and laced with an unmistakable Italian accent—spoke.

"What is a beautiful woman like you doing here… all alone?"

Scarlett turned, slowly, already half-smiling out of habit.

The man standing behind her was tall, well-dressed in a tailored navy suit, his dark hair slicked back with precision. He held a coffee cup in one hand, his eyes boldly appraising her with a smile that had probably worked on a hundred tourists before her.

Her smile shifted, polite but guarded.

"I'm not alone," she said smoothly, glancing toward Jeff across the lobby. "Just waiting for a friend."

"Lucky friend," the man replied, stepping a little closer. "You have the kind of beauty that makes time stop."

Scarlett arched a brow, the compliment sliding off her like silk. "And you have the kind of charm that probably works better on women who haven't had their morning coffee yet."

He chuckled, clearly not deterred. "Ah, but I like a woman with fire."

"This woman's not available."

As she responded, neither of them noticed the tall figure approaching quietly from behind.

Brad.

He'd just stepped off the elevator, phone in his pocket, shirt crisp and sleeves casually rolled to his forearms. He spotted Scarlett immediately—but stopped short when he saw the man in the navy jacket speaking to her, standing a little too close, smiling a little too easily.

Brad didn't rush.

He walked toward them slowly, silently, his gaze flicking over the stranger as he closed the distance. His steps were smooth, quiet over the marble, his expression unreadable.

The man was mid-sentence— "In Rome, beauty like yours should never be left unaccompanied…"—when Brad stepped up behind him.

"Funny," Brad said, voice calm and cool, "I was just thinking the same thing."

The man startled slightly, turning to see who had spoken.

Scarlett's eyes widened as she realised Brad was suddenly right there—close, grounded, quietly powerful in a way that made her pulse skip.

The stranger looked between them, something unreadable flickering in his eyes.

"Ah," he said lightly, adjusting his collar. "The friend."

Brad smiled—but it didn't quite reach his eyes. "Boyfriend, actually."

Scarlett's breath caught for a moment, but she didn't correct him. Didn't need to.

The man gave a short nod, his charm slipping into something cooler. "My mistake."

"I'm sure it happens often," Brad said, tone still even but edged now, a thread of warning beneath the words.

The man offered a tight smile, then turned and walked away without another word.

Scarlett exhaled, turning to Brad. "You're good at that."

He raised a brow. "At what?"

"Appearing out of nowhere and making someone rethink their whole approach."

He stepped closer, his hand brushing hers before linking their fingers together. "Was he bothering you?"

"No," she said with a soft smile. "But I'm glad you showed up."

Brad leaned in just enough that only she could hear. "Me too."

They walked off together toward Jeff—who was watching from across the lobby with an expression halfway between smug and swooning.

Scarlett didn't look back.

She didn't have to.

Brad was right there.

The three of them had breakfast at a sun-drenched café tucked along a quiet Roman side street. Awnings fluttered in the breeze, the scent of espresso and warm pastries curling through the air. Scarlett sat between Jeff and Brad, their table dotted with cappuccinos, fruit, and flaky cornetti that melted on the tongue.

Jeff was in rare form, narrating their walk from the hotel with dramatic flair, exaggerating the "charming menace" of the man who had approached Scarlett in the lobby.

"I mean, I turned around and saw Mr. Espresso trying to sweep you off your feet— and then boom," he gestured theatrically toward Brad, "Captain Brooding appears like a Roman god in denim and ruins his whole day."

Scarlett laughed, sipping her coffee. "Captain Brooding?"

Brad raised a brow at her. "Is that what we're calling me now?"

Jeff winked. "Better than Captain Overprotective."

Brad smirked but didn't argue, and Scarlett couldn't help but smile at how easily the two of them bantered now.

The rest of the day passed in a blur of cobblestone streets, historic piazzas, and gelato eaten too quickly under the hot Italian sun. Scarlett lost herself in the rhythm of it—the casual way Brad reached for her hand without needing to ask, the light jokes Jeff made whenever the two of them got too dreamy-eyed.

They tossed coins into fountains, wandered through markets, and took blurry selfies that captured nothing and everything all at once. Brad even smiled in a few, something Scarlett had learned was rare.

That night, they found themselves at a cozy trattoria tucked into an ivy-covered alleyway, the kind of place only locals seemed to know about. A violinist played somewhere nearby, soft notes floating on the air between bites of pasta and shared carafes of wine.

It was after dessert, when plates were mostly cleared and conversation had quieted, that Jeff glanced at his phone and casually said, "By the way, our ferry to Santorini leaves the day after tomorrow. Early."

Scarlett's hand froze around the stem of her wineglass.

She didn't look at Brad. Didn't dare. Her eyes stayed on the candle flickering between them, even as something heavy pulled low in her stomach.

The day after tomorrow.

So soon.

Her smile didn't slip, but it felt tight. Fragile. Like if she blinked too long, he'd see right through it.

Brad didn't speak immediately. She could feel his eyes on her, the weight of his silence louder than any question.

Jeff, oblivious, kept talking about flights and weather apps and ferry schedules.

Scarlett finally took a sip of her wine, hoping the cool liquid would ease the burn in her throat.

It didn't.

Because the truth was—she didn't want to leave.

Not yet.

And worse… she wasn't sure how to ask him to stay. Or if he would.

So, she kept smiling.

And didn't meet his eyes.

Chapter Seventeen

They returned to the hotel beneath a canopy of stars, the city behind them still humming with life even as the hour stretched toward midnight. The streets had quieted, but the air still carried the warmth of the night—and the weightless sense of something unspoken, something neither of them wanted to end.

Inside the lobby, the world slowed.

It was quiet—cool marble floors gleaming under soft golden light, a hush of late luxury settling around them. Scarlett walked between Jeff and Brad, her heels clicking softly with each step. Her hand was nestled in Brad's; their fingers interlaced like it was second nature.

Brad's thumb brushed lightly over her knuckles, an unconscious rhythm that steadied them both. It wasn't possessive—it was protective. Reassuring. Like he was anchoring her to something solid in a world that kept shifting.

They were almost to the elevator when a voice sliced clean through the air.

"Scarlett."

She froze.

The sound of her name—familiar, too familiar—pulled her to a stop. Slowly, she turned, her hand still in Brad's.

Sean stood by one of the lobby columns, dressed like he hadn't left the hotel all day. His shirt open just enough to look intentional, his posture relaxed in a way that felt entirely rehearsed.

His gaze landed on her like a claim. "Can we talk? Alone."

Before Scarlett could answer, Jeff stepped forward, sharp as a blade. "Not happening."

Brad didn't speak, but his entire body shifted beside her—subtle but unmistakable. He didn't tighten his grip, didn't move, but Scarlett felt it in the air around him. A quiet alertness. Like still water holding the weight of a coming storm.

Scarlett looked between them—Jeff bristling, Brad unreadable—and then back at Sean.

"It's okay," she said at last, her voice steady. "Just a minute."

Jeff turned to her, brows low. "You sure?"

She nodded. "I'm sure."

Jeff stepped back, reluctantly, but didn't go far. Brad stayed beside him, silent and watchful—muscle coiled beneath the surface. Steel beneath stillness.

Scarlett walked a few steps toward Sean, crossing into the chandelier's soft glow. Her arms remained folded, chin lifted. She wasn't that girl anymore—the one who used to mistake his charm for something real.

But even as she stood tall, Brad's eyes tracked her every movement, unreadable. Unwavering.

As soon as she and Sean were out of earshot, he turned on her.

"What the hell are you doing holding that guy's hand?" he bit out, voice low but thick with restrained fury.

Scarlett met his gaze without flinching. "I've told you—we're done."

"You don't mean that. You and I belong together. You just need—"

"No, Sean," she said, her voice firm, clear. "We're done. I don't need anything from you. Please… go. Don't follow me, don't text me, and don't try this again."

She turned to walk away.

But he grabbed her arm—hard—yanking her back so fast she stumbled straight into his chest.

Before she could react, his arms snapped around her like a trap, and he crushed his mouth to hers—hard, bruising, desperate.

Scarlett gasped, her hands pushing at his chest, struggling to break free.

"No—"

Brad moved before anyone else could breathe.

One heartbeat he was beside Jeff—

The next, he was between them, his hand clamping down on Sean's wrist with brutal precision.

"Let. Her. Go."

His voice was low, controlled. Lethal. Steel wrapped in ice.

Sean tried to twist away, but Brad didn't flinch. His body was unmoving. His expression, flat and unreadable—except for the storm boiling beneath it.

"I said," Brad growled, "let her go."

Sean bared his teeth. "She's mine—"

Brad leaned in, voice like a blade.

"She was never yours. Not now. Not ever."

Scarlett tore out of Sean's grip the second it loosened, stumbling back.

Brad's other hand caught her waist without looking, steadying her like it was instinct. Like he'd never let her fall.

Then he turned back to Sean, every word cold and exact.

"If you ever touch her again, you won't walk away from it. Do you understand me?"

There was something in his eyes—not rage. Something worse.

That still, dangerous calm honed by years of knowing exactly how much damage he could do.

Sean froze. He saw it. He felt it.

And he believed it.

He ripped his arm free and glared. "This isn't over."

"Yes, it is," Brad said, unmoving.

Scarlett stepped beside him, her voice cutting like glass.

"Walk away, Sean. And don't come back."

Sean's eyes lingered on her for one beat too long—then he turned and stormed out of the lobby, the doors hissing shut behind him.

Jeff let out a sharp breath and muttered, "Jesus."

Brad finally turned to Scarlett, his hand still hovering near her waist like he wasn't quite ready to stop protecting her. "Are you okay?"

She nodded, but her voice came out a little shakier than she meant it to. "Yeah. I'm okay."

Brad searched her face, his brows drawn tight with concern. Then, softer, more careful: "Are you sure?"

Scarlett tried to smile, but it faltered. Her pulse still raced beneath her skin, a jittery echo of adrenaline she couldn't quite shake. "I didn't expect him to grab me like that," she admitted, her voice barely above a whisper.

Brad's jaw clenched. He didn't say anything right away, but his hand came to rest gently on the small of her back. It wasn't possessive—but it was definitely protective. Grounding. As if he needed to keep her close. Just in case.

Jeff stepped forward, glancing between them. "You're white as a sheet," he said gently. "How about we get a drink? Just one. Something to take the edge off."

Brad didn't look away from Scarlett, but his tone softened. "Might be a good idea."

Scarlett hesitated, then gave a small nod. "Okay. Yeah. I think I need something to calm down."

Brad moved with her as they headed toward the bar, his presence steady and unshakable at her side. His hand remained at the small of her back—not guiding, not gripping—just there. Quietly claiming space. Like a silent shield between her and whatever might try to reach her again.

When Scarlett eased onto the barstool, her eyes lifted to his. The low light caught the hard angles of his face, but it was his eyes that held her. There was steel in them—not fury, not panic, but something calmer and far more dangerous.

A vow.

You're safe. And no one touches you like that again.

Jeff stepped up beside them, his voice lighter but no less concerned. "Brandy," he told the bartender. "Make it a double."

Scarlett offered a faint smile, but it didn't quite reach her eyes.

When Jeff handed her the drink, she nodded her thanks and took a sip—then another, quicker this time. The warmth spread through her chest, not just from the alcohol but from the weight of Brad's gaze still anchored to her face.

She met it with a steadier breath. Not perfect. But steadier.

They sat in silence for a few beats, the hum of the bar around them a comforting blur. Then Jeff leaned an elbow against the counter and glanced at Brad.

"That guy's always been a loser," he muttered, just loud enough for them to hear. "Scarlett dated him for, what? A month? Months ago. He still can't let it go."

Scarlett gave a humourless laugh. "I thought he had."

Jeff scoffed. "Yeah, well, clearly, he followed you here like some desperate rom-com villain. Only not charming. Or romantic."

Brad's expression didn't change, but his hand gently closed over Scarlett's where it rested on the bar.

"You're not dealing with him again," Brad said, quiet but certain.

Scarlett didn't answer right away—but she didn't let go of his hand either.

And in that moment, something inside her began to settle. Slowly. Quietly. Like the first deep breath after a storm.

She finished the brandy in one last sip, then straightened her spine and set the glass down with quiet finality.

"I don't want to think about him anymore," she said, her voice clearer now. "Thank you for stepping in."

Brad gave her a small, tight smile. Not casual. Not easy. But real. "You don't have to thank me."

She squeezed his hand once before letting go.

They rose from the bar and crossed the quiet lobby together. Jeff trailed behind them, still casting occasional glances toward the entrance like he expected Sean to slink back in. Brad walked beside Scarlett, his hand hovering just near hers—not clinging, not urging. Simply there. Steady. Watchful.

When they reached the elevator, Scarlett leaned lightly into Brad's side. She didn't say a word.

She didn't need to.

He didn't either—but when the elevator doors slid shut behind them, his hand found hers again. Their fingers laced together like they belonged there.

The ride up was quiet—comfortable but charged with something low and simmering. Scarlett stood between Brad and Jeff, the hum of the elevator rising beneath their feet. Her hand remained in Brad's, their touch quiet but tethered. Like an anchor in the middle of everything that had almost spiralled out of control.

Brad stood tall beside her, his jaw tight, eyes forward—but inside, he was anything but still.

He replayed it—Sean's grip on her arm, the flash of fear in her eyes, the way her breath had hitched. And though it was over now, the memory lived sharp beneath his skin.

He hadn't expected to feel this—this need to protect her like she was already his.

But she was. And that terrified him more than anything.

No one would touch her like that again. Not while he was breathing.

He didn't care what came next—what confessions still waited, what fallout was looming. He'd make it right. For her.

The elevator chimed softly. The doors slid open to their floor.

They stepped into the muted light of the hallway, the air quieter somehow— thicker, like it held something unspoken.

Scarlett's steps slowed as they approached the hallway's fork—the familiar point where her suite lay one way, Brad's the other. She stopped walking.

Chapter Eighteen

Brad didn't notice she'd stopped walking until the gentle tug at his hand pulled him back. He turned—she was still standing at the fork, eyes on him, like she was waiting for him to say what came next.

No questions. No demands.

Just… a pause. A moment suspended in the hush of the corridor.

He could've let go. Said goodnight. Stepped back.

But he didn't.

Because he didn't want to leave her alone tonight.

Hell, he didn't want to be alone.

His hand was still wrapped around hers, and he took another step forward, gently tugging her with him—almost like he hadn't even considered the possibility she wouldn't follow.

Scarlett looked from him to Jeff, a silent question in her eyes.

But Jeff just smiled knowingly and gave her a wink. "Have a good night, you two," he said, voice light and easy. "See you in the morning."

Before she could say a word, he was already strolling toward their suite, keycard in his hand, whistling to himself like he'd never had a single doubt about how this would go.

Scarlett turned back—only to find Brad watching her with that quiet, unreadable look that made her insides flutter. He didn't say anything. He just lifted their joined hands and gave her fingers a small, sure squeeze.

Then, without a word, he took a slow step backward toward his door.

She followed.

Willingly.

Her choice made for her in the most effortless way.

And when they disappeared into his suite and the door clicked softly shut behind them, the world outside ceased to matter.

All that remained was them.

As soon as the door clicked shut behind them, Brad turned and gently tugged Scarlett into his arms.

She came willingly, her body soft against his, her fingers curling into his shirt like she'd been waiting all day to be this close.

Their eyes met, the room silent except for the soft thud of their breathing. And then, at the exact same moment, they both spoke.

"I want to come to—" Brad began, then stopped himself.

"I want you to come to—" Scarlett said just as quickly—and froze.

They stared at each other, the air between them thick with something tender and uncertain.

Brad swallowed hard, a thousand thoughts colliding behind his steady gaze.

Scarlett blinked, her voice cautious but hopeful. "What were you going to say?"

He hesitated.

This was the moment he could tell her. Should tell her. That he hadn't just met her by chance. That he'd known Alec for years. That he hadn't been in Rome just to enjoy the sights.

But he didn't.

Instead, he gave her a faint, crooked smile—one that didn't quite reach his eyes.

"I was going to say… I want to come to Greece."

Her breath caught. "You do?"

"Yeah." He reached up and touched her cheek, his thumb brushing lightly over her skin. "If you'll have me."

She smiled, soft and radiant, a bloom of relief lighting up her face. "I was going to ask you the same thing."

Brad let out a quiet breath, wrapping his arms around her more tightly. But guilt pressed at the edges of his chest like a weight he couldn't shake. She looked at him like he was hers already.

And God help him; he wanted to be.

But the truth still lingered—unsaid, unspoken—between them.

"I wasn't sure if you'd want that," Scarlett murmured, her voice trembling slightly. "I didn't want to make it awkward."

"I want to spend more time with you," Brad said, his tone low. "If you'll let me."

She leaned in, their foreheads brushing. "I want that too."

They stood there for a moment, swaying slightly in the quiet, wrapped in something fragile and real. Brad kissed her then—slow, searching, trying to lose himself in her warmth, in her softness. Trying to forget, just for now, that he hadn't earned this moment the way she thought he had.

And still, he didn't let her go.

Because even with the truth between them—unsaid and heavy…

Brad didn't want to let her go at all.

He showed her the only way he knew how.

They made love slowly, like they were trying to hold onto something slipping between their fingers. His hands traced the shape of her, his mouth kissed away every unspoken word, and she clung to him like it might be the last time.

Later, as the night stretched long and quiet, Scarlett lay awake in Brad's arms, her head resting against his chest. His breathing was steady, sleep-softened, one arm draped over her waist as if to keep her anchored there beside him.

She was falling for this man. She knew it.

Not just for the way he touched her or looked at her like she was the only thing in the room—but for who he was when no one was watching. The gentleness, the quiet protectiveness, the way he held her like she mattered.

And it scared her.

Because this was a holiday. A brief escape. And holiday flings? They didn't last.

She knew that. She'd told herself that going in.

But now?

Now she didn't want to let him go.

She wanted more mornings like the one before. More nights where she fell asleep with his heart beneath her ear. More of the quiet safety she felt when his arms were around her and the world disappeared.

She was glad he was coming to Greece with them. He had wanted to—had chosen to.

And that meant something.

Still, reality whispered. Brad had his life. She had hers.

Maybe they weren't meant to collide beyond this holiday—beyond these perfect, borrowed days that felt too good to last.

But she wasn't ready to let go.

Not yet.

Even as she knew, deep down, that after Greece… she'd have to.

And that truth—the weight of it—hurt more than she'd expected.

So, she closed her eyes and let herself melt into him, breathing in the steady rhythm of his chest beneath her cheek.

Letting the moment stretch a little longer.

Letting his warmth hold back the dawn.

Because when morning came… goodbye would follow.

Greece didn't feel like a destination anymore.

It felt like a countdown.

Not a beginning—

But the edge of the end.

Still, she wasn't going to waste a second.

She would hold on to this—

To him—

With both hands.

Because this thing between them—fragile, fleeting, and impossibly precious—

Might never feel quite the same again.

The next day blurred past in a whirlwind of shops and bustling Roman streets, sunlight spilling across cobbled alleys and elegant piazzas. Scarlett moved with purpose, her eyes scanning boutique windows like a general surveying a battlefield. Jeff kept pace beside her, armed with cappuccinos and caustic commentary, the two of them locked in a rhythm only best friends could maintain.

They visited high-end ateliers tucked behind ivy-covered facades, charming leather workshops with the scent of fresh hide lingering in the air, and glittering fashion houses where stylists greeted Scarlett like royalty. At one point, she held up two gowns—one midnight blue, the other emerald silk—and turned to Jeff with a dramatic sigh.

"Do I want to look like the night sky... or jealousy incarnate?"

"Neither," Jeff replied dryly. "You want to look like you already own the building, and the blue screams 'take me seriously.'" He turned to Brad. "Back me up here."

Brad had barely said a word since they started. Not because he wasn't interested, but because watching her—watching them—was entertainment enough. He smiled slightly, then nodded. "The blue."

Scarlett rolled her eyes. "Traitors, both of you," she said, but the smile tugging at her lips gave her away. She handed the emerald back to the assistant.

Hours passed like minutes, the day unfolding in a blur of golden sunlight and cobblestone charm. Laughter floated easily between them—warm, unguarded, the kind that came only with comfort and connection. They paused for rich espresso at a café tucked beneath flowering vines, and later shared scoops of pistachio and blood orange gelato that melted too fast in the afternoon heat.

In a quiet side street, Scarlett lingered inside a small jewellery boutique, its windows framed in gilded ironwork. Her eyes lit up at the sight of a pair of delicate moonstone earrings—pale, iridescent, like captured moonlight. "They're beautiful," she murmured, admiring them but placing them back with a quiet sigh.

Brad said nothing. But minutes later, while she and Jeff debated handbags next door, he quietly returned and bought them.

Later, they paused again near a crumbling fountain where a street violinist played a haunting melody that curled through the air like smoke. Scarlett stood still beside him, her expression soft, dreamy. And Brad—arms full of shopping bags, heart impossibly full—thought he could stay in that moment forever.

Brad followed, quiet and steady, weighed down with glossy shopping bags looped over both arms. He didn't complain once. Not when Jeff dumped an armful of scarves into his hold, not when a delicate heel box nearly tumbled from the top of the pile, and not even when Scarlett swept into yet another boutique with a gleam of purpose in her eyes.

He just carried it all—silently, contentedly—with a quiet smile tugging at his lips.

He hadn't known what to expect from this trip. Certainly not this: the three of them laughing until they cried over Jeff's impersonation of a pushy French salesclerk, or the way Scarlett leaned into him without thinking when they stopped to rest on a bench, sipping bottled water in the shade.

Never in his life had Brad imagined that carrying a woman's shopping bags could make him this happy.

But this wasn't just any errand.

It was for her. And that made all the difference.

Every step through those cobbled streets, every smile she threw over her shoulder, every time she asked for his opinion on a dress, he tucked the moment away like something sacred.

That night after dinner, Scarlett returned to her suite to pack. The soft glow of the hallway lights danced across her face as she turned to Brad, her fingers trailing lightly down his arm.

"Do you want me to come to your suite when I'm done?" she asked, voice low, almost shy.

He didn't hesitate. "Yes. Of course."

Because the thought of being apart from her — even for a little while — settled in his chest like an ache. A dull, hollow pull that only eased the second she was back in his arms.

"Being away from you," he added quietly, "feels like something's missing."

Her lips curved, soft and knowing, and then she turned and disappeared into her suite, leaving him standing there with that familiar ache already creeping back in.

Thirty minutes suddenly felt like a lifetime.

Chapter Nineteen

Early the next morning, just after dawn broke across the horizon, the three of them boarded the ferry bound for Santorini.

The port was already buzzing—tourists dragging rolling luggage behind them, locals loading cargo, voices rising and mingling with the sharp cries of seagulls overhead. The ferry itself was massive, its white hull gleaming beneath the soft golden light of morning. Passengers moved up the ramp with practiced efficiency, a mix of sleepy anticipation and rustling excitement trailing behind them.

Scarlett clutched her tote bag and blinked against the wind as they climbed aboard, Jeff at her side humming a tune from the hotel's playlist, Brad just behind them, their hands brushing every so often.

It would be nearly eight hours before they reached Santorini—an island wrapped in legend, suspended on cliffs above the Aegean like a dream. The ferry would cut south across the cobalt-blue waters, stopping briefly at Naxos and Paros before curving west toward the island's iconic whitewashed villages and sun-drenched vistas.

They found a quiet spot on the deck, away from the tourist chatter and camera flashes, and settled into a trio of cushioned seats by the railing. Wind tugged playfully at Scarlett's hair as she pulled on her sunglasses and leaned into the moment—the salty tang of the sea air, the rhythmic churn of water beneath them, and the soft heat of Brad's thigh pressed against hers.

She glanced sideways at him, catching the way his eyes were already fixed on the horizon, calm and unreadable, like he was trying to make sense of something far beyond the waves.

Maybe they both were.

But for now, the journey had begun.

And Santorini waited on the other side.

A place of sunsets and secrets.

Of beauty and, maybe, endings.

But Scarlett wasn't thinking about endings—

Not yet.

She was still holding onto beginnings.

Brad leaned against the ferry's railing, the wind tousling his hair as the massive vessel sliced through the Aegean Sea. Below, the water churned in endless shades of blue—ribbons of sapphire and slate streaked with frothy white where the hull broke through.

He wasn't used to this kind of peace.

Not the open sea, not the sunlight warming his shoulders, not the soft weight of Scarlett leaning beside him with her head tipped back and sunglasses shielding her eyes from the morning glare.

He watched her from the corner of his vision.

She laughed at something Jeff said—a carefree, effortless sound that tugged at something deep in his chest—and then turned her face toward the wind, her hair dancing wildly around her shoulders like the breeze belonged to her.

God, she was beautiful.

Not just in the obvious way, though that hit him like a gut punch every time she looked at him. But in the way she carried herself—open, curious, a little guarded, but always alive. She didn't need anyone to complete her. And maybe that's why he wanted to be the one standing beside her so badly.

This wasn't what he'd expected when he took the job.

Protect Alec's sister. Keep your distance. Stay detached.

Easy on paper.

Except it hadn't been simple the second she smiled at him and started unravelling every line he'd drawn for himself.

And now?

Now they were sailing toward Santorini, and he was falling harder by the hour.

He glanced at her again, and this time, she was looking at him too. The corners of her mouth lifted, subtle but sure, and she nudged her knee against his like it meant something. Maybe it did.

Brad forced a smile in return, but it didn't quite reach his eyes.

Because beneath the pull of the sea and the charm of the moment, the truth sat heavy in his chest—unspoken and slowly eating away at him.

She didn't know the full truth. Not yet. And that was starting to weigh more heavily than he liked.

And every mile they travelled brought him closer to a point where he'd have to tell her.

About Alec.

About why he'd really shown up in Rome.

About how this had never been chance… even if everything about her felt like fate.

He exhaled slowly, glancing out at the wide horizon. Naxos was still hours away. Then Paros. Then finally, Santorini.

Plenty of time to figure out how to say what needed to be said.

But for now, Scarlett leaned her head on his shoulder, and his arm curled instinctively around her, holding her there like he never wanted her to move.

At the moment, she was here. With him.

And that had to be enough.

For now.

The ferry rocked gently as it pulled into Naxos, the first of the major stops along the way. Brad stood on the deck, sunglasses on, arms folded loosely over his chest as he watched the port come into view—whitewashed buildings rising in tiers, climbing the hillside like bleached steps to the sky.

Scarlett appeared beside him, holding an iced coffee in one hand, her hair pulled up into a loose knot that did nothing to hide the sun-kissed curve of her neck. She bumped his arm with her elbow.

"Pretty, huh?"

Brad glanced sideways at her. "Beautiful."

He meant the island.

He meant her more.

Naxos was a quick stop—barely enough time to stretch legs or take photos from the deck. Tourists disembarked, others climbed on. The buzz of change swept through the ferry like a shifting tide.

Jeff rejoined them with a pastry in hand. "Okay, if Santorini isn't more impressive than this, I want a refund."

Scarlett laughed, the sound light and easy, and Brad let himself soak it in.

Paros came next—smaller, more subdued. The harbor was quieter, the buildings cozier, dotted with pops of pink bougainvillea and sea-washed doors painted a dozen shades of blue. Scarlett leaned over the railing, squinting against the sun.

"Paros feels… peaceful."

Brad nodded. "Still think you want to move here for good?"

"Maybe," she said, teasing. "You coming?"

He smirked. "You first."

She grinned and turned back toward the view, but Brad caught the flicker of hesitation in her eyes—something soft, uncertain. Like they were both aware that this wasn't just sightseeing anymore. It was memory-making. Attachment-forming.

And Santorini was waiting.

By the time the ferry began its final descent into Athinios Port, Santorini unfolded before them like a painting come to life. Steep cliffs carved by volcanic fire, white houses stacked high on ridgelines, the caldera cradling deep, endless blue.

Brad had seen a lot of places in his life. But nothing hit like this.

"Whoa," Jeff said under his breath, for once without a single sarcastic comment.

Scarlett didn't speak. Her fingers found Brad's, threading through his like it was instinct now, and she just stared—awed, silenced by the sight of it all. The sun was lowering in the sky, casting the island in a warm, golden wash, and everything shimmered with the glow of something otherworldly.

"It doesn't look real," she murmured.

Brad gave her hand a gentle squeeze. "It's real."

And somehow, so was this.

Her fingers in his.

The ache in his chest that had nothing to do with distance or ferry rides.

And the knowledge that what they were walking into might be the beginning…

…or the beginning of the end.

The ferry docked with a soft jolt. The terminal buzzed with tourists, luggage, and shuttle buses, but Brad kept close—his arm around Scarlett, his eyes quietly tracking every detail around them like instinct.

Not just because of the job.

But because he couldn't not care anymore.

As they stepped off onto the sun-soaked pavement of Santorini, the wind picked up slightly, warm, and fragrant with salt and the faintest trace of lemon trees.

Scarlett turned to look at him with that open, radiant smile he was quickly becoming addicted to.

"Ready for our next adventure?"

Brad nodded once.

He was ready for the island.

He just wasn't sure if he was ready for what came after it.

Chapter Twenty

The car wound its way up the cliffside, the sea stretching endlessly to their left, glittering under the afternoon sun. Whitewashed walls flashed past the windows, the occasional blue dome rising like punctuation against the sky. When the car finally stopped, it was in front of a stone gate wrapped in flowering vines and a hand-painted sign that read Villa Eleonas.

Scarlett stepped out first, brushing her hair back from her face as she looked up at the charming, sun-bleached facade.

"I found it online months ago," she said, almost shyly. "I thought it looked like a dream."

Brad shaded his eyes from the sun as he grabbed his bag. "You weren't wrong."

Jeff was already ahead, whistling as he wheeled his suitcase toward the gate. "Okay, if there isn't a plunge pool and at least one place to drink wine while judging people from a distance, I want a refund."

Scarlett laughed, but her eyes were on Brad as he pulled his bag from the trunk and walked toward the gate. He paused before following her through it.

"Scarlett…" he said, his voice lower now, hesitant. "Are you absolutely sure you want me staying here? I can book something nearby, it's no problem. I don't want you to think I'm… taking advantage of the situation."

She turned to face him fully, her smile faltering just a little. The sun framed her face, casting golden light in her hair, but her eyes were serious—quiet and searching.

"You think I'd invite you if I didn't want you here?" she asked softly.

He hesitated, then gave a faint shrug. "I just… I don't want to assume."

For a moment, she said nothing. Then her expression shifted—just slightly. A flicker of worry in her brow. She took a small step closer.

"If you're uncomfortable," she said gently, "that's different. I won't be upset if you'd rather stay somewhere else, Brad. I promise. But I invited you because I want you here. With me."

He exhaled, the tightness in his chest loosening a little. "So, you're sure?"

"I'm sure," she said with a small, genuine smile. "Unless… you're not?"

Brad looked at her—really looked—and saw the vulnerability in her eyes, the quiet question beneath her words.

He stepped forward and brushed a knuckle down the curve of her cheek. "I'm not uncomfortable," he murmured. "Far from it. I just needed to hear that you were sure."

"I am," she said, voice barely above a whisper.

"Then I'm staying."

She smiled again—relieved this time. Brighter.

"Good."

They stood there for a moment, the soft rustle of the sea breeze and Jeff's distant commentary about the villa's "perfect Instagram angles" drifting around them.

Then Scarlett reached for his hand and laced her fingers through his.

"Come see our view," she said.

And with that, she led him through the gate—toward the villa, the island, and a few more borrowed days that neither of them wanted to end.

The villa was everything Scarlett had described—and more.

Sunlight streamed through arched windows as they stepped inside, illuminating pale stone floors and whitewashed walls accented with soft blue shutters. The open-plan living area was airy and bright, filled with rustic wood furniture and linen-covered cushions in muted sea-glass tones. Sheer curtains billowed gently in the breeze from the terrace doors, letting in the scent of salt and citrus.

To Brad, it felt like the kind of place you'd see on a postcard and assume was fake— too perfect to be real. But this was real. And Scarlett was here. That made it better.

Jeff dropped his bag with a dramatic sigh and called out, "Claiming the big room with the best light for my skincare routine unless someone fights me for it."

Scarlett just laughed and tugged Brad down a hallway lined with small paintings of the caldera. At the end was a wide set of double doors painted ocean blue. She pushed them open and stepped inside.

"This one's ours," she said.

Brad followed her in—and stopped.

The bedroom was simple, but beautiful. White linens dressed a large bed tucked against a wall of windows, where sheer curtains framed an endless stretch of sapphire sea and jagged cliffside. The ceiling beams were exposed wood, soft with age, and the tiled floor beneath their feet was cool and hand-laid, patterned with pale blue and grey mosaics.

Across from the bed was a private terrace, its doors open to a small table and two chairs, and beyond them… Santorini in full bloom. White villas spilled down the cliffs in layers like frosting, domes and rooftops glowing under the late afternoon sun. Far below, the Aegean shimmered like glass, sailboats scattered like pearls on its surface.

Brad walked slowly to the terrace doors and stepped outside, the warm breeze lifting his hair as he took in the view.

"Holy hell," he murmured.

Scarlett appeared beside him, her shoulder brushing his. "Worth the ferry?"

He looked at her then—at the way the light kissed her cheeks, how her eyes reflected the blue of the water—and smiled.

"Yeah. Worth everything."

She blushed, just a little, and leaned her head against his arm.

He let the silence stretch, comfortable and full, before glancing back inside at the room again. "You planned all of this?"

"I booked the villa for Jeff and me weeks ago," she said softly. "But—I'm glad I get to share it with you."

He looked at her then, eyes searching. "Are you?"

Scarlett's gaze didn't waver. "Yes."

Brad stepped closer, cupping her face gently in his hands. "You're full of surprises."

"And you're full of secrets," she said softly—not accusing, just honest.

Brad's smile faltered. The words landed gently, but they struck deeper than she could've known. Because she was right.

He did have secrets.

Ones he hated keeping from her.

He opened his mouth, wanting—needing—to tell her then. To lay it all out. The truth about Alec. About why he was really here. But the words caught somewhere between guilt and fear, choking on the weight of what it might cost.

Before he could speak, Scarlett rose onto her toes and kissed him—slow, certain, anchoring.

"We're here now," she whispered against his lips, her breath warm. "That's what matters."

And he let the truth stay buried a little longer. Just to hold onto this moment.

Just a little longer.

He kissed her back, pulling her into him as the sea breeze curled around them and the sound of the waves echoed faintly below.

This place, this moment—it felt like a pause in time.

And as the sun dipped lower toward the horizon, casting long golden shadows over the white rooftops of Santorini, Brad knew he would carry the memory of this view—of her—for the rest of his life.

Their first night in the villa unfolded under a sky dusted with stars and wrapped in the gentle hush of Santorini's sea breeze. The windows were open, letting in the scent of salt and bougainvillea, and the distant sound of waves lapping the cliffs far below.

Scarlett padded barefoot across the cool marble floors, her sundress traded for one of Brad's T-shirts that hung off her shoulders, soft and worn. She looked completely at ease—yet still impossibly beautiful—and it tugged something deep in Brad's chest. Something that felt dangerously close to forever.

He leaned against the doorframe of the bedroom, watching her as she moved around the space. Their room was bathed in warm, amber light from the bedside lamps, the terrace doors open behind her, revealing the moonlit shimmer of the caldera. The bed was wide, low, with white linens and sheer curtains tied back to the posts like something out of a dream.

"You okay?" she asked, catching him staring.

Brad nodded slowly. "Yeah. Just… taking it in."

She crossed to him and slid her hands up his chest. "The view's nice," she teased, tilting her head. "But I think you've got it backwards."

He gave a quiet laugh and caught her hips, pulling her flush against him. "I've had a lot of nights in a lot of places," he said, voice low, "but none of them felt like this."

She rested her cheek to his chest, fingers curling into the fabric of his shirt, like she was anchoring herself there.

They didn't rush things that night.

There was no urgency.

Only the soft rustle of sheets, the murmured hush of her name against his skin, the way her hands moved like she was learning him all over again.

Brad memorised everything—the sound of her sighs, the way she said yes like it meant more than permission. Like it was a surrender.

They made love slowly, like they were building something.

Something they weren't quite ready to name.

Scarlett had drifted off, her breathing soft and even, one hand still resting lightly against his chest. They lay tangled in the quiet aftermath, their bodies warm beneath the linen sheets, skin still humming with the echo of closeness.

The night stretched around them, hushed and endless.

Brad reached up and gently brushed a damp strand of hair from her cheek. He watched her sleep for a long moment, taking in the peaceful curve of her lips, the way she seemed to fit so perfectly in the space beside him.

"I don't want this to end," he whispered—half confession, half prayer.

Scarlett stirred, murmuring something unintelligible, shifting just slightly closer.

He let out a quiet breath, pulled her fully into his arms, and held her like he could keep the moment suspended—keep her safe, keep her his—for just a little longer.

Outside, the wind stirred the olive trees and whispered across the terrace, brushing cool fingers against the whitewashed walls of the villa.

Inside, everything was still. Everything felt like hers.

And for the first time… it felt like his too.

Even if he didn't deserve it.

Not yet.

Chapter Twenty-One

Brad woke to the kind of pleasure that blurred the line between dream and reality.

A slow, building heat pulsed through him, dragging him from the edge of sleep. His breath caught in his throat, a low, guttural sound slipping free as awareness took over. He blinked against the soft morning light filtering in from the terrace, the world still hazy—until he looked down.

Scarlett.

Between the sheets, her hair spilled like silk across his thighs, her touch and mouth working him with devastating focus. The sight of her—so completely unselfconscious, so intent on him—made his entire body tense with pleasure and disbelief.

His hands found her hair, not to guide, but to anchor. To remind himself this was real.

She felt incredible—her movements skilled, unhurried, like she had all the time in the world and no desire to rush a single second. And when the pleasure finally fractured through him, stealing his breath and curling his toes, she stayed with him. Never flinched. Never looked away.

Brad groaned again, deeper this time, one hand sliding down to cup her shoulder as the aftershocks rolled through him like waves. She didn't move until the tremors had fully subsided, until he was boneless beneath her, undone in the most intimate, vulnerable way.

When she finally looked up, her lips curved into a soft, knowing smile. Mischief and warmth danced in her eyes, but it wasn't teasing—it was something deeper. Something closer to love.

Brad reached for her, pulling her gently up into his arms, heart still hammering against his ribs.

"You're going to ruin me," he murmured, his voice rough with sleep and wonder.

Scarlett let out a quiet laugh—but it was warm, content, full of that same quiet mischief and something far more permanent.

In one fluid motion, Brad rolled her onto her back, settling beside her, their legs tangled in the sheets. She raised an eyebrow, still smiling. "Brad… what are you doing?"

"Returning the favour," he said, kissing her shoulder, her collarbone, the edge of her jaw.

Then lower.

His mouth found her with aching precision, tongue sliding slowly through her slick heat. Scarlett's back arched as a gasp caught in her throat, her fingers flying to the sheets, to his hair, to anything she could hold on to.

Brad moved with focus, with reverence—each flick of his tongue a promise, each stroke coaxing another helpless sound from her lips. Her thighs trembled against him, and he gripped her hips to steady her, anchoring her to him as he lost himself in the rhythm and taste of her.

She was beautiful like this—open, unguarded, unravelling in his hands.

When she shattered, she cried out his name—raw, breathless. Her body arched, trembling, her fingers fisting in the sheets as wave after wave rolled through her.

Brad held her through it, grounding her as her world broke open around them both.

Later, they lay in the quiet aftermath, limbs tangled, skin still humming. The city stirred softly outside, but here—in the hush of morning light and heartbeat stillness—they were the only two people in the world.

Brad smiled, pressing a kiss to her forehead. "I could get used to waking up like this."

Scarlett returned the smile, warm and content, then pressed a soft kiss to his chest—right over his heart. "Good."

They stayed tangled in each other for a few more quiet minutes, then reluctantly rose. A shared shower followed—filled with steam, laughter, and the occasional stolen kiss—before they dressed and stepped out onto the sun-warmed terrace for breakfast.

Jeff was already there, lounging in a chair with his sunglasses on, a mimosa in hand and a spread of croissants and fruit laid out on the table. He glanced up as they arrived and grinned like he knew exactly what kind of night they'd had.

"Took you two long enough," he said, lifting his glass in a lazy toast. "Happy morning-after."

Scarlett rolled her eyes fondly and sank into the chair beside him. Brad joined her, pouring himself a coffee, grateful for the illusion of normalcy.

But then her phone rang.

Scarlett reached for it, glancing at the screen. Her brows lifted. "It's Alec."

Brad went still.

His fingers curled slightly around his coffee cup, tension sliding down his spine like ice water. If she told Alec he was here—if she so much as hinted—they were going to have a serious problem. A blowup.

Because she still didn't know.

Didn't know that the man she'd fallen in love with, the man who had just made her come undone in his arms, was only in her life because her brother had hired him.

To protect her.

Brad's heart pounded behind his ribs. One word. That's all it would take. One, "Alec, I met someone, his name is Brad"—and the entire fragile truth would come crashing down.

Scarlett looked up, phone in hand, expression unreadable. "Should I answer it?"

Brad forced a steady breath and gave her a small nod—careful. Measured. "It's your brother. You should."

Scarlett narrowed her eyes slightly at his tone, like she picked up on the edge beneath the calm. But she didn't press.

She tapped the screen and lifted the phone to her ear.

"Hey, Alec."

Brad turned toward the skyline, pretending to admire the view—while every muscle in his body coiled tight, waiting to see if this was the moment everything unravelled.

Behind him, Scarlett's voice was low and polite. The call went on for a few minutes—nothing heated, no names mentioned. No "Brad" slipping through. Just measured responses. Pauses. Nods he couldn't see.

And then… a sigh.

She hung up.

Jeff, always the first to cut through tension, lifted his sunglasses. "Is everything okay?"

Scarlett gave a small, practiced smile. "Yeah." But her tone lacked conviction. It wasn't the confident, fire-edged Scarlett Brad had come to know.

Brad turned back, his gaze immediately locking onto hers. He noticed the subtle shift—the way she didn't quite meet their eyes, the way her hand lingered near her phone like it still held weight.

He reached over, gently covering her fingers with his. "What is it?"

Scarlett hesitated. Then she looked down at their joined hands and exhaled slowly, her shoulders deflating just a little.

"It's Alec," she said quietly. "It's like… there's nothing there anymore. No warmth in his voice. Just clipped answers and questions like he's reading from a script. Like he's checking boxes." She shook her head slightly. "We used to be so close. He was my best friend."

Her voice cracked just barely on the last word, and Brad felt it like a gut punch.

She glanced up again, eyes glassy but not yet spilling. "We used to talk about everything. And now it's like… like he's a robot. Efficient. Cold. Like I'm just one more thing on his calendar."

Jeff reached across and squeezed her arm in quiet support, but Brad didn't let go of her hand.

He wanted to tell her the truth.

That Alec wasn't cold because he didn't care—he was distant because he did. Because he'd asked Brad to step into the shadows and protect her in ways he couldn't.

But now, watching the hurt flicker in her eyes, Brad realised that silence might be the very thing pushing her further from the brother who had meant the world to her.

He shifted slightly, turning to face her more fully. His thumb brushed gently along the back of her hand.

"Scarlett…" His voice was low, careful. "Have you ever really sat down and told Alec how you feel?"

She blinked at him, surprised by the question. "What do you mean?"

"I mean," Brad said, steady and sincere, "have you looked him in the eye and said, *'You're shutting me out. You've changed. And it hurts'*? Not hinted. Not tried to guess what he's thinking. Told him the truth. The whole truth."

She looked away for a moment, lips pressing together. "No," she admitted quietly. "Not really. I guess I've been… waiting. Hoping he'd just come back to me on his own."

Brad nodded, his gaze unwavering. "I get that. But maybe he doesn't realise how far he's drifted. Or maybe he thinks he's doing the right thing by keeping his distance. People convince themselves of all kinds of crap when they think it's protecting someone."

Scarlett looked back at him, studying his face—maybe wondering if he was speaking from experience. He was.

Brad gave her hand a gentle squeeze. "When you get back, sit him down. No distractions. No soft landings. Make him listen. Make him understand exactly what he's risking by shutting you out."

She swallowed hard, her throat working. "And if he won't listen?"

Brad's voice softened, but his eyes didn't waver. "Then you've done everything you can. And if he still doesn't want to be the brother you need…" He paused. "Then you stop carrying that guilt. That weight. That's on him—not you."

Silence fell between them, but it wasn't heavy this time. It felt like clarity.

Scarlett leaned into Brad's shoulder, her voice barely above a whisper. "You really believe that?"

"I do," he said. "And you deserve more than unanswered calls and polite detachment. You deserve the brother who used to fight for you."

She nodded slowly, her cheek against his arm.

Brad didn't push. He just stayed there, holding her hand, letting the strength of his presence do what words sometimes couldn't.

Letting her know she wasn't alone.

From across the table, Jeff raised an eyebrow and took a slow sip of his cappuccino. "Well, damn," he said with a smirk. "Didn't know we had a philosopher in our midst."

Scarlett let out a soft, surprised laugh, wiping the corner of her eye with the pad of her finger. "Right? Who knew the hunk came with built-in wisdom."

Brad chuckled, rubbing the back of his neck. "I have my moments."

Jeff leaned back in his chair, clearly enjoying himself. "No, seriously—if this whole private security empire thing ever gets boring, you should write self-help books. 'Protecting the Heart: Emotional Security in a Dangerous World.' I'd buy five."

Scarlett laughed again, more freely this time, her fingers still curled in Brad's.

Brad looked over at Jeff with a wry grin. "You laugh, but I could put your quote on the back cover."

"Oh, please do," Jeff said, raising his glass. "As long as there's an acknowledgements page. And maybe a dedication."

Scarlett shook her head, her smile lingering as she looked between them.

The days slipped past like silk through fingers—sun-drenched, salt-kissed, and impossibly full. Five whole days in Santorini, each more golden than the last. Mornings began with coffee on the terrace, the Aegean stretching endlessly below, and ended with wine, laughter, and the soft rustle of linen sheets tangled around warm bodies and whispered promises neither of them dared speak aloud.

They had walked narrow stone alleys lined with blooming bougainvillea and postcard-worthy rooftops, fingers brushing. They'd talked for hours under shaded tavern awnings, about everything and nothing. They'd laughed until they cried over Jeff's dramatic takes on Greek mythology and questionable hat choices. And they'd danced—God help Brad—they had danced.

Santorini glowed beneath a watercolour sky, the sun slipping behind the caldera in a blaze of molten orange and rose. The air was warm, laced with sea salt and the faint rhythm of bouzouki music drifting up from the tavern below. Lanterns swayed overhead, casting flickers of gold across the terrace where locals danced and tourists sipped their wine, cheeks flushed pink from sun and drink.

Scarlett spun barefoot across the stone floor, her laughter light and unrestrained. Her linen dress fluttered around her knees, her hair undone, tumbling over her shoulders in a way that made Brad forget how to breathe.

"You're terrible at this," she giggled, trying to pull him back toward the makeshift dance circle.

"I told you I don't dance," he said, half-laughing, letting her tug him forward like he didn't even have a choice.

"And yet here you are," she teased, swaying closer. "Trying."

He was. For her, he was trying everything. Even this.

They moved awkwardly at first—his steps unsure, her timing off because she was too busy laughing. But then something shifted. Maybe it was the rhythm. Maybe the wine. Or maybe it was simply the way Scarlett looked at him—unguarded, radiant, like the weight of the world had fallen away for just one night.

By the time the music slowed, their hands had found each other more naturally. Her palm rested against his chest; his arm curled protectively around her waist. Their feet moved less. Their eyes did the talking.

The final notes faded into the warm buzz of applause. Scarlett leaned back slightly, smiling up at him. Her skin was warm. Her lips flushed. And her eyes—God, her eyes—sparkled with mischief and something softer beneath it.

"You're not so bad," she said, voice teasing but thick with emotion.

Brad's hand slipped to the small of her back, anchoring her there. "And you're beautiful," he murmured.

She tilted her head, lowering her voice. "Still think that?"

His answer never made it to his lips.

Because in the next breath, she leaned in—slowly, deliberately—and kissed him.

The kind of kiss that silenced the world. The kind that lingered long after the music stopped.

And the memory of it clung to him, even as morning broke.

Chapter Twenty-Two

The soft hush of the sea drifted in from the open terrace doors, mingling with the gentle rustle of the curtains. The sheets were still tangled around them, warm with the echoes of the morning's closeness, but reality was waiting—uninvited and persistent.

She had to leave today.

Her flight back to New York was scheduled for late afternoon. A driver would take her down the cliffside roads to the port, where a private transfer waited to ferry her to the airport on the mainland. From there, it was a long-haul journey home—private jet, terminals, sleek town cars.

Back to reality.

It had all been planned weeks ago, neat, and uncomplicated.

Brad held her closer without thinking, his hand splayed across her bare back as if he could memorise the feel of her—her warmth, her softness, the way she seemed to fit perfectly against him.

He didn't want to let her go.

Not just because of how she felt in his arms. Not just because the silence with her was more comforting than words had ever been with anyone else. But because there was still a truth he hadn't told her.

The one that mattered most.

She knew the outlines of who he was—his security firm, his military career, the scars that didn't always show. She knew about his childhood too. The system. The string of foster homes. The way he'd learned to survive without needing anyone.

But there was more.

One truth still sat lodged in his chest like a stone.

The real reason he'd met her.

Alec.

Her brother had reached out weeks ago—offered to hire him, to keep an eye on Scarlett while she travelled. Not because she was in danger. Just… because. Because

Alec didn't trust easily. Because he wanted someone watching over his little sister from a distance, even if she didn't know it.

Brad wasn't taking the money.

But he had taken the assignment. And if it hadn't been for Alec's request… he never would've crossed paths with Scarlett Hale.

That was the part she didn't know.

The part she deserved to.

And she would know. He'd make sure of it.

Just… not now. Not like this. Not as she packed her bags and prepared to walk out the door. He needed to talk to Alec first. He needed to be honest—with both of them.

Scarlett stirred against him, murmuring something soft and unintelligible, her fingers brushing lightly over his ribs before settling again.

She had no idea how much she'd shifted his world.

But time was slipping through his fingers like the tide outside their window—and the truth was coming, whether he was ready or not.

If Scarlett found out before he told her… it wouldn't just end this. It would destroy what they'd barely begun.

She was a blend of in. And she didn't even know she was risking her heart on a man who hadn't told her the whole story.

She also didn't know how deeply he felt for her.

Not just desire. Not just the quiet companionship they'd fallen into so effortlessly.

But something more.

Something real.

And she needed to know that too. Not in a rush of words at the airport. Not in a panicked goodbye.

But when the timing was right.

When he could look her in the eyes and tell her everything.

Because whatever this was between them… it wasn't over.

Not by a long shot.

Scarlett stood on the villa's terrace, the morning sun brushing her skin with golden warmth. Below, the Aegean sparkled like liquid glass, and the breeze carried the faint scent of citrus and salt. Inside, she could hear the distant rush of water—Brad in the shower, steam fogging the bathroom mirror.

Jeff wandered out with two coffees, handing her one without a word before sinking into the cushioned lounge chair beside her.

For a while, they sat in companionable silence, sipping and watching the world wake up around them.

Then Jeff glanced over, one brow arched. "So," he said, drawing the word out like it was a conversation starter and a warning all at once. "Has he asked to see you when you get back?"

Scarlett didn't look at him right away. She stared at the sea instead, a small crease forming between her brows.

"No," she said finally, her voice soft.

Jeff didn't say anything for a beat, just sipped his coffee.

"Do you want him to?"

Scarlett let out a breath, almost a laugh—but not quite. "Yeah. I do."

Jeff gave her a knowing side-eye. "And yet you're pretending you don't."

"I'm not pretending anything," she said, a little defensively. "I'm just not… pushing it."

He raised an eyebrow. "So, you're playing it cool."

She shook her head. "I just don't want him to feel obligated. If he wants to see me, he knows where I am. He has my number, my address, my everything. If this meant something to him, he'll reach out."

"And if he doesn't?"

Scarlett's smile wavered. "Then I have some wonderful memories. That's more than most people get."

Jeff leaned over and bumped her shoulder gently. "You're braver than you think, you know that?"

Scarlett glanced at him, her voice barely above a whisper. "I don't feel brave. I feel… careful."

She paused, then added quietly, "I'm not chasing anyone. If he wants me in his life, he'll find a way."

He made her feel safe. Known. But part of her wondered if he realised just how much of herself, she'd already handed over.

But sometimes when Brad went quiet—too quiet—she felt something shift. Like he was holding a piece of himself just out of reach. And maybe she was a fool for trusting it would come out when it mattered.

Jeff smiled—soft, sincere, touched with a trace of protectiveness. "And if he doesn't, he's an idiot."

Scarlett laughed under her breath, the sound small and bittersweet, like something tucked between hope and resignation.

Silence settled for a moment, comfortable and fragile.

"There is one thing I have to do when I get back," she said, her eyes still on the horizon.

Jeff turned his head. "What's that?"

"Brad helped me see that it's time I finally confront my brother. Really talk to him. No more sidestepping. No more pretending everything's fine." She paused, drawing in a breath. "I need to know if Alec still wants me in his life—as a sister, or just… as a spectator."

Jeff's gaze softened. "That's been a long time coming, Scarlett. I'm glad Brad helped you see that."

"Me too," she murmured. "I need my brother back."

The sun had begun its lazy descent behind the caldera, casting Santorini in a golden haze that made everything feel too beautiful to leave. Warm light spilled across the courtyard of Villa Eleonas, painting long shadows over the cobbled stones and whitewashed walls. The car waited just outside the gate, engine quietly humming, the luggage already packed.

Scarlett stood beside Jeff, both of them ready to leave—back to New York, back to reality. Brad was staying one more night. The villa was still theirs until morning, and she had insisted he keep it.

"You might as well enjoy the view one more night," she'd said with a smile that didn't quite reach her eyes. "Besides… I like knowing someone will be here for one last sunset."

Now the time had come. Brad stood with his hands in his pockets, his frame still and quiet as the weight of goodbye pressed in.

Jeff turned to him first, extending a hand with a grin that tried to lift the mood. "It was good to meet you," he said. "You're not so broody anymore."

Brad chuckled and shook his hand, gripping it firmly. "Thanks. It was good to meet you too."

Jeff pulled him into a brief hug—the kind men shared when something real had been built. Then he turned to Scarlett. "I'll be in the car," he said, giving her space with a soft squeeze to her arm.

Scarlett turned to Brad, the breeze catching the hem of her dress and the ends of her hair. Her carry-on was slung over one shoulder, sunglasses pushed to the top of her head, her eyes bare and clear.

"You've changed me," Brad said, his voice low and rough.

She blinked at him, her heart tugging. "In good ways, I hope."

"Better than good."

She stepped closer, lifting her hand to his chest, resting it there like she could feel everything he wasn't saying. "I'm not asking you for anything, Brad," she said softly. "I'm not expecting… anything. But I hope you know—if you want to find me again, you can."

He nodded, his throat tight. "I will."

Scarlett leaned in, brushing her lips over his—slow, lingering, a quiet imprint she knew would stay with her long after the flight home. He kissed her like a man holding on to a secret—one he knew might cost him everything.

And still, he didn't say it.

When she stepped back, her hand lingered on his chest for one last second.

"Bye," she whispered.

"Bye," he murmured.

She turned without another word and walked toward the car where Jeff waited, her steps steady but reluctant.

Brad didn't move until the car pulled away, the tyres crunching on the gravel, the sight of her disappearing beyond the gate. Only then did he let out the breath he'd been holding, his hands still hanging loosely at his sides like they didn't know what to do without her.

The courtyard was silent now, the air thick with everything left unspoken.

He had one night left on the island.

And then a confession he had to make to two very important people.

Chapter Twenty-Three

The elevator doors opened with a soft chime on the top floor of Hale Enterprises, and Scarlett stepped out into the sleek, marble-floored reception of her brother's penthouse office. Floor-to-ceiling windows flooded the space with late afternoon light, casting a golden glow across the minimalist furniture and glass walls. The skyline of Manhattan stretched beyond the windows—sharp, glittering, imposing.

Alec Hale's secretary looked up from her desk and offered a warm smile. "Miss Hale. He's expecting you. You can go right through."

Scarlett returned the smile with a polite nod, smoothing her palms down the front of her coat as she crossed the expansive office foyer. Her heels clicked softly against the polished floor, echoing in the hush that seemed to wrap around the space.

She paused at the double doors, then pushed them open without knocking.

Alec stood near the windows, phone to his ear, suit jacket draped over the back of a nearby chair. As she stepped in, he glanced her way and held up a finger—one second. Then he wrapped up the call quickly, his voice crisp and controlled.

"Make it happen. I want numbers by Friday."

He ended the call, set the phone on his desk, and turned toward her with a smile that was equal parts surprise and warmth.

"Look who finally decided to visit," he said, crossing the room. "Back from the Greek Isles, no less."

Scarlett smiled faintly as he leaned down and kissed her cheek.

"You look rested," he said, stepping back to study her. "Tanned. Like someone who drank too much wine and made at least one questionable purchase."

Scarlett let out a short laugh. "That's... not inaccurate."

He gestured for her to sit, but she stayed standing.

"Holiday was good?" he asked, tone casual. "Jeff survived?"

She nodded. "It was incredible."

Alec gave her a small, amused look. "That's good to hear. You needed the break."

Scarlett hesitated, then drew a breath and met his eyes.

"But that's not why I'm here."

Alec's brows lifted slightly. "No?"

She shook her head slowly. "I need to talk to you, Alec. Really talk."

Something in her tone made the room still. Alec stepped back slightly, tension flickering at the edge of his expression.

"All right," he said carefully. "Then let's talk."

Scarlett stood by the edge of her brother's office, the city sprawling behind her like a painting she couldn't feel. Alec sat on the arm of one of the leather chairs, arms crossed loosely, but his gaze was sharp—focused entirely on her.

She took a breath, steadying herself. "When Mum and Dad died… I feel like I lost you with them."

Alec's mouth opened, the beginnings of protest on his lips.

"Scarlett—"

"No," she cut in gently but firmly. "You need to hear this."

He fell silent.

"You buried yourself in work," she said, voice low but clear. "And at first, I understood. We all grieve differently. But it's been years, Alec. And the truth is— I don't feel like you want me in your life anymore. I feel like I'm just… this obligation. An inconvenience."

"That's not true," he said quickly, eyes narrowing.

"Isn't it?" she asked, her tone sharpened by the ache in her chest. "Have you ever even met Jeff?"

Alec blinked. "No, but I know about him."

Scarlett nodded once, the tiniest, bitter smile tugging at her lips. "Jeff is the most important person in my life besides you. He's been there through everything. He knows all my flaws, all my fears—and he loves me anyway. And you don't even know what he looks like."

Alec's jaw tightened. He shifted, straightening his posture. "I've kept tabs. I make sure you're safe. You have everything you need."

"I don't need things, Alec," she said softly. "I needed my brother."

Silence fell between them, thick and uncomfortable. Outside, the late sunlight bled orange across the glass, turning the office gold. Scarlett crossed her arms, holding herself together.

"I'm not saying this to hurt you," she added after a moment. "I'm saying it because I miss you. And I'm tired of pretending that what we have now is okay."

Alec looked at her then, really looked at her—and for once, the CEO mask slipped just a little.

"I didn't realise you felt that way," Alec said quietly, his voice stripped of the usual polish, the practiced composure.

Scarlett held his gaze, steady and unwavering. "I know you didn't. That's why I'm here."

There was a beat of silence. Then Alec exhaled, long and slow, and rubbed a hand across the back of his neck.

"Look, Scarlett... when Mum and Dad died, I felt like I had to hold everything together. Keep it all the same so you'd feel safe. Secure." His voice faltered slightly. "And somewhere along the way, that just... consumed me."

Scarlett's expression softened, but her voice didn't waver. "The reason I went on this holiday... was because I woke up one morning and realised, I'm changing into something I don't want to be."

She paused, her throat tight, then added with a bittersweet smile, "You know people call me the ice queen now."

Alec frowned. "That's ridiculous."

"Is it?" she asked quietly. "Have you ever looked at the photos of me from those charity balls and galas? I do look like an ice queen. Cold. Controlled. Untouchable."

Her voice cracked just slightly at the edges, but she pushed on.

"I can't go on like that. I don't want to live a life that looks perfect and feels empty. I want to be the girl who danced barefoot in the grass. The girl who laughed more than she cried."

Alec stared at her, eyes dark with something that looked like guilt—or maybe grief.

Scarlett swallowed hard. "I want to be her again. But I can't do it without letting go of some of what's broken between us. I need my brother back. Not just in title, but in truth."

The room felt still, the weight of her words settling like dust on old memories.

For a long moment, Alec said nothing.

Then—very softly—he nodded.

"I get it. And I'm sorry," he said, his voice rough with emotion he rarely let show. "You're the most important person in my life, Scarlett. I love you. But I see what you're saying… I've been holding on so tight to what I thought I was supposed to be, I didn't see what you actually needed."

He looked at her then—really looked. "I didn't mean to shut you out. I just… I didn't know how to let myself grieve without falling apart. So, I buried it. All of it. Including you."

Scarlett blinked, fighting the burn in her eyes.

"I don't want to be distant anymore," Alec continued. "I don't want to be the guy who only shows up for speeches and photo ops. I want to know your life. Your people. I want to know Jeff. I want to be your brother again."

Scarlett took a step forward, her voice trembling. "That's all I've wanted."

Alec opened his arms, hesitant but genuine. "Then let's stop pretending we're fine. Let's actually fix this."

She didn't hesitate.

She crossed the room and hugged him—tight, unguarded, like the years of distance could be erased if they both held on long enough.

And for the first time in a long time, they both believed maybe it could.

Alec pulled back slightly, his hands still resting on her shoulders. "How about we have lunch tomorrow?" he asked gently. "I'll clear my schedule. You and I can really talk about your holiday."

Scarlett nodded, the smallest smile tugging at the corners of her mouth. "I'd like that."

"And on Saturday night…" he paused, almost tentative, "if Jeff is free, I'd like to meet him."

A single tear slipped down her cheek—not from sadness, but relief.

"Yes," she whispered, her voice catching. "He'd like that too."

Alec reached up and brushed the tear away. "Good. It's time I start showing up— for both of us."

Chapter Twenty-Four

It was just after 11 a.m. when Brad was called in.

He adjusted the cuffs of his shirt, his fingers brushing briefly over the envelope in his jacket pocket—the cheque. Still untouched.

He hadn't come here for money. He hadn't come to finish a job.

He was here to come clean.

To take responsibility.

To ask for a second chance—not from Alec Hale, the billionaire CEO, but from Alec, the man who used to call him a friend.

And maybe—if life was kind—from Scarlett.

This morning, he'd woken with a jolt, drenched in sweat. In the dream, Scarlett had looked at him with betrayal carved into every line of her face.

"You lied to me."

Over and over.

A voice he loved turning into something he feared.

It still echoed in his chest.

The office door opened. Alec was already standing.

He stepped forward and extended his hand, his grip firm, unreadable.

"Brad. Good to see you. My sister's home safe and sound. Thanks to you."

Brad shook his hand, but there was no satisfaction in it. Just a low hum of nerves beneath his skin. "I need to talk to you. About Scarlett."

Alec nodded, gesturing to the chair across from his desk. "Sit."

"I'd prefer to stand." Brad reached into his jacket and pulled out the envelope. "Here's the full amount you transferred for the job."

Alec took it, frowning. "What's this?" He glanced inside, then looked up, confused. "Brad, you did the job. Why are you giving this back?"

"Because I didn't do the job the way you intended," Brad said. His voice was steady, but the tension in his shoulders gave him away. "Somewhere along the line, it stopped being about surveillance or protection. I fell for her, Alec."

Alec's jaw tightened, the weight of the confession settling slowly before fully hitting. He blinked once, then twice, the shift in his expression subtle—but unmistakable.

"You what?"

Brad didn't flinch. "I fell in love with Scarlett."

The room seemed to freeze, silence crackling in the space between them like a wire pulled too tight.

Alec slowly placed the cheque on his desk, his fingers lingering on the envelope as if it might anchor him. Then his hands dropped to his sides.

His voice was low—measured, but laced with fury barely held in check, his breath sharp through his nose.

"Please tell me you didn't sleep with my sister."

Brad didn't flinch. He held Alec's gaze, even as his stomach turned.

"I did."

The words landed like a crack of thunder in the room—loud even though they were spoken quietly. Final. Irrevocable.

Alec's jaw clenched, his breath catching for half a second before he turned away, pacing once toward the window like he couldn't stand still. His hands curled into fists at his sides.

"When?" he asked tightly, his back still turned.

"After we got to know each other. After it was real. And before you say it—no, I didn't plan any of it. I didn't go looking for it. But I'm not going to lie to you, Alec. I love her."

Alec turned, fury in his eyes now, voice razor-sharp.

"Don't you dare talk to me about love. You were supposed to protect her, not touch her. You were the one person I trusted with her—and you slept with her."

Brad took a step forward, his own voice tight with emotion. "I know I crossed a line. But I didn't use her. I didn't manipulate her. What happened between us—every second of it—was real."

Alec's laugh was hollow. "Real? You mean the part where you were lying to her every single day?"

Brad didn't respond. Because there was no defence. Just truth. And fallout.

Alec took a slow step forward, his voice sharp and cold now, honed like a blade.

"She doesn't know, does she?"

Brad's silence said everything.

Alec's nostrils flared. "You were paid to protect her. You were hired to be there. And you let her believe it was a coincidence. You let her fall for you while you kept the one truth that mattered buried."

Brad swallowed hard, his jaw tense. "I was going to tell her—"

"When?" Alec snapped. "After you proposed? After you moved into her apartment? After she found out on her own?"

He stepped closer, eyes burning.

"She trusted you, Brad. I trusted you. And you let her believe it all just… happened. That you were just some guy in the right place at the right time."

Brad's voice was quieter now, steadier despite the tension crawling through his chest. "It stopped being a job the second I got to know her. I turned the money down. I gave it back. I would never have touched her if I didn't—"

"But you did touch her," Alec cut in, ice laced through every word. "And you never told her why you were there. You think that cheque makes it right?"

He leaned in, voice low and seething.

Just then, the intercom buzzed.

"Mr. Hale, your sister is here for your lunch meeting."

Alec's eyes never left Brad's. A slow, sharp-edged smile curled at the corner of his mouth—one that didn't reach his eyes.

"Perfect timing," he murmured. "Let's see how Scarlett feels about your confession, shall we?"

Before Brad could speak, Alec pressed the intercom.

"Send her in."

"Alec, wait—" Brad started, but the office doors were already opening.

Scarlett stepped inside, her expression instantly lighting up when she saw Brad.

"Brad!" Her smile widened. "What are you doing here?"

She crossed the room and reached for his hands without hesitation, leaning in to kiss his cheek. The warmth in her touch made something twist painfully in his chest.

But before he could answer, Alec's voice cut through the reunion—hard, cold, and deliberate.

"Scarlett, allow me to introduce you properly… to the man I paid to watch you."

The words hit like gunfire.

Scarlett froze.

Her smile vanished.

She stepped back slowly, her eyes snapping to Alec, then to Brad, confusion giving way to dawning horror.

"…What?" she whispered.

Her hands fell away from Brad's as if she'd been burned.

She shook her head slightly. "What is he talking about?"

Brad took a step toward her. "Scarlett—I can explain."

But her expression was already crumbling.

And Brad knew—this wasn't the moment he'd wanted.

It was the one he'd feared.

Scarlett's gaze snapped to her brother, fury igniting behind her eyes.

"You paid someone to watch me?" she demanded, her voice sharp with disbelief.

"Are you serious?"

Alec stood his ground, arms folded tight across his chest.

"I was worried about you," he said, his voice clipped. "You were travelling with someone I didn't know."

Scarlett's eyes flared.

"That's on you," she snapped. "You never bothered to meet my best friend. You didn't ask. You didn't care. You didn't trust me."

She shook her head, her voice cracking.

"That's what this was. You didn't think I could handle my own life."

Alec's mouth tightened, but he didn't argue. Couldn't.

Scarlett turned to Brad then—slowly, cautiously, like even looking at him took effort now.

Scarlett blinked, like the floor had shifted beneath her. The air felt thinner, harder to pull into her lungs. When she finally spoke, her voice was raw—barely more than a whisper.

"Was any of it real?"

The question didn't need volume to devastate. It landed like a quiet blow to the chest—soft, sure, and shattering.

Brad's throat worked. He stepped toward her instinctively.

But she took a step back.

Still holding his gaze, still waiting for an answer.

"Yes," he said quietly, fiercely. "All of it was."

And she didn't say a word. Not yet.

She just stood there—still, trembling—her heartbreak painted in silence.

Then, softer, more broken:

"Is your name even Brad Jenkins?"

He hesitated for half a second. Just long enough to hurt.

"No," he said. "It's Brad Allen."

Tears welled in Scarlett's eyes, blurring the two men standing before her—one her brother, the other the man who had just broken something inside her she hadn't even known was fragile. She blinked fast, brushed them away quickly with the back of her hand, like she could erase what she felt just as easily.

"Scarlett, you don't—" Brad started, his voice thick with regret.

She cut him off sharply. "No. I don't want to hear excuses."

Her words were quiet but sharp enough to draw blood.

She turned toward Alec then, her expression a mixture of disbelief and wounded fury.

"Did you announce this to hurt me? Or to make me look like a fool?"

Alec's confident exterior faltered. He shifted on his feet, jaw tightening.

"Neither," he said, more carefully now. "But you needed to know."

Scarlett let out a shaky breath, like the moment itself was pressing down on her ribs, squeezing the air from her lungs.

"I can't believe this," she whispered, voice raw and trembling.

Then—louder, sharper, cutting through the silence like glass—

"I can't believe either of you."

Her eyes, still wet, swept over both men—her brother, who had betrayed her trust in the name of protection, and Brad, who had betrayed her heart in the name of silence.

And then she turned.

No more words. No more tears.

She walked out, heels echoing against marble, head held high even as her world cracked underneath her.

The door clicked shut behind her.

And for the first time in a long, long time, neither man had anything to say.

Chapter Twenty-Five

Brad collapsed into the nearest chair, elbows on his knees, head in his hands. His heart was still pounding, his mind a blur of her voice— *'Was any of it real?'*—playing on a loop.

Across the room, Alec slammed his palm against the desk with a sharp crack. "Damn it," he hissed. "Just when I was starting to get her back."

Brad looked up slowly, jaw clenched, eyes dark with fury—and something deeper. Shame. Grief. Devastation.

"This is your fault."

Alec turned, eyebrows raised. "My fault?" he snapped. "You're the one who lied to her."

"I didn't tell her, and that's on me. But I didn't go in there with an agenda," Brad shot back. "You built the whole damn lie."

"I hired someone to protect her," Alec said coldly. "Not seduce her."

Brad stood, his whole frame tight with emotion. "I didn't plan that! I didn't expect to feel anything for her. But I did. And I would've told her the truth. I came here to do that—until you ambushed her with it like a damn power play."

Alec's nostrils flared, his voice like ice. "She deserved to hear it."

"She deserved to hear it from me," Brad bit out.

Silence fell between them—thick, bitter, and heavy with everything that had just gone wrong.

Brad dragged a hand down his face, his eyes flicking toward the door Scarlett had just walked through, as if willing her to come back.

"She'll never look at me the same way again," he said quietly, voice thick with regret.

Alec didn't argue.

Because they both knew it might be true.

Brad turned to him, the anger giving way to something raw. "Do you feel good now? You always have to be in control—was this worth it?"

Alec's jaw flexed. "No," he said tightly. "I don't feel damn good."

Brad stepped forward, voice taut with everything he was trying not to yell. "I encouraged her to talk to you. I wanted her to have that with you again. Because I actually care about her. This wasn't a job. It wasn't a game."

Alec scoffed, but Brad didn't stop.

"I never thought I'd fall in love. Hell, I didn't even believe in it. Thought it was just something that happened to other people."

He paused, swallowing hard.

"But I fell. Hard. And I know you think I crossed a line—maybe I did. But I swear to you, Alec —I love her."

Alec stared at him, silent for a long beat, his expression unreadable.

And for the first time since everything had exploded, neither of them was just angry anymore.

They were both something worse.

Helpless.

Alec's voice, when it finally came, was quieter. Searching.

"You really do," he said. Not a question. Just quiet disbelief.

Brad met his gaze without hesitation. "Yes. I damn well do. I want to marry her."

Alec exhaled, the anger finally bleeding into something more desperate. "We need to fix this."

Brad let out a bitter breath, his hands spreading in disbelief. "How? You saw her. She looked at me like I was a stranger—like I was the lie."

Alec dragged a hand through his hair, pacing a few steps before turning back. "She's hurt, Brad. But she's not made of stone. You should know that better than anyone. If what you had was real—"

"It was real," Brad cut in, his voice fierce, aching.

"Then don't give up now," Alec said. "You want to marry her? Fight for her. Show her that the lie didn't undo the truth."

Brad stared at him, jaw tight. "I don't even know where to start."

Alec looked him dead in the eye. "Start with the truth. All of it. No more holding back."

Brad swallowed hard. "And if she never forgives me?"

Alec's voice dropped. "Then at least she'll know you meant it."

Silence stretched, thick with tension and hope and everything that had just broken.

But underneath it… something still intact.

The chance to make it right.

Or at least try.

Scarlett slid into the back seat of the waiting limousine, the door clicking shut behind her with a soft finality. The moment the partition rose between her and the driver, her composure crumbled.

She hadn't even told the driver where to go. She couldn't. Not yet.

She pressed a trembling hand to her mouth, trying to hold it in, but the pressure was too much. The betrayal, the humiliation, the heartbreak—it all surged at once.

The first sob broke free, quiet, and sharp. Then another. And then the floodgates opened.

Tears streamed down her cheeks as she curled into herself, her designer coat bunched in her lap, makeup smudging with every swipe of her fingers. Her chest ached, her breath coming in shallow bursts, like her lungs had forgotten how to work properly.

Was any of it real?

The memory of her own voice echoed in her head, small and cracked, and Brad's answer—*yes, all of it was*—haunted her more than if he'd said nothing at all.

Because she had wanted to believe it. Still wanted to.

And that hurt more than anything.

She leaned her head back against the seat, eyes squeezed shut, silent now but not calm. Her heart felt like it had shattered in the quietest, most brutal way.

She had trusted him.

She had trusted both of them.

And they had both kept the truth from her.

The city passed by in a blur outside the tinted glass, but Scarlett didn't look. She just sat there, lost in the storm of what she thought she knew, and what she could no longer believe.

By the time the car turned down Fifth Avenue, her face was streaked with tears, her hands limp in her lap.

But her eyes—though swollen—had begun to harden.

Because beneath all the pain… something else was stirring.

Resolve.

The apartment was quiet, dimly lit by the soft glow of a single floor lamp near the window. Scarlett sat curled on the couch, knees tucked beneath her, a blanket draped around her shoulders. Her eyes were red, her expression distant—numb.

The elevator dinged just past 6:00 p.m.

Scarlett startled slightly, then stood, smoothing her hands down her arms as if she could erase the remnants of the day. Her heart knew before her ears confirmed it— Jeff.

The door opened, and there he was, still in his work clothes, his bag slung over one shoulder. His eyes found hers instantly, taking in her swollen eyes, the set of her jaw, the heaviness she couldn't hide.

He dropped his bag without a word.

Opened his arms.

And she went.

No hesitation. No words. Just the thud of her steps across the floor, then the solid comfort of his arms closing around her. She buried her face in his shoulder, the sob she'd been holding in all evening catching in her throat.

Jeff held her tighter, one hand cradling the back of her head, the other wrapped firmly around her back.

"I've got you," he whispered. "I've always got you."

Scarlett didn't reply. She didn't need to.

Because for the first time that day, she felt safe enough to break.

Jeff pulled back just enough to look at her, his hands still resting on her arms, steadying her.

"What the hell were they thinking?" he said, voice sharp with protective fury. "Your brother hires a guy to spy on you, and that guy—he falls for you? Do they not realise how messed up that is?"

Scarlett let out a brittle laugh, more pain than humour. She shook her head.

"They weren't thinking," she said hollowly. "It was a blend of a lie. Brad wasn't just there—he was paid to be there. To watch me. Like some mission."

Jeff's jaw clenched. "Unbelievable."

Scarlett's voice cracked as she added, "And I let myself believe it was real."

Jeff wrapped his arms around her again, pulling her back into his chest.

"Hey," he murmured, "you felt something real. That's not on you, Scar. That's on them."

Scarlett's voice trembled as she stepped back, just enough to meet Jeff's eyes.

"I was being strong… thinking that it was real on both sides," she said, barely holding it together. "Thinking that he'd want to be part of my life. That maybe, for once, something good would stay."

Her lips quivered, and she blinked rapidly, trying to hold back the tears that had already claimed most of her day.

"But now I know it's over." Her voice cracked on the last word. "And that hurts more than anything. Because I fell in love with him, Jeff. I didn't mean to—I fought it—but I did. Completely."

Jeff's heart broke for her. He gently pulled her close again, holding her like he could absorb some of the pain.

"I know you did," he whispered. "And he was a damn fool to break something so real."

Scarlett closed her eyes, breathing in shaky gasps, letting herself be held. Letting herself fall apart just a little more—because here, with Jeff, it was safe to do so.

Scarlett's voice was barely a whisper against Jeff's shoulder.

"I feel like a fool."

Jeff pulled back just enough to look at her, his hands still resting on her arms, steady and grounding.

"Hey," he said gently but firmly. "You're not a fool. You're someone who believed in something good. You opened your heart. That doesn't make you weak, Scarlett—it makes you brave."

She shook her head, eyes rimmed red. "I should've known. I should've seen it coming."

"No," Jeff said, his voice rising slightly with emotion. "You shouldn't have to live your life waiting for the rug to be pulled out from under you. Loving someone shouldn't come with suspicion as a condition. You trusted him because he earned it. He's the one who broke that trust. Not you."

Scarlett let out a shaky breath, and a tear slipped down her cheek.

"I just... I don't know how to come back from this."

Jeff gently tucked a strand of hair behind her ear. "You don't have to come back all at once. You just have to take the next step. And when you're ready... we'll figure out the rest. Together."

Chapter Twenty-Six

It had been a week since Brad had seen Scarlett.

Seven days of silence. Seven nights of staring at the ceiling, haunted by the look on her face when the truth came out.

He'd called—more times than he could count. Every call went to voicemail.

He'd sent flowers—her favourite kind, handpicked, not just ordered. They were declined at the door.

He'd gone to her apartment, standing in the foyer like a man with nothing left to lose, only to be told by the concierge—firmly, painfully—that he wasn't welcome.

Now, he sat in his office, still wearing the same shirt from the day before, the collar wrinkled, the sleeves pushed up like he couldn't remember rolling them. The lunch someone had left hours ago sat untouched on the table beside him, the coffee cold.

His appetite was gone.

Sleep, a distant memory.

And the only thing louder than the quiet of the room was the ache of missing her.

He'd messed up. He knew it. Maybe beyond repair.

Maybe he didn't deserve forgiveness. But God, he missed her.

Her laugh—sharp, sudden, real.

Her stubborn streak that met his own and matched it without fear.

The way she looked at him like she saw through every scar, every failure—and didn't flinch.

He missed her voice in the morning, rough from sleep and soft with trust.

He missed her hand in his at night, that silent promise that somehow, against the odds, he'd become someone she could lean on.

And worst of all, he missed the way she made him feel like he was becoming someone better.

Someone worth loving.

And now… he wasn't sure if he'd ever get the chance to prove it.

Just then, the intercom buzzed, jarring him from the spiral.

"Mr. Allen, there's a Jeff Bozeman here to see you."

Brad blinked.

Of course. Scarlett's best friend. Her ride-or-die.

He leaned back in his chair with a sigh, jaw tightening.

Great.

Her best friend had come to rip him a new one.

And honestly? He probably deserved it.

"Send him in," Brad said, scrubbing a hand down his face.

A moment later, the door opened, and Jeff walked in, dressed in dark jeans and a crisp button-down, his usual easy confidence dulled by something heavier. He shut the door behind him and just stood there, looking at Brad for a long, silent beat.

Then, finally—

"Good."

Brad frowned. "Good what?"

Jeff dropped his bag on the chair by the door and crossed his arms. "You look like shit."

Brad gave a bitter half-laugh. "Thanks."

Jeff shrugged. "That tells me you actually care."

Brad leaned forward, elbows on his knees again, the weight of the past week settling even heavier. "I do. More than I've ever cared about anything in my damn life."

Jeff studied him a moment longer, then stepped further into the office and dropped into the chair across from Brad.

"Well," he said simply, "let's talk about how you're going to fix it."

Brad blinked. "What… you'll help me?"

Jeff nodded, expression steady. "I love Scarlett. I'd do anything to make her happy. And I'm hoping I'm right in thinking… you could make her happy, too."

Brad swallowed hard. "How is she?"

Jeff's expression softened—sad, knowing. "She hides it from everyone else, but I can see it. She's hurting, Brad. Badly."

Brad dragged a hand through his hair, his voice thick. "God, I never meant to hurt her. I fell for her so fast, I didn't stop to think. I just fell."

He let out a bitter laugh, low and raw. "I kept telling myself I'd find the right moment. That she deserved the truth, and I'd give it to her. But then… I just kept waiting. Hoping I could protect what we had for a little longer."

Jeff studied him in silence, letting the words settle.

"I didn't expect her," Brad went on. "Not like that. Not to matter so much. But the second she started trusting me, looking at me like I was someone she could count on… I was already gone."

He looked up, eyes tired, voice hoarse. "I was stupid. I thought love would fix the lie—but love doesn't erase betrayal. I know that now."

Jeff exhaled and leaned forward, resting his elbows on his knees. "Then the only thing you can do now is prove it wasn't all a lie. Show her that what you feel is real. That it always was."

Brad nodded slowly, like the weight of that truth had finally settled fully on his shoulders. "I'll do whatever it takes."

"Good," Jeff said quietly. "Because if you break her again—I won't just come here to talk next time."

Despite everything, Brad almost smiled. "Fair enough."

Scarlett stood by the floor-to-ceiling windows of her penthouse apartment, the city sprawling beneath her like a glittering sea of lights. The evening sky was fading into deep indigo, the last traces of daylight slipping away.

It had been a week since she had seen her brother. A week of silence stretching out between them, filled with unanswered questions and unspoken pain.

Her phone sat silent on the marble countertop. He'd called a few times, but each time she'd told him she needed space—time to think, to breathe, to figure out what she even wanted anymore.

She reached for her makeup kit and carefully brushed concealer under her eyes, trying to mask the dark circles that had settled there. The reflection staring back at her in the mirror was tired—haunted—but she forced herself to steady her hands.

Every brushstroke was an attempt to reclaim a piece of herself, to present strength when inside she felt anything but.

The elevator dinged, declaring his arrival. Her heart thudded unevenly in her chest.

She smoothed her dress, took a deep breath, and turned toward the door.

Tonight, the silence would finally be broken.

The elevator doors slid open, and he stepped out.

"Hello, Alec," she said softly.

He closed the distance between them, his eyes warm as he reached for her.

"Hi, sis," he whispered, pressing a gentle kiss to her cheek. "How are you?"

"I'm okay."

"I missed you."

"I missed you too."

"I'm sorry. I shouldn't have hired Brad to protect you. I only did it because…, I love you."

She looked into his eyes, her voice soft but steady. "I know. But you need to stop trying to be my father and start being my brother."

Alec's expression shifted—guilt, then something heavier. Regret.

"I will," he said quietly. "I promise."

He ran a hand through his hair, then sighed. "I don't want us to go back to the way we were. You were right about me being distant. Always too busy. Always trying to manage everything from a distance like it made it easier."

Scarlett didn't say anything—just watched him.

"This week… it made me realise how much I miss you," he continued. "Not just as my sister. As the one person I should've been showing up for all along. One I don't want to lose."

Her eyes glistened, but she didn't cry. Not this time.

"I don't want to lose you either," she said. "But if you want to be in my life—really in it—then it has to be as equals. Not as the man who makes decisions for me behind my back."

Alec nodded slowly, the weight of her words sinking in. "Okay. No more secrets. No more control. Just… me being your brother. If you'll have me."

Scarlett stepped forward and wrapped her arms around him. "I'll always have you. But from now on, we face things side by side."

He hugged her back tightly. "Side by side," he murmured. "I can do that."

They stood there for a moment—siblings, finally grounded in honesty—before Alec pulled back just enough to look at her.

"Have you seen Brad?"

Scarlett shook her head. "No. He's tried. Called, sent flowers. Even came by the apartment." Her voice faltered as she looked down. "But I wasn't ready."

Alec nodded, quietly processing that. "What about now?"

Her eyes flicked away, uncertainty clouding her expression. "I don't know, Alec. I don't know if I can trust him. He kept something from me—something huge."

"I get that," he said gently. "I do. But I would trust Brad with my life. I did trust him—with my life, more than once, back in the military. And I trusted him with you. Because I believed he'd keep you safe… He loves you."

Scarlett's lips trembled, but she held firm. "Does he? I mean, really—does he really care about me? Or was I just some mission that got out of hand?"

Alec didn't answer right away. He stepped back, leaned his hip against the edge of the kitchen counter, and folded his arms.

"I've known Brad for fifteen years," he said finally. "I've seen him in combat, in crisis, in some of the worst situations imaginable. And I've never seen him fall apart the way he did when you walked out of my office."

Scarlett blinked, startled by the quiet weight of that confession.

Alec went on. "He looked like a man who lost something he didn't think he'd ever find. And believe me, Brad doesn't fake emotion. If he said he loves you… he meant it."

Her breath hitched, but she didn't speak. Not yet.

So, Alec took one last step forward. "You don't have to forgive him tonight. Or tomorrow. But don't shut the door forever just because it hurts now. He didn't come into your life by accident, Scarlett. And I don't think you fell for him by accident, either."

Chapter Twenty-Seven

The golden glow of the chandelier cast soft light across the elegant penthouse. The sounds of distant music and city traffic filtered in through the balcony doors, but inside, everything was still.

Scarlett stood in front of the full-length mirror, adjusting the delicate diamond clasp at the back of her neck. The strapless red gown hugged her curves like it had been made for her—sparkling under the light, dramatic and unforgettable. Her dark auburn hair was swept into a sleek chignon, a few soft tendrils framing her cheekbones. The diamond necklace and matching earrings caught the light with every small movement.

Jeff leaned against the doorframe behind her, watching her silently for a moment— his expression somewhere between admiration and pride.

"You look absolutely gorgeous," he said finally, voice warm with sincerity.

Scarlett gave a soft smile, her fingers pausing at her earring. "Thanks, Jeff. But you're biased."

He walked toward her, fixing the edge of her wrap gently across her shoulders. "I mean, yes," he said with a playful grin, "I'm completely biased—but I'm also right."

She let out a quiet laugh, eyes meeting his in the mirror. "This feels… surreal. Like I'm wearing someone else's life for the night."

Jeff's smile faded just slightly, his tone more serious. "It's your life, Scar. You've earned every second of it. Every diamond, every spotlight, every compliment."

She turned to face him, something soft and vulnerable in her expression. "Even after everything?"

"Especially after everything," he said without hesitation. "You didn't let it break you. You're still standing—stronger than you've ever been."

Scarlett blinked, a sheen of emotion rising in her eyes. She didn't speak for a moment, just nodded, gathering herself.

Jeff held out his arm. "Shall we, birthday girl?"

She took it, squeezing his hand gently. "Let's go."

And together, they walked out into the night—her chin a little higher, her steps a little steadier, the sparkle of her dress catching the light like embers refusing to burn out.

The grand chandelier overhead shimmered like a thousand tiny stars, casting warm golden light over the polished floors and glittering gowns. The room was alive with soft music and the low murmur of conversation, laughter, and clinking glasses.

Brad stood near the base of the sweeping staircase, straightening the cuffs of his crisp white shirt beneath the jet-black tuxedo. His jaw was tight, his hands fidgeting in a way that betrayed nerves he rarely let show. Next to him, Alec stood tall in his own tux, a glass of champagne untouched in his hand.

Alec glanced sideways at him. "Don't stuff this up, Brad."

Brad shot him a look. "Thanks for the pep talk."

Alec didn't smile. His eyes were serious. "I mean it. This is her birthday. Her night. If you're going to say something, make sure it's the truth. And make damn sure it's not too late."

Brad exhaled slowly, scanning the room as though he might spot her among the crowd. "Do you think she'll even talk to me?"

"I don't know," Alec admitted. "But I'm hoping so."

Brad turned to look at him, surprised at the softness in his voice.

Alec's gaze drifted to the ballroom entrance. "I just want her to smile again."

Brad nodded, swallowing hard. "So do I."

They both turned their attention to the stairs as the music shifted—something soft, elegant. A hush fell over the nearby guests. And then—

There she was.

Scarlett, on Jeff's arm.

Descending the stairs like royalty—poised, untouchable, breathtaking. The strapless red gown clung to her like liquid fire, shimmering with every graceful step. Her dark auburn hair was swept into a flawless chignon, diamond earrings sparkling like frost beneath the chandeliers.

Brad's breath caught.

But it wasn't the gown or the diamonds that stole his voice.

It was the absence of her smile.

That radiant, unguarded light he'd seen when she laughed freely, when she looked at him like maybe—just maybe—she was falling.

Gone.

In its place was the mask. Polished, perfect. The ice queen persona she wore when the world became too cruel to touch her.

And he'd put it there.

Alec leaned in. "That's your cue."

Brad barely heard him. His pulse thundered in his ears. Because just then, Scarlett looked up—

And for the briefest, breathless moment… their eyes met.

And he felt the full weight of what he'd broken.

Scarlett paused halfway down the grand staircase, her fingers tightening on Jeff's arm as if the luxury around her had turned suddenly hollow. The soft hum of music, the quiet clink of crystal, the polite murmur of the crowd—all of it faded as her eyes locked onto one person.

Brad.

He stood beside Alec, striking in a tailored black tuxedo, but it wasn't the sharp suit that held her still. It was his gaze—anchored to her, unmoving, like she was the only person in the room who mattered.

Her breath caught.

Jeff felt her hesitate and leaned in just enough to keep it between them.

"What is he doing here?" she whispered, her voice barely more than a breath.

Jeff followed her line of sight, then returned his calm gaze to her.

"I invited him," he said quietly.

Scarlett's head snapped toward him, her expression betrayed and disbelieving.

"Why would you do that?"

Jeff didn't back down. He turned to face her fully, his voice steady as he gently took both of her gloved hands in his.

"Because you love him. And he loves you."

Her eyes glistened. She shook her head, a flicker of protest forming.

"How do you know?"

Jeff gave her a soft, knowing smile.

"Because I've seen the way he looks at you when you're not watching. Like you hung the stars. I've heard the guilt in his voice when he talks about you. The way it guts him."

He squeezed her hands gently.

"And if I didn't believe—truly believe—that he cares for you more than anything, I would've kept him out of this building myself. But I know he does. And I think… so do you."

Scarlett blinked rapidly, the shimmer in her eyes threatening to spill. Her gaze returned to Brad—still standing there, still watching, still waiting like she was the answer to every question he'd ever had.

Her grip on Jeff's hands tightened.

"I don't know if I can trust him again."

Jeff nodded. "Then don't. Not yet. But maybe… give him the chance to earn it back."

She was quiet for a beat, breath trembling in her throat. Then, so softly it almost wasn't meant to be heard—

"He broke something in me."

Jeff didn't speak at first. He just brushed his thumb over her knuckles with quiet reverence.

"Maybe he did," he murmured. "But I've also seen what he built in you. How you lit up when he was around. If anyone has the strength to rebuild what's broken… it's you."

Scarlett held his gaze, searching, uncertain. Then she turned her eyes back to Brad across the ballroom.

Her heart was hammering. Her knees didn't quite feel steady. But something shifted.

Resolve, maybe. Or the ghost of hope.

And slowly—one breath, one decision—she took a step down.

Then another.

Brad held his breath.

She'd stopped halfway down the staircase—frozen in place, her hand clutching Jeff's arm, her elegant red gown catching the light like fire.

He couldn't hear their words from where he stood, but he could feel the weight of them. The intensity in her eyes, the disbelief, the hurt. And for a terrible, aching second, he thought she might turn around and walk away.

His pulse pounded.

He didn't know if she'd come to him. Couldn't expect her to. But God, he hoped.

He prayed.

If she gave him even the smallest chance—if she forgave him, even a little—he would spend the rest of his life proving he deserved it. Proving she'd never have to question him again.

He didn't blink. He didn't breathe.

And then—

She moved.

One step. Then another.

The breath he'd been holding left his lungs in a shaky rush.

Hope—real, trembling, impossible hope—unfurled in his chest like dawn breaking over a long, dark night.

His eyes didn't leave her. Not for a second.

She was still coming toward him.

And for the first time in ten days, Brad let himself believe—

Maybe all wasn't lost.

Maybe… just maybe… it was the beginning of something new.

Scarlett stopped in front of him.

Her eyes met his—clear, searching, unreadable. But she didn't turn away.

Brad's voice was low, reverent. "You look breathtaking."

Her expression didn't shift, but something flickered in her gaze. Something that made his heart stumble.

Behind them, the music changed—soft, slow, unmistakably the start of the first dance. A spotlight swept the edge of the dance floor, waiting.

Brad swallowed hard.

This was it.

He bent his arm and held it out to her, a quiet offering. Not assuming. Not expecting. Just hoping.

He wouldn't blame her if she turned away.

But then—

Her gloved hand slipped gently from Jeff's arm.

And found Brad's.

Warm. Light. Trembling slightly against his.

Brad looked down at where her fingers rested on his forearm, then up into her face, barely able to believe it.

She didn't smile. But she didn't let go.

And that alone nearly undid him.

In silence, they stepped forward together onto the dance floor, the crowd parting like a tide.

And as he placed one careful hand at the small of her back, the other guiding her hand to his chest, Brad realised—

This wasn't forgiveness. Not yet.

But it was a beginning.

And that… was everything.

A quiet sigh nearly escaped her lips.

It felt too good—dangerously good—to be back in his arms.

His touch was gentle, tentative, like he was afraid to push too far, too fast. But his hand at her waist fit like it had always belonged there, and the warmth of his body drew hers in before she could stop it.

The music swelled softly around them, but all she could hear was the steady thrum of her heart—racing, confused, alive.

She didn't know what this meant yet.

Didn't know if she could trust him again.

But for this moment…

Being held by him felt like home.

And God help her—

She'd missed it.

Chapter Twenty-Eight

They danced in silence, the world falling away with each slow turn.

At first, Scarlett moved stiffly—her spine straight, her hand resting lightly in Brad's as though uncertain whether to stay. But with every breath, every measured step, the wall between them began to crack.

Brad felt it. The subtle shift in her body. The softening of her shoulders. The way her fingers curled just slightly against his. Bit by bit, she let herself lean in.

And he didn't push. Didn't speak.

He simply held her with a tenderness he hadn't dared to imagine days ago, his hand at the small of her back steady and warm. Like an anchor. Like home.

Her cheek brushed his shoulder, just barely, and he pulled her in—closer this time.

She came willingly.

Their faces were so close now, the scent of her perfume wrapping around him, familiar and intoxicating. The music swelled softly, but it was her breath he listened to. The way it caught. The way it eased.

Brad lowered his head, his lips just near her ear.

"Happy birthday, sweetheart," he whispered, his voice rough with emotion.

Scarlett didn't answer right away. But her fingers tightened against his chest, and for a moment—just a moment—she closed her eyes.

And that was enough.

It wasn't forgiveness.

But it was a beginning.

The final notes of the waltz drifted through the air like a sigh, and the ballroom erupted into polite applause. Around them, couples began to part, laughter rising and glasses clinking as the celebration resumed.

But for Brad, the world narrowed to the woman in his arms.

He didn't want to let go.

His hand lingered at her waist, his other still cradling hers, until the moment could stretch no longer. Slowly, reluctantly, he stepped back.

"Can we talk, Scarlett?" he asked quietly, his voice rough around the edges. "Please."

For a heartbeat, she said nothing—just looked up at him, her expression unreadable beneath the shimmer of chandelier light. Then she gave a small, almost imperceptible nod.

Brad exhaled, something like relief breaking through the fear.

"Come with me," he said gently.

He placed his hand just beneath her elbow—not possessive, just a guide—and led her through the crowd. Heads turned. A few whispers stirred. But no one stopped them.

They stepped through the tall French doors onto the terrace beyond the ballroom. The city stretched before them in a sea of lights, skyscrapers glittering against the inky sky. A soft breeze lifted a strand of hair from her temple.

Just as Alec and Jeff had promised, the terrace was empty. Reserved. Private.

Jeff's words echoed in Brad's mind: 'Then it's all up to you.'

Brad turned to face her, the noise of the party muffled behind the glass doors.

No more audience. No more pretence.

Just them.

And finally, the truth.

She looked at him calmly, her expression unreadable but open. She didn't speak—just stood still, steady, waiting.

Ready to listen.

Brad's heart thudded, the weight of the moment pressing down on his chest. But her silence wasn't rejection—it was permission. So, he stepped closer and gently took both of her hands in his.

His thumbs brushed over the backs of her gloves, grounding him.

"The first thing you need to know is…" he began, his voice low, rough with emotion, "yes—every second was real."

He saw her eyes flicker, but she didn't look away.

"I love you, Scarlett," he said, barely above a whisper. "More than I ever thought possible. More than I knew I could love anyone."

The words hung between them, raw and trembling.

"And if I could go back and do it differently—tell you the truth from the start—I would. In a heartbeat. But I didn't. I messed it up. And I'll live with that for the rest of my life."

His grip on her hands tightened slightly, not in desperation, but in quiet sincerity.

"But what we had… what I felt… what I still feel—it was never part of the mission. It wasn't strategy or convenience or some job gone wrong. It was you. It was always you."

Her breath hitched—just slightly—but she didn't pull away.

So, he kept going.

"I know I broke something in you. I hate myself for that. But if there's even a small piece of you that still believes in us… I'll spend the rest of my life proving I'm worthy of it."

He paused, searching her eyes.

"Just say the word, and I'll fight like hell to earn your trust back. No more lies. No more hiding."

A silence stretched between them.

He didn't beg.

He didn't plead.

He just waited—hope flickering like the city lights behind them—holding on to the only truth that mattered.

He loved her.

And he always would.

Scarlett's voice was steady, but quiet. Heavy with emotion she hadn't let herself feel until now.

"The day I saw you in my brother's office..." she began, eyes fixed on his, "I was so happy to see you."

Brad didn't move, didn't breathe.

"I wasn't sure why you were there," she continued. "But for a moment, I let myself believe it was because you wanted a life with me."

"I do," Brad said, instantly—his voice fierce, certain. "I do want a life with you, more than anything."

She nodded slowly, the hint of a tremble in her chin. "Then Alec told me the truth. Why we met. Why you were in Rome."

She looked down for the first time, her hands tightening in his.

"And I felt... betrayed. Used. Like none of it had been mine."

Brad opened his mouth, but she shook her head gently. "Let me finish."

He nodded, silent again.

She took a breath, steadying herself. "Then I started thinking about it. About you. About everything."

Her eyes rose to meet his again, sharp and searching. "You're a professional, Brad. You know what you're doing. You're trained. Controlled. You don't make mistakes like that."

A pause. A heartbeat.

"So, I thought... why? Why did he bump into me at the market? Why strike up a conversation? Why smile like it was real?"

Brad's chest rose and fell, barely containing what threatened to spill out.

Scarlett's voice softened, almost a whisper. "Because if it was just a job, you would've stayed in the background. Watched from a distance. You wouldn't have made it personal."

Her hands were still in his, but her eyes... her eyes were asking the only question that mattered now.

"Was it ever just the job?"

Brad leaned in, his voice raw, reverent. "No. It stopped being just the job the second you looked at me like I wasn't invisible. The second you laughed at that stupid tomato joke comment."

A soft, broken smile tugged at her lips.

"I didn't expect you, Scarlett. I didn't expect to feel anything. But I fell—and I never stopped falling."

Tears shimmered in her eyes, but she held them back.

Because this—right now—was the truth she'd been waiting for.

And finally, she was hearing it.

Brad's voice dropped, thick with emotion. "I watched you for two days, Scarlett… and I just couldn't stay away."

He lifted one of her hands, brushing his thumb over her knuckles.

"I had to talk to you. Not because you're the most beautiful woman I've ever laid eyes on—though you are," he added, with a faint, wistful smile. "It was more than that."

She stayed quiet, her gaze locked on his, her breath shallow.

"It was your strength," he said, his voice rough. "Your grace. The way you moved through the world like it couldn't touch you, but I could see underneath… that it already had."

He swallowed hard.

"You shine, Scarlett. Even when you don't mean to. Even when you try not to. That first day at the market—I saw the way you smiled at the woman selling flowers. The way you helped the little kid who fell over. And I realised… that tough persona you show the world? That's your armour. But underneath it…"

He shook his head slowly, reverently.

"There's so much heart."

Scarlett's lips parted slightly, her throat working.

"I saw the press photos. You looked like every other bored, untouchable heiress. I figured you were cold. Distant."

He paused, letting out a breath.

"But I couldn't have been more wrong."

Her eyes shimmered again, but this time, she didn't look away.

"The second you looked at me like I mattered—I knew. I wasn't working anymore. I was already yours."

He reached up, gently brushing the back of his fingers along her cheek—soft, reverent, like she was something precious he was afraid to break.

"I saw you, Scarlett," he said, his voice barely above a whisper. "And I've never stopped seeing you. Because I love you. I will always love you."

Chapter Twenty-Nine

Her eyes filled, but this time she didn't blink the tears away.

"I love you too," she whispered, the words raw and honest, pulled straight from her heart.

Brad's breath caught. For a moment, he couldn't speak. Couldn't move. He hadn't dared to hope he'd hear those words from her.

But he didn't assume—he couldn't. Not after everything.

So, he asked, quietly, carefully, "Will you ever forgive me?"

Scarlett reached up and laid her hand gently over his heart. Her thumb moved in slow, soothing circles through the fine fabric of his jacket.

"I already have," she said softly.

And just like that… the weight he'd been carrying for days—weeks—lifted.

Not completely.

But enough to breathe again.

Enough to believe again.

Enough to begin.

Brad bent his head and kissed her—softly, reverently. Like a man who knew exactly what he almost lost.

Scarlett kissed him back without hesitation, her hand curling into his lapel, holding him close.

When he pulled away, his forehead rested lightly against hers for a breath before he reached into his pocket.

"I bought you something," he said, his voice low and a little rough.

He opened his hand and nestled in his palm was a ring—an emerald-cut diamond, large and luminous, set in a sleek band of platinum. It caught the terrace light and shimmered like it held every unspoken promise between them.

Scarlett's breath hitched.

"I know you might not be ready to wear this on your left hand," Brad said quietly. "But it's yours. For when you are. For if you ever are."

His gaze locked with hers.

"No pressure. No timeline. Just… my heart. In your hands."

Scarlett gave him a watery smile, her eyes still glistening from the emotions of the moment.

"You think you're going to get away with not getting down on one knee?" she teased, her voice soft but steady.

Brad's breath caught—then his eyes lit with sudden, unmistakable hope.

Without hesitation, he dropped to one knee on the terrace floor, the lights from the city casting a golden glow around them.

He held the ring out properly this time, reverently, like it was an extension of his very soul.

"Scarlett," he said, voice thick with emotion, "you are my heart. My soul. My beginning and my home."

He drew a deep breath, steadying himself, even though he already knew his life would rise or fall on the next words.

"Would you marry me? And let me love you for the rest of our lives?"

"Yes, Brad," she whispered, tears slipping down her cheeks now, unchecked. "I will. I will love you for the rest of our lives."

Brad let out a shaky breath, overwhelmed with a joy so fierce it nearly dropped him again.

He stood slowly, reverently, and took her left hand in his, sliding the ring onto her finger with a tenderness that made her heart ache in the best possible way.

Then he leaned in and kissed her—soft, slow, full of everything they had survived and everything they still had left to build.

And this time, Scarlett kissed him back without hesitation. Without fear.

"Well, thank the Lord," Jeff said, leaning casually in the doorway to the terrace, arms folded and grinning like he'd known all along. "You two finally came to your senses."

Scarlett let out a breathy laugh, wiping at her cheeks. "Were you listening the whole time?"

Jeff shrugged. "Not the whole time. Just the important part—like the part where you said yes."

Brad chuckled, slipping his arm around Scarlett's waist as she leaned into him.

Alec stepped out behind Jeff, his smile warm and a little wry. "Scarlett, I can see why you like this guy," he said, nodding toward Jeff. "He's annoyingly right most of the time."

Jeff shot him a smug look. "Told you I was good for more than wardrobe critiques and snide commentary."

Scarlett laughed again, the sound lighter than it had been in weeks. "You're both impossible."

Brad glanced between Jeff and Alec, then looked down at her, his voice quiet but full of gratitude. "I'm glad he believed in me… even when I didn't."

She tilted her head, her smile tender as her fingers curled around his. "You're lucky. You have no idea how close he came to banning you from the building."

Brad smirked, eyes soft. "Remind me to send him something expensive."

Jeff called out from behind them, deadpan, "I accept cars. And beachfront property."

"Come on, you two," Alec said, his voice warm with pride. "It's time to celebrate my little sister's birthday… and her engagement to my best friend."

Scarlett let out a soft laugh, cheeks flushed, her hand still tucked in Brad's.

Jeff grinned and nudged Brad as they followed Alec. "No pressure or anything."

Brad just shook his head, smiling like a man who couldn't believe his luck.

Together, they stepped back into the golden light of the ballroom—where music played, glasses clinked, and the night still shimmered with possibility.

Brad stayed by Scarlett's side all night, his hand never far from hers, his presence a steady comfort in the swirl of celebration. The ballroom glowed with golden light and laughter, filled with the hum of music, champagne flutes clinking, and the soft rustle of silk and satin.

But for Brad, the rest of the world had faded to background noise.

Because she was in his arms.

When the music slowed, he guided her onto the dance floor again, pulling her close. Scarlett moved into him without hesitation, her head resting lightly against his shoulder, her fingers splayed over his heart, steady beneath her palm.

Brad closed his eyes for a moment, breathing her in—jasmine and something softer, something distinctly her.

He'd nearly lost her.

And yet, here she was. With him. Loving him.

He pressed a kiss to her temple, his voice a quiet whisper meant for no one but her. "I still can't believe you're mine."

Scarlett smiled, her voice muffled against his tuxedo. "That makes two of us."

Brad's arms tightened around her. He didn't need a spotlight, a toast, or a stage. He didn't need the applause or the congratulations.

All he needed was this.

Her—dancing with him, choosing him.

And as they moved together, slow, and sure beneath the chandelier's golden glow, gratitude swelled in his chest like a tide. For her forgiveness. For her strength. For her love.

Later that night, the city lights twinkled far below as the elevator doors slid open to Scarlett's penthouse. The hush of the late hour wrapped around them like a warm cocoon, the noise of the party left behind, replaced by the quiet rhythm of home.

Scarlett stepped inside first, the soft click of her heels on the marble floor echoing in the stillness. She paused just inside the foyer, then let out a sigh of relief as she slipped off her shoes.

"That's better," she murmured, flexing her toes and dropping the heels by the wall.

Before she could take another step, Brad was there—moving behind her with a quiet, mischievous energy. His arms slid around her waist, and before she could protest—he scooped her up.

"Brad!" she laughed, startled, her arms flying around his neck.

"I've been wanting to do this all night," he said, grinning as he carried her across the room like she weighed nothing.

He made his way to the couch, still holding her close, and then sat down with her cradled in his lap. His hands didn't leave her—one at her waist, the other brushing a stray tendril of hair from her face.

Scarlett settled against him, her fingers tracing absent circles on the lapel of his jacket. Her laughter faded into a soft, contented hum.

"I thought I was the reckless one," she teased, her voice husky with affection.

Brad's eyes sparkled as he leaned in, his forehead resting lightly against hers. "Turns out recklessness is contagious. Especially when love i's involved."

She smiled, nestling closer, her bare feet curling against the couch cushions.

And for a long moment, they simply sat there—wrapped in each other, the night quiet around them, the world paused—exactly where they wanted to be.

"I remember you, you know," Scarlett murmured, her fingers idly tracing the buttons of Brad's shirt as she curled against him.

Brad glanced down, curiosity flickering in his eyes. "What do you mean?"

She leaned back just enough to meet his gaze, a slow, knowing smile tugging at her lips. "I didn't realise it at first… not when you showed up in Rome. But the day I saw you with my brother—it all came back." Her eyes gleamed with mischief. "Soldier boy."

Brad blinked, caught off guard. Then a low laugh rumbled from his chest. "You're kidding."

Scarlett's grin widened, delight playing across her features. "Nope. The Hamptons. My parents' estate. You were barely out of uniform and trying to blend in like a proper gentleman."

A beat passed. Then Brad let out a groan of recognition. "You followed me around all weekend asking about sniper positions and covert tactics."

"And you kept dodging the questions like you were under interrogation," she teased. "I remember dancing barefoot in the garden, and you watching from the shadows like I was a puzzle you couldn't quite solve."

"You were sipping lemonade like you belonged in a Tennessee Williams play," he said, grinning. "And yeah, I was watching. You were impossible to ignore."

"You were so serious back then," she said softly, her fingers brushing his jaw.

"And you were too charming for your own good," he murmured, pulling her a little closer. "Even then."

She rested her forehead against his. "Maybe we were always supposed to find our way back."

Brad's voice dropped, tender and certain. "This time, I'm never letting you go."

Epilogue

Three Months Later...

Alec watched Brad pace across the plush carpet of the church's side room, arms folded and jaw tight.

"You're going to wear a hole in the floor if you keep that up," Alec said dryly.

Brad shot him a look. "What time is it?"

Alec glanced at his watch. "Five minutes later than the last time you asked."

Brad huffed and ran a hand through his hair, tension radiating off him in waves.

Alec leaned casually against the doorway, amused. "Why did you agree to wait three months if you were going to spend every day acting like a man on the edge?"

"You insisted on waiting," Brad reminded him. "Said your sister deserved more than a rushed wedding."

"She does." Alec shrugged. "No sister of mine is getting married with some half-assed ceremony. Scarlett deserves the best. Besides…" He smirked. "I wanted more time with her before you stole her away."

Brad stopped pacing, his eyes softening despite himself. "I would've married her the same night I proposed."

Alec chuckled. "Yeah. I know. That's why I made you wait."

Brad didn't argue. He just looked toward the doors, the anticipation sharpening in his chest. In minutes, she'd be walking toward him. His future wrapped in white satin and wildflowers.

Meanwhile, in the bridal suite, Jeff was gently adjusting Scarlett's veil, his fingers careful and practiced.

"You look absolutely gorgeous," he whispered, stepping back to admire her.

Scarlett met his gaze in the mirror, her eyes already shimmering. "Don't you dare," he warned, wagging a finger. "If you cry, I cry. And then your makeup's ruined, and I'll have to murder the makeup artist for failing us all."

Scarlett let out a shaky laugh, brushing at the corner of her eye. "I can't believe this is really happening."

Jeff smiled and squeezed her shoulders. "Believe it, babe. This is your forever."

She nodded slowly, breathing in deep.

And somewhere, down the hall, Brad straightened his tie one last time.

Then the music began.

And nothing else mattered.

Brad stood at the altar, the quiet murmur of hundreds of guests behind him, the soft rustle of silk and lace filling the vaulted air of the chapel. Alec stood tall beside him as best man, expression calm but knowing.

As the first notes of the processional echoed through the space, Alec leaned in and murmured, "No turning back now."

Brad didn't flinch. "I don't want to turn back," he said quietly. "Your sister is the best thing that's ever happened to me."

Alec gave a small nod. "I know."

Then it happened. A collective breath from the crowd—sharp, audible. A quiet, stunned kind of gasp that rippled like a wave through the pews.

Brad glanced at Alec. He wasn't looking at him anymore—his gaze was fixed down the aisle, a proud smile curving his lips.

Brad turned.

And the world simply… stopped.

First came Jeff, striding confidently down the aisle as Scarlett's man of honour, his tux impeccable, his expression full of mischief and affection. But Brad barely saw him.

Because just behind Jeff—

There she was.

Scarlett.

Her dark auburn hair was swept back in soft, romantic waves, a few tendrils framing her radiant face. She wore a gown that looked like it had been made from moonlight—soft, flowing layers of silk and lace that shimmered as she walked. The bodice hugged her gently, detailed with delicate embroidery that glinted with each step she took. The veil floated behind her like a whisper of wind, anchored by a jewelled comb at the crown of her head.

Her eyes found his instantly—bright, brimming, and locked on him like there was no one else in the room. Her smile was soft, real, glowing with a joy that hit Brad straight in the chest.

She was breathtaking.

And she was his.

Brad felt his heart swell, his lungs tighten—his feet somehow both grounded and weightless. He'd never known he could love someone this much. Never known he could need someone like this.

And as Scarlett walked slowly, gracefully toward him, everything else faded—the guests, the music, the months they'd waited.

All that existed was this moment.

She was a vision. But it was her face—her eyes—that undid him.

He'd never seen anything more radiant.

Alec said something—probably a joke—but Brad didn't hear it.

He only saw her.

His future.

And forever, waiting just a heartbeat away.

The ceremony was intimate, heartfelt. Every word laced with meaning. Every vow, a promise spoken with trembling certainty.

Brad couldn't take his eyes off her. Not for a second.

Scarlett's hands trembled slightly as she slid the ring onto his finger, her voice steady but thick with emotion.

And when she said, "I do," something inside Brad settled.

Anchored.

Like the world had finally clicked into place.

He'd thought nothing could match the moment she walked down the aisle.

He'd been wrong.

Because standing across from her now, hearing her call him her husband-to-be, seeing her eyes glisten with unshed tears…

That was everything.

The priest gave a warm smile as he closed the book in his hands. "By the power vested in me… I now pronounce you husband and wife."

Brad didn't wait.

The words were barely spoken before he pulled Scarlett into his arms and kissed her—deep and sure and full of every moment they'd shared, every obstacle they'd overcome, every ounce of love he hadn't known how to carry until her.

The guests erupted into applause, but neither of them heard it.

It was just them.

Heart to heart.

Home.

When he finally pulled back, her smile was brighter than sunlight, her fingers still curled against his chest like she never wanted to let go.

"You didn't give him time to finish the sentence," Scarlett whispered, eyes dancing.

"I wasn't waiting another second," Brad murmured back. "You're mine now."

"Always," she said softly.

And hand in hand, they turned toward forever.

The door clicked shut behind them with a soft finality, muffling the distant echo of laughter and clinking glasses from the grand ballroom below. The bridal suite at The Plaza was breathtaking—timeless elegance with sweeping views of the city glittering beyond floor-to-ceiling windows. But Scarlett barely noticed.

Because Brad was carrying her across the threshold, his arms strong around her, his tux jacket long gone, his shirt slightly wrinkled from hours of holding her close.

She laughed softly; her head tucked beneath his chin. "You really didn't have to carry me."

Brad's voice was low, rough with affection. "I've waited three months to do this. You think I'm skipping the classic?"

He paused just past the doorway, then looked down at her. "You good?"

Scarlett nodded. "Better than good."

He kissed her forehead, slow and sweet, before gently setting her down. Her heels clicked on the polished floor as she took a breath, turning in a slow circle to take in the room—gold accents, a fireplace already lit, and a bottle of champagne on ice by the bed.

She looked back at him. "They pulled out all the stops."

"They were supposed to," he said, stepping closer. "It's not every day the most incredible woman I've ever met becomes my wife."

Scarlett smiled, a little shy despite everything. "I'm still not used to hearing you say that."

"My wife?" Brad whispered, pulling her gently into his arms. "Get used to it. I'm not planning on calling you anything else."

They stood there for a long moment, wrapped in silence and the golden hush of the suite. Her hands settled against his chest, her fingers tracing the steady beat of his heart beneath the white dress shirt.

Brad touched her cheek, brushing a lock of hair away. "You know... all night, people kept coming up to me saying how lucky I am."

Scarlett tilted her head. "Are you?"

He leaned in, lips brushing hers. "I'm the luckiest man alive."

Her breath caught as he deepened the kiss—slow, unhurried. Everything they hadn't said during the chaos of the day poured into that moment: reverence, relief, devotion.

When they finally pulled apart, Scarlett's eyes glistened, not with tears—but with something deeper.

Peace. Joy. Home.

She let her forehead rest against his. "I still can't believe this is real."

Brad exhaled, his thumb stroking her hip. "It's real. It's you and me. And no one's taking this from us."

She nodded, her voice barely above a whisper. "Promise me we won't forget tonight."

Brad pulled her closer. "I promise. But just in case…"

He reached into the inner pocket of his suit vest and pulled out a small Polaroid photo—the two of them taken by Jeff just before their first dance, laughing like no one else existed.

Scarlett stared at it, her hand covering her mouth. "You kept that?"

"Every second with you, I'll keep," he said.

Then, without another word, he scooped her up again, this time carrying her straight toward the oversized bed covered in white linen and rose petals.

And as the lights of the city glittered behind them, Brad and Scarlett disappeared into the quiet of the night—no longer bride and groom, but husband and wife.

And everything ahead of them was just beginning.

The End

Undercover Billionaire

Alison Reid

A complete standalone romance

Previously published individually

Chapter One

Harper Jameson sat at her desk, fingers hovering above the keyboard as the office buzzed quietly around her. The familiar hum of fluorescent lights blended with the rhythmic tapping of computer keys and the occasional hiss from the espresso machine down the hall, a low, droning symphony of routine that had long ago faded into background noise.

It was another ordinary Monday at Veridian Dynamics.

Ordinary—except for the storm that kept tightening inside her chest.

She drew in a slow breath, held it, and exhaled as though she could press the ache out of her body and leave it on the desk beside her. Her gaze returned to the spreadsheet glowing on her monitor—headcount reports, training schedules, PTO balances. Columns and rows, black text in neat little boxes. Nothing about it should have made her stomach knot. Nothing should have made her pulse trip over itself.

But everything had felt different since that night.

A month. Thirty days since her world quietly, brutally, came undone. Thirty mornings she'd woken up and reached for a life that no longer existed, only to feel her fingers close around air.

She had come home early from a client meeting that evening—her arms full of policy updates and draft proposals, her thoughts full of him. She had even swung by his favourite Thai place, the one where the green curry always made him grin, the one he swore could fix any bad day. She'd pictured his smile when he saw it, pictured the way his hand would brush her hip as he leaned in to kiss her.

But there was no fixing what she walked into.

Because when she opened the door of the apartment they had chosen together— painted together, laughed in, made a home out of—she didn't find candles lit or music playing. She didn't find the warmth of someone waiting for her.

She found Billy Bailey—her fiancé of two years—standing shirtless in their living room, smirk curling his lips, while his assistant fumbled with the buttons on her silk blouse. Lipstick smeared. Bra strap slipping. Eyes daring Harper to react, as though she were the intruder, as though she should have expected it all along.

They hadn't even bothered with the bedroom.

In her own home. The place where her sweaters hung beside his pressed shirts, where her favourite mugs sat on the shelf beside his protein powder and unopened cookbooks. A life built piece by piece—reduced to rubble in a single glance.

"Just a mistake," Billy had said. His voice was flat, casual, irritated even. As if he'd forgotten to take out the trash or misplaced a bill. As if her outrage was the true inconvenience.

It wasn't the betrayal that shattered her.

It was the indifference.

The way he stood there, breathing hard, hair rumpled from someone else's hands, and expected her to absorb it. To forgive and forget, the way she always had with the little things he never apologized for. To let this slide, as though it were nothing more than a speed bump on the smooth road of their future.

But this wasn't a bump.

This was a wall.

She hadn't screamed. Hadn't thrown anything, hadn't demanded an explanation. The pain struck like a stone dropped into deep water—sharp, shocking, and then sinking fast, dragging everything with it.

She remembered the calm. Cold, foreign calm. The way her body moved on autopilot, her fingers sliding the diamond ring from her hand, holding it out to him as though she were returning a library book. Her voice was steady, even detached.

"You should go now."

Four words. Final. Unyielding.

Billy blinked, uncomprehending, as though he still had a claim on the moment, a right to her ear, a chance to fix it.

"Harper—"

She turned her back before he could finish.

She didn't cry that night. She didn't cry the next day either. She went to work, answered emails, even led a staff meeting with a smile that felt less like an expression and more like a shield strapped to her face.

The tears came three days later.

In the shower. Alone. Hot water pounding down her skin as her knees gave way, as she crumpled to the floor and wrapped her arms around herself, the sound of her own heartbreak drowned out by the rush of the faucet. For five minutes she let it happen—five minutes of raw, ragged grief of tasting the bitter edge of what she'd lost.

And then she swallowed it down.

She stood up.

And she made herself a promise.

Never again.

Since that day, Harper had buried herself in work. She was the first one in every morning, the last to leave every night. Her inbox gleamed, her deadlines were flawless, her posture was iron. Every smile was measured. Every wall rebuilt brick by deliberate brick.

Because she had learned something brutal, something unforgettable:

When love is misplaced, it doesn't just break you.

It humiliates you.

And no matter how persistent, how magnetic, how devastatingly handsome the next man might be—Harper Jameson was done. She would not fall again.

Not ever.

But now, with Billy still working in the same building—just two floors up in his sleek, glass-walled office where he used to send her winks, lunch orders, and the occasional heart emoji—Harper felt the emotional whiplash wearing her thin, layer by layer.

It wasn't just the awkwardness.

It was the audacity.

He acted as though nothing had happened. Still forwarded policy updates and compliance notes with the same clipped professionalism he'd used before shattering their engagement like a cheap ornament dropped on tile. No apology. No acknowledgment. No flicker of regret. Just bullet points, attachments, and an unnerving ability to behave as though their history had been archived, deleted, and permanently erased from memory.

Worse—he hadn't stopped trying to win her back.

Flowers in glossy wrapping that she left unopened in the break room. Late-night texts glowing on her phone screen, unread, their previews alone enough to sour her stomach. That smug, infuriating smile in the corridor, a silent, self-assured message that whispered, we'll get past this, as though she were the unreasonable one for walking away.

Two weeks after the breakup, he'd cornered her in the underground parking garage. His tie was loosened, his cologne faint but familiar, his tone pitched low and intimate, as if the sound alone could erase what he'd done. He had stepped in close while she fumbled with her keys, his shadow stretching across her car door like an oil stain.

"I miss you," he murmured, eyes soft with the kind of artificial vulnerability she'd once mistaken for sincerity. "It was a moment of weakness, Harper. One mistake. What we have… it's too strong to throw away like this."

One mistake.

Her grip on the door handle tightened until her knuckles turned white. Rage had simmered under her skin, hot and unrelenting, but her voice—when it came—was ice. Controlled. Precise.

"A mistake," she told him, turning to meet his gaze head-on, "is forgetting to sign a document, Billy. What you did was a choice."

He blinked, caught off guard by her clarity, by the absence of the softness he'd always relied on. But still—he persisted.

Persistent in the way only a man could be when he had never truly faced consequences. When he believed charm was currency, and accountability an option.

And every time she passed him in the hallway, saw his name bold in her inbox, or overheard a giggling intern gush about how good he looked in his navy suits, Harper felt the pressure mounting. Quietly. Inwardly. Like water pressing against the walls of a dam.

It was exhausting.

The effort it took to appear unbothered. To sit in meetings and smile with practiced ease. To hold her posture rigid while her past walked freely around the building as though he still owned it—and by extension, a piece of her.

She wasn't heartbroken anymore—that wound had begun to scab, jagged and permanent. But his presence—so close, so smug, so unapologetically there—was its own slow poison. A daily drain. A reminder of everything she had trusted, everything she had lost, and the silent humiliation of being made to feel like she was the one at fault for not forgiving him.

And she was tired.

Tired of pretending she hadn't been hurt.

Tired of pretending she wasn't still angry.

Tired of carrying the weight of his choices while he strutted two floors above, untouched, unbothered, and unrepentant.

Her intercom buzzed, sharp and sudden, slicing through the quiet of her office. Harper jumped, pulse quickening.

"Harper, new employee's here for orientation. Alexander Dawson. He's early," Melanie's voice came through—bright, efficient, with that brisk cheerfulness that always reminded Harper of someone winding a clock.

Harper blinked, dragging herself back into the present. Right. The new systems engineer. She'd skimmed his résumé only once—relocated from London, strong credentials, glowing recommendations. Oddly vague about his prior roles. Something about the vagueness had pricked her HR radar, but she hadn't had the luxury of time to dig deeper.

"I'll be right out, Mel," she answered, her voice even, smooth, professional.

She hung up, smoothed her palms down the front of her navy blouse, and squared her shoulders. Her reflection caught briefly in the darkened monitor: polished hair, neutral lipstick, eyes calm and unreadable. A woman in control.

Professional. Always professional.

Even when her world had cracked open.

Even when the past lingered two floors above, watching.

Clipboard in hand, heels striking a steady rhythm against the polished floor, Harper stepped into the reception area. Her mask was firmly in place—measured smile, level gaze, composed stride. She was ready to greet the new hire.

But Billy got there first.

"Harper," he said, voice smooth, practiced, like a man delivering lines he'd rehearsed in the mirror. He materialized beside her without warning, like a shadow she could never fully outrun.

Her smile didn't falter, but her spine did.

"Yes, Billy?" she replied, tone clipped, eyes already searching past him toward the waiting area. There—by the windows—sat a tall man, dark-haired, absorbed in something on his phone. Him, no doubt. The new engineer. But she couldn't reach him. Not until she peeled off the barnacle clinging stubbornly to her day.

Billy stepped closer. Too close. That subtle violation of space that once might have felt familiar, comforting. Now it made her skin crawl.

Before she could move back, his knuckles brushed her cheek.

A ghost of a touch. Intimate. Invasive.

"When are you going to forgive me?" he murmured, as though forgiveness were inevitable, as though time itself should have smoothed away his betrayal.

Harper's hand rose—measured, firm—and she guided his wrist away, her grip quiet steel.

"Billy," she said, her voice calm but edged with iron. "This is inappropriate. And the answer is never. Stop asking. It's never going to happen."

He blinked, stunned by the finality. As if, for the first time, the reality had truly cut through his arrogance.

"You don't mean that."

She gave him a smile so tight, so clipped, it was the same one she reserved for unreasonable clients demanding the impossible in half the time.

"I have a new employee to induct," she said, already stepping past him.

"They can wait," he countered, moving into her path again, stubborn as stone. "You and I—what we had—that matters more."

Her patience frayed, snapping like overstretched thread. "Not here," she hissed, voice low, sharp as a blade. From the corner of her eye, she caught the receptionist's quick glance before Melanie ducked back to her screen, pretending not to see.

Billy's jaw flexed. His voice hardened. "Where, then? You never answer my calls. You pretend I don't exist. You won't even open the door when I come by."

Her grip tightened on the clipboard, edges biting into her palm. The air between them thickened, heavy and oppressive, like a room with no windows.

"I don't owe you anything," she said through her teeth. "Not answers. Not time. And definitely not forgiveness."

She stepped sideways, brushing past his shoulder—

But his hand shot out, catching her arm. Gentle, yes, but insistent. A restraint.

"Harper, please. Don't throw us away."

Her heart pounded, not with longing but with fury. The sheer nerve of him. Still playing the victim. Still pretending she was the one at fault for refusing to play along.

She looked down at his hand wrapped around her arm, then back up, her stare cold enough to shatter glass.

"No."

One word. Crisp. Icy. Absolute.

She yanked her arm free with a sharp, cutting breath and turned—

Only to find herself inches from the new hire.

Tall. Broad-shouldered. Dark hair. Green eyes that met hers with a steady calm. Observant. Unreadable. And very clearly aware of everything he'd just witnessed.

Perfect. Just perfect.

The last thing Harper needed was to make a terrible first impression—especially not in front of a new hire. Especially not now, with her ex still radiating entitlement in the hallway like a cologne cloud that refused to dissipate.

But the man standing before her didn't look like any IT guy she'd ever met. Not even close.

He was tall—too tall, really—with shoulders that tested the limits of business casual, the kind of frame that made office space feel suddenly smaller. His dark brown hair curled slightly at the ends, just unruly enough to suggest he either didn't bother taming it—or worse, couldn't. The kind of hair that refused to obey, that carried its own stubborn personality. And his jawline… dear God. Why did it have to be that jawline? All hard lines and faint shadow, sculpted like he'd been ripped from a high-end fragrance campaign and dropped into her office purely to test her resolve.

Then he smiled.

God help her, he smiled.

It wasn't a full grin—more suggestion than declaration. Casual. Confident. A little amused. Like he already knew something she didn't. Like he'd caught her staring and was gentleman enough not to point it out.

And something inside her chest flickered. Uninvited. Dangerous. Inconvenient.

She cleared her throat, snapping her professional mask back into place. "Alexander Dawson?"

He tilted his head slightly, posture easy. "Alex, please. And you must be Harper Jameson."

British. Of course he was British. Because clearly, the universe hadn't finished toying with her yet. That smooth, velvety accent could melt the resolve of women with ironclad boundaries—and hers were still patched together with tape and stubbornness.

She forced a polite, neutral expression and extended her hand. "Welcome to Veridian Dynamics."

Their hands met—warm, firm, steady. The kind of handshake HR liked to preach about in orientation slides. Unremarkable in every way… except for the sharp, electric spark that zipped up her arm, hot and undeniable, like static from carpet in winter. Only this didn't feel like static. This felt alive.

She told herself it was nothing. A fluke. Science, not chemistry.

"Thank you," he said, his gaze lingering just a fraction too long. "Excited to be here. I've always wanted to see what Australians are really like outside the travel brochures."

Her brow arched, dry humour sliding easily into her tone. "We bite less than the brochures imply. Most days."

His laugh came low and unhurried—deep enough to reverberate, rich enough to slip beneath defences without bothering to knock.

Harper pulled her hand back like it had singed her skin. Nope. Not this time. Not again.

"Let's get you started," she said crisply, tucking her clipboard under her arm with military precision. "Orientation isn't glamorous, but I promise we only haze new hires on Fridays."

"I'll mark my calendar," he replied, falling into step beside her as though he'd been walking with her for years.

She kept her stride brisk, posture straight, every inch the consummate professional. But awareness prickled at her edges. She was too conscious of him walking next to her—tall, composed, unhurried. A touch too relaxed for someone on his first day. He didn't fidget, didn't posture. He observed. Like he'd done this before. Like he belonged.

She didn't want to notice.

He was an employee. She was HR. There were rules—clear, explicit rules. Her rules. She'd written half of them herself. No office dating. No exceptions.

And after Billy, she wasn't breaking a single one.

Still… her mind betrayed her, cataloguing details she shouldn't care about: the way his shirt sleeves were rolled just high enough to reveal strong, capable forearms. The way his gaze moved through the office—not entitled, not calculating, but curious, open. And the way he didn't push forward to lead. He let her lead. Not because he wasn't capable, but because he recognized it was her domain.

Respect. A rare commodity. And far more dangerous than a smile.

Danger, she thought. Danger dressed in tailored shirts and an accent designed to ruin lives.

She paused at the boardroom door, forcing her hand steady as she pushed it open and gestured him inside. "Here we are. I hope you brought your enthusiasm. There's a whole PowerPoint waiting for you."

He grinned—slow, deliberate, and devastating. This time it was full, the kind of grin that could disarm armies. "Can't wait. I live for HR slides."

Her eyes narrowed, though her lips betrayed her with the smallest twitch. "Careful. That kind of sarcasm earns you extra policies to memorize."

"I'll take my chances," he replied easily, already stepping across the threshold like the room belonged to him.

Harper lingered a beat longer at the doorway, clipboard pressed tight against her ribs. Longer than she should have.

Because no matter how professional she forced herself to appear—no matter how many times she repeated the mantra that she was done with charming smiles and ruinous accents—something deep in her gut warned her that this man wasn't just a storm drifting through.

He was the shift in air pressure before lightning cracked the sky.

And Harper Jameson, despite every rule she had written and every wall she had built, wasn't entirely certain she wanted to stay dry.

Chapter Two

Alex adjusted the stiff collar of his off-the-rack button-down shirt and let his gaze drift over the reception area of Veridian Dynamics' Sydney office. Fluorescent lights. Neutral carpet. A faint hum of printers and polite morning chatter.

It was all so… ordinary.

The company was his. Technically. He owned every inch of this sleek Australian branch—from the ergonomic chairs to the server racks quietly humming on Level Four. But for the next month, no one here would know that.

That was the point.

No title. No privilege. No Dawson name. Just Alex, Systems Engineer—slightly overdressed, suspiciously polished for IT, but officially one of the team.

The bet had started like most foolish decisions in Alexander Dawson's charmed but complicated life: too much whiskey, a roaring fireplace, and Theo Clarke lounging in a leather armchair like the bastard child of Oscar Wilde and the devil himself.

They were halfway through a bottle of GlenDronach, city lights glittering through the towering windows of Alex's Mayfair penthouse. The skyline stretched beyond the glass like a promise he no longer believed in. Alex had been ranting—bitter, raw, tired—about the latest woman who'd walked out of his life, designer heels clicking, disappointment trailing behind her like a shadow.

"Annie said she loved me," he muttered, tossing back the last of his drink. The scotch burned nothing but his temper. "But what she really loved was the jet and the Amalfi sunsets."

Theo grunted knowingly, swirling his own glass as if it contained the universe's secrets. "They all fall in love with your lifestyle, not you," he said, voice lazy but precise, lips curling around the truth like a blade. "Your money. Your name. Your power. Strip all that away… and what are you?"

"Still me, I imagine," Alex scoffed, jaw tightening. "Are you implying I have nothing but money and power to offer a woman?"

"That's exactly what I'm saying. Sure, you're good-looking, but you're self-absorbed. And you aren't really interested in her, are you?"

"I'm not self-absorbed…!" he said, mock outrage in his voice.

Theo laughed. "Oh yes, you are. Name two things you actually learned about Annie."

"She…" Alex hesitated, wracking his memory. "…she liked diamonds."

Theo shook his head, amusement and exasperation mixing in his eyes. "What woman doesn't like diamonds? Something personal, Alex. What colour were her eyes? How old was she?"

Alex blinked, flustered.

Theo leaned forward, eyes gleaming with challenge. "You don't know, do you?"

Alex frowned. "Okay… no. I think her eyes were hazel," he admitted reluctantly.

Theo's grin widened, slow and knowing. "Exactly. You don't want to know those women, Alex. You just want a bauble on your arm when it suits you."

Alex's jaw tightened. "That's not true."

"Be honest with yourself," Theo said, his tone calm but cutting. "It is. Your arrogance and entitlement would turn most women off. But they don't see it—because they're too distracted by your bank account and everything that comes with it."

Alex stared at him, disbelief flaring. "Are you serious? Is that what you really think of me?"

Theo shrugged, unflinching. "I've known you since we were kids, and I love you like a brother. But when it comes to women, you've turned into an arrogant bastard." A smirk tugged at his mouth.

Alex was too stunned to speak—offended, but with a flicker of something else beneath it.

Then Theo leaned back and said casually, "Tell you what. I bet if you didn't have the money, the name, the tailored suits, or the chauffeured cars… you couldn't make a woman fall for you. Not really."

Alex let out a sharp, incredulous laugh. "That's ridiculous. Of course I could."

"Prove it," Theo challenged. "One month. Make a woman fall for you—not your fortune."

"A month?" Alex scoffed, lifting a brow. "What is this, a Jane Austen novel?"

"I'm serious," Theo said, tone lowering, the kind of seriousness that usually ended in spectacular chaos. "No wealth. No reputation. Just you. Could you win a woman's heart then?"

Alex waved it off as drunken nonsense, a passing challenge. But later, in the dark silence of his penthouse—after Theo left and the city quieted to a low electric hum—the words wouldn't leave him. They whispered in the corners of his mind, gnawing at something he didn't want to name.

What if Theo was right?

What if, stripped of polish and privilege, he was nothing special at all? What if beneath the charm and tailored suits, there was nothing worth loving? What if every woman who'd ever smiled at him had really fallen for the Dawson brand—not the man behind it?

By morning, the question had settled in his chest like a weight. And then, somewhere between defiance and doubt, it hardened into a dare.

He picked up the phone before breakfast. "I'm in," he said the moment Theo answered.

A pause. "Pardon?"

"The bet," Alex clarified. "One month. One million pounds to the winner."

Theo's laughter crackled through the line, bright and disbelieving. "You're actually doing it?"

"Watch me," Alex said, his voice low, steady—more conviction than he'd felt in years.

And now, here he was.

Wearing a department-store button-down instead of a bespoke Italian shirt. A company-issued laptop bag slung over one shoulder in place of his usual leather briefcase. His Rolex, tucked away in a drawer back in London, replaced by a modest Seiko. No headlines. No private driver. No tailored suits. No entourage.

Just him.

Alex Dawson, anonymous cog in the very machine he secretly controlled.

It was madness. The kind of reckless stunt that would look ridiculous in hindsight—another chapter in a future memoir titled '*Things I Shouldn't Have Done but Did Anyway*'.

But beneath the layers of wealth and carefully curated charm, past the armour of old-money detachment, lay a truth he could no longer ignore:

He wanted to know.

Could someone love him—truly, wholly, without the billions? Without the penthouse view, the private jet, the boardroom authority?

Could someone fall for just… him?

The thought unsettled him more than he cared to admit.

He rolled his shoulders back, masking the tension, schooling his features into something neutral. Friendly. Approachable. Not the billionaire playboy the tabloids claimed to know.

Just a new hire. Just Alex.

He hadn't expected much. A few awkward conversations in the break room. Maybe a polite brush-off over stale coffee and company memos. He'd pick someone pleasant, play the part, survive the month, and return to London—bet won, ego intact, heart untouched.

What he hadn't expected was *her*.

Harper Jameson.

The name had been tucked into his orientation schedule, sitting innocuously between an HR briefing and a software demo. But nothing—not the crisp precision of her emails, not the professional poise in her profile photo—could have prepared him for the moment she stepped into the room.

She was the answer to a question he hadn't even fully formed yet.

Tall, composed, quietly radiant—Harper moved like someone who didn't just belong in a room, but subtly commanded it. Her long strawberry-blonde hair shimmered under the sterile office lighting like spun copper. Her deep blue eyes scanned the surroundings with sharp, unflinching focus. She wasn't seeking attention.

But God, she had it.

Presence. Real, effortless presence. Unapologetic. Unbothered. She moved like she had nothing to prove and no time for games.

And Alex, for all his careful planning, forgot the script in his head.

Then came the disruption.

"Harper."

A man's voice intruded—casual, on the surface, but weighted with unmistakable entitlement. He materialized beside her like a shadow that refused to fade.

"Yes, Billy," she replied, tone even, polished. Civil—just barely. Her posture remained straight, her smile steady, but her eyes… they were already calculating, searching for an escape. Strategic. Controlled.

Billy.

Even the name sounded smug.

Alex's jaw tightened as Billy stepped closer—too close. The kind of close that ignored boundaries because it assumed they no longer existed.

Then Billy lifted a hand—knuckles drifting toward Harper's cheek in a gesture that, to a stranger, might have seemed intimate.

But not to Alex. Not when he saw Harper's reaction.

She caught his wrist midair.

Not forceful. Not dramatic.

Just final.

Like someone trained to defuse tension without sparking an explosion. She lowered his hand with the ease of a seasoned diplomat and the authority of a woman who had drawn this line before—and expected it to be respected.

Controlled. Poised. Unshaken.

"When are you going to forgive me?" Billy asked softly, a faint curl of wounded pride in his voice, as if the world could not exist without her eventual acquiescence.

Alex watched her carefully—shoulders square, stance steady, voice unwavering.

"Billy, this is inappropriate," she said, tone cool and crisp. "And the answer is never. Just stop. It's never going to happen."

That's when it hit him—just how much strength lived in her silence.

She wasn't theatrical. She didn't need drama to make a point. But God, she *was* powerful.

A slow, unfamiliar burn ignited beneath Alex's ribs—equal parts protectiveness and admiration. She doesn't need rescuing, his mind noted. But he'd step in anyway if she asked. Hell, if she even hinted she wanted it.

Billy blinked, stunned as if the word no were a foreign concept. Like rejection had always been a temporary detour, not an immovable wall.

"You don't mean that," he said, disbelief threading his tone.

Her smile sharpened into angles. Professional. Polished. The kind she probably reserved for arrogant board members and cocky vendors who underestimated her.

"I have a new employee to induct," she said, voice steady, eyes forward.

Alex's ears pricked. Was that her signal? Her escape route? A calculated pivot? Or merely a line drawn to keep the past at bay?

"They can wait," Billy insisted, voice brittle, edging into petulance. "You and I— what we had—that's more important."

Harper's spine straightened, silk shifting against steel.

"Not here," she said, sharper now. Edged. The line between composed and cornered visible in the tightening of her posture.

Instinct pulled Alex forward. His mask as *Systems Engineer Alex Dawson* wavered, cracks forming in the careful performance. Every fibre of him screamed to intervene, to shove Billy back, to erase the tension tightening Harper's eyes.

But he stopped.

He watched.

He measured.

Was this his moment to act? Or hers to command?

Billy pushed anyway. Voice rising, brittle around the edges. "Well, where then? You never answer my calls. You pretend I don't exist. You won't even open the door when I come to your place."

Christ.

Alex's jaw clenched.

The possessiveness in the man's tone. The persistence. The delusion. It crawled under his skin like rot. But Harper—she stood unmoving.

Chin lifted. Shoulders squared. Eyes forward. Unyielding.

"I'm not obligated to give you anything, Billy. Not answers. Not time. Not forgiveness."

And that—*that*—was the most stunning thing Alex had seen in years.

Not her beauty. Not her poise.

It was her refusal to explain herself.

She started to walk past Billy, clipboard gripped tight, eyes fixed ahead. But entitlement had a habit of clinging.

Billy grabbed her arm.

Not aggressively.

But wrong.

The kind of grip that said *mine,* not may I.

He turned her toward him. "Harper, please. Don't throw us away."

Alex's fists curled at his sides, blood humming beneath his skin like distant thunder. A step closer and he wouldn't be Systems Engineer Dawson anymore—he'd be the man dragging Billy out by his tie, making him regret every second of entitlement.

But Harper… Harper didn't flinch.

She stared down at the hand on her arm like it was an object she could examine, dissect, label, and discard. Then she lifted her gaze—slow, deliberate—into Billy's eyes with a cold so precise it didn't need volume to be heard.

"No."

One word. Clean. Final. Irrefutable.

She wrenched her arm free with effortless grace, drew a steady breath, and turned.

Like he no longer existed.

Like he had *never* existed.

And in that moment, Alex didn't care about the bet. Or the million pounds. Or even the meticulous plan he had crafted.

All he could think was, *Christ, she's extraordinary.*

Their eyes met.

His sharp green gaze—steady, unreadable, barely still. Hers—cool, composed, but flickering faintly at the edges, as if something beneath the surface had stirred and refused to settle.

It wasn't a long exchange. Barely a few seconds.

But in that silence, something passed between them.

Awareness. Recognition. Caution.

She was tall—nearly eye level with him in her heels. Elegant, yes, but not in a flashy or curated way. There was nothing forced about her. Every inch of her presence— posture, gaze, the quiet command in the way she stood—felt grounded, deliberate, unshakable.

And then there was that figure… *Focus*, he told himself. Eyes up. Intentions clean.

Then she smiled.

And God help him—it knocked the air right out of his lungs.

"Alexander Dawson?" she asked, voice crisp, calm, efficient.

It wasn't flirtatious. It wasn't cold. It was simply competent. And for some reason, that shook him far more than any sultry greeting ever could.

He managed a practiced smile, the one he usually reserved for heads of state or hostile shareholders. "Alex, please. And you must be Harper Jameson."

She extended her hand.

Warm. Confident. The handshake of someone who knew exactly who she was and had no need to prove it to anyone. No flirtation. No hesitation. Just presence.

He took it.

And a jolt of awareness shot through him like a live current—swift, sharp, undeniably human. Her grip was firm, assured. It should have been a simple handshake.

But somehow, it lingered.

Or maybe he did.

For one heartbeat too long, he held on. Just long enough to memorize the warmth of her skin, the precision of her grasp, the way it grounded him when he hadn't realised he'd been drifting.

Then he let go—casually, or at least as casually as he could hope, just before it could be noticed.

"Welcome to Veridian Dynamics," she said, stepping back into her neutral stance. Every note of her tone, every millimetre of posture, the unruffled way she reclaimed control of the moment—it was flawlessly professional.

He liked the way she said it—like the company belonged to her. Like she *was* Veridian.

Like she was the one he'd need to impress.

And for the first time in a very, very long while, Alexander Dawson wasn't thinking about himself. Not the bet. Not the challenge. Not proving Theo wrong.

He was thinking about her. About the quiet, magnetic power she carried like second skin. About how she moved through the world with a grace that commanded attention without demanding it.

And, uncomfortably, about just how much danger he'd wandered into without even realizing it.

"Thank you," he said, slipping back into charm like a well-worn jacket, though it felt tighter across the chest than it ever had before. "Always wanted to see what Australians are like outside the travel brochures."

Her eyebrow arched—just enough sass to draw a spark of amusement to her otherwise polished expression. "We bite less than the brochures imply. Most days."

He laughed. Genuinely.

And the sound startled him. *When had he last done that?* Not the polite laugh for fundraisers. Not the calculated one for a photo op. This was real. Unplanned. Unfiltered.

She was sharp. Dry. No-nonsense.

And not for a single second was she trying to impress him.

Which intrigued him all the more.

And yet—she didn't smile back.

No flutter. No reaction. She simply turned, smooth and composed, already moving toward the task at hand.

Unfazed. Unmoved. Unimpressed.

"Let's get you started then. Orientation isn't glamorous," she said, leading the way with clipped efficiency, "but I promise we only haze new hires on Fridays."

He followed, falling into step beside her as if it were instinct. "I'll mark my calendar."

As they walked down the corridor, he noticed the subtle ways the other employees responded to her. Nothing overt. No bowing or fawning. But there were glances. Quick nods. Quiet respect. An ease of recognition that ran deeper than hierarchy.

She didn't demand attention.

She earned it.

Not through force, but through the kind of presence that made people straighten a little more when she passed.

She was beautiful, yes. Striking even. But that wasn't what made his pulse skip.

It was the self-possession. The quiet command of her body and mind. The way she carried herself as if she had nothing to prove and no patience for nonsense. She didn't rush to fill the silence between them.

And somehow, that made the silence feel… shared. Comfortable. Even intimate.

Which, inconveniently, meant this little bet had just gotten a hell of a lot more complicated.

Because something had shifted inside him.

Not strategy. Not ego. Not even the thrill of the challenge.

Something real.

And he hadn't even started the game yet.

She reached a sleek glass door and gestured with a smooth sweep of her hand. "Here we are. I hope you brought your enthusiasm. There's a whole PowerPoint waiting for you."

He grinned as he stepped inside. "Can't wait. I live for HR slides."

Her lips twitched—almost, but not quite, a smile. "Careful. That kind of sarcasm earns you extra policies to read."

"I'll take my chances," he said, stepping further into the room, unaware of how quickly the space between them had shrunk in a single, quiet moment.

And as the door clicked shut behind them, the air shifted again.

It wasn't romantic. Not yet.

But it was something.

And for the first time in longer than he cared to admit, Alexander Dawson wondered if maybe—just maybe—this was the kind of risk worth taking.

Chapter Three

Alex Dawson was not accustomed to shared workspaces, fluorescent lighting, or malfunctioning coffee machines.

Yet here he was.

Perched in a beige cubicle amid the chaos of Veridian's open-plan Sydney office—surrounded by the ceaseless clatter of keyboards, the faint but persistent odour of someone's unfortunate tuna lunch, and the rising tension of what sounded like a full-blown printer war in the next row.

Not metaphorically. The man in the adjacent cubicle was loudly narrating his battle with the machine as if it had personally insulted his mother. Every beep, every paper jam, every squeal of misfed toner earned a running commentary.

Alex stared at the screen of his assigned laptop. It blinked at him in judgment, cold and unrelenting.

The email client refused to load. The spreadsheet labelled *"PASSWORD MASTER (USE THIS ONE FINAL).xlsx"* was already locked by another user. And a software suite called SprocketNet—which sounded like something engineered in the Windows XP era—had crashed twice and opened a third time, only to display a 404 error in Comic Sans.

So, *this is purgatory*, he muttered under his breath, attempting yet again to access the onboarding portal. The browser froze. Then spontaneously closed.

A head popped up from the adjacent cubicle like a curious meerkat.

"Hey, you new?"

The man couldn't have been older than twenty-five. His hair defied gravity with the wild confidence of someone who'd clearly never feared humidity, and a neon pink post-it note clung to his forehead like a badge of honour.

Alex blinked. "Yes. Alex Dawson."

"Gavin. Welcome to the pit." The younger man grinned as if surviving the chaos were a badge of pride. "You code?"

"I… dabble," Alex replied diplomatically.

Which wasn't a lie. He had, in fact, once taken a crash course in Python—and used it successfully to program a smart coffee machine that still refused to make anything but espresso.

Gavin laughed like Alex had delivered the punchline of the century. "Don't worry, mate. No one knows what they're doing the first day. Fake it till you make it."

Alex nodded with a touch more solemnity than the moment required. Now that, I can do, he thought wryly, a flicker of amusement tugging at the edges of his composure.

Then, movement caught his eye.

Across the open floor, Harper Jameson strode down the hallway with clipboard in hand, her walk brisk, efficient, and entirely self-possessed. Her hair was tied back now, revealing the clean line of her neck and the way her shoulders squared, carrying an invisible weight with effortless ease.

She wasn't looking his way—too focused on corralling whatever minor chaos this floor had cooked up before noon—but he saw her.

And more importantly, he *watched* her.

There was something magnetic about the way she moved—composed but not cold, fast-paced but never rushed. He had seen powerful women before, women who wore ambition like armour or weaponised charm to get what they wanted.

Harper didn't do either.

She wasn't trying to impress anyone.

And yet… she did.

There was something in that effortless control that held his attention. A woman like her didn't just walk away from a man like Billy Bailey unless she had made a deliberate, final decision. No drama. No flinching. Just clean, quiet certainty.

It lingered in his mind like a fine scotch—sharp, smooth, impossible to forget.

"Earth to Alex," came Gavin's voice, waving a bent paperclip like a wand in front of his face.

Alex blinked, caught. Subtle. Smooth. He said nothing.

Gavin followed his gaze, then let out a low, knowing whistle. "Ah. Right. Harper."

Alex didn't confirm or deny it. He simply raised an eyebrow slightly and waited.

Gavin, undeterred, leaned back in his chair, lacing his fingers behind his head, grinning with the satisfaction of a man who lived for office gossip and the glory of delivering it.

"Mate, every straight man in the building is in love with her. And probably a few who aren't."

Alex kept his expression neutral, but a flicker of something flared in his chest. He didn't like being lumped in with the crowd. He wasn't here to admire Harper Jameson from afar. He was here on a mission. A bet.

Though, disturbingly, that mission felt less simple by the minute.

"We were practically doing cartwheels when she broke off her engagement to that tosser Billy from legal," Gavin continued, unprompted. "Never understood what she saw in him. Slick hair, smug smile, dead eyes. Total muppet."

Alex's jaw twitched slightly.

The idea of Harper—*his Harper*, a voice in his head insisted, far too possessively— being discussed so casually, so publicly, irritated him in a way he couldn't rationalize.

Gavin wasn't done.

"You'll have to get in line though," he added, chuckling as if this were all harmless fun. "She's got that don't-even-try aura. But man, when she smiles? Half the department forgets their passwords."

Alex offered a polite smile, but it didn't quite reach his eyes.

Because while Gavin saw Harper as an unattainable office goddess, Alex saw something else entirely.

Not just beauty. Not just mystery. Something deeper.

She was sharp-edged and steel-spined. The kind of woman who didn't give away her attention cheaply, who didn't trust easily—and not because she was jaded, but because she'd earned the right to be discerning.

He respected it.

Which was infuriating.

Because it meant she was going to be harder to win than he'd anticipated. Not just because she was guarded, but because she deserved more than charm, deception, or half-truths.

And worse—she wasn't just a challenge now.

She was a temptation.

One that made him wonder—dangerously—if he was already too far in to walk away clean.

Before he could ponder further, Gavin leaned in again, lowering his voice as if about to share state secrets.

"You'll also wanna watch out for the one they call Shelley."

Alex looked up, puzzled. "Shelley?"

"HR dragon," Gavin said gravely, nodding toward a desk in the corner. "Red nails, eyes like lasers, devours interns for breakfast. Had a guy cry in the stairwell once because he filed the wrong payroll form."

Alex raised an eyebrow. "That's oddly specific."

"I'm just saying—if she offers you a peppermint, run. It's a trap. She reels you in with the mint, then smacks you with policy."

Alex smirked. "Duly noted."

He returned his attention to the screen, scrolling through a tech manual that read like Greek written in Morse code. Calm, professional—on the surface. Beneath, he was furtively Googling acronyms under the desk, praying no one noticed.

He made it through lunch without outing himself, choosing to eat outside alone— half to keep his cover, half because Harper had been in the break room, and he wasn't ready to sit across from her yet.

When he returned, he found a sticky note on his monitor. In precise, immaculate handwriting:

IT meeting moved to 3pm. Boardroom B. —H.J.

Just initials. Efficient. No flourish. Still, his stomach did a little flip.

It was going to be a long month.

By 3pm, he had managed to locate Boardroom B, show up on time, and even nod intelligently through the first fifteen minutes of technical jargon. He took notes, asked questions that wouldn't reveal too much, and survived the initial onslaught of corporate vernacular.

Harper sat near the front, legs crossed, notebook open, her pen moving quickly. She didn't look at him once.

But when the meeting ended and everyone shuffled out, she paused.

"Settling in?" she asked, glancing at him briefly.

Alex smiled, a playful tilt to his lips. "Still waiting for my welcome balloon and ceremonial coffee mug."

Her mouth curved—just barely. "Budget cuts."

He chuckled. "Tragic."

A pause.

"Let me know if you need anything," she said, nodding once, efficient, and precise. "We like to support new hires. Within reason."

Before he could answer, she turned and walked away, heels clicking lightly against the polished floor.

Alex sat there a beat longer than necessary, trying to remember what this whole charade was supposed to be about.

Oh, right. The bet.

He was supposed to *win* it.

So why, already, did it feel like he was the one in over his head?

Alex was in the process of setting up his monitor when the scent of eucalyptus—and a sort of corporate intimidation—slithered into the air.

"Alexander Dawson," a clipped voice said from behind him, each syllable sharp and deliberate, like a court summons delivered in perfect English diction.

He turned to find a tall, rail-thin woman hovering at the edge of his desk. Her hair was scraped into a severe bun, her lipstick the exact shade of dried blood, and her scarlet nails clicked ominously against the clipboard she held like a weapon forged from pure authority.

"Shelley," she said without offering a hand. "HR compliance officer. Orientation forms weren't submitted before noon."

Alex blinked. "I didn't realise there was a deadline."

Her eyes narrowed behind sharp-rimmed glasses, cutting into him with a precision that could've punctured steel. "It was in the packet. Page four. Paragraph six. I trust you read the packet?"

He was about to answer when Gavin, at the neighbouring desk, muttered under his breath, "Run. Now."

Shelley snapped her head toward him like a serpent sensing movement. "Something to add, Mr. Cooper?"

Gavin straightened immediately, shaking his head. "No, ma'am."

Alex resisted the urge to laugh. Shelley's reputation was no exaggeration. She was the kind of woman who could make grown men fear open-plan offices, fluorescent lighting, and malfunctioning coffee machines all at once.

Shelley turned back to Alex, clipboard still in hand. "If you're unclear on deadlines, we can schedule a time for basic comprehension training. I believe there's a remedial program for new hires."

Alex's mouth twitched. "That won't be necessary."

He was about to bluff his way through an apology when a new voice cut through the tension like a scalpel through silk.

"Shelley."

It wasn't loud. It didn't need to be.

Harper.

She stood a few steps away, clipboard in hand, eyes fixed squarely on the HR dragon. Calm. Controlled. Cool as arctic glass. Unyielding.

Shelley's spine visibly straightened.

"Ms. Jameson," she said, every word clipped with efficiency.

Harper's tone didn't change. "You'll speak to Mr. Dawson with professionalism and courtesy. He's a new employee, not a disciplinary case."

Shelley opened her mouth—probably to protest—but Harper didn't give her the chance.

"If there's an issue with form submission, flag it with me. I'll take it from there. Understood?"

A long pause. Shelley's jaw flexed like a coiled spring, then she nodded. "Understood."

"Good." Harper's gaze didn't waver. "Return to your desk, please."

Shelley turned on her heel and marched away, the scent of eucalyptus trailing behind her like a vanishing storm cloud, leaving only the faint echo of authority in her wake.

Alex blinked. "Well. That was…"

"Shelley," Harper finished for him, expression impeccably unreadable.

"I was warned about the peppermint," he offered, deadpan.

Harper's lips twitched just slightly. "Smart man."

Their eyes met again—an unspoken thread tightening between them. She glanced at his screen, then back at him.

"Don't worry about the forms. You've got time."

"Thanks," he said, the word carrying more weight than mere gratitude for paperwork.

Harper nodded once, then turned away, her stride unhurried but unmistakably commanding. As she disappeared around the corner, Alex leaned back in his chair, exhaling slowly.

Gavin leaned over, eyes still wide. "See what I mean? Harper's the best. She actually gives a damn about people. Not just the job—us."

Alex let out a quiet chuckle, still watching the space where Harper had vanished. "I think I'm in the wrong profession."

Gavin grinned. "Mate, welcome to Veridian. The drama's free."

But Alex barely heard him.

Because Harper Jameson wasn't just beautiful—she was sharp, composed, quietly commanding. She didn't just walk into a room. She shifted the entire balance, like the air itself bent around her without effort or fanfare.

And for the first time in a long while, Alex felt something he hadn't expected to find down here—intrigue.

Maybe he'd come to Sydney for a bet.

But looking at the path Harper had just taken, a sudden suspicion struck him:

He might've just stumbled into something real.

And this?

This was only the beginning.

Chapter Four

Alex awoke to the screeching of a garbage truck outside his window, a sound that could only be described as the mechanical equivalent of a slow, painful death.

He groaned and rolled over—straight into the hard, unyielding edge of a twin mattress that seemed stuffed with broken promises, crushed dreams, and a generous sprinkling of sawdust.

His eyes cracked open.

The ceiling above him was a masterclass in disappointment: faded beige, cracked in two corners, and crowned with a single flickering bulb that swung ever so slightly, as if haunted by some petty ghost of better days. The shadows it cast jittered across the walls like extras in a low-budget horror film.

Right.

Sydney.

The bet.

The flat.

He exhaled slowly and dragged his hands down his face. His neck popped angrily. His lower back protested politely but firmly. The pillow—thin, sad, utterly unhelpful—might as well have been a folded tea towel.

The room was small enough that he didn't need to stand to take it all in. A kitchenette huddled in one corner, home to a dented kettle and a toaster that had already betrayed him twice that week. The bathroom door hung slightly ajar, revealing a sink the size of a cereal bowl and a shower stall barely wide enough to turn around in. The water pressure had all the conviction of a whisper. The coffee he'd made that morning tasted like regret brewed over existential dread. The toast was charred on one side, uncooked on the other.

He was starting to understand—deeply, personally—why people hated Mondays.

Still, he dressed with meticulous precision. A button-down shirt (slightly off-the-rack, which irritated him more than it should), slacks pressed with a $19 iron that hissed like a defensive cat, and shoes sporting scuff marks he hadn't seen since prep school.

He caught a glimpse of himself in the mirror before leaving. Rumpled. Under-caffeinated. Somehow both overdressed and entirely out of place.

He missed his driver. He missed the smooth hum of his Jaguar waiting curb side. He missed the scent of fresh espresso and polished marble in his Mayfair penthouse. He missed his bed—cloud-soft, sheets probably costing more than this entire flat. He missed silence. Clean air. Predictability.

He missed his life.

And yet…

As he crossed the lobby of Veridian Dynamics and stepped into the elevator, something stirred in his chest. A low, insistent thrum of anticipation. That strange, almost forgotten flicker of restlessness that had nothing to do with money, prestige, or control.

It had everything to do with Harper Jameson.

The office was alive with motion—phones ringing, conversations overlapping, someone shouting about a broken espresso machine in the break room as if it were a national emergency. But none of it registered.

Because there she was.

At her desk, expression cool and composed, typing with a precision that made everyone else's chaos seem almost criminal. Her hair was swept up today, a soft twist revealing the elegant curve of her neck. She wore a navy blazer that mirrored her eyes—calm, impenetrable, quietly commanding.

She didn't smile when she looked up. She didn't need to.

Her gaze landed on him for the briefest second, and something passed between them. Not a spark—nothing so obvious—but a thread of unspoken awareness. A taut, invisible line neither had drawn but both could feel.

"Morning," she said simply, her voice smooth, measured, unhurried.

"Morning," he replied, just slightly slower.

And just like that, the stiff neck, the burnt toast, the dreadful instant coffee, the relentless buzz of fluorescent lights—all of it faded to background noise.

Because for the first time since arriving in Sydney, since agreeing to this absurd bet that had stripped him of every luxury he'd taken for granted, Alex Dawson wasn't thinking about what he'd lost.

He wasn't thinking about the mattress. Or the malfunctioning shower. Or the fact that he was pretending to be someone he wasn't.

He was thinking about her.

About how, in the most ordinary of places, Harper Jameson somehow made the world feel sharper. Clearer. More alive.

Maybe that was worth enduring the lumpy bed and the instant coffee.

Maybe, it was worth a hell of a lot more.

The break room smelled faintly of burnt coffee and disappointment—specifically in the form of a half-eaten loaf of banana bread with a passive-aggressive Post-it note clinging to its plastic wrap:

"Help yourself, but don't eat it all, thanks – Janine."

Alex stood near the staff bulletin board, pretending to study a flyer for a workplace meditation seminar ("Breathe Through the Budget Cuts") while covertly observing Harper across the room. She stood by the window, backlit by the morning sun, sipping from a ceramic mug that bluntly declared:

Don't Make Me Use My HR Voice.

He couldn't help the smile tugging at his mouth. Of course she had a mug like that.

The last of the orientation forms had been filled out that morning—painful, ink-bleeding biro and all. Now they were clutched in one slightly smudged hand as he approached her, careful not to appear too eager.

"Harper," he said, voice calm, measured, the kind of tone one used for high-stakes investors—or skittish thoroughbreds.

She looked up, eyes narrowing with polite scepticism—the same precise, appraising look she'd given him yesterday when Shelley had cornered him near the lift. "Alex. All settled in?"

"As settled as a six-foot-three man can be on a twin mattress," he replied dryly. "I brought my completed forms. Thought you might appreciate how well I colour inside the lines."

A faint smirk tugged at her lips—barely visible, but enough to feel like a minor victory.

She took the forms, flipping through them with effortless precision, fingers fast and exact. "No HR violations yet. I'm impressed."

"Give it time," he teased, leaning in slightly. "I hear you devour interns for breakfast."

Her lips twitched, amused. "That's Shelley."

"Ah." He lowered his voice conspiratorially. "She offered me a peppermint. I declined. Barely escaped with my life."

Her laugh was quiet, restrained, but real. For a heartbeat, Alex felt like he'd glimpsed something private, a tiny window into her guarded world. Not wide open, just slightly ajar.

"You're adjusting faster than most new hires," she said, still flipping through the paperwork. "Especially coming from the UK. Bit of a climate shock, isn't it?"

He shrugged, adopting a casual air, though every inch of him was alert, studying her. "The sun is aggressive. The birds sound like demons. Someone advised carrying bug spray like cologne. But… the people are warm. Real."

Her eyes lifted ever so slightly. "We are who we are. No airs, no graces."

"Refreshing," he said, holding her gaze. A small pause followed, weighted with the unspoken.

Harper cleared her throat and returned to the forms. "These are fine. I'll get them scanned into the system today. Let me know if you need help with anything else."

Professional again. Efficient. Someone used to holding the world at arm's length. Yet Alex caught it—the subtle flicker of curiosity behind her calm, controlled exterior. She was studying him, just a little.

"I might take you up on that," he said, quieter now. "You seem like someone worth learning from."

She blinked once. Not dramatic. But a shift—a tiny crack in the glass of her composed armour.

Before she could respond, Gavin burst in like a Labrador on espresso, clutching two sausage rolls and hollering, "Oi, new guy! Did anyone tell you the trick to claiming the good coffee mug?"

Harper glanced at the forms one last time, then at Alex, expression composed, unshaken. "Welcome to Veridian, Alex. Don't let Gavin corrupt you."

"Too late," he murmured, lips curving.

She turned, stride purposeful, mug in hand, her presence shifting the space around her with every step.

Alex watched—not with the casual admiration every other man seemed to feel, but something slower-burning, deeper.

Harper Jameson wasn't just beautiful. She was sharp-edged, self-contained, utterly unapologetic. She didn't try to impress. She didn't have to. She carried herself like someone who had rebuilt more than one part of her life with her own bare hands.

He had come here chasing a game. A bet. A challenge.

But Harper?

She was the kind of challenge that could rewrite the rules entirely.

And perhaps the very reason this whole ridiculous charade might cost him far more than he'd ever bargained for.

The conference room buzzed with early morning chatter, the scent of burnt coffee and blueberry muffins drifting lazily through the air. Alex slipped into a seat near the middle of the long table, ignoring the curious glances directed his way. People were still sizing him up, still trying to place the "new guy from London."

Harper stood at the head of the table, tablet in hand, her strawberry-blonde hair pulled into a sleek, no-nonsense ponytail. She looked cool, focused, entirely at ease—like this room, this team, answered to her. And judging by the way the chatter fell silent the moment she cleared her throat, they did.

"Morning, everyone. Let's jump in."

Alex straightened instinctively. Harper had the kind of presence that didn't ask for attention—it claimed it, effortlessly, without even seeming to try.

"First up—thank you to everyone who's helped welcome our new systems engineer, Alex Dawson. Alex, welcome again."

He nodded, offering a polite, measured smile. "Happy to be here."

A faint ripple of amusement passed around the table, and Gavin leaned over, whispering with a grin, "They're still placing bets on how long the *new guy from London'* will last."

"Nice," Alex murmured under his breath. "Warm welcome."

Harper arched a brow at them—fully aware of the exchange—but let it slide with practiced patience.

"Now, for the calendar: the team-building weekend is coming up—Hunter Valley, one week from Thursday. Three nights. Yes, there will be wine tasting, hiking, and some trust falls—if Marcus from marketing gets his way."

Groans and laughter followed in equal measure.

Alex tilted his head. "Trust falls?"

"You'll survive," Harper said smoothly, not missing a beat.

She flipped to the next item. "Also, the Christmas party is two weeks from Friday. RSVP is required. And before anyone asks—yes, it's at the Harbourview again. Yes, there will be an open bar. No, you cannot bring five friends."

Gavin raised a hand. "Can we vote on the music this year? Last year was… traumatic."

"If anyone submits a playlist with more than two Mariah Carey songs," Harper said dryly, "I will shut it down personally."

More laughter erupted. The room was hers. And Alex couldn't look away.

She transitioned seamlessly into HR updates, project timelines, and a brief but barbed reminder about interdepartmental professionalism—which Shelley clearly absorbed, judging by the stiffening of her posture across the room.

"And lastly," Harper said, voice crisp and deliberate, "Veridian prides itself on a culture of respect. That means treating colleagues—new or otherwise—with decency. If you have an issue, raise it with your manager or with me directly. Passive-aggressive emails and territorial attitudes are not how we operate here."

No one dared speak. The message was clear.

"Questions?" she asked, glancing around.

Silence.

"Great. Meeting adjourned—except for Alex."

Chairs scraped as people rose and filed out. Gavin shot Alex a cheeky thumbs-up before disappearing down the hallway.

When the room was empty, Harper finally turned her attention fully to him.

"How are you finding things?"

"Still getting used to decaf coffee and shared walls," he said with a grin. "But your team's been fantastic. You, especially."

"Flattery this early in the morning?" she asked, arms crossed loosely. "Ambitious."

Alex shrugged, eyes twinkling. "Just calling it as I see it."

She paused, studying him for a beat longer than strictly necessary. "I meant what I said—Veridian has no space for egos or games. We've worked hard to build trust here."

"And I respect that," Alex replied sincerely. "It's… refreshing."

Her gaze softened, just slightly. "The Hunter Valley trip will be a good way for you to get to know everyone. Just… don't share a room with Gavin. You'll regret it."

"Duly noted."

"And the Christmas party?" she added, raising a brow.

"I have a suit," he said with a smile. "And an aversion to Mariah Carey."

Harper's smile—real, easy, unguarded—hit him like a brief, electric jolt. For a second, Alex forgot this was all supposed to be part of a bet. He didn't want to play a role around her.

"Get back to work, Dawson," she said, turning back to her tablet, her posture commanding yet effortless.

"Yes, ma'am," he replied, a small grin lingering.

He left the room, but her smile stayed with him, shadowing his thoughts for the rest of the day, a quiet reminder that this month was going to be far more complicated than any wager could predict.

Chapter Five

Alex adjusted the strap of his laptop bag and stepped into the late afternoon heat of the underground car park, exhaling slowly. The air was thick and stifling, a stark contrast to the clinical chill of the office. It smelled faintly of engine oil, concrete dust, and the lingering tang of summer sweat.

Friday. Somehow, he'd made it through his first week—barely breathing, barely sane.

No personal assistant anticipating his next move. No chauffeured town car waiting with the engine running. No espresso machine humming in the background of his Mayfair penthouse like a quiet promise of control.

Just a shoebox-sized apartment with paper-thin walls and a neighbour who treated 3 a.m. drum solos as a spiritual calling.

He deserved the weekend off. The suite he'd quietly booked at The Langham overlooked the harbour, offered Egyptian cotton sheets, a minibar stocked with Dom Pérignon, and—most importantly—silence.

He rounded the row of cars, keys in hand, already half-lost in thoughts of a long, hot shower and a night free from the pretence of being someone he wasn't.

Then a voice cut through the air—sharp, familiar, and trembling on the edge of fury.

"Billy, just stop."

Alex's head snapped up. Instinct surged before thought.

Ten metres ahead, beside a faded red hatchback, stood Harper. Her body angled away, one arm raised in a protective gesture. The tension radiating from her was almost visible, crackling in the humid air like a live wire.

And then he saw him—*Billy Bailey.*

Polished, smug, confident, clad in an overpriced suit that screamed entitlement. He was too close, too bold, hands gripping Harper's upper arms possessively, as if she were still his to command.

Something dark surged through Alex. Heat pooled in his chest. Pulse spiked.

He moved forward before he even realised he'd made a decision.

"Come on, Harp," Billy coaxed, voice slick, practiced. "She meant nothing to me. You know you miss me."

Harper's reply cut through him like a whip—cold, controlled, furious.

"Then maybe you should've kept your pants on. I don't do second chances for cheaters," she snapped, tone steel wrapped in fire.

She shook her head, attempting to step back, but Billy moved faster. His mouth crashed onto hers without warning.

Alex saw red.

Harper recoiled immediately, shoving at Billy's chest with every ounce of her strength. "Billy, I said no!" she gasped.

But he didn't let go.

As she tried to move around him, his hand clamped down on her wrist in a bruising grip.

Her breath hitched. Her body froze for a heartbeat. And Alex could see it—the flash of fear, the sharp intake of breath, the tiniest flicker of panic in her eyes.

That was it.

The line. Crossed.

"Hey!" Alex's voice cut through the concrete air, sharp and echoing like a gunshot.

Both heads snapped toward him. Harper's eyes widened—relief? Surprise? Both, maybe. Billy's jaw clenched, rigid, defiant.

Alex walked forward with measured purpose, each step deliberate, a predator's calm precision. His green eyes were cold, unwavering, carved from stone.

"Let her go."

Billy scoffed, still holding Harper's arm. "This doesn't concern you, mate."

Alex's voice dropped, syllables deliberate, sharp. "Let. Her. Go."

There was something beneath the words—a quiet, lethal weight. Fury tempered by control. A warning that needed no theatrics.

Billy hesitated, the smirk faltering just slightly, before releasing her arm with a reluctant shove, stepping back as if trying to reclaim some shred of dignity.

"We were just talking," he said, forcing the casual tone of a man pretending nothing had happened.

Harper folded her arms across her chest, more shield than posture, cheeks flushed, breath uneven.

"That didn't look like talking."

Alex stopped beside her, close enough to offer protection but careful not to crowd. The space between them buzzed with tension—coiled, dangerous, but contained.

"You should leave. Now."

Billy's smirk deepened, eyes flicking back to Harper like a man claiming his territory. "You're making a mistake."

Alex didn't flinch. "She already made one. You."

Billy's jaw tightened. His cocky veneer cracked for a heartbeat before he spun on his heel, muttering under his breath as he stalked toward his car. One last scowl thrown over his shoulder, then he disappeared behind a concrete pillar.

The silence that followed was heavy, almost tangible.

Alex turned to Harper, voice softer now, grounded. "You okay?"

She nodded, fingers gripping her car keys tightly, a tremor betraying her calm. "Yeah. Just… caught off guard."

He exhaled slowly, trying to tamp down the residual surge of protective anger. "He put his hands on you."

She shrugged, almost dismissively, but the lightness in her voice was forced. "It's not the first time he's been pushy. I usually handle it."

Alex's gaze held hers, steady, assessing. Strong? Undeniably. Resilient? Absolutely. But no one should have to 'handle' that alone. Not ever.

"You shouldn't have to." His voice was low, sincere, edged with quiet fierceness.

Harper blinked, a flicker of vulnerability crossing her features—surprise, gratitude, uncertainty all wrapped in one fleeting expression.

"I'm fine," she murmured. "Thanks for stepping in."

He didn't speak again immediately. Just nodded, jaw tight, eyes lingering on her a fraction too long. Protective. Watchful. Silent reassurance in the still air between them.

Then, as if deciding in mid-breath, he said, "I was going to grab dinner. There's a place near my flat. Would you… want to come?"

Harper hesitated.

Billy's unwanted kiss still lingered in memory like oil on her skin. She wanted to scrub it away, pretend it never happened.

But here with Alex, she didn't feel weak. She didn't feel exposed. She felt… seen.

Still, she shook her head gently. "Sorry, I can't. My friend's in town from Perth."

She moved toward her car, paused, and glanced back. Her voice softened. "Thanks again, Alex. Really."

He watched her car pull away, red taillights fading into the dusk like the remnants of a bad dream.

He remained rooted to the spot, muscles coiled, fury still simmering beneath the surface.

Finally, almost absently, he reached into his pocket and pulled out his phone, the world around him momentarily receding as his thoughts stayed fixed on her.

The line clicked alive. "James."

Alex's voice dropped low—controlled, precise, dangerous enough to make the air in the carpark feel thinner.

"I need you to do something. And I want it done fast."

A beat of silence on the other end. "Go on."

"There's an employee in the Sydney office. Name's Billy Bailey. Legal. I want him gone."

He let the words hang; eyes locked on the empty parking space where Harper had been a moment before. The fluorescent-lit concrete around him felt suddenly colder.

"I don't care how—transfer, redundancy, scandal. Just make it happen."

James's pause deepened; Alex could hear the calculator-clack of a mind weighing options. "Timeline?"

"Yesterday." Alex's voice was flat, iron. Then he added, softer but with lethal intent, "And James—make sure he never gets to harass another woman again."

Another measured pause. Then, quietly: "Understood."

The call ended with the soft click of a line going dead. Alex slid the phone back into his pocket and exhaled, the breath leaving him like steam in winter. The weight of what he'd asked—what he'd set in motion—pressed down on him in the same way the damp concrete pressed against his shoes.

He had crossed a line. Maybe several.

He'd promised himself the month would be a game, a dare to prove a point. But whatever pretence he'd brought to Sydney felt thin and fragile now, blown away by the memory of Billy's hand around Harper's wrist, and the fear that flitted across her face.

When it came to Harper Jameson, the rules had changed.

This was no longer about a bet, or pride, or proving Theo right. This was about keeping her safe.

And Alex had no intention of taking any chances.

The night settled like velvet over Sydney, the city alive with a symphony of distant horns, laughter spilling from rooftop bars, and the steady hum of traffic weaving through the air. Yet in the quiet corners—the streets away from neon signs and pulsing clubs—something had shifted. Something invisible but undeniable, a tension threaded through the city's hum.

Harper entered the Langham Hotel's elegant restaurant, her heels clicking softly against the polished marble floor. Warm, golden light bathed the room, casting flattering shadows across every surface. Near the bar, a pianist coaxed low, languid notes from the keys, each one a soft caress in the ambient glow. The scent of polished wood mingled with the subtle perfume of gardenias from a towering floral arrangement near the entrance, filling the air with understated luxury.

She spotted Clara immediately—always radiant, even when trying not to be. Her soft blue dress hugged her just enough to flatter her figure, while her copper hair fell in relaxed waves around her shoulders. A wineglass twirled lazily in her hand as she waved Harper over with the kind of effortless charm that seemed to announce her presence without demanding attention.

Beside her sat Jonathon Bennett, Clara's older brother. Tall, composed, impeccably dressed in a crisp navy blazer, and tailored trousers, he was every inch Sydney elite. His brown eyes locked on Harper the moment she appeared, unreadable yet penetrating, carrying a flicker of something Harper couldn't immediately name. Recognition. Concern. Maybe something deeper. His gaze cut through the background chatter, the clatter of silverware, the low hum of conversation—it was acute, precise, unwavering.

Harper offered a polite, restrained smile. "Hey, you two. Thanks for waiting."

Clara stood, giving her a quick hug. "You look exhausted. Sit, sit. I already ordered your ravioli—you're welcome."

"You're a lifesaver," Harper murmured, sliding into the chair beside her. The tension in her shoulders eased slightly as she reached for her water glass, fingers brushing the cool condensation. Across the table, Jonathon's gaze remained steady, unwavering.

"You look like work chewed you up," he said finally, his voice low, deliberate, scanning her face for the details she hadn't spoken aloud. "Rough week?"

"You could say that," Harper replied, glancing quickly at Clara before taking a sip. "Let's just say… Billy's not exactly taking no for an answer."

Clara's wineglass landed on the table a little too forcefully. "What did he do?"

Harper hesitated, throat tightening. "Nothing I couldn't handle. Just… persistent. And completely out of line."

Jonathon's posture shifted in an instant—from relaxed to coiled, taut with barely concealed tension. His jaw twitched once, subtle but deliberate. Harper noticed; he always gave himself away in the smallest movements.

"Did he put his hands on you?" he asked, voice quieter now, steel threading the edges.

Harper met his steady brown eyes—silent, protective, and quietly, hopelessly in love with her, though he'd never said it aloud. He didn't need to.

"He tried," she murmured softly. "Someone stopped him."

Clara leaned in, eyes wide. "Who?"

Harper lowered her voice, careful. "It was the new systems engineer. Alex."

Clara's eyebrows shot up, and a mischievous grin tugged at the corner of her lips. "Interesting."

Jonathon remained silent. He lifted his wineglass slowly, measuring, calculating, the subtle flare of his nostrils betraying irritation. His hand tightened around the stem, his grip precise. He didn't like it. Not one bit.

"He needs to back off," he said finally, voice low but edged with authority. "Or I'll make sure he does."

Harper offered a faint, appreciative smile. "Thanks, Jon, but it's under control."

Clara scoffed, tossing her hair over her shoulder. "Still—one text and I'd have been here in heels and earrings, swinging a clutch like a weapon."

Harper laughed, surprised at herself. "You always say that."

"Because it's true," Clara replied, mock solemnity in her tone as she raised her glass. "No one messes with my best friend."

Jonathon's gaze flicked to Clara for a brief moment, then returned to Harper— steady, unwavering, and just a touch too tender to be casual. The silence between them stretched, heavy with unspoken words and restrained emotion. He wouldn't push. He never did. But she could feel it nonetheless: a quiet promise, a readiness lurking beneath the surface, patient and enduring.

"I didn't want to make a thing of it," Harper said finally, exhaling with a tired, wry smile. "Tonight's for unwinding. Please—tell me about Perth. About your new job. About literally anything else."

Clara shot her a look that clearly said, *we're circling back to this later*, but then launched into a story about a new coworker—an intern bold enough to wear Crocs to a client pitch and somehow land the account anyway.

Harper laughed again, more freely this time, letting herself lean back into the easy rhythm of their company. For a while, she allowed the cadence of Clara's storytelling, the gentle clink of silverware, and the soft murmur of other diners to lull her into something resembling peace.

But even as she relaxed, Jonathon's gaze occasionally found her again—quiet, calm, patient, and somehow carrying more weight than it should. He would never overstep; that wasn't his way.

And yet the unspoken truth between them lingered like a charged current, hovering in the space they shared, waiting for the right moment to be named.

Alex was halfway through his scotch when he saw her.

He had come to the Langham's restaurant seeking quiet. Anonymity. A tucked-away booth near the back, a dim light above, a glass of Macallan in his hand, and no one asking questions. The kind of sanctuary that let a man disappear in plain sight. He'd wanted to disappear—just for the night. Just long enough to stop thinking about her.

But then Harper walked in—and every thought he'd tried to outrun came roaring back like a tidal wave.

She stepped into the room with effortless grace, as if every space she entered had been waiting for her. Her presence didn't simply draw attention—it commanded it, held it captive. Her strawberry-blonde hair shimmered beneath the warm golden light, swept off her shoulders in soft waves that caught and reflected every glow. She paused just inside the doorway, scanning the room, and smiled—bright, genuine, untouched by pretence.

It was like watching sunlight fracture through a cloudy sky.

Alex froze.

She hadn't seen him—of course she hadn't. Why would she be looking for him? They barely spoke at work unless it was about schedules or system reports. Still, his heart tripped over itself, stupidly hopeful, as if she might glance his way.

But she didn't.

And he couldn't look away.

She wore a form-fitting emerald dress that hugged her curves with understated elegance, the kind that whispered rather than shouted. It seemed sculpted for her alone. The rich green pulled the blue from her eyes, made her skin glow, and set her hair ablaze like molten copper. At the office, she was all crisp blouses and practical heels—the armour of professionalism. But here? Harper was unguarded. Poised. Devastating.

He noticed the subtlety of her makeup—barely there but masterfully applied. A hint of liner accentuated her ocean eyes, a sweep of blush highlighted the angles of her cheekbones. She never wore makeup at work. She didn't need it. But tonight, she looked like a woman who knew her power—and wasn't afraid to wield it.

She moved through the restaurant with quiet confidence, each step purposeful, the subtle click of her heels blending with the low hum of clinking glasses and soft piano music. Her presence shifted the room, a gentle storm stirring everything in its path.

She reached a table near the centre, where a woman with fiery red hair jumped up to embrace her. Beside her sat a man in a sharp navy blazer—tall, composed, radiating the effortless assurance of someone entirely at home in the world. Their greeting was warm, familiar, built from years of friendship and easy laughter.

But it was the man who drew Alex's gaze.

He watched Harper too closely, too intently. There was something in the way his eyes lingered on her, the way his smile held after hers faded. Protective. Reverent. As if he saw not just the woman she was, but the woman she could be—and was already guarding her future in his mind.

A tight coil of envy twisted in Alex's chest.

He knew that look. He'd worn it himself—in private, fleetingly, when no one was watching. The difference here? This man wasn't hiding it. Every glance, every small gesture was raw, unrestrained. The way he leaned in when Harper laughed, the way his gaze tracked her every move—it spoke plainly: he loved her.

And Harper—perhaps she noticed. Perhaps she didn't. Or perhaps she was pretending not to.

Alex took a slow sip of his scotch, letting the burn cut through his thoughts.

Did she attract every man within a five-block radius? It certainly felt that way.

He hadn't meant to end up here. He'd just wanted a quiet meal, a refuge for thought. But now, watching her across the room—alive, radiant, adored—he was reminded of something he'd spent the week trying to suppress.

Harper Jameson wasn't just beautiful.

She was magnetic.

And the pull was getting harder to resist.

He wasn't supposed to fall for her. That wasn't the plan. She was the HR manager—professional, off-limits, sharp, and far too smart to fall for a man like him. Especially if she knew the truth.

But none of that mattered tonight. Not the rules, not the bet, not the secrets he hadn't yet found the courage to reveal.

Tonight, she looked like a woman a man didn't walk away from.

And Alex wasn't sure he could.

Chapter Six

Alex remained seated in the dim corner booth, shrouded in shadow and the low hum of piano music. His posture was deceptively relaxed—one arm draped along the back of the leather seat, the other resting near his glass—but his eyes, sharp and unblinking, betrayed the truth.

From his vantage point, he had a clear view of the table near the window—though he wished he didn't. Because he couldn't stop watching her.

Harper.

She sat with the redhead—and the man. The stranger who seemed far too comfortable in Harper's orbit.

They talked non-stop, Harper and the woman, their laughter rising like champagne bubbles—effortless, warm, unfiltered. The kind of laughter that didn't ask for attention but turned heads anyway. Harper leaned in often, her eyes bright, her smile easy, her entire body alive in a way Alex had only glimpsed at the office. Seeing her like this was different. Freer. Lighter. The weight she carried between 9 and 5 seemed momentarily set aside.

The man, however—he wasn't laughing. Not like they were. He spoke occasionally, offered the occasional comment, even smiled now and then. But mostly… he watched Harper. Not distractedly. Not politely.

Intently.

Like she was something rare and fragile. Like he'd memorized every nuance of her expressions and still hadn't grown weary of the view.

Alex studied him—the easy lean of the shoulder, the subtle tilt of his body toward her, the faint, almost imperceptible smile when she laughed. That wasn't indifference. That was practiced affection. Familiarity. Shared history.

And then it happened.

As the three rose to leave, the man's hand slid gently—naturally—over the small of Harper's back. Not accidental. Not tentative. Confident. Possessive. The sort of gesture that suggested it had been done a hundred times before and would be done a hundred times more.

Alex's fingers tightened around his glass.

He didn't like it.

He didn't like it one damn bit.

What unsettled him most wasn't the man's touch. It was Harper's reaction—or rather, her lack of one. She didn't pull away. She didn't flinch or step aside or even seem surprised. If anything, she leaned into it. Just slightly. Just enough. The kind of unconscious response born from trust, habit, intimacy.

Alex's chest constricted.

This wasn't some harmless dinner among old friends.

His jaw clenched, teeth grinding behind the cool mask he wore. He told himself it didn't matter. That it shouldn't matter. She was a colleague. A name on an org chart. A line item in a bet that had begun as a joke.

But it did matter.

Because that small, silent gesture—the subtle press of a palm to her back—felt too intimate. Too practiced. Too real. It carried the quiet certainty Alex recognized in himself from a long-ago love—the certainty that claimed space without apology.

And right now, someone else occupied the space Alex hadn't even earned the right to want.

He watched them leave, their laughter trailing behind like perfume. Harper glanced back once—not at him, not for him, just toward the room—before the door closed behind her.

Only then did Alex exhale. Long. Slow.

He lifted his scotch, took a deliberate sip, and set the glass down with quiet finality.

If he wanted a chance with Harper Jameson, sitting in the shadows wouldn't suffice.

He'd have to step into the light.

And he'd have to do it soon.

Because someone else was already standing exactly where he wanted to be.

Outside the Langham's grand entrance, the Sydney air was warm and carried the faint sweetness of jasmine, mingling with the distant hum of the city—horns, chatter, the occasional siren, all weaving into a soft urban lullaby. Streetlights cast a golden glow across the pavement, stretching shadows long and gentle. Harper stood with Clara and Jonathon beneath the portico, phone in hand, waiting for her taxi. The evening lingered around them—laughter, wine, shared stories, and the weight of unspoken things.

Clara linked her arm through Harper's with the ease of long friendship, her voice low, warm, familiar. "We still on for tomorrow?"

Harper nodded, brushing a strand of hair from her cheek as a breeze teased it. "My place at eleven. I'll make pancakes."

"You'd better," Clara teased, narrowing her eyes in mock warning. Then she leaned in, pressing a quick kiss to Harper's cheek. "Goodnight, gorgeous."

Jonathon stepped forward, slower, more measured, his expression softened by something careful, quiet. "Text me when you get in?"

"I will," Harper replied, offering a gentle smile. "Thanks for dinner. Both of you."

He bent to kiss her cheek—just a touch longer than necessary. Lingering. "Sleep well, Harp."

She climbed into the taxi, tilting her hand in a final wave through the open window. They watched in silence as the car pulled away, its taillights fading into the night. A hush settled over the portico, that heavy, familiar quiet that comes only after moments of significance.

Eventually, Clara looped her arm through Jonathon's and nudged him with a knowing grin. "Come on, tragic hero. Let's get a drink."

They made their way back through the revolving doors into the Langham's marble-floored lobby, the hush of the night giving way to soft lighting, gleaming chandeliers, and the muted murmur of the hotel bar. The space was sleek, low-lit, humming with quiet conversation, wrapping them in a cocoon of familiarity. They slid into a corner booth, the ritual comfortable and grounding.

That's when Alex saw them.

He'd been nursing a scotch at the far end of the bar, trying to temper the storm of his temper, trying to keep the tension at bay. He had watched Harper leave.

Watched the way Jonathon's eyes followed her. And now, seeing them return without her, something inside him shifted, cold and sharp.

Without a word, he rose and made his way toward the booth, careful to remain unnoticed—but not silent.

Clara tossed her clutch onto the seat beside her and leaned back, draping an arm along the booth like a queen surveying her kingdom. Her eyes sparkled with mischief, her tone soft yet teasing. "So…" she drawled, letting the word hang in the air. "Harper's looking well, don't you think, Jon?"

Jonathon gave a quiet, almost wistful laugh, swirling the red wine in his glass. "She's always beautiful to me, Clara. You know that."

Clara arched an eyebrow, not missing a beat. "Then why haven't you told her?"

"Told her what?" he asked, though his voice carried no real confusion. He knew exactly what she meant.

"That you're head over heels in love with her, of course."

A few feet away, Alex stiffened, the rim of his glass paused at his lips.

Jonathon didn't speak immediately. His gaze fell to the table, and he pressed his thumb against the edge of his glass, jaw tightening as if the words themselves were painful to hold.

"Because it wouldn't change anything."

Clara's smile softened into something contemplative. "You don't know that."

"Yes, I do," he said quietly, each word deliberate, weighted with certainty. "She doesn't see me that way. Not really. And I'd rather be in her life as a friend than not at all."

Clara exhaled, warm eyes shifting between frustration and admiration. "You know, brother… you're a good man. But sometimes good men miss their shot because they're too noble." She gave him a half-teasing, half-sincere look. "I'd love to have Harper as my sister-in-law."

Jonathon didn't respond. He stared into his drink, the silence heavy with meaning, more telling than any confession could have been.

A few feet away, hidden behind the high booth divider, Alex's eyes dropped to the amber swirl in his glass, the ice cracking faintly as he gripped the tumbler. His jaw tightened. Fingers curled loosely around it.

So, it wasn't just Billy.

Harper Jameson wasn't merely admired.

She was cherished.

By men who knew her history. Her laugh. Her gentleness. Who had stood beside her for years while he'd been half a world away behind a penthouse window and a billion-dollar shield. Men who probably deserved her.

And yet, something stirred inside him—low, sharp, igniting in his chest like a match catching fire.

Not jealousy. Not exactly.

Something more dangerous.

Longing.

He wasn't ready to give up—certainly not before he'd even begun.

Not by a long shot.

Alex finished the last sip of his scotch, the melting ice clinking softly against the glass as he set it down on the polished bar. The crowd had thinned, voices fading into a low murmur behind him, but his mind was anything but quiet. Thoughts spun like smoke—thick, restless, impossible to pin down. He could feel the tension coiling in his chest, the kind that made the blood thrum in his temples.

He stood, adjusted the cuff of his shirt with a practiced precision honed over years of boardrooms and gala dinners, and made his way to the elevator. A short ride later, the doors slid open onto the top floor of the Langham, revealing the hushed opulence of his penthouse suite. Marble floors gleamed beneath soft recessed lighting, walls of glass offered panoramic views of the city, and everything smelled faintly of polished wood and quiet luxury. Underneath it all shimmered the kind of wealth most people could only dream of.

It should have felt like relief—after a week trapped in a generic flat that smelled vaguely of stale coffee and fluorescent despair—but the silence here did not soothe. Instead, it pressed against him, loud in its emptiness.

He shrugged off his jacket, loosened his tie with a sharp tug, and moved toward the vast window overlooking the Sydney skyline. The city glittered below, alive, and indifferent. A symphony of lights, horns, and distant laughter played without care for him or his schemes.

His phone buzzed.

He glanced at the screen and exhaled. Theo. Of course.

With the resigned patience of a man expecting nonsense, Alex answered. "What?"

Theo's voice crackled through the speaker, amusement clear in every word. "Just checking in. So… have you made a woman fall for you yet, or are you still charming HR dragons and pretending to know what a server rack is?"

Alex didn't smile. He paced slowly to the window, the city lights flickering across the glass beside his reflection. Jaw tight, exhaling slowly, he muttered, "She's not just any woman."

There was a pause on the other end. "Oh?" Theo's tone shifted, still amused but threaded now with genuine curiosity. "Do tell."

Alex's fingers tapped lightly against the cold window frame, thoughts tangling like the lights below. "She's… sharp. Observant. She sees everything. And she doesn't care who I am—or at least, who I usually am. She treats me like everyone else."

"Well, that's the point, isn't it?" Theo chuckled. "You wanted someone who didn't know you were obscenely rich. Someone who didn't fall at your feet the moment you walked into a room."

"I didn't think it would be this bloody hard," Alex muttered, running a hand through his hair, tugging at it as though it might help unravel the knot of thoughts and feelings coiled inside him.

"You have to work for it now, don't you?" Theo laughed, his tone sharp with mischief. "Do you even know what colour her eyes are?"

"Yes," Alex said, a faint edge of pride in his voice. "As a matter of fact, I do."

"Well, that's progress," Theo replied, amusement lingering.

"I want to know a lot more than that," Alex murmured, almost to himself.

Theo laughed again—rich, smug, but carrying a thread of warning. "Careful, mate. Sounds like she's already under your skin."

Alex said nothing. His silence was heavy, taut with unspoken truths and simmering frustration.

After a beat, Theo's voice softened, threading through the tension like a tether. "Don't forget the terms of the bet. A month, remember? Three weeks left."

Alex ended the call without another word, letting the quiet stretch around him like a living thing, dense and unyielding.

He stood at the window, staring at the sprawling city below—and at his reflection staring back. For the first time, he didn't fully recognize the man in the glass. Not the tailored suit. Not the carefully controlled expression.

Because beneath all the detachment, beneath the carefully cultivated control, something real had begun to stir.

For the first time in years, the stakes weren't about pride. Or money. Or winning.

They were about her.

And the terrifying, undeniable possibility that he'd already begun to lose.

The next morning, exactly at 11am, the buzzer sounded.

Harper opened the door to find Clara and Jonathon standing there like perfectly coordinated models—Clara in a flowy sundress and oversized sunglasses, Jonathon in a crisp white tee and chinos, holding a box of fresh strawberries.

"Right on time," Harper said, stepping aside.

"We were raised to respect punctuality," Clara teased as she swept into the apartment, placing her sunglasses carefully on the entryway table. "Also, we were promised pancakes."

Harper laughed. "Then you shall have pancakes."

Jonathon held out the strawberries. "Figured you could use these. They're from that market you love."

"Perfect," Harper said, gesturing them inside. "Come on, make yourselves at home."

Her apartment wasn't large, but it had an effortless elegance. Pale timber floors, soft grey walls, and brass accents whispered of taste and understated luxury. A stack of art books sat on the coffee table beside a vase of fresh peonies. The kitchen was compact but modern—marble counters, brushed-gold fixtures, and an espresso machine that screamed, *serious about caffeine.*

Jonathon wandered over to the bookshelf. "You've rearranged your classics," he noted.

"I was bored last weekend," Harper replied with a shrug.

Clara leaned over the kitchen counter. "Tell me you have that blueberry maple syrup I love."

Harper pulled it from the fridge with a wink. "You doubted me?"

They spent the next hour in the kitchen. Harper flipped pancakes like a pro while Clara set the table, and Jonathon brewed coffee, the air filling with the warm scent of butter and berries, laughter echoing off the walls.

"Remember that disastrous camping trip to Rottnest Island?" Clara asked between bites, eyes watering from laughter. "When Jon forgot the tent poles?"

"I was twelve!" Jonathon groaned, throwing his hands in the air.

Harper nearly choked on her orange juice. "And we all had to sleep under an upside-down canoe."

"That was your idea," Jonathon pointed at her.

"It worked, didn't it?"

Clara wiped her mouth with a napkin. "Harper Jameson—engineering solutions to male incompetence since birth."

"You're just jealous you didn't think of it," Jonathon muttered.

Clara grinned. "I'm not as smart as Harper."

Jonathon watched her closely—the way he always did when he thought she wasn't looking. But today, Harper noticed. Their eyes met, holding for a beat longer than usual, the air between them thick with something unspoken.

A softness flickered in Jonathon's gaze—warm, familiar, like an open door she'd always hesitated to walk through.

But then—Alex.

Unbidden, he flashed into her mind. That crooked smile. The way his eyes tracked her like she was the only person in the room. He'd been doing that—haunting the edges of her thoughts—since the moment they met.

Harper blinked, looking away, her heart nudging against a truth she wasn't ready to name. Too many feelings. Too many what-ifs.

And just like that, the moment passed.

Clara clapped her hands. "Okay, I'm clearing the plates. You two, bring the coffee to the lounge. I'm not moving after this feast."

They drifted into the living room. Harper curled up in the armchair while Jonathon lounged comfortably on the couch opposite her. The space between them was warm, effortless—a quiet understanding that didn't need words.

It felt like family.

Sunlight poured through the windows, casting a golden glow that softened every edge. The sweet scent of pancakes lingered, mingling with their quiet laughter and easy conversation.

For now, in that perfect moment, nothing else mattered.

That was enough.

Chapter Seven

All week, Alex barely saw Harper.

She moved constantly—coordinating schedules, finalising headcount, confirming room allocations for the upcoming Hunter Valley team-building retreat. Every time he passed her office, she was on the phone or deep in conversation, brows drawn tight in concentration, her voice clipped with authority.

It frustrated him more than he cared to admit.

Not just because he missed her presence—but because he hated how much he noticed her absence.

On Wednesday afternoon, Gavin—ever the office commentator—leaned against Alex's desk with a grin. "You'll like the retreat," he said. "Wine, sunshine, no signal. Last year, two of the married ones ended up sneaking off together."

Alex didn't even crack a smile. "Charming," he muttered, his tone deliberately cool.

He loathed cheaters. Nothing made his blood run colder.

Billy Bailey came to mind—and conveniently, by Wednesday, Billy was gone. No one knew exactly why. The whispers in the office were vague but persistent, curling around the cubicles like smoke.

"I heard Harper made it happen," one intern said near the kitchen.

"Well, she is in charge of HR," someone else countered, a hint of awe—or fear— in their voice.

Alex knew better. He had orchestrated it. And he wasn't sorry about it.

He hadn't forgotten the look on Harper's face that night in the car park—the sharp spike of fear, the way Billy's hand had gripped her arm, and the quiet, contained fury that had flared in her eyes when he'd stepped in.

Billy's sudden departure felt like justice. Clean. Swift. Necessary.

And in the background of that justice, Alex felt a flicker of satisfaction, though he wouldn't have admitted it to anyone—not even himself.

Thursday finally arrived, bringing with it the long-anticipated team retreat to the Hunter Valley. For most of the staff, it promised wine tastings, open skies, and a welcome escape from the city grind.

For Alex, it meant one thing—he'd be spending an entire weekend in Harper Jameson's orbit. Even if it was technically a work trip… even if half the Sydney office would be crammed onto the same coach.

A company bus had been arranged for the journey from headquarters to the vineyard estate. Predictably, Gavin led the charge to the back with a six-pack and a playlist that hadn't been updated since 2009. Alex, however, had a very different destination in mind.

He spotted Harper near the front, talking with one of the junior managers, her posture relaxed but commanding, the kind that drew attention without demanding it. The moment she turned to board, he slid into the empty seat beside hers before anyone else could even think to try.

She glanced at him with a warm, slightly amused smile. "Strategic seating, Mr. Dawson?"

"I prefer to call it tactical," he said, settling in beside her. "Long bus ride. Figured I'd choose good company."

Harper raised an eyebrow, but the corner of her mouth lifted in acknowledgment. "I suppose I'll allow it."

As the bus rumbled to life and merged onto the motorway, Alex leaned back, stealing a glance at her. "Did you have a good weekend?"

She nodded, tucking a strand of hair behind her ear. "Yeah. Spent most of it with friends from Perth. They came over for a few days—felt like home again, if only for a moment."

He tilted his head. "You're from Perth?"

"Born and raised. Old money, old schools… the whole cliché," she said with a soft laugh. "Two older brothers who still think I'm twelve."

Alex grinned. "I'm guessing you were the golden child?"

"I was the diplomatic one," she replied, smirking. "Which made me their favourite target… and protector, depending on the day."

He chuckled, then she tilted her head toward him, curiosity sparking in her eyes. "What about you? Any siblings?"

"No," Alex said quietly. "Just me and my mum now. My father past three years ago… heart attack."

"I'm sorry," she said gently, her tone softening with genuine concern.

"Thank you," he said, glancing out the window before meeting her eyes again. "It was sudden. But… it changed things for me. Made me look at life a little differently."

She studied him, thoughtful. "You don't talk about it much, do you?"

"No," he admitted. "Still working on this whole 'opening up' thing."

Harper smiled, a flicker of warmth in her expression. "Well, you're doing fine so far."

And as the countryside unfurled outside—rolling hills in shades of green and gold—their conversation stretched out, natural and effortless, the kind that made the distance between strangers shrink.

By the time the Hunter Valley came into view, Alex had learned more about Harper Jameson than he had in an entire week at the office.

And without even trying, he'd revealed more of himself than he had to anyone in years.

Well—everything except the part about being a billionaire and owning the very company he pretended to work for.

That little detail… could wait.

The welcome dinner was in full swing—laughter rolling from the long tables strung beneath fairy lights, wine glasses clinking, conversations overlapping like a tide of noise. The Hunter Valley evening was warm, the air rich with eucalyptus and faint smoke from the outdoor grills.

Everyone seemed at ease. Everyone except Alex.

Two women from accounts had him cornered, their compliments too polished, their questions a shade too direct. He offered practiced smiles, murmured polite replies, nodded at stories he wasn't hearing. None of it mattered.

Because across the courtyard, he'd caught the flash of strawberry-blonde hair.

Harper.

She stood with two department heads, both leaning in closer than necessary, laughing far too loudly at every word she said. Alex watched the way she smiled—polite, professional—but her body angled subtly away from them, her fingers tightening around her wineglass. And then, almost imperceptibly, her gaze flicked toward the back doors.

A heartbeat later, she slipped out.

He didn't hesitate. With a murmured excuse and a half-smile, he didn't mean, Alex left his corner and followed.

The quiet outside was immediate, a balm. The moon hung silver and high, casting long shadows across the rows of vines. The night smelled of earth and crushed leaves, cool air brushing against his skin. Ahead, Harper walked slowly along a gravel path, her heels dangling from one hand, the hem of her soft dress whispering against her knees.

"Harper," he called gently.

She turned, startled, eyes widening before softening. "Oh—you scared me."

"Sorry." He slowed as he caught up, his voice low. "Needed some air. Those women inside? Ruthless."

She laughed—an unguarded, melodic sound that hit him square in the chest. "I'm sure you can handle yourself, Alex."

He stopped walking. Something flickered in his gaze, sharp, intent. "Say that again."

Her brow arched. "What?"

"My name." His voice was quiet but firm, the kind that carried more weight than it should. "Say it again."

For a moment she studied him, then tilted her head, a smile tugging at her lips. "Alex."

He stepped closer, closing the last of the distance until only inches separated them. Her scent—something warm with a citrus edge—wrapped around him, pulling him in.

"There," he murmured, his voice rougher now. "That's better."

Silence stretched between them, not awkward but alive, humming with everything unspoken. The kind of silence that wasn't empty at all—it was full, heavy, begging to break.

Harper looked up at him, her smile fading into something softer. "You're not what I expected."

"I get that a lot," he said quietly, his gaze steady on hers. "But neither are you."

She drew in a breath, her eyes flicking to the glow of the retreat behind them, where laughter still carried on the breeze. "I should probably go back in."

"Do you want to?" he asked. No teasing in his tone this time. Just honesty.

Her hesitation was brief but telling. Her eyes met his, wide and clear in the moonlight.

"No," she admitted softly.

Neither of them moved.

The vineyard hushed around them, the world narrowing to two steady heartbeats and the fragile space that kept them apart. One breath, one step, and that barrier would dissolve.

"Harper," he whispered, his voice stripped of all his usual control. "I like you."

Her lips curved gently. "I like you too."

But he shook his head, holding her gaze, every word deliberate. "No. I mean—I like you. More than I probably should."

Her breath hitched, and in that charged moment, the air between them thickened—alive with everything both of them were trying, and failing, not to say.

And then, she broke it, her voice quiet but resolute. "Oh, Alex... it can't happen."

He took a half-step closer, careful not to touch her, but close enough to feel the warmth radiating from her skin. "Why not?"

"Because we work together. Because I've been down this road before. Because you're..." She shook her head, words faltering. "You're different, and that scares me."

His jaw tightened—not in anger, but in careful restraint. "I'm not Billy."

"I know that," she said quickly, eyes searching his. "But that doesn't make this—us—a good idea."

"Do you feel it?" he asked softly, leaning just enough to meet her gaze. "This… between us?"

Her silence spoke louder than words.

"Yes," she admitted finally. "But sometimes feeling something isn't enough."

He nodded once, deliberately slow. He didn't push. Didn't argue. Didn't break the fragile line she'd drawn.

"Okay," he said quietly. "But I'm not going anywhere. And I'm not pretending I don't want this."

She looked at him then—really looked—and for a heartbeat, the air between them felt charged with possibility, like it could tip into something more.

But instead, she offered a soft, regretful smile, then turned, walking back toward the soft glow of the lights.

Alex stood alone in the moonlight, hands buried in his pockets, her scent lingering in the cool night air. He didn't move. He didn't breathe out the tension. And he knew—whatever this was—it was far from over.

Harper left him there under the gentle sweep of moonlight and made her way back to the main building, the crunch of her heels on gravel the only sound keeping her tethered to reality. Her heart hammered against her ribs—loud, insistent, frustratingly hopeful.

She shouldn't have stopped. Shouldn't have looked back. Shouldn't have let him burrow under her skin so completely, so fast.

But she had. And he had.

By the time she reached her room, her hands trembled slightly as she slid the keycard into the lock. The moment the door clicked shut behind her, she leaned back against it, exhaling like she could calm the storm raging inside her chest.

She felt it—the pull. The spark. The dangerous, exhilarating tension that defied logic but refused to be ignored.

And it terrified her.

Not because Alex wasn't kind or genuine. Not because he wasn't sharp, infuriatingly charming, impossibly handsome.

But because he was.

Because she'd done this before. Gotten tangled with a charismatic colleague who said all the right things… until he didn't. Until he shattered her trust and left her to gather the pieces under the unforgiving gaze of everyone else.

She wasn't going to be that girl again.

No matter how much her heart leaned toward him. No matter how much she wanted to believe he was different.

Harper pushed off the door and moved to the window, gazing down at the moonlit vineyard stretching below. Somewhere out there, Alex was still standing alone in the night, quiet but present, impossibly close despite the distance.

She drew the curtain shut.

And whispered to herself, "It's better this way."

But even as she slid under the covers, cocooned in the stillness of the room, her thoughts betrayed her.

Because for the first time in years, she didn't want to be alone.

Chapter Eight

The morning sun filtered through the sheer curtains of the vineyard estate's meeting hall, casting a soft golden glow across the wide wooden floorboards. Staff milled about with coffees and croissants, their chatter bouncing off the high ceilings and mingling with the faint scent of fresh pastries. Outside, the sprawling fields glistened with dew, promising a day of sunshine, awkward icebreakers, and the usual corporate competitiveness.

Alex sipped black coffee from a paper cup, scanning the gathering crowd with quiet attention. Harper stood near a table, clipboard in hand, dressed in slim black trousers and a crisp white blouse. Efficient. Composed. Unflappable. Absolutely untouchable.

But then her eyes flicked up—and caught his. Something unspoken passed between them. Not a smile exactly, but something heavier: recognition. Last night hadn't vanished into the dark. It lingered, settling quietly between them.

"Alright, everyone!" Harper's voice rang out, clear and commanding. "Let's get started."

Groans rippled through the room like a low wave.

"Don't worry," she added, flashing a grin. "There's no trust fall. Yet."

A few nervous laughs scattered through the group. Alex allowed himself a small, reluctant smile.

She divided them into teams—colour-coded lanyards, playful group names, light-hearted banter. Alex ended up on Team Green, much to Gavin's obvious delight.

"This is fate," Gavin said, slapping a green ribbon around Alex's neck. "We're going to crush this."

"Because we both have a healthy sense of competition?" Alex asked dryly.

"No," Gavin said, grinning. "Because you look like the kind of guy who hates to lose."

He wasn't wrong.

The first exercise was a problem-solving challenge—a mock "minefield" set up with cones and blindfolds on the back lawn. One partner guided, the other walked blind.

To Alex's quiet delight, he was paired with Harper.

She handed him the blindfold, a faint smirk tugging at her lips. "You trust me?"

He looked her directly in the eye. "With my life."

The words slipped out before he could stop them. Her eyes flickered—but she said nothing. She merely gestured for him to put the blindfold on.

"Okay," she instructed as he stood amid the cones. "Start by stepping forward—three slow steps."

He obeyed, arms out slightly for balance.

"Now left. No, your other left."

"Harper, are you trying to kill me?"

She laughed—free, unguarded, and entirely disarming. "Maybe a little."

"Charming," he muttered.

He moved again, guided by her calm, clear, sometimes teasing voice. With every step, her instructions became quicker, more confident. He trusted her tone, her rhythm. There was something intimate in the exchange—a subtle dance of control and surrender that left his pulse just a little faster.

Finally, she said, "Okay, you're through."

He peeled off the blindfold, blinking into the sunlight. She stood only a foot away, smiling broadly.

"Not bad, Mr. Dawson."

"Couldn't have done it without you," he said smoothly, though his chest carried a little extra weight.

A nearby whisper floated over from someone else about *chemistry*, and Harper stepped back, professionalism snapping back into place like armour.

The next exercise was a scavenger hunt around the vineyard—teams racing to solve riddles and collect clues. It should have been silly. Probably intended to be. But somehow, Alex found himself laughing more than he had in years.

At one point, Harper and Mel, the ever-chatty receptionist, crouched over a wine barrel labelled Cabernet, debating a cryptic clue.

"I'm telling you, *'Where the secrets ferment'* means the cellar," Mel insisted, pointing a manicured nail at the vineyard map.

"No," Harper countered, brow furrowed, hands gesturing animatedly. "It's a play on words. 'Bottling room'—that's where things get sealed."

Alex leaned against a nearby fence post, arms crossed, watching quietly. But as his gaze lingered on Harper—her expressive face, the rapid flick of her eyes, the way she tucked a stray strand of hair behind her ear—amusement gave way to something tighter. Sharper.

She was brilliant. He already knew that.

But she was also warm. Playful. A little fierce.

And completely, maddeningly captivating.

By late afternoon, the sun hung high overhead, casting a golden sheen across dusty shoes, flushed cheeks, and sun-kissed arms. The scavenger hunt had ended in a breathless victory lap for Team Green, and Harper called for a break under the shaded veranda. Lemonade was passed around in sweating glasses, tart and sweet, offering a brief reprieve from the relentless heat.

Mel dropped onto the bench beside Harper with a theatrical groan, fanning herself with a folded event itinerary.

"This was fun in theory," she complained, voice dripping with mock drama. "In practice? My calves are submitting a formal complaint."

Harper laughed, a low, melodic sound that drifted across the patio, softening the tension of the day. She turned just as Alex approached, moving through the group with easy confidence.

"Good day?" she asked, tone casual but edged with a faint caution.

"The best I've had in a while," he replied, sincere. "Though Gavin is threatening a rematch over the wine barrel clue."

"Let him try," she said, a teasing glint dancing in her eyes. "You earned that win."

Their eyes met—a glance meant to be simple, fleeting. Yet it lingered.

Too long to be accidental.

Not long enough to be fully confessed.

Before either could speak again, Gavin's booming voice shattered the moment.

"Afternoon tennis, anyone? Or should we skip straight to poolside drinks and wildly embellished tales of triumph?"

The spell broke. Harper looked away first, back to safe ground. Back to duty. Back to business.

The line was redrawn—neat, professional, deliberate.

But the air between them?

Still charged.

Still humming.

Still unresolved.

And the weekend—oh, the weekend—was far from over.

That night, the vineyard grounds shimmered beneath a blanket of stars, the kind that seemed endless, as though the whole valley had been draped in silver light. Someone had built a bonfire in the clearing behind the main house, its flames crackling, sending up sparks that vanished into the dark. The glow flickered across a semicircle of Adirondack chairs, painting faces in warm gold and turning wine glasses into tiny stained-glass lanterns balanced on knees.

Laughter rolled lazily through the night—unguarded, softened by a full day of sunshine, games, and too much competition. Mel was in the middle of a ridiculous story about Gavin accidentally texting a heart emoji to the CFO, and Clara was doubled over, wheezing so hard she nearly spilled her drink.

Harper sat with a wool blanket draped over her lap, a glass of red cupped loosely in her hand. Firelight danced in her eyes, catching the wild strands of her hair stirred loose by the wind. Her cheeks were still pink from the sun, her smile soft, unforced. She looked… different. Relaxed in a way Alex had never seen before. Unguarded. For once, not carrying the weight of being the most composed person in the room.

Alex sat two chairs down, nursing a whiskey, content to watch rather than speak. Every so often, he caught the curve of her smile, the quiet shift of her shoulders beneath the blanket, and it tugged at something deep inside him.

Then Clara rose to fetch marshmallows, and Mel dragged Gavin into some chaotic glow-stick version of truth-or-dare, leaving the space beside Harper suddenly empty.

He hesitated.

And then he stood.

And crossed it.

"Room for one more?" he asked, nodding toward the vacant chair.

Harper glanced at him, her eyes half-shadowed by firelight. "It's your team retreat," she said lightly, scooting the blanket just enough to make room. "Technically, I work for you."

"That's not what I asked."

A pause. Then the faintest curve tugged at her mouth. "Yes. Sit."

He did.

For a while they simply watched the flames. The silence wasn't awkward—it brimmed, alive with things unsaid. The kind of silence that felt like its own language.

"They really like you," Harper said at last.

"Who?"

"The team. Gavin. Even Shelley, and she's a tougher critic than she'll ever admit."

"I like them, too," he said. And then, turning his gaze fully on her: "And you?"

Her brows lifted, amused. "Do I like them?"

He shook his head, voice low, direct. "No. Do you like me?"

That startled a soft laugh out of her. "Direct, aren't you?"

"Only when it matters."

Her eyes lingered on his, searching, peeling past the easy charm. Looking for the truth beneath it.

"I don't know yet," she admitted quietly. "Some days, yes. Some days, I think there's more to you than you let on."

"And the other days?"

She turned back to the fire, the flames catching gold in her hair. "On the other days, I'm still figuring you out."

He leaned in—just enough that she could feel the warmth of him, close but not touching, the subtle pull he carried without effort.

"Then I'll make it easier," he murmured. "I'm not who I pretend to be. But I want you to see the real me."

Her breath caught, and when her eyes met his again, the fire cracked softly between them, filling the silence with possibility.

"Alex," she whispered, almost fragile, "you don't have to be perfect. Only real."

The moment stretched—breathless, fragile, suspended between fear and want. Something shifted. Not fireworks. Not a kiss. But something quieter, heavier. A gravity neither could deny.

She didn't move closer. Neither did he.

But the space between them wasn't the same anymore.

Then a voice rang out from near the food table: "S'mores time!"

The spell broke like glass.

Harper rose first, wrapping the blanket tighter around her shoulders, retreat disguised as composure. She glanced back at him, eyes glinting in the firelight.

"You're good at that," she said.

"At what?"

"Leaving things just unresolved enough to keep someone wondering."

He smiled faintly, though it didn't reach his eyes. "So are you."

The air was crisp, sharp with dew and laced with the faint sweetness of lavender drifting from the bushes that bordered the vineyard path. Above them, the sky stretched wide and endless, painted in pastels—peach, rose, violet—slowly surrendering to gold. The rows of grapevines, heavy with fruit, caught the morning light like scattered jewels, each drop of moisture sparkling as though the whole valley had been dusted with glass.

Alex walked with his hands shoved into his pockets, each breath puffing into faint clouds in the chill. He hadn't slept. Not after the bonfire. Not after the way her voice had trembled when she told him he didn't have to be perfect, only real. And definitely not after she disappeared into the dark without a word, leaving him with nothing but the echo of her absence.

He crested a low hill—and stopped.

Harper stood at the edge of the path, wrapped in a grey hoodie and black leggings, her arms crossed tightly across her chest. Her hair was loose, tousled by the breeze, her gaze fixed on the vineyard that lay bathed in dawn's hush. She looked softer like this, almost breakable, though he knew better than to mistake her silence for fragility.

He could have turned back. Given her the space she clearly wanted.

He didn't.

"You always up this early?" His voice was quiet, but steady.

She turned, startled. "I could ask you the same."

He walked toward her, stopping a few feet away, close enough to feel the chill radiating between them. "Couldn't sleep."

Her eyes dropped; she nudged a pebble with the toe of her sneaker. "Me neither."

For a while, the only sound was the rustle of vines in the breeze and the far-off call of a bird breaking the stillness.

Then he asked, careful but direct, "Why'd you leave last night?"

She hesitated. "I was tired."

"Harper," he said gently, firmly, "don't lie to me."

That pulled her gaze up to his. Her eyes—stormy, uncertain, edged with hurt—locked on his. "I wasn't lying."

"You didn't even say goodnight."

"I didn't think I needed to."

His jaw tightened, though his tone stayed even. "Something shifted between us last night. I felt it. And I think you did too."

Her arms wrapped tighter around herself. "That's exactly why I left."

He stepped closer, the gravel crunching beneath his shoes. "Why? Because it felt real?"

Her answer was a whisper. "Yes. And I don't trust real."

The words caught him off guard. His breath stilled in his chest.

She turned back toward the horizon as if its rising light could steady her. "I've been there before. With someone who said all the right things. Promised I was safe. And when it fell apart… it broke something in me."

Alex's voice was low, measured. "I'm not him, Harper."

Her shoulders sagged slightly, her reply almost too soft to hear. "I know. But that doesn't make it easier."

He closed the distance until he was beside her—not touching, but close enough that she would feel his presence like a quiet promise. "You told me last night I didn't have to be perfect. Only real. Doesn't that go both ways?"

That made her turn, really look at him. Her expression was raw, stripped of defences, as if every wall she'd carefully built had cracked under the weight of honesty. "You scare me, Alex."

His voice broke on the edges of restraint. "Why?"

"Because the way I feel when I'm around you… it's not simple. It's not something I can control. And if you're not who I think you are—if I let myself fall and I'm wrong—I won't come back from that."

The truth hit him hard, sharper than he expected. Because beneath her fear was the very thing he was hiding: the fact that she didn't really know who he was.

She wanted real. And he was living a lie.

His throat tightened. His fists curled inside his pockets.

"I don't have all the answers," he said finally, slow, and deliberate. "And I've made mistakes. But last night—whatever that was—that was real. I'm not walking away from it."

She didn't respond. Just turned her face back toward the sunrise, her profile washed in gold.

He stayed beside her in silence, matching her stillness even as his thoughts roared. She wanted truth, and he was drowning in deception.

If he told her now, he risked losing her.

If he kept the lie, he risked never deserving her.

The sun climbed higher, gilding the vines, and the silence stretched between them, taut and unyielding.

And Alex knew—something had to break. And soon.

Chapter Nine

Mismatched mugs, half-eaten pastries, and bowls of fruit cluttered the long wooden table. Sunlight slanted through the pergola, casting striped shadows over the group as they laughed and traded stories from the day before. The air smelled faintly of coffee and citrus, comforting and ordinary—everything Alex wanted, and everything that made it impossible to focus.

Harper sat to his right, close enough for Alex to catch the faint scent of her perfume—something soft, clean, and achingly familiar. Her hair was loosely braided now, the casual hoodie from that morning replaced by a crisp white linen shirt that caught the light every time she moved. She laughed at something Mel said, the sound light and effortless… yet distant enough to strike him square in the chest, sharp as a stone.

She was here. But not entirely.

Just like him.

"Earth to Alex," Gavin's voice cut through the fog. Perched casually across the table, he smirked behind his coffee mug. "You look like someone just told you we're out of coffee."

Alex blinked, forcing a smile. "Just thinking."

"That's new," Mel teased, earning a ripple of laughter from the table.

He lifted his black coffee to his lips, the bitter liquid doing little to clear the fog clouding his mind. Across the table, Harper glanced at him once—brief, unreadable—before returning to her conversation with Mel.

Alex tried to focus on the others. Gavin's animated retelling of the barrel puzzle debacle. Mel's dramatic reenactment of slipping in the vineyard mud. The laughter, the clinking mugs, the bright morning sunlight—it all drifted past him like smoke. Nothing anchored him. Nothing stuck.

Because all he could think about was what Harper had said.

'If you're not who I think you are… I won't come back from that.'

And he wasn't. Not really.

They sat amid coworkers, casual acquaintances, and harmless chatter, but none of them knew the man he truly was. Not Harper. Not Mel. Not even Gavin, who had already suggested grabbing drinks next week in the city.

They thought he was Alex Dawson, a transfer from London, a systems engineer.

Not Alexander Dawson, billionaire CEO of Veridian Dynamics. Not the man who had walked into this on a bet, never expecting to feel anything—and yet now feeling everything.

A clatter of cutlery snapped him back. Harper had dropped her knife, and as she bent to pick it up, her hand brushed the back of his leg beneath the table. She froze, then straightened, expression carefully neutral, as though nothing had happened.

He wanted to reach out. Say something. Anything.

But Gavin's voice cut through the tension again. "So, Alex," he said, a glint of knowing amusement in his eye, "how's the corporate culture down here treating you? More laid back than London, I assume?"

Alex stiffened. Subtle. But Harper noticed.

He schooled his features, forcing his tone flat, controlled. "Very different. But refreshing."

Gavin nodded, already turning the conversation toward today's plan. But the damage was done. Harper's gaze lingered, just a fraction too long, and Alex felt the weight of it pressing against him.

She was sharp. Intuitive. She'd start putting things together if he wasn't careful.

And yet, for the first time since this charade began, Alex wasn't afraid of being discovered.

He was afraid of hurting her.

Of watching that warmth in her eyes vanish the instant she discovered the truth.

Of losing the fragile trust they'd begun to build, thread by delicate thread.

His fork hovered above his plate, untouched. The coffee had gone cold. Around him, the morning moved on—light and easy—but inside, he was unravelling.

Because the question was no longer just *if* he should tell her.

It was *when.*

And what kind of man he'd be if he didn't.

The next team-building exercises kicked off after breakfast, and to Harper's secret delight—and Alex's visible dread—there were trust falls.

They returned to the grassy clearing behind the meeting hall, where the morning sun had burned off the last of the mist, leaving the dew-slick grass sparkling. Staff members formed wobbly lines in their assigned teams while a young facilitator, clipboard in hand, radiated boundless energy as he explained the rules with the earnest conviction of someone who truly believed in the transformative power of organized vulnerability.

Alex stood with his arms crossed, watching a junior analyst topple backward into Gavin's waiting arms.

"She's really going for it," Harper said, stepping beside him, a coffee cup cradled between her hands, the aroma of roasted beans rising into the warm air.

"She's half his size," Alex murmured. "Low risk."

Harper's lips twitched. "Are you scared, Mr. Dawson?"

"I'm cautious," he corrected. "There's a difference."

"Mm. Spoken like a man who's about to fall flat on his back."

He arched a brow. "Are you catching me?"

"No," she said brightly. "Mel is."

His head snapped toward the petite receptionist, who was currently adjusting her sunglasses and chatting animatedly about nail polish with Shelley. He turned back to Harper, mock horror etched across his face. "You're joking."

She grinned. "Don't worry. I'll supervise."

One by one, team members stepped forward, fell back, and laughed as they were caught. It was awkward, yes—but laughter came easier now. Yesterday's stiffness had melted into camaraderie, thanks in no small part to Harper's warm, steady leadership. And maybe, Alex admitted silently, to a certain green team victory that Gavin couldn't stop bragging about at every opportunity.

Then it was Alex's turn.

He eyed the semicircle behind him: Gavin, Shelley, Mel—enthusiastic but wildly underqualified.

"You're stalling," Harper called from the sidelines, arms crossed, a teasing smile lifting her lips.

He shot her a look. "If I die, tell my tailor he was right about the double stitching."

"Noted."

With a slow, measured breath, he closed his eyes—and let himself fall.

A split second of weightlessness.

Then arms—many, slightly uneven but firm enough—caught him.

Cheers erupted. Someone clapped. Mel squealed, "We did it!" as if they'd just won the World Cup.

Alex stood, brushing grass from his sleeves, and turned to Harper with narrowed eyes. "You're enjoying this."

"Immensely."

"Good to know," he said, stepping a little closer, his voice lower, more intimate. "I'll remember that when it's your turn."

She blinked. "Excuse me?"

"Oh, it's only fair," he said, already gesturing toward the facilitator. "I believe it's in the team-building handbook—page three."

A ripple of amusement ran through the group as Harper's name was called.

She hesitated. "I—"

"No backing out now," Alex said. "Unless you're scared."

That got her. She handed off her coffee, rolled her shoulders, and stepped forward with mock seriousness. "Alright. Just... don't let me crash."

"Wouldn't dream of it."

She turned, exhaled slowly—and fell.

He caught her. Clean, smooth, without hesitation. Her body pressed briefly against his, enough to feel the warmth radiating from her, the faint scent of lavender mingling with something uniquely, unmistakably him. Then she straightened, brushing a stray strand of hair from her face.

Their eyes met.

There it was again. That thrum of something just beneath the surface. A gravity neither of them could shake, drawing them closer even as they stood upright, socially acceptable distance maintained.

"Well done," Alex said quietly. "Told you I wouldn't drop you."

She looked up at him, cheeks faintly flushed, lips curved in a small, almost shy smile. "No. You didn't."

Another moment passed—brief, breathless—before Gavin loudly called for a group photo, scattering the tension with forced poses and bad angles.

But the feeling lingered.

Not just between them.

Within them.

Something had shifted.

And neither of them could pretend it hadn't.

The farewell cocktail party was in full swing—the final afternoon of the team-building retreat. Streamers crisscrossed the open-air patio, casting a festive glow over clinking glasses, bursts of laughter, and the mellow strumming of a live acoustic guitarist. Off to the side, a small bonfire crackled, sending flickers of golden light across the crowd, the scent of toasted marshmallows mingling with the crisp summer air.

Alex leaned against one of the tall cocktail tables, a beer in hand, talking with Gavin and two others from their department—Brandon from finance and Jai from IT. They were swapping stories from the retreat, rehashing the obstacle course with exaggerated flair, and yes—Gavin was still bragging.

"I'm just saying," Gavin said, gesturing with a lime wedge, "no one expected the green team to win. We were the underdogs. The scrappy team."

"You memorised the trivia sheet," Brandon shot back, "that wasn't scrappy. That was obsessive."

"I call it prepared," Gavin replied smugly, tapping his temple.

Alex chuckled, taking a slow sip of his beer, finally letting himself relax. It had been a good day. Harper had looked stunning earlier—wearing a deep blue dress that skimmed her knees and made her eyes glow under the bright afternoon sun. She'd been laughing with Mel near the bar, occasionally glancing his way, and each time his chest had tightened just a little.

He didn't know what it meant. Not yet. But he was hoping.

Then Gavin's expression shifted. His smile faltered, replaced by a frown that sharpened into a scowl. "What is he doing here?"

Alex followed his gaze without thinking.

And there he was.

Billy Bailey.

Cutting through the crowd with a purposeful stride, eyes locked on Harper.

Alex's jaw clenched, his knuckles tightening around the cold bottle in his hand.

Billy looked as slick as ever—expensive blazer, meticulously styled hair, and that insufferable, self-satisfied confidence that screamed entitlement. Several heads turned as he passed, clearly surprised to see him. He wasn't part of the team. He wasn't invited. And yet, there he was—zeroing in on Harper with a determined swagger that sent a sharp, hot edge of territorial instinct racing through Alex's chest.

"What the hell," Jai muttered under his breath. "Didn't he get fired?"

Alex didn't answer. He was already moving.

Across the patio, Harper had just handed Shelley a drink when she turned—and froze.

Her eyes widened, a flicker of shock and unease passing across her features as she took in the man striding toward her. The light-hearted laughter around them dimmed in her perception, replaced by the unmistakable tension that made the hair on her arms prickle.

Alex's mind narrowed. Every step Billy took forward only sharpened the urgency in him, the need to be between Harper and the danger she hadn't yet recognised.

And in that instant, the party—the music, the chatter, even the warm sun—faded into background noise.

All that existed was Harper.

And the man who had no business standing in her way.

Billy smiled like he had every right to be there. "Harper."

She stiffened. A cold spike of dread shot down her spine, coiling in her stomach.

"What are you doing here?" she asked, arms crossing defensively.

"I needed to talk to you." His voice was low, rehearsed, every syllable carefully measured—not even pretending to be casual. "Alone."

"I'm at a work retreat," she said, steadying herself. "This isn't appropriate."

"Neither was disappearing on me without a proper conversation." His tone dipped into something coaxing, manipulative. "You never gave us a real chance to talk about what happened. You can't just throw two years away on one mistake."

Alex's grip tightened around his beer bottle. Every muscle in his body screamed to step in—but this was Harper's moment, and she was holding her ground.

"We already talked." Her voice was tight, but steady. Don't let him get to you. "You just didn't like what I had to say. And I didn't throw it away—you did."

Alex moved without hesitation, jaw clenched, pulse hammering in his temples. He slipped in beside Harper—close enough to mark his presence, careful not to touch her, but close enough to make his point.

"Everything alright here?"

Billy's smile faltered, just for a flicker. "Ah. You again. Go away."

Alex didn't blink. "No. You're trespassing."

Harper's hand brushed Alex's arm, fleeting, a silent thank-you. "Billy, this is Alex Dawson." Her voice remained steady, though her knuckles whitened around the glass she held. "He's the systems engineer—part of our Sydney team."

Billy's eyes narrowed, scanning Alex like he was a rival in a game he'd already lost. "Funny. You don't look local."

"And you don't look invited," Alex shot back, calm but sharp.

Mel appeared beside Harper as if summoned by instinct, her eyebrows arched in icy judgment. "You should leave, Billy. Before someone calls security. Again."

Billy's jaw ticked. "I'm not here to cause trouble. I just… I just need to talk to Harper."

"We already talked," Harper replied, voice cool and unwavering. "Nothing you say will change how I feel, Billy."

Her throat tightened, but her spine remained straight. "Please leave."

For a long beat, he studied her—frustration flickering across his face, then something darker, a trace of regret. Finally, he turned and stalked away, disappearing into the night like a bitter aftertaste.

Silence fell, thick and heavy.

Then Mel exhaled, a soft, wry laugh escaping. "Well. That was dramatic."

Alex glanced at Harper. Her shoulders were stiff, but her composure unbroken. Strong. Fierce.

"You okay?" he asked quietly, voice low.

She nodded, taking a small, steadying breath. "I will be."

He didn't press her. Just stayed, a solid presence at her side—warm, protective, unspoken.

And when she finally lifted her gaze to meet his, Alex saw it: a shift in her eyes.

Not just gratitude.

Not just relief.

Trust.

Real, unshakable trust.

And in that instant, Alex realised—it was worth more than a hundred hollow victories, more than any prize or point he could ever claim. This mattered.

Chapter Ten

The bus hummed softly beneath them as it wound along the curling coastal roads, the late afternoon sun slanting golden through the wide windows. Shadows stretched long across the seats, painting everything in a muted glow. Alex had managed to slip into the seat beside Harper again—not by chance this time, but with quiet determination.

She hadn't reappeared until boarding, slipping back in without a word—no goodbye, no explanation, just a silent return and carefully averted eyes.

He'd almost gone searching for her after Billy stormed off, frustration chewing at his chest like glass. But he hadn't known what room she was in, and barging through the halls of the retreat would've made him look controlling, possessive—everything she didn't need. She needed space. And he was trying—God, he was trying—to respect that.

Now, seated next to her again, he didn't press. He just waited. The quiet between them wasn't strained, exactly—it was delicate. Fragile. Something knitting itself back together in real time.

Harper stifled a yawn and blinked toward the window, lashes lowering against the sunlit glass.

"Tired?" Alex asked, voice pitched low, careful.

She nodded without turning to him. "Didn't sleep much."

For a moment he hesitated, then let instinct win. He reached down and closed his hand gently over hers. Her fingers twitched at the contact... but she didn't pull away.

That small allowance landed like a victory. Monumental.

She exhaled, soft and weary, then leaned over, her head finding his shoulder. Her hair brushed his jaw, fine strands tickling, and her body slowly relaxed into him, her warmth seeping through his shirt like sunlight thawing frost.

Alex went utterly still, afraid that even breathing too deeply might break the spell.

Within minutes, her breathing evened out. She was asleep.

He turned his head slightly, careful, and let himself look at her—the faint furrow in her brow smoothed as she drifted deeper, her lips parting in unguarded peace. She looked so different like this. Not the woman who kept her chin high and her emotions neatly locked behind polite smiles. Not the guarded, careful Harper she let the world see.

His chest ached with something he didn't have a name for.

He didn't know what tomorrow would bring. Whether she'd pull back again. Whether that wall she kept around herself would rise higher.

But tonight, here on this bus, she was with him. Trusting him enough to rest. Enough to lean on him.

And that was enough.

For now.

It was late evening when the bus hissed to a stop outside the Veridian Dynamics Sydney office, brakes sighing like they, too, were relieved the journey was over. Around them came the shuffle of bags, the low murmur of voices, colleagues shifting back into workday reality. The weekend retreat was already being folded away.

Alex didn't move.

He looked down at Harper, still leaning lightly against him, her hand still curled in his.

"Harper," he said softly, brushing a strand of hair from her cheek. "We're back."

Her eyes fluttered open, slow, and hazy. For a moment she seemed caught between worlds, uncertain of where she was, then her gaze found his.

She blinked, sat up, smoothing her hair with a hand. "Sorry," she murmured. "I didn't mean to—"

"You don't need to apologise," Alex interrupted gently. "You needed rest."

The bus emptied around them until only the two of them remained. The driver flicked a glance at them in the rearview mirror—patient but pointed.

Alex rose and offered his hand. She accepted without hesitation this time, letting him help her with her bag. Together, they stepped down onto the pavement.

Sydney was alive around them—traffic rushing past, voices carried on the cooling night air, the endless rhythm of the city resuming its pace. Their colleagues peeled away into rideshares or toward the parking garage, waving quick goodbyes until only the two of them lingered, caught in a moment neither seemed ready to break.

Alex turned to her. He didn't speak. Just looked at her, steady, the quiet intensity in his eyes saying more than words could.

Harper shifted her weight, then lifted her gaze to meet his.

"I walked in on Billy," she said, her voice low, even. "With his assistant. In my own apartment."

Alex didn't flinch. He didn't gasp or widen his eyes. He just listened, still and rooted, letting her unburden herself.

"He called it a mistake," she went on, a bitter laugh edging her words. "Like forgetting to buy milk. Like we hadn't been together for two years. Like we hadn't been engaged for a few months."

Alex's hands curled into fists at his sides, his pulse beating sharp and steady in his ears.

"I'm sorry," he said quietly. It wasn't perfunctory. It wasn't pity. It was something fiercer—anger wrapped in tenderness, as though he longed to tear the past apart with his bare hands and carry the weight of the wound for her.

Her gaze dropped to the pavement, lashes lowering like a shield, before lifting again. Her eyes were sharp, but beneath the steel was hurt that hadn't healed. "I'm finding it hard to trust again. That's why I don't do… this." She gestured between them, a small, weary flick of her hand. "That's why I keep things simple. Safe."

Alex drew in a slow breath, his chest tight, every word pulling at something raw inside him.

"I'm not him, Harper."

"I know," she said quickly, almost too quickly. Then softer, as if the truth itself scared her. "That's the terrifying part."

They stood there, suspended in a silence that felt like the edge of something vast.

Then Alex extended his hand again—not out of obligation, not for help, but simply open. Steady. Waiting.

Harper looked at it.

And then, with a breath that trembled just a little, she took it.

Alex walked beside Harper in silence as they made their way toward the underground car park. The low hum of fluorescent lights filled the space, mixing with the sharp, steady clack of her heels against the concrete. Their earlier conversation lingered between them, fragile and unspoken, like smoke that hadn't quite dispersed.

He didn't try to fill the silence. He didn't need to. He just stayed close, his presence steady at her side.

When they reached her car, she paused, keys dangling loosely from her fingers. She turned to him with a small, softened smile that didn't quite reach her eyes but warmed him all the same.

"Thanks for… staying behind," she said.

"Anytime," Alex answered. And he meant it—more than she could know.

She hesitated, as though she might add something more, but instead opened her door. "See you tomorrow?"

"Yeah," he said quietly. "Tomorrow."

She slipped inside, closing the door with a muted thud. For a moment she lingered, glancing at him once through the glass before starting the engine. Then she was gone, headlights slicing through the dim garage as she drove out into the night.

Alex remained where he stood, watching the taillights disappear, reluctant to move. Finally, he turned and crossed to his own car—an unassuming silver sedan that looked utterly out of place. Worlds away from the sleek black Jaguar that usually waited for him in London.

He slid into the driver's seat, shut the door, and leaned back against the headrest. His chest rose and fell in a slow, deliberate exhale, the weight of the evening pressing heavy against his ribs.

That was when his phone buzzed.

He didn't need to check the screen. He already knew.

With a resigned sigh, Alex answered. "Theo."

"Mate!" Theo's voice exploded down the line, brash and smug as ever. "Just checking in on your little outback experiment. You got a woman on the hook yet, or what?"

Alex pinched the bridge of his nose, fatigue threading through him. "I don't think this bet is a good idea anymore."

A beat of silence. Then Theo laughed—loud, sharp, disbelieving. "Oh no, you don't. You're not backing out now. It's only been two weeks. You've got two more to go."

Alex stared through the windshield, the city lights blurring. Harper's face rose unbidden—how her shoulders had tensed when Billy appeared, how she'd leaned into him on the bus, the quiet tremor in her voice when she finally trusted him with her truth.

"Harper's not some conquest," he said flatly.

"Harper," Theo repeated, amused. "Nice name. What's she like?"

Guilt crawled beneath Alex's skin. "She wouldn't appreciate being discussed like that."

Theo scoffed. "Since when did that ever stop you? When have you *ever* cared about the women you date?"

"I'm not dating her."

"Oh, so she's playing hard to get. Or she just not interested?"

Alex said nothing. The silence stretched, heavy and telling.

Theo broke it with a chuckle that grated. "You knew the rules—one million pounds, four weeks, no money, no name. Just charm. Just you."

The words landed harder than they had the night the wager was made, dragging across Alex's conscience like chains.

His jaw tightened. "I'll talk to you later."

And before Theo could reply, Alex ended the call. The silence that followed felt louder than anything Theo could've said.

For a long moment he just sat there, phone heavy in his hand, the quiet roar of the city beyond the garage pressing against the windows.

Then, without another word, he started the engine and drove into the night—more conflicted, more unsettled, than he'd ever admit to anyone.

Monday morning arrived with its usual chorus of clattering keyboards and the hiss of the espresso machine, but there was a charge in the air—an undercurrent of anticipation that only came in the week before Christmas. The Sydney office had slipped into holiday mode. A wreath hung crookedly on the glass door, tinsel spiralled around monitor stands, and someone had swapped out the scent diffuser for cinnamon and pine, filling the space with warmth that felt both festive and faintly distracting.

In the conference room, the team gathered for their final Monday meeting of the year. Harper stood at the front, clipboard in hand, poised yet approachable. She wore a forest-green blouse—simple, elegant, but striking against her strawberry-blonde hair, which was pulled neatly into a ponytail.

"Good morning, everyone," she began, her voice calm but carrying a spark of cheer. "First of all, thank you for your participation at the team-building retreat. I know some of you were sceptical about trust falls and vineyard obstacle courses—" a ripple of laughter moved through the room, "—but I truly appreciated the enthusiasm and openness. If you have suggestions for the next one, feel free to email me or drop by my office."

Her gaze swept the group, steady but warm. "Just a quick reminder—the Christmas party is this Friday. After that, the office will be closed until January 2nd. Please remember that even while we're on break, we still represent Veridian Dynamics. Whether it's on social media or at company events, let's keep professionalism in mind."

Several heads bobbed in agreement, while others glanced down at phones to check calendars.

"That's all from me. I'll be around most of the day if you need anything."

As the meeting broke into quiet chatter and shuffling papers, Alex didn't move. He sat rooted in place, gaze fixed on Harper. At the front, she leaned in toward Mel and Gavin, smiling, her posture easy, her laughter unforced—completely in her element. Professional. Composed. Unreachable. And something inside him twisted.

One more week.

That's all he had before the holiday break scattered them to different corners of the world. One more week before daily proximity dissolved into silence, before the fragile thread tying them together was tested by distance, time, and the secrets he still hadn't told her.

The thought struck him hard—sharp, unexpected, and unsettling in its depth. After everything—the retreat, the trust fall, her head resting against his shoulder on the bus—it wasn't about the bet anymore. It hadn't been for days.

He didn't want to win. He wanted her. Not as a conquest. Not as a prize. Not as some reckless victory to hold over Theo.

He wanted her entirely. Honestly. Without conditions. Without the shadow of a lie between them.

And the clock was ticking.

His jaw tightened, the truth pressing heavy in his chest, immovable and suffocating. "I can't keep lying to her," he muttered under his breath, the words raw, scraped from somewhere deep.

What had begun as a foolish wager had shifted beneath his feet, transforming into something he couldn't control. Somewhere between the vineyard dawn and the fragile weight of her trust, the rules had been rewritten.

This wasn't strategy anymore.

It was betrayal.

Alex stepped into the break room, the familiar aroma of burnt toast and bitter instant coffee hanging in the air like an old habit. He spotted Harper by the window, stirring sugar into a mug, her posture relaxed but her expression distant, wrapped in thought.

"Hey," he said, keeping his tone casual, light enough to mask the pull in his chest. "Any plans for the Christmas break?"

She glanced over her shoulder, a soft, fleeting smile tugging at her lips. "Yeah. Heading to Perth to see my family. It's been a while."

"That sounds nice," Alex said, moving a step closer, careful not to crowd her. "Big gathering?"

She shrugged, the morning light catching the warmth in her eyes. "Just my parents, my brothers, and the neighbours. It's a tradition—we all get together every year."

Alex's mind drifted to the weekend before—the guy at the restaurant who had looked at Harper like she hung the stars. "The friends that were here that weekend?"

She nodded, faint amusement in her expression. "Yeah. Clara and I have been best friends since school. Her brother and mine are practically inseparable. It's like one big extended family, really."

He felt a sharp pang in his chest. Jealousy? Or the hollow ache of knowing she had a place where she belonged—where warmth and tradition wrapped around her like a protective cloak—while he didn't.

"We attend a New Year's Eve party every year," she added, her tone airy, almost playful. "Dancing, drinking, too much food. The usual chaos."

"Sounds a lot better than my plans," he said with a crooked, self-deprecating smile. "My mum's off on a cruise, so… it'll just be me. Sticking around the city, probably catching up on sleep—or regretting all my life choices."

Her expression softened, a fleeting wistfulness passing over her features. For a heartbeat, he thought she might say more—something unspoken hovering on the edge of her lips, an invitation to step into her life, even just for a moment.

But it never came.

She just nodded, eyes dipping briefly to the floor. "Still," she said gently, "a quiet Christmas doesn't sound so bad."

But it didn't. Not really. Not for either of them.

Harper busied herself with tidying the sugar packets beside the coffee machine, though they were already neatly arranged. Her fingers moved with purpose, but her mind spun uncontrollably.

She couldn't believe it—she'd almost invited him. Home. To Perth. To her family. To her real life. What had she been thinking?

Maybe it was the way he'd looked at her—honest, a little lonely, hiding it behind that charming smile. Or maybe it was the way he truly listened when she spoke, as if she were the only person in the room, as if she mattered more than anyone else.

She shook her head, trying to ground herself. This wasn't supposed to be anything. He was just a colleague. A handsome, charming, quietly magnetic colleague who made her pulse quicken in ways she hadn't felt in years.

And yet…

The words had almost escaped her lips.

You could come with me.

She didn't say it. Couldn't. It was too soon, too intimate, too impossibly hopeful.

Still, the truth lodged itself firmly in her chest.

Some part of her wanted him to say yes.

Some part of her wanted him there.

Some part of her wanted to believe he would stay.

Chapter Eleven

To Alex's mounting frustration, he had barely seen Harper all week.

A passing glance in the hallway. A fleeting nod across a crowded room. A brief meeting where she had strategically taken the far end of the table. Nothing more.

How was he supposed to get closer to her if she was never around? The days slipped through his fingers like grains of sand—slipping, scattering, leaving him increasingly desperate. With each passing hour, his chances to connect, to speak, to touch the edges of her world… they were dwindling.

Friday arrived far too quickly.

The final day in the office. Possibly the last time he'd see Harper—at least in this life he'd constructed under a carefully crafted false identity. The thought lodged like a jagged stone in his chest, heavy and unwelcome.

The Christmas party was being held at the Harbourview, a sleek rooftop venue adorned with twinkling lights and a sweeping panorama of Sydney Harbour. Ironically, it was only a short walk from his modest flat, a reminder of the life he usually led—unremarkable, unnoticed.

He planned to walk there, but his mind was already ten steps ahead, pacing through the entire evening in meticulous detail. Every second, every glance, every opportunity to speak to her—he needed to seize it. Tonight, there would be no hiding. No half-measures. No games.

Tonight, he had one mission: win Harper Jameson over. Not as a challenge. Not for a bet.

For real.

He had dressed with careful intention: a dark blue suit that hugged his frame perfectly, a crisp white shirt, the collar left casually open at the neck, no tie. Sharp enough to command attention, relaxed enough to seem effortlessly himself—the version of himself he wished he could always be in her presence.

But the moment he stepped into the Harbourview, he froze.

There she was.

Harper.

Her hair swept up in an elegant style, soft tendrils brushing the curve of her neck—an exposed line of skin that made his pulse stutter. Around it, a delicate necklace glinted, the stones deep crimson like rubies, catching the light in a way that drew his eyes instinctively to her collarbone.

And the dress.

Red. Bold. Fitted in all the right places, flowing where it should flow, with a daring slit that ran high along one leg, leaving him painfully aware of every curve. She looked…

Breathtaking.

Not merely beautiful, not just alluring.

Regal. Radiant. Untouchable.

And yet achingly familiar, like a figure he had been dreaming of long before he even realised he was.

He swallowed hard, the weight of it pressing on his chest. Tonight, had just become a thousand times harder—and infinitely more important.

He forced himself to step forward, his stride measured, confident on the outside, while his heart pounded like a drum in his chest, threatening to betray him with each step. She hadn't seen him yet—she was laughing softly at something the bartender had said while handing her a drink, and the sound made his stomach twist.

Then she turned.

Their eyes met.

He opened his mouth, words ready to escape—but nothing came out. For the first time in a long, long time, Alexander Dawson—the billionaire, the negotiator, the charmer—was utterly, completely, speechlessly disarmed.

Harper arched an eyebrow, a playful smile tugging at her lips. "Don't you scrub up nice."

He exhaled a quiet laugh, finding his voice at last. "You can talk. You look… stunning."

"Thank you." Her cheeks flushed the faintest pink, and she glanced down for a moment, clearly flattered, a subtle shimmer in her eyes betraying her amusement.

Before he could respond, they were interrupted. A couple of department heads made their way over, grins wide, brimming with holiday cheer. One pressed a kiss to Harper's cheek; another draped an arm just a little too snugly around her waist, holding her close for a greeting that lingered a touch too long.

Alex's jaw tightened, and he slipped his hands casually into his pockets, keeping himself from doing something rash.

She laughed politely, gently disentangling herself, but her eyes flicked toward him—checking, measuring his reaction.

He didn't say a word—but his gaze spoke volumes.

She turned back to him, that teasing curve of a smile returning. "Jealous, Mr. Dawson?"

He tilted his head, smirking. "Territorially observant."

Her laugh was low, warm, and musical. "You're impossible."

"But you're still talking to me," he murmured, voice dropping just slightly.

"I suppose I am," she replied, a faint blush in her cheeks.

The music swelled behind them, a soft current that seemed to dissolve the crowd around them. For a moment, it was just the two of them, the world narrowing to the hum of holiday lights and shared tension.

It was a sit-down dinner, much to Alex's relief—less room for her to drift away. He stayed close, matching her pace until the seating arrangements were finalised.

To his quiet satisfaction—and Graham's obvious irritation—Alex was placed on Harper's right. Graham, the overly familiar department head, landed on her left.

Dinner began. The soft clinking of cutlery mingled with murmured conversation, creating a gentle rhythm. Alex leaned slightly toward Harper.

"So," he murmured, voice pitched low, meant only for her, "how are you finding the evening so far?"

Before she could answer, Graham chimed in. "It's been lovely, hasn't it, Harper? I was just telling Rachel from marketing, no one lights up a room quite like you."

Harper gave a polite smile. "That's kind of you."

Alex bit the inside of his cheek, suppressing a groan. He tried again. "Are you returning on January second?"

Graham, of course, cut in once more, launching into a self-congratulatory story about a pitch he once led in Singapore, name-dropping half the room with gleeful precision.

Alex's jaw twitched. He barely tasted his food; attention narrowed entirely on Harper—and the mounting urge to strangle Graham with his overpriced silk tie.

When dinner finally ended, the soft strains of music drifting across the room, Alex didn't hesitate. As Harper reached for her clutch, Graham rose with a self-satisfied grin.

"Harper—"

"Dance with me," Alex said, already standing, extending his hand with quiet authority.

Harper blinked in surprise, then a smile curved her lips as she placed her hand in his. "I didn't know you danced."

"I do tonight," he replied, the corner of his mouth lifting in a hint of mischief.

Before Graham could sputter a protest, Alex was leading her onto the dance floor, her hand snug in his, the quiet victory settling through him like a warmth he didn't want to let go of.

The music swelled around them, soft and slow, the kind of melody that demanded closeness. Alex placed one hand gently on Harper's waist, the other enclosing hers. She rested her free hand lightly on his shoulder, and for a moment, they simply stood there, suspended in the hush between songs, feeling the gravity of being near each other.

Then they began to move.

Harper's breath caught. He was warm, steady, his touch confident yet gentle. She could smell his cologne—subtle, masculine, and expensive—and the way he was looking at her... like she was the only woman in the room. Her heart fluttered, a tight lump forming in her throat.

This might be the last time she saw him. The thought hit harder than it should have.

"You're a good dancer," she murmured, her voice quiet, almost hesitant.

His lips curved in a small, private smile. "You make it easy."

The compliment sent a flush up her neck. She lowered her eyes for a moment, then glanced back up. "It's strange, but… I think I'm going to miss you."

Alex faltered, just for half a heartbeat. His arms tightened slightly around her, instinctive and protective. She was going to miss him.

He looked down at her, the soft glow of fairy lights casting gold across her features, her body fitting perfectly against his. She belonged there—in his arms. It felt natural, inevitable.

He wanted to tell her everything. About the bet, about the truth, about how completely he'd changed. But not yet. Not while she smiled at him like that.

"I'm going to miss you too," he admitted, voice low and rough with the emotion he didn't bother to hide.

They danced on, swaying slowly as the world blurred around them. Just for now, it was enough—enough to hold her, enough to pretend the hours weren't slipping past too quickly.

Two more songs passed. Neither was ready to let go. The music, the lights, the warmth of her body pressed close—it was intoxicating. It was easy to forget that time was running out.

Eventually, Harper pulled back slightly, breathless, eyes shining. "I need some air," she murmured.

He nodded, guiding her gently through the crowd and out onto the terrace. The cool night air wrapped around them like a balm, a welcome contrast to the warmth inside. City lights shimmered across the water, the hum of laughter and music fading behind the glass doors.

No one else was out there. Just them. Silence. Stars. Possibility.

Harper walked to the edge of the railing, hands bracing the metal, gazing out at the sparkling water. Alex followed, standing close, resisting the urge to touch her. She looked impossibly beautiful in the moonlight—elegant, glowing, untouchable.

Then he noticed it—mistletoe, hung quietly from the pergola beam above them. Subtle, deliberate.

He glanced at her, a slow, playful smile tugging at the corner of his mouth. "Well… it's tradition."

Harper turned, saw it, and laughed softly, a light, airy sound. "Of course it is."

Their eyes locked.

Neither moved at first. The space between them crackled with unspoken words—things he hadn't confessed, things she hadn't dared to admit. But the moment stretched, fragile, full of possibility.

He stepped closer, breath brushing hers, closing the last inches. "May I?" he asked, voice low, reverent.

Harper hesitated barely a heartbeat… then nodded.

Alex cupped her face gently, thumb brushing her cheek, leaning in. Their lips met—soft at first, tentative, then deeper, drawn by the pull that neither could resist.

It wasn't just tradition. It was something real. Something inevitable.

When they finally parted, Harper's eyes searched his, wide, stunned, breathless.

"What was that?" she whispered.

Alex's chest tightened, heart pounding. "Something I should've done a long time ago."

"Harper," he murmured, voice husky from the kiss, "I need to tell you something."

Before he could continue, she spoke, voice barely above a whisper. "I need to tell you something, too."

He froze, sensing the gravity in her tone.

She looked up at him, eyes wide, yet resolute. "I want you to take me home."

Alex blinked, stunned. "What?"

"To your home," she clarified quickly, cheeks flushed with warmth. "I know it sounds impulsive. I just… I don't want this night to end. I want to be with you."

Her words struck him like lightning—hope and longing crashing together in his chest.

He was stunned. This was what he had wanted all along—her, choosing him. Not for a bet. Not for a game. For him.

But the truth pressed at his ribs, heavy and sharp. She didn't know who he really was. Not yet.

His hand reached for hers, fingers brushing hers with careful hesitation. "Harper… are you sure?"

She nodded, eyes bright with certainty. "I've never been more sure."

His heart thudded violently. He should tell her now—before they crossed a line that couldn't be uncrossed. But what if she walked away? What if this one perfect night shattered everything between them?

He glanced back through the glass doors. Laughter, music, the world they'd just stepped out of. Then he looked back at her—the woman who had unknowingly changed everything.

Maybe… just one more night. One moment that was theirs alone—untouched by truth, untouched by consequence.

"My flat's nearby," he said quietly. "Do you mind walking?"

She shook her head, her hand tightening slightly around his. "No. I'd like that."

He kissed her again—slower this time, lingering just long enough to burn the moment into memory—then whispered, "Let's go."

They walked in silence, hand in hand, into the soft Sydney night. Behind them, the music and laughter of the Christmas party faded into memory, replaced by the quiet rhythm of the city—the distant hum of traffic, the rustle of leaves, the soft brush of a summer breeze that danced between them, warm and teasing.

Alex could hardly believe she was beside him—choosing him, trusting him. Yet with every step toward his modest flat, the weight of his secret pressed heavier against his chest.

He should have taken her to the penthouse at the Park Hyatt—the suite with harbour views, marble floors, and impossibly elegant interiors. That's where a man like him would normally take a woman like her.

But tonight, he wasn't a billionaire. He was just a man walking home with a woman who had no idea who he really was.

They reached the building. He hesitated outside the door, thumb hovering near the keypad, gathering courage.

"It's not much," he admitted finally, voice low. "Just… don't expect anything fancy."

Harper turned to him, eyes soft, steady, sincere. "I don't care, Alex. I'm not interested in your possessions—or your lack of them."

Something tightened in his chest. No one had ever said that to him before. And actually meant it.

"Right," he said, forcing a smile, though his throat felt tight and raw. "Well… welcome to my humble abode."

They stepped inside. The flat was modest—clean, simple, but undeniably lived-in. A second-hand couch, a tiny kitchen, stacks of books and magazines on the side table, a hint of life in every corner.

The door clicked shut behind them, and silence wrapped around Alex like a noose.

She was here. With him. Trusting him.

And he was lying to her with every heartbeat.

He watched her take in the space—small, sparse, nothing like the life he'd left behind in London. She didn't flinch. Didn't frown.

When she looked at him again, there was nothing but warmth and affection in her eyes.

His throat tightened.

He didn't deserve this.

He didn't deserve her.

For a split second, he almost told her everything.

But then her hand reached for his, her touch soft and grounding, and the war inside him fell silent.

He kissed her—slow, soft, aching—and told himself he'd find the courage tomorrow.

Chapter Twelve

Alex pulled Harper into his arms, their mouths meeting in a kiss that was deep, slow, and searching. There was no rush—only need, only presence. He kissed her as if he had to memorise every second for the rest of his life—every taste, every sigh, every tremble of her lips against his.

His hands traced down her sides, fingertips grazing over the curve of her waist, committing every line, every contour, to memory like a cartographer charting a sacred, forbidden map. He found the zipper at the back of her dress and drew it down, inch by aching inch, the soft rasp of fabric the only sound between them, a private whisper of desire.

The dress slipped from her shoulders and fell in a silken sigh to the floor, pooling around her feet with a gravity all its own.

Alex stepped back just slightly, letting the air shift between them. His eyes darkened, reverent, as they roamed over her body with an intensity that was both worshipful and hungry. She stood tall beneath his gaze—confident, unflinching—in red lace that clung to her like a second skin. The firelight from the nearby lamp bathed her in gold, casting soft, teasing shadows that accentuated every curve, every line, every exquisite detail.

"You are so beautiful," he murmured, voice thick with awe, as though words could never contain what he truly felt.

Her breath hitched—not from uncertainty, but from the weight of the moment. The intensity of his gaze undressed her far more thoroughly than any clothing ever could. There was no hesitation, no shame—only want, and the thrill of being utterly seen.

She reached for him, fingers curling over the lapels of his jacket, sliding it from his shoulders. It fell behind him, forgotten, a discarded barrier. She moved with quiet determination, undoing his shirt one slow button at a time. Each brush of her fingers against his skin—warm, taut, and achingly alive—made his pulse stutter.

When the last button surrendered, she pushed the fabric aside and let her hands glide across his chest, featherlight but deliberate. He closed his eyes, grounding himself in her touch, imprinting it into memory as if it were the only reality that mattered.

"I've wanted this," she whispered, the confession hanging in the space between them like a vow, fragile and absolute.

"So have I," he breathed, voice low, husky with something feral and tender all at once. "More than I can ever say."

He kissed her again—fierce, insistent, filled with longing and promise—as they moved together toward the bedroom, leaving hesitation, doubt, and restraint behind.

She still wore her heels—tall, elegant, devastatingly sexy—and the sight of her standing there in nothing but lace and those heels stole his breath, leaving him teetering on the edge of reason, utterly undone.

Alex stood beside the bed, shirtless, his breath shallow. For a moment, he didn't touch her—he simply looked. Like a man starving who had finally found the thing that would sustain him. Then, slowly, reverently, he dropped to his knees before her.

He wrapped his arms around her hips, drawing her close. His lips brushed the soft skin of her waist, then trailed lower to the gentle curve of her belly, lingering there as she tangled her fingers in his hair, her nails lightly scraping his scalp.

Her breathing stuttered, the air around them thick with anticipation.

With hands that were steady but unhurried, he hooked his thumbs into the waistband of her panties and slid them down her legs. She stepped out of them, her gaze never wavering from his. There was trust in her eyes now—pure and unspoken. And something more—something soft and aching beneath the heat.

He looked up at her once, seeking her permission. She nodded, the movement barely there.

Then he leaned in, kissing her again—lower this time. Soft, reverent. Worshipful.

A quiet gasp escaped her lips as her hand gripped his shoulder, her body arching into his touch.

There was no rush, no desperation—only a slow, unfolding surrender.

He worked her with devastating precision, every movement purposeful, every stroke meant for her and her alone. Harper clutched his shoulders, her breath turning ragged, her thighs trembling beneath his hands. He could feel her unravelling, piece by piece, each moan a testament to her pleasure.

When she shattered, it was with a cry that tore through the silence—his name on her lips, raw and sacred, a prayer spoken into the night.

He stayed with her, holding her through every tremor, every pulsing wave, his hands firm on her hips, anchoring her to the moment.

Only when the last of her convulsions faded did he lift his head.

Then, tenderly, he ran his hands down her legs and undid the delicate straps of her heels. One, then the other. He slipped them off with reverent care, as if they were priceless. As if she was.

He rose slowly, his mouth tracing the journey back up her body. Her thighs, her hips, her stomach—each kiss a promise, each lick a reminder that she was his entire focus.

By the time he reached her mouth, she was trembling again. He paused, just for a moment, meeting her gaze. Something passed between them—vulnerability, desire, maybe even the fragile beginning of love.

Then he kissed her—deep, slow, and consuming—until the line between them disappeared completely.

As their mouths moved together, he reached behind her and unhooked her bra with practiced ease. The lace slipped from her shoulders and dropped to the floor. He cupped her breasts, his thumbs rasping over her hardened peaks, drawing a soft gasp from her lips.

Harper's hands found his belt. She unfastened it with quiet urgency, fingers slipping beneath the waistband of his pants, sliding down to cup his firm backside. She pulled him closer, her lips brushing against his jaw.

Their bodies pressed together—skin to skin, heart to heart—every inch of contact igniting something deeper.

She met his gaze, breathless and bold. "I want you."

Alex let out a low groan, the sound dragged from somewhere deep in his chest. "I want you too. So damn much."

Her fingers slid his trousers down his hips, and he stepped out of them. His arousal sprang free—hot, hard, and aching—and she cupped him gently, drawing another shaky breath from his lips.

But then he paused, his body tense with sudden awareness.

"I don't have any condoms," he murmured, voice tight with regret.

Harper didn't flinch. "I've been tested. I haven't been with anyone since… Billy. And I have an IUD."

Relief broke over his features like sunlight through clouds. "I was tested recently too," he said, his voice rough with emotion. "And I haven't been with anyone either."

In that moment, the last of the distance between them disappeared.

Alex lowered Harper gently to the bed, following her down. He braced himself above her, his eyes locking with hers—heat and hunger and something so much softer lingering there.

Her hands found him, sure and steady, and he groaned at her touch, the sound unguarded and real.

She explored him slowly, her fingers mapping out every inch of him. Her touch was reverent, full of curiosity and need.

Then, with a sly smile and a spark in her eyes, she pressed lightly on his chest.

"Lie back," she whispered.

He obeyed, breath catching as she knelt between his legs, her eyes never leaving his. The air between them crackled with heat, anticipation coiling like a live wire. Her fingers slid slowly up his thighs, featherlight, deliberate—each inch of contact unravelling him.

Then her mouth joined the dance—hot, wet, and devastatingly skilled. She teased him first with her tongue, the lightest flicks that sent shudders down his spine. When she finally took him into her mouth, deep and slow, his hips jerked helplessly in response.

"Harper…" he choked out, her name torn from him like a plea, a prayer, a confession.

His hand flew to her hair, fingers threading through the silken strands as he tipped his head back with a broken gasp. She set a rhythm—sensual, maddening, reverent. Her mouth and hands worked in perfect sync, and it wasn't just about pleasure; it was devotion, exploration, the kind of intimacy that unravelled him from the inside out.

It wasn't just lust—it was something deeper, richer, dangerous in its intensity. Something neither of them had dared name. But in that moment, it was everything.

His breath came in ragged gasps, chest rising and falling with a raw desperation. Tension coiled deep in his core; every nerve lit with fire as she brought him to the brink with merciless grace.

"I need to be inside you," he rasped, his voice rough with need, thick with emotion.

Harper lifted her head slowly, lips swollen, cheeks flushed, her eyes gleaming with heat and something achingly tender. Without a word, she rose and straddled his hips, her thighs trembling slightly—not from fear, but from the weight of anticipation.

Their eyes met, locked, and time seemed to stall.

There was trust there. Hunger. The kind of desire that stripped you bare.

She reached down, guiding him to her entrance, and slowly—agonisingly—lowered herself onto him, inch by inch, until he was fully seated inside her. A shared gasp broke between them, sharp and reverent.

She was warm, wet, and perfect. He cupped her face, brushing his thumb along her cheekbone as if memorising her. Then she began to move—slow, rolling motions that stole his breath, that made his hands clench hard on her hips.

He met her thrust for thrust, their rhythm building with every grind of her hips, every sigh that escaped her parted lips. She tipped her head back, riding him with abandon, her hair tumbling down her back like molten fire. Her body trembled as her climax overtook her, her soft cries breaking free as she clenched around him.

He held her close, anchoring her through every ripple of release, kissing the sweat-dampened curve of her shoulder, her collarbone, her throat.

And then, he shifted.

With fluid strength, he lifted her and gently turned her onto her knees, her back arching instinctively. He positioned himself behind her and slid back into her with a deep, unrestrained thrust.

She cried out, her hands bracing against the mattress, back arching into him.

He gripped her hips, pulling her back into him with each thrust, his pace steady, then wild, then reverent all over again. One hand reached around to cup her breast, fingers rolling over her sensitive peak until she whimpered, her whole body shivering beneath him.

"God, Harper," he groaned, voice hoarse, his lips trailing along her spine. "You feel so good."

Her name spilled from his lips like a mantra, a song, a desperate prayer.

Their bodies moved in perfect sync, a slow burn that erupted into wildfire. There was no space between them, no hesitation—just raw, electric intimacy.

"Harper, please—I can't…"

But he never finished.

She shattered first, body clenching around him, a cry ripping from her throat that echoed through the room like thunder. Her release triggered his own, a groan torn from deep in his chest as he surged into her, spilling every last ounce of control.

They collapsed in a tangle of limbs and heat, her back flush against his chest, his arms wrapping tight around her middle like he never wanted to let go. They stayed joined, still connected in every way that mattered.

Her heartbeat thundered against his. He buried his face in her neck, pressing soft, reverent kisses to her damp skin.

"That was…" he whispered against her shoulder, his voice thick, almost awed. "You're incredible."

She turned her head slightly, meeting his eyes over her shoulder, a small, breathless smile curving her lips. "So are you."

He kissed her again, slow, and deep, sealing the promise neither of them had spoken yet—but both had undeniably begun to believe.

She didn't speak—she didn't need to. Her hand found his beneath the sheets, fingers weaving through his in a quiet act of devotion. That single, tender gesture said everything words couldn't. In that intimate tangle of limbs, warm skin, and shared breath, the world fell away. There were no doubts, no questions—only them.

Their bodies remained joined for a few more still moments, hearts pounding in sync, eyes closed as if afraid to break the spell. When he finally slipped free from her warm, slick heat, a soft sigh escaped them both—bittersweet and full of aching satisfaction.

Harper pressed a kiss to his chest, then quietly slid out of bed. Her bare feet padded across the floor, her silhouette glowing softly in the golden light of the bedside lamp. The bathroom door clicked shut behind her, leaving a brief hush in her wake.

Alex lay still, one arm flung across the sheets, the other tucked behind his head. The sheet had slipped low on his hips, revealing the sharp lines of his torso, still sheened with the heat of their lovemaking. But his eyes were only for her—his Harper—moving like poetry even in the half-light.

When she returned, fresh-faced, her hair falling in soft waves over her shoulders, he propped himself up on one elbow, gaze devouring her with quiet intensity.

He reached out a hand, his voice a low, magnetic pull. "Come back to me."

She didn't hesitate.

Crawling onto the bed, she slipped back beneath the covers and curled into him, her bare skin pressing to his. Their mouths met in a slow, unhurried kiss—less frantic now, but no less consuming. It was a kiss that spoke of belonging. Of possession. Of something neither of them dared name out loud.

He wrapped his arms around her like he was anchoring himself, like letting go would mean losing something vital.

But holding her wasn't enough.

His lips brushed across her cheek, her jaw, her neck—trailing fire. Then he shifted, easing her onto her back, settling between her thighs. He gazed down at her with reverence, like she was something sacred.

"I need you," he murmured, his voice thick with emotion and desire.

Her answer came in a breathless moan as he slid into her again—slow, deep, deliberate. A low groan escaped him, raw and primal, as their bodies found that same perfect rhythm, as natural as breathing. Every thrust was reverent, an unspoken vow whispered through movement instead of words.

They moved together like tide and moon—drawn, inevitable, bound by something far greater than desire. Her fingers clawed at his shoulders, urging him closer, deeper, until her soft cries spurred him on. His control frayed with every pulse of her body around him, every trembling sigh that spilled from her lips.

When her body arched beneath him, trembling with release, he followed—losing himself completely in her, in the moment, in everything they were becoming.

Later, when exhaustion overtook them, they drifted into sleep wrapped in each other's arms, skin against skin, breaths syncing in a gentle lullaby. The world outside ceased to matter. For a few blissful hours, there was no past, no future—only the warmth of shared connection, of hearts beating in perfect time.

But in the quiet early hours, when the city was still and the moon painted silver shadows across the bed, Alex stirred.

Soft lips brushed over his.

He blinked into the dim light, vision slowly sharpening until he saw her—Harper—straddling him in the hush of morning, her body silhouetted by the soft spill of moonlight through the curtains. Her hair tumbled around her shoulders, eyes dark with a different kind of need.

"Good morning," she whispered, her voice velvet, brushing another kiss to his lips—slow, deep, full of promise.

His hands found her hips instinctively, as if they belonged there. He was still groggy, caught between sleep and waking, but desire surged through him the moment their bodies touched.

"I don't think I'll ever get enough of you," she murmured, her lips grazing his.

He barely had time to reply before she rose just enough to guide him into her again, her breath catching as she sank onto him inch by inch. A low, tortured groan escaped his throat, hands tightening on her waist.

"God, Harper…"

She began to move—slow, languid, sensual—riding him with a grace that made his heart thunder. Her palms braced on his chest, her eyes locked on his, filled with something deeper than lust. There was longing there. Need. A desperate ache to make this last, to etch this moment into forever.

Their bodies moved in harmony, a slow rhythm that built like the steady pull of the tide. There were no words—only sighs, low moans, and the soft slap of skin against skin. Each motion drew them closer, until their moans blended, their breathing faltered, and they fell over the edge together.

She collapsed against his chest, boneless and trembling, her heartbeat a wild staccato against his ribs. He wrapped his arms around her, holding her tightly, anchoring them both in the afterglow.

He kissed her temple, his lips lingering there, reverent. "Good morning," he murmured against her skin, his voice low and rough.

She smiled, eyes still closed, her fingers lazily tracing small circles on his chest.

"If this is how mornings start with you…" she breathed, "…I might never leave."

He tightened his hold, burying his face in her hair, breathing her in.

He didn't answer.

Because deep down, part of him already knew—he didn't want her to.

Chapter Thirteen

Alex had taken a quick shower, steam still curling through the flat as he stepped back into the living space, hair damp, the clean scent of soap clinging to his skin. The sound of running water hummed faintly behind the bathroom door, echoing in the quiet. He tugged on a fresh T-shirt, then held out another for Harper.

It looked comically large in her hands, but when she pulled it over her head, the fabric transformed—falling loose around her curves, the hem brushing her bare thighs in a way that made his throat run dry. She glanced over her shoulder at him, eyes sparkling with mischief, lips curving in a smile that threatened to undo him all over again.

Then she disappeared into the bathroom, the door clicking shut, leaving him alone with the ghost of her touch and the vivid memory of her skin beneath his hands.

While she showered, Alex drifted into the kitchen, needing something to anchor him before he drowned in the sheer intensity of her. He cracked eggs into a bowl, whisking with more force than necessary, the scent of bacon sizzling soon filling the air. The stovetop hissed and popped, the aroma wrapping around him like comfort—warm, grounding, startlingly intimate.

It felt domestic.

It felt... right.

By the time he plated eggs, toast, and bacon, he sensed her presence behind him. Her arms slipped around his waist as if they belonged there, her damp hair cool and fragrant against his back. She pressed a slow kiss to the side of his neck, the softness lingering until heat rippled through him.

"Mmm," she murmured against his skin, her voice husky with sleep and satisfaction. "I'm starving."

He turned his head, grinning. "For food, I hope."

Her laugh was low and silky, the kind that brushed over his skin like velvet. "That too."

He pivoted in her embrace, brushing damp strands from her cheek before kissing her—unhurried, lazy, a kiss that said don't go anywhere. When he finally pulled back, his voice was warm, teasing. "Sit. Breakfast is served."

She slid onto a stool at the narrow counter, legs bare, skin glowing, wearing only his shirt and a smile. Her damp hair tumbled over one shoulder, her eyes sleepy but luminous. Something shifted inside Alex's chest—something dangerous and deep. A pull he couldn't fight. Wouldn't fight.

He sat beside her, pretending to focus on his food, though every nerve sharpened at the brush of her leg against his, light and deliberate. She took small bites, slow and teasing, licking her fork like she knew exactly what she was doing. Over the rim of her coffee cup, she gave him sly glances, turning eggs and toast into foreplay.

"Is this how you always eat breakfast?" he asked, his voice low, amused—and entirely aroused—as she swiped yolk from the corner of her mouth with her fingertip, then slipped it between her lips.

"Only when the company's good," she said, tone all innocence. She leaned forward, plucked a piece of bacon from his plate, and held it between her fingers before biting into it with agonising slowness. "Mmm. Crispy. Just how I like it."

He groaned, half laugh, half surrender. "You're going to kill me."

She gave a lazy shrug, one bare shoulder slipping free of the oversized collar. The neckline slid just enough to confirm what he already suspected—she wasn't wearing anything beneath.

"You started it," she teased, voice dipped in mischief. "Showing up at the Christmas party, looking all hot and mysterious."

He shook his head, watching her like she was the most impossible, fascinating puzzle. "I didn't know you were like this," he murmured, almost to himself.

She arched a brow, lips curling. "Like what?"

"Cheeky. Sensual. Bloody irresistible."

Her smile turned wicked as she leaned in, fingers trailing up his arm, each touch deliberate. "Get used to it, Dawson."

And there it was again—that quiet, seismic shift inside him. That ache that wasn't just desire, but something softer, far more dangerous.

Because he had gotten used to it. To her. To this.

And the truth was terrifying.

Because now, he didn't want it to end.

As Harper sipped her coffee and swiped another piece of toast from his plate, Alex smiled on the outside, letting out a soft laugh when she nudged his foot under the counter. But inside, he was unravelling, strand by strand.

The guilt sat heavy in his gut, a weight pressing down with every breath, coiling beneath his skin like a spring ready to snap.

It's not that bad, he told himself. I'm just wealthy. That's all. She didn't fall for the billionaire. She fell for me—the man I am with her.

But even as he clung to that reasoning, the fear slithered through the cracks, sharp and insistent.

What if she felt betrayed?

What if she looked at him and saw nothing but the lie?

Because it had started as a game. A bet. A test of pride, ego, and cleverness. A challenge about love, gold-diggers, and cynicism.

Somewhere along the way, though, the rules had changed. She had changed everything.

He watched her tuck a strand of hair behind her ear, smile at something innocuous on the kitchen counter, completely unaware of the storm coiling within him.

She leaned over suddenly, brushing toast crumbs from his shirt, then kissed his jaw—a quick, affectionate touch that sent heat spiralling through him.

"You've gone quiet on me," she said, voice teasing but curious.

He blinked, forcing a smile that didn't quite reach his eyes. "Just thinking."

"Dangerous," she murmured, giving his thigh a playful nudge before returning to her coffee.

Alex held her gaze for a beat longer, chest tight, pulse thrumming with a rhythm he couldn't quite hide.

Soon, he promised himself. Soon, I'll tell her.

Just… not today.

Today, she was here. Smiling. Barefoot in his shirt. Stealing his bacon. Filling his apartment—and his life—with warmth he hadn't realised he'd been starving for.

And he couldn't bear to lose her. Not yet.

They spent the entire day wrapped in each other like a secret—laughing until their stomachs ached, watching old movies with the volume turned low, and making love with a kind of abandon that made time irrelevant. Outside, the world kept spinning, oblivious. But inside Alex's modest flat, time slowed, melted, and reshaped itself around them.

Between stolen kisses and whispered jokes, between the rustle of sheets and the hum of her sleepy laughter, everything else faded. It wasn't just about the physical— it was about the comfort, the connection, the sanctuary they built from nothing more than tangled limbs, sunlight filtering through slatted blinds, and hearts beating in synchrony.

By evening, they were curled on the floor in front of the coffee table, limbs loosely intertwined in a makeshift nest of throw pillows and a fleece blanket he'd yanked off the back of the couch. Takeaway containers were scattered around them—boxes of Thai food, their shared favourite, giving off the scent of basil, chilli, and something warmly familiar that felt like home.

Harper wore his shirt again—just his shirt—and it fell loosely over her curves, the hem brushing the tops of her bare thighs in a way that made his throat dry. Her legs were tucked beneath her, toes brushing lightly against his thigh in a quiet, unconscious rhythm. Her hair was a tousled, beautiful mess from their long, lazy afternoon, and her cheeks still glowed with the soft flush of contentment.

Alex handed her a spring roll with one hand while taking a long sip of beer with the other, letting the fizz dull the gnawing ache in his chest that had returned like an unwelcome guest. She looked so at ease, so real and radiant in the flickering lamplight—and he felt like an imposter in his own skin.

His voice came out too casual, too measured, as he glanced around the small flat. "This doesn't bother you?"

Harper looked up mid-bite, blinking, a dab of sweet chilli sauce catching on her lower lip. She licked it off without thinking, and he nearly forgot his question.

"What doesn't?"

"This place," he said, gesturing vaguely with the bottle, trying to keep his tone light. "Not having more than this? No city view. No smart fridge. No walk-in wine cellar."

She paused, chewing slowly, expression curious—amused, even. "We have Netflix and pad Thai. I'm thriving."

He let out a short huff of laughter, but it didn't ease the pressure tightening in his chest. "I'm serious. You could have more. You should have more."

She set the spring roll down carefully, concern touching her expression. "Alex…"

"You're smart. Beautiful. You could be living in some penthouse with champagne and someone who—" He broke off, swallowing hard, shaking his head. "Someone who can actually give you everything."

She studied him for a long moment, eyes clear and steady—the ocean-deep clarity that always seemed to read him better than he could read himself.

"You think I want a penthouse more than I want you?"

He couldn't answer. His throat tightened around the truth. Around the fear.

"I like this," she said gently, her voice soft as rain. "I like you. The version of you who hogs the blanket, burns toast, and forgets where he put his socks."

A dry laugh slipped out of him. "Sexy."

She smiled, that lazy, fond smile he was starting to crave like oxygen, and crawled closer, shifting through pillows until her shoulder rested against his. "I don't care about the size of your apartment or the number in your bank account. I care about how you make me feel."

"Harper…" His voice cracked. He turned to look at her, heart thundering in his chest. Her presence always disarmed him, but this—this was different. She was so certain. So unwavering. And he felt like a man made of glass.

She reached for his hand, threading her fingers through his, grounding him. Her grip was warm, steady, unflinching.

"Are you okay?"

He nodded automatically, but it felt false. Like everything he hadn't told her. "Yeah. Just… wanted to hear you say it."

"Say what?"

"That this—" he motioned between them, their hands, their mess of takeaway and shared smiles "—is enough."

She didn't hesitate. She leaned in and kissed him, soft and certain, the kind of kiss that gave everything without asking for a thing in return.

"I don't need more than this," she whispered against his mouth. "You're my more."

And that—God, that—nearly undid him.

His heart twisted hard in his chest. The words hovered on the tip of his tongue: *I haven't been honest. I'm not who you think I am.* He opened his mouth, desperate to confess, to come clean.

But instead, he kissed her. Slower this time. Deeper. With a quiet desperation that curled through him like smoke. His hand slid around her waist, pulling her into his lap, anchoring her there like maybe if he held her tightly enough, he could press pause on time. On consequences. On the truth.

He buried his face in the curve of her neck, inhaling her scent—faint shampoo, warm skin, safety. Her fingers threaded through his hair, nails gently grazing his scalp, and he closed his eyes against the swell of emotion rising sharp and unforgiving.

Even in her arms, wrapped in the warmth of her trust, the guilt clung to him like a second skin. The truth hovered just outside the glow of the room, a storm cloud edging closer with every heartbeat.

And he knew—*he knew*—it couldn't stay buried forever.

After dinner, Harper stood and stretched with exaggerated laziness, her arms reaching toward the ceiling, a soft sigh slipping from her lips. Her hair fell in loose waves around her face, tousled from the lazy day they'd spent wrapped around each other. The hem of Alex's shirt—still the only thing she wore—rose higher on her thighs with the movement, drawing his attention like a magnet.

Her eyes sparkled with mischief as she looked down at him, one corner of her mouth lifting in a wicked smile.

"What?" Alex asked, still lounging on the floor, his back against the couch, grinning like a man who knew he was in trouble—and couldn't wait for it.

She didn't answer. Instead, she reached for the first button of the shirt, her fingers moving slowly, deliberately. One by one, she slipped each button free, revealing smooth, golden skin beneath. Her hips swayed subtly as she moved, rhythm in every motion, like she was dancing to a song only she could hear.

He leaned back on his hands, eyes fixed on her, caught somewhere between amusement and awe.

"This is new," he murmured, voice low, like he didn't dare speak too loudly and break the moment.

"It's a thank you," she said, grinning as she let the shirt slide down her shoulders. The fabric whispered against her skin as it fell, catching briefly at her elbows before she shrugged it off completely. She caught it in one hand before it hit the floor and tossed it toward him.

She wore nothing underneath.

He caught the shirt in his lap but didn't look down at it. His gaze stayed locked on her, breath catching in his throat.

"Jesus, Harper…"

She gave a playful little spin, laughing softly as her hair flared around her shoulders, and then turned to face him again. The warm light from the lamp behind her cast a golden halo around her silhouette, softening every curve, making her look like something from a dream he wasn't ready to wake from.

Then she stepped closer, stopping just between his bent knees. His hands lifted instinctively to touch her, to pull her in—but she took a single step back, just out of reach, raising a teasing brow.

"Uh-uh. No touching."

He groaned, tilting his head back with a sound of pure agony. "Oh, you're killing me."

"Good," she whispered, leaning in and pressing a slow, teasing kiss to his mouth. Her lips brushed his with maddening softness, tasting, promising.

That was all he could take.

With a low growl of need, he surged to his feet, closing the space between them in an instant. She laughed—a breathless, delighted sound—as he scooped her into his arms, her bare skin warm against his. Her arms locked around his neck, and her legs curled around his waist as he carried her to the bedroom, like she weighed nothing at all.

He laid her down on the bed like she was breakable, like this was sacred—and then something shifted.

The laughter fell away, replaced by something deeper, rawer. His mouth found hers again—hungry, desperate, consuming. The kiss wasn't gentle. It was everything he'd held back, everything he couldn't say out loud, poured into the press of lips and the slide of tongues and the tight, aching grip of his hands on her hips.

His hands roamed her body like a man memorising her by touch—her ribs, her waist, the dip of her spine. He kissed her like he couldn't breathe without it, like letting go might kill him. And the way she arched into him, her fingers clawing gently into his shoulders, her gasps catching on the edge of his name—she didn't want him to stop.

She didn't want gentle. She wanted him.

Every kiss, every touch, every deep thrust became a vow he didn't know how to speak aloud:

You're everything… I don't want to lose you.

You're the only real thing I've ever known.

He poured it all into her—love, fear, guilt, and longing—until they were tangled again, breathless, lost in each other, the world beyond their bodies forgotten.

But even as she lay beneath him, trembling and glowing and whispering his name like a promise—

—the truth still burned quietly behind his ribs, waiting.

And he knew the clock was ticking.

The night had been a blur of whispered endearments, teasing fingers, soft laughter, and tangled sheets. Again and again, they found each other in the quiet dark—drunk on each other's breath, hungry for connection, greedy for closeness. The kind of hunger that wasn't merely skin-deep or about heat—it was about being truly seen, about being chosen, about belonging. Every touch felt more intimate than the last, as if their bodies were speaking truths their mouths hadn't yet dared to voice.

There was urgency, yes—but threaded through it was something gentler, more reverent. Each kiss was a prayer, each sigh a confession. They moved as though memorising every curve, every freckle, every hitch in breath in case the moment was fleeting in case the morning unravelled it all.

For Harper, it felt like falling and flying at once.

She had known passion before. She had known desire. But this—this quiet, aching intensity—was something entirely different. It wasn't lust alone. It was recognition. Like her soul had leaned in and whispered, Oh. It's you.

She'd never known this kind of safety—this unspoken understanding between two people who didn't need to pretend. She saw him, raw and real, and he saw her. And for the first time in years, that didn't scare her. It made her ache in the best, most terrifying way.

They spoke in half-words and broken whispers, laughing into each other's mouths, tangled together like threads that could never again be separated. Eventually, sleep came—not because they ran out of words, touch, or feeling, but because their bodies had surrendered to the kind of peace that only follows being thoroughly, reverently, and lovingly unravelled.

And the world, for a little while, fell blissfully quiet.

Morning arrived slowly, slipping through the curtains in soft, golden streaks that painted the walls in warm, liquid light. The air was thick with the scent of skin, the faint trace of jasmine rice lingering from dinner, and the unmistakable memory of the night they'd shared, heavy and intimate.

Harper stirred first, shifting languidly under the covers, her brow furrowing as she stretched like a cat across the tangled sheets. Muscles pleasantly sore. Lips still tingling from his kisses. But before she could fully rise, she felt it—the unmistakable weight of a gaze. Heavy. Intimate. Devoted.

She blinked up, and her breath caught.

Alex was already awake, propped on one elbow beside her, tousled hair falling into his eyes, bare chest rising and falling in steady rhythm. His gaze was fixed on her face as though she were the first sunrise he had ever seen—and he feared missing a single moment.

"Morning," she murmured, voice husky with sleep, a shy, uncertain smile tugging at her lips.

He leaned in and pressed his lips to her shoulder, featherlight, reverent, careful—as if she might vanish if he kissed her any harder.

"Still incredible," he whispered, his words brushing her skin like silk, soft and sure.

She blushed, heat rising to her cheeks, but she didn't look away. Something in his eyes made her heart stutter. Something tender. Awed. And yet, beneath the softness, she glimpsed a flicker of something else—hesitation? doubt? a shadow of fear?

It passed too quickly for her to name, leaving only a faint trace, a memory of something unspoken.

She reached up, tracing her fingers slowly along his jaw, exploring the angles of him with a gentleness that mirrored his own. "You always look at me like that."

"Like what?"

"Like I'm going to disappear."

Alex didn't answer right away. His eyes softened, but his silence spoke volumes.

Instead of words, he slid his hand along her waist, fingers curling around her like he needed to anchor her to this moment. To him. He pulled her closer until there was no space left between them—no room for doubt, no room for fear.

"Because I keep wondering how the hell I got this lucky," he admitted, voice low, almost awed.

Her breath hitched, and she smiled—but it was bittersweet, threaded with an ache she hadn't expected to feel. Her chest throbbed with the intensity of trust regained, with the courage it had taken to surrender again. Naked, exposed, yet utterly safe, she rested against him, her soul quietly unfolding.

Hope. Dangerous, unsteady, irresistible hope.

They made love again—slow this time. Almost reverent.

No teasing. No games. No hurry. Just the raw, aching need to feel everything. To be present. To speak with hands what their mouths still couldn't say. Every movement was deliberate. Every touch a silent vow:

I see you.

I choose you.

Please don't disappear.

It was unhurried, grounding. Like time had folded in on itself. Like the world had paused just for them. Outside that bed, nothing existed—not the past, not regrets, not the truths that still lived in shadow.

They held each other as if the moment could stretch indefinitely, limitless, and sacred.

Eventually, Harper lay draped against his chest, her palm resting over his heart, listening to its steady rhythm beneath her ear. Her hair spilled across his skin like molten copper, catching the sunlight now streaming freely into the room, painting golden lines across their bodies. It was perfect. It was still. It was everything.

And yet.

She couldn't shake the feeling. Something unspoken lingered in the air—silent, almost invisible, yet impossibly heavy. Like a door left slightly ajar. Like a word trapped behind teeth, aching to be freed.

Alex stared at the ceiling, unmoving, his hand tracing lazy circles along her spine. But inside, the guilt gnawed with a vicious persistence, scraping against his ribs with every beat of his heart. Sharp. Insistent.

Because he had all the chances in the world to tell her the truth. To unburden himself, to set it free.

And he hadn't.

Chapter Fourteen

Alex was the first to slip out of bed, leaving behind the soft, warm weight of Harper still curled beside him. Her cheek rested against the pillow, lips slightly parted, one bare shoulder peeking out from beneath the sheets. Her hair fanned around her like molten copper, tangled just enough to look effortless, ethereal—like something out of a dream.

He stood there for a long moment, simply watching her—so peaceful, so unguarded. So trusting.

And he hated himself for the secret he carried.

Every gentle breath she took felt like a silent vote of confidence in him, and it burned. Because the version of himself she knew—the modest IT guy, the man who lived simply, who made her laugh at the office—was only half the truth. And every hour he stayed silent, that lie grew heavier, pressing against his chest.

He slipped into the bathroom, letting the hot water cascade over him, bracing his hands against the slick tiles. Steam rose, curling around him like it could wash away the sharp edges of guilt cutting through his insides. But no heat, no water, no moment of solitude could soften it. He closed his eyes and admitted the truth he'd been running from since the moment he met her: she deserved better. She deserved the whole truth.

When he emerged, towel slung low on his hips, Harper stirred at the sound. She blinked up at him, sleepy and soft-eyed, her gaze lighting up with a smile that made his chest tighten painfully. She pressed a quick kiss to his jaw as she passed and padded barefoot into the bathroom, leaving a trace of warmth and fragrance in her wake.

That simple, effortless gesture—it nearly undid him.

She trusted him. And he was lying with every glance, every touch, every whispered word from the night before.

He exhaled sharply, raking a hand through his damp hair. Enough.

He had to tell her. No more dodging. No more rationalising. After breakfast, he'd sit her down and lay it all out—the truth about who he was, about the bet, about how it had started as a reckless game and become something terrifyingly real, raw, and impossible to walk away from.

Hopefully, she'd love him enough to forgive him.

She might leave. She probably would.

But at least she would leave knowing the truth—not the fantasy he'd built around them.

Trying to calm the storm in his mind, he dressed in joggers and a T-shirt and headed to the kitchen. He needed something to occupy his hands. Bacon sizzled as it hit the pan. Eggs whisked. Coffee poured. Two mugs were set on the table with muscle memory, more than any conscious thought. Anything to delay the inevitable.

For a few blessed minutes, he allowed himself the illusion of normalcy—just a man making breakfast for the woman he loved.

And he did love her. Fiercely. Completely.

But even that fragile illusion couldn't last. Because love demanded honesty. And she was about to learn everything.

Then—

A sharp knock at the door.

Alex froze.

His pulse spiked, adrenaline surging with a clarity that sliced through his morning haze. Who the hell could that be?

He glanced toward the bathroom. The water was still running. Harper wouldn't have heard.

Another knock. Louder. More insistent.

His stomach twisted. No one ever came to this flat. No deliveries. No neighbours. Yet someone was standing on the other side of that door, shattering the fragile peace he'd built with Harper like a stone through glass.

He wiped his hands on a dish towel and walked toward the door, every step measured. Instinctively, his eyes scanned the flat—the clothes they'd left strewn across the living room, the faint trace of Harper's perfume lingering in the air, her bra draped casually over the back of a chair.

Whatever this was, it wasn't nothing.

He hesitated. Then opened the door.

Alex's heart sank before he even spoke. "What the hell are you doing here?"

Theo Clarke.

The smug bastard stood in the doorway, every inch the aristocratic menace—tailored trousers hugging his hips, white shirt open just enough to be infuriatingly cocky, sunglasses shoved into the chaos of his dark hair. His grin was maddening, sharp as a knife.

"I thought I'd come and check on your progress," Theo said breezily, stepping inside as if the flat were his private playground.

Alex's arm shot out instinctively, blocking him from moving further. "Are you insane? You can't just show up here."

"I was in the neighbourhood," Theo replied smoothly, hands in his pockets, as if that explained everything.

"You're in Australia," Alex snapped.

"Well," Theo drawled, tilting his head, "Sydney's lovely this time of year. You can hardly blame me for being curious. I've invested, what, a million pounds in this little wager of yours?"

Alex stepped sideways, deliberately positioning himself between Theo and the slightly ajar bedroom door. "You have to leave. Now."

Theo arched a perfectly sculpted brow. "You're not exactly rolling out the red carpet. That a sign things are going well?"

"Keep your bloody voice down," Alex barked, eyes flashing. "She's here."

Theo's grin widened, wicked and knowing. "So, I was right. You and the pretty HR manager. I had a feeling." He leaned in slightly, lowering his voice with mock conspiratorial charm. "I must say, you look properly wrecked. I take it the lady's fallen for the charm of our mysterious systems engineer?"

Alex said nothing, jaw tight, shoulders coiled like a spring ready to snap.

Theo's grin broadened, smug as ever. "I'll take that as a yes. Well then—game over. You win the bet. She loves you. I'll wire the money."

"It's not like that anymore," Alex muttered, voice low, hard, carrying the weight of the truth he hadn't yet shared.

"What do you mean?" Theo asked, eyes gleaming with amusement and curiosity.

Before Alex could answer, a soft, deliberate pad of bare feet sounded behind him.

He turned—too slow.

Harper stood in the doorway, a towel wrapped snugly around her, damp strawberry-blonde hair clinging in loose tendrils to her collarbone. Her skin glowed from the shower, warm and luminous, but her face was sharp, alert, confusion and curiosity flickering in her eyes as they moved between the two men.

And then Theo, in the worst possible timing imaginable, let out a long, appreciative whistle.

"You weren't kidding," he said, voice low, eyes twinkling with something deeply infuriating. "She's stunning."

Harper's expression didn't waver. Her gaze fixed on Alex, steady and piercing.

Then, her voice calm and icy as a blade, she asked:

"What bet?"

Alex turned quickly. "It's nothing."

"Don't lie to me," she said sharply, voice ringing with authority and disbelief. "I heard him. He said something about a 'pretty HR manager'—or is there another one you were talking about?"

"Harper," Alex said, palms raised in surrender, "it's not important. I swear, it's—"

She cut him off with a glare that pinned him in place. Her eyes flicked to Theo, then back to Alex. "Tell me about the bet."

"Don't," Alex warned, his voice low, tense.

She didn't flinch. She just looked at him, and the weight of her stare made his chest tighten, like he'd been caught in the crossfire of his own lies.

Theo shifted uncomfortably, clearly realising the joke had curdled into something far too real. "He bet me a million pounds," he said slowly, dragging out each word as though measuring the impact. "That he could make a woman… fall in love with him… without her knowing he's rich."

The silence that followed was suffocating, thick with disbelief and unspoken accusation.

Harper's gaze didn't waver. She looked at Alex as if seeing him for the first time—not the man she had fallen for, but the stranger behind the mask.

"Alexander Dawson," she said softly, voice trembling with quiet horror, the pieces falling into place. "The Alexander Dawson. CEO and owner of Veridian Dynamics."

Alex's mouth opened, but no words came out. Nothing could articulate the guilt, the panic, the heartbreak all at once.

She took a slow, deliberate step back, creating distance that mirrored the chasm opening in her heart.

"Was any of it real?" she asked, her voice barely more than a whisper, fragile yet sharp enough to cut.

"Yes. Of course it was," Alex said quickly, desperation cracking his tone. He stepped toward her, hands reaching out—but she recoiled, as though his presence burned her skin. "Harper, please. I never meant for you to find out like this—"

Her eyes snapped to Theo, accusation blazing.

"I had to fall in love with him?" she asked, incredulous, voice trembling now, sharp with the sting of betrayal.

Theo froze. For once, the smug mask was gone. His jaw tightened, and shame flickered across his face. He nodded once, stiffly, almost too small in the enormity of what he'd done.

Harper let out a breath—sharp, uneven, almost a laugh—but there was no humour in it. Only disbelief. Only betrayal. Her eyes glimmered with icy clarity, cutting through Alex like a blade, making him feel naked, exposed, and utterly helpless.

She stared at him—beyond the lies, past the intimacy, straight into the core of him.

"Well then," she said, voice steady, controlled, but laced with venom, "congratulations."

Her eyes flicked briefly at Theo, then back to Alex, and the words she spoke next landed like shards of glass.

"You owe Alexander Dawson one million pounds."

Alex flinched, the weight of her words colliding with the weight of his guilt, and then—without another sound—she moved.

With a grace that belied the fury simmering beneath her skin, she crossed the room, snatched her bra from the back of the chair, and spun on her heel, leaving him frozen in the wreckage of everything he'd hidden.

The bedroom door slammed behind her with a crack that ricocheted through the flat like a gunshot, sharp enough to make Alex flinch.

He froze, heart lodged in his throat, every muscle taut.

"Harper—" he choked out, already stepping forward, but the words caught in his chest.

The silence that followed was suffocating. It swallowed the room whole.

No footsteps. No voice. No forgiveness hovering just beyond the door.

Just the echo of his own ragged breathing—and the weight of everything he hadn't said crashing down around him like falling masonry.

Alex moved to the bedroom door, knocking softly, voice hoarse and ragged.

"Harper… please, can we just talk? Let me explain—"

The door swung open before he could finish. She stood there, framed by the hallway light, her red dress clinging like armour, chin lifted in defiance. But her eyes—her eyes betrayed her, shimmering with pain she fought so hard to bury.

She didn't look at him.

"Do you have a car here?" she asked Theo, voice sharp, controlled, almost weaponised.

Theo blinked. "Uh… yes."

"Well then," she said, each word deliberate, slicing through the tension, "you can drive me home."

Alex stepped forward, desperation breaking through the taut restraint in his chest. "Harper, please. Don't do this. I love you. I never meant to hurt you. I—I can't lose you."

For a heartbeat, her gaze flicked to him. And for one fragile second, hope flared—maybe she would stay. But then her eyes hardened, distant, and shuttered, closing him out completely.

She turned to Theo. "Now."

"Yes, ma'am," he muttered, already moving toward the door.

Alex reached out, hand brushing her shoulder, pleading without words. "Just let me explain—"

She stepped back sharply, voice icy, cutting.

"Get your hand off me."

Alex let his arm drop as if she had branded him.

Without another word, she turned and walked out, her movements controlled but heavy with unspoken fury.

Theo followed but paused just before crossing the threshold.

He glanced back at Alex. For once, there was no smirk, no careless quip—only a flicker of something quieter, almost human. Guilt. Regret. A silent admission that the game had gone too far, that hearts had been broken along the way.

Then he turned and disappeared down the stairs.

The flat was left in near silence.

Only the fading echo of her heels lingered, and the ragged, uneven breath of a man who had just lost everything that truly mattered.

Theo drove her home in silence after she gave him the address.

She stared out the passenger window the entire ride, eyes tracking the blur of passing streetlights and traffic, but she saw none of it. Her heart pounded beneath her ribs, relentless, as though trying to escape. Her thoughts were a jumble of white noise, chaotic and hollow. Her body felt numb, hollowed out by disbelief.

She didn't cry. Not here. Not in front of him.

Her pride wouldn't allow it.

When Theo finally pulled up outside her building, she unbuckled her seatbelt with mechanical detachment. Her hand hovered over the door handle when his voice, soft and tentative, broke the silence like a fragile thread.

"Harper…" he said, almost unsure he had the right to speak. "I'm sorry."

She didn't look at him. She couldn't. If she did, if she allowed herself that single glance, she might shatter.

"I didn't mean for it to happen like this," he continued, the guilt in his tone raw, like a wound he couldn't stop reopening. "He didn't either. I mean… it started as—God, it was stupid—but he loves you."

That word hit her like a sucker punch to the ribs. *Love.*

Don't say that word. Not now. Not when it meant everything and yet nothing.

Her grip tightened on the door handle until her knuckles ached, white against the metal.

"You've got nothing to apologise for," she said, voice low, brittle, each word measured like a blade. "I didn't fall in love with you."

Theo flinched, and she saw it from the corner of her eye—the small, fleeting movements, a breath caught, a jaw clenching—but she didn't allow herself to look directly at him.

She stepped out of the car, head held high, shoulders squared, chin set like stone.

She didn't look back as the door closed behind her. Didn't glance over her shoulder as Theo pulled away, his car shrinking in the sunlight. She didn't allow herself to feel—not yet.

She pressed the elevator button with a hand that trembled only slightly, waiting as it hummed, creaked, and climbed floor by floor, the seconds stretching longer than they should have.

And then, the moment she stepped inside her apartment and the door clicked shut behind her—

She fell apart.

Her back hit the door as though her body could no longer support her upright frame. Her knees buckled, and she slid to the floor in one graceless, surrendering motion, legs folding beneath her like discarded paper.

And then—

She cried.

Not the polite, controlled crying she'd allowed herself after Billy. Not the quiet tears of disappointment.

No—this was something older, something primal.

It started quietly, a tight clench in her chest, face crumpling, eyes squeezed shut, hands fisted into the fabric of her dress as if sheer willpower could hold her together.

Then the sobs broke free.

Racking, shuddering, raw. Each gasp ripped from her chest in waves, stealing her breath, hollowing her out.

Because she had let herself love him. Fully. Recklessly. Completely.

She had let herself believe, even for a moment, that this time might be different. That this man—this version of Alex, barefoot and burnt-toast-messy, with the way he looked at her like she was the only thing that made sense in his world— was real.

But he wasn't.

And it had all started with a lie.

She buried her face in her hands, sobbing harder, not just for the deception, but for everything it had cost her.

The trust she'd painstakingly rebuilt.

The walls she'd lowered.

The future she had allowed herself to imagine—mornings tangled in sheets, nights wrapped in his arms, a life not built on wealth or secrets, but on something achingly, impossibly real.

She had fallen in love with him.

And now, she didn't know if she could ever forgive him for letting her believe he was someone else. Not when the man she'd loved had been hiding behind a mask the entire time.

And still—through the heartbreak, the humiliation, the gnawing emptiness in her chest—one truth cut deeper than all the rest:

She still loved him.

God help her, she still loved him.

Chapter Fifteen

Alex collapsed onto the couch like a man who'd been hit by a freight train.

His elbows dug into his knees, hands laced behind his neck, head bowed so low he could barely draw a full breath. Each inhale was shallow, rasping. Each exhale felt like a betrayal.

What the hell was he going to do now?

His mind spun in a cyclone—chaotic, vicious, unrelenting. Thoughts collided like jagged glass, slicing through every rational defence he tried to cling to. But beneath the noise, beneath the panic, beneath the self-loathing, one truth throbbed like an open wound:

He loved her.

God, he loved her.

Not casually, not superficially. This wasn't convenient. It wasn't rational. It wasn't fleeting. This was soul-deep, earth-shattering, life-altering. Real. And now… it was in pieces. Shattered. He had shattered it.

He'd broken something fragile, something rare. Something he might never get back.

And it was his fault. Every jagged, burning, gut-wrenching bit of it.

Alex sat there, staring at the carpet as though the fibres held some secret key, some answer he could cling to. But they didn't. Nothing did.

Then the door creaked open behind him.

Footsteps. Hesitant. Measured.

Theo's voice followed, low, almost reverent.

"That's one hell of a woman."

Alex didn't move. Didn't even lift his head.

"I know," he whispered, voice cracked and raw, like sandpaper against steel.

Theo lingered, the usual arrogance stripped away. His hands shoved deep in his pockets, shoulders stiff, stance tense. He looked uncertain—like he didn't know whether to apologise, or leave, or maybe punch the wall.

"She didn't say much," Theo murmured. "No yelling. No crying. Didn't even glance at me. Just gave me the address, climbed into the car, and stared out the window like I wasn't even there."

Alex's jaw clenched until it ached.

"She was proud," Theo continued, more to himself than to Alex. "Held it together the whole time. Until the end. That's when I saw it."

"Saw what?" Alex rasped, voice raw and ragged.

"The heartbreak," Theo said softly, almost reverent. "The kind that guts you from the inside out. Cuts you open and leaves your chest hollow, like you'll never be the same again."

Alex finally lifted his head. Bloodshot eyes, hollowed and rimmed red from self-recrimination, met Theo's.

"Yeah," he said bitterly. "She trusted me."

"And we betrayed that," Theo's voice was heavy with guilt. "I never should've made that bet."

"I never should've taken it," Alex admitted, voice rough, almost a growl.

A heavy silence pressed down, thick as fog, suffocating, unyielding. Regret swirled in the air like smoke—too late to undo, too real to ignore.

Theo studied him. Really studied him.

Alex didn't look like a billionaire right now. Not the confident, arrogant man who always had the next move planned, the next step calculated.

He looked... broken. Hollow. Every fibre of him weighed down by guilt, love, and fear.

And Theo, for the first time in years, didn't have a single quip. Not one. No joke, no smug remark, no clever line. Just silence.

"I don't know if she'll ever forgive you," Theo said after a long pause, each word deliberate, heavy. "But if she does... if she even gives you the chance to try..."

Alex's hollow, hopeless eyes met his.

"You fight like hell, mate," Theo said quietly.

Alex gave a single, bitter laugh, dry and ragged. "You think I don't know that?"

Theo said nothing. He just lingered for a moment longer, studying Alex with something that was part guilt, part awe, part recognition.

Because Harper hadn't stormed out screaming.

She hadn't thrown things or collapsed into tears in the street.

She had walked away with every shred of her dignity intact; heartbreak folded neatly behind eyes that were steady, unflinching, resolute.

And that kind of strength? That kind of grace?

It left even someone like Theo stunned.

Without another word, he turned and walked toward the door.

But just before stepping out, he paused, glanced over his shoulder.

"Don't wait too long," he said quietly, voice low, serious. "Some things… they don't stay broken forever. But only if you're brave enough to fix them."

Then he was gone.

And Alex sat there, in the suffocating silence, surrounded by everything he'd built—wealth, success, power—

Except the one thing that had ever truly mattered.

The one thing he had shattered with his own hands.

The one thing he could never, ever get back… unless he was brave enough to fight.

By the time Harper peeled herself off the floor, the sun had dipped low, spilling long amber streaks across her apartment like brushstrokes of fire. Her body felt hollow, drained, every muscle heavy from hours of crying. Her throat was raw, her eyes swollen, but through the fog of exhaustion, one need pulsed steady and undeniable.

She couldn't sit with this alone.

With trembling hands, she reached for her phone. Her thumb hovered, then pressed the familiar contact. The line rang once, twice—

"Hey, gorgeous," Clara answered, her voice all warmth and sparkle, as if the world hadn't just ended.

Harper's own voice cracked, raw. "Clara…"

The shift was immediate. Concern sharpened Clara's tone. "What's wrong, babe?"

"I've done it again."

A pause. "Done what again?"

"Fallen for a liar," Harper whispered, the words fragile but laced with bitterness.

And then it all came out. The bet. The lies. The Christmas party. The truth detonating in her chest like shards of glass. Every word spilled like confession, jagged and unpolished, but once she started, she couldn't stop.

Clara didn't interrupt. She just listened, her silence steady and sure, like an anchor Harper didn't know she needed.

When Harper finally ran out of breath, there was only the faint sound of Clara inhaling on the other end. And then—

"That absolute piece of garbage," Clara exploded. "He bet on you. What is he— twelve? No, worse—twelve and emotionally stunted?"

Harper closed her eyes. The silence on her end said everything.

Clara's voice softened, though the steel never left. "Oh, babe. I'm so sorry. You didn't deserve that. You opened up, you trusted him, and he played you. I swear, I want to punch him. No—stab him with a cocktail umbrella. Slowly. Twist it for emphasis."

Harper almost smiled. Almost.

"I should've known," she murmured. "I always do this. I always…"

"No, Harper," Clara cut in firmly. "You don't. You fall for the wrong men because you're good. Because you see the best in people, even when they don't see it in themselves. That's not a weakness. That's your damn superpower. He didn't deserve an ounce of it."

Harper let out a shaky breath, her chest loosening just enough to let air back in.

"I hate that I can't be there," Clara said fiercely. "If I could, I'd storm over right now with a bottle of wine, a shovel, and a playlist called 'Vengeance, but Make It Classy.'"

That earned a wet, broken laugh. The first since everything shattered.

"I'm flying to Perth tomorrow," Harper whispered.

Clara didn't miss a beat. "Good. Come home. I'll be waiting with wine, junk food, and possibly a dartboard with his face on it. We'll cry, scream into pillows, and then figure out how to glue your heart back together piece by piece."

Harper's lips curved, faint but real. "Thanks, Clara."

"Anytime, babe. I love you."

"I love you too."

When they hung up, the silence in Harper's apartment wasn't quite as crushing. It still pressed in, heavy, but there was a thread of calm woven through the ache now. Clara's voice still echoed in her chest, fierce and certain, a reminder she wasn't completely alone.

But there was one last thing Harper had to do. One final cut to sever the tie for good.

She walked to her desk, opened her laptop, and stared at the blank glow of the screen. Her fingers hovered over the keys, trembling for only a second before she began to type.

Her resignation letter was short, professional, final. No explanations. No second chances. Just a clean, precise end.

When she finished, she sat there, cursor blinking, breath uneven. She hovered over the Send button, her hand tightening into a fist. Just for a heartbeat.

And then she clicked it.

Done.

She snapped the laptop shut and released a shaky exhale that felt like tearing free of chains.

There was no way she could work for him now. Not after everything.

Tomorrow, she would go home. Tomorrow, she would put distance between herself and Alexander Dawson.

But tonight, here in the quiet ruins of her apartment, Harper finally chose herself.

And she was done.

The next morning, Harper stood by the window, the early sunlight spilling gold across the city skyline. Her suitcase sat by the door, packed, and zipped, a silent sentinel to the life she was leaving behind. She hadn't slept much—her mind too restless, her heart too bruised—but there was a strange clarity in her exhaustion, a stillness she hadn't felt in weeks. It was as if, finally, her heart had stopped spinning, even if only for a moment.

She took one last, lingering look around the apartment as her phone buzzed on the counter. A new message—from Billy, of all people.

I miss you. Call me. It's Christmas.

Her thumb hovered over the screen for just a second, and then she deleted it. Without responding. The past had nothing left to offer her. No comfort. No warmth. No place in her future.

No more going backward.

She slipped on her coat, shouldered her bag, and pulled the door closed behind her. The soft click echoed in the quiet hallway, a punctuation mark on the chapter she was leaving behind.

Downstairs, the taxi waited. Its engine hummed softly in the cool morning air as the driver lifted her suitcase into the trunk. Harper slid into the back seat, hands folded tightly in her lap, her fingers brushing the cold leather as if it could steady the storm inside her.

"Where to?" the driver asked.

"Airport, please," she replied, voice steady, though her stomach twisted with every meter the car rolled forward.

As the vehicle pulled away from the curb, Harper didn't look back. Not at the building. Not at the skyline. Not at the city that had seen her heart rise and fall in the space of a few short weeks.

Perth was waiting. Clara was waiting. And maybe—just maybe—somewhere down the long road ahead, healing would be waiting too.

Harper exhaled, a slow, deliberate breath, as if releasing the weight of what she was leaving behind. The city shrank behind her, the past a fading blur in the rearview mirror. For a brief, fragile moment, she thought of what could have been something real.

A sharp knock shattered the heavy silence that had swallowed the apartment whole.

Alex didn't move at first.

He sat slumped on the edge of the couch, still in the same clothes from yesterday—shirt wrinkled, buttons half undone, hair sticking up in uneven tufts. His eyes were bloodshot, hollowed from a night without sleep, and his jaw was clenched so tight it throbbed. Around him, the apartment was dim and stale, curtains half-drawn, the air itself thick with grief. It felt like even the walls knew she was gone.

The knock came again—firmer this time, impatient.

With a groan, Alex dragged himself upright, every step weighted, as though guilt had seeped into his bones and made them heavy. Part of him didn't want to answer. He wanted to sink back down, stay in the dark, let the world pass him by. But another part—God help him—prayed it might be her.

He opened the door.

Not her.

Theo.

Alex's expression darkened instantly. "What do you want?"

His voice was rough, scraped raw by silence and sleeplessness.

Theo, infuriating as ever, held up two takeaway coffees like a peace offering. "I come bearing caffeine. And help."

Alex just stared, unimpressed. "Help with what?"

Theo brushed past him without waiting for permission, dropping the cups on the counter. "With getting her back, obviously."

Alex let out a humourless, bitter laugh, raking a hand through his tangled hair. "You think coffee's going to fix this?"

"No," Theo said evenly, his tone stripped of its usual smugness. "But maybe a plan will."

"I don't need a plan," Alex snapped. "I need a damn time machine."

He started pacing the room, restless, his hands opening and closing at his sides. "She's never going to talk to me again. She was already hurt by a bastard who broke her trust, and then I—" His voice cracked, raw. "I made her believe again. And then I destroyed it."

Theo didn't interrupt.

For once, there was no smirk, no teasing. Just quiet sincerity.

"Yeah," Theo said softly. "You did."

Alex stopped pacing, eyes narrowing. "You're not supposed to agree with me."

"I'm not here to sugarcoat it," Theo replied. "You messed up. Badly. But you also fell in love with her. And if that means anything—if she means anything—you don't get to just sit here like some tragic Shakespearean hero in a rundown apartment, mourning his own mistakes."

Alex looked away, jaw clenched so hard his teeth ached. "She's probably already on her way to Perth."

"So?" Theo's brows lifted. "Get on a bloody plane."

"She's gone, Theo."

"Then go find her." Theo's voice sharpened. "Jesus, Alex—what's your alternative? Sit here staring at the floor while she disappears from your life forever?"

Alex hesitated.

Theo stepped closer, his voice low, urgent. "You made a mistake. But I've known you a long time, and I've never once seen you look at anyone the way you look at her. You love her."

"I do," Alex whispered, like it physically hurt to admit.

"Then do something about it," Theo said. "Because that kind of love? It doesn't come around twice."

Alex's hands trembled—whether from adrenaline, fear, or the faintest spark of hope, he couldn't tell. He took one breath. Then another.

And bolted for his phone.

"James," he said the moment his assistant answered, voice clipped and urgent. "Get the jet ready for Perth. I need Harper Jameson's address there—immediately."

There was a pause. "Perth? Sir, is this about the HR manager from Sydney—Harper Jameson?"

"Yes," Alex snapped. "That Harper Jameson."

Another pause. Then James said cautiously, "She resigned yesterday. Effective immediately."

Alex froze. His blood ran cold.

"What?"

"She emailed late last night. No notice period. No explanation. Just… gone."

He closed his eyes, the weight of it slamming into him like a wrecking ball. He hadn't just broken her heart—he'd driven her away from everything.

"Find her address," Alex said hoarsely. "I don't care how. Send it to me the second you have it."

"Yes, sir. The jet will be ready in forty-five."

Alex hung up and stared blindly out the small window.

Below, the city glittered indifferently. Above, the sky was beginning to pale with dawn.

"She quit because of me," he murmured, the words jagged in his throat, finally landing somewhere deep and unrelenting.

Theo watched him carefully. His voice, when it came, was softer. "Then give her a reason to start again. With you."

Alex turned slowly. For the first time in hours, his eyes were clear. Not broken. Not hopeless. Focused.

"I'm going to Perth."

A grin tugged at the corner of Theo's mouth. "Good. Because you'll need someone to stop you from making an even bigger mess. I'm coming with you."

Alex didn't reply.

He was already moving.

The warm, earthy scent of eucalyptus wrapped around Harper the moment she stepped outside the terminal, curling through her chest like a half-forgotten memory. She paused on the pavement, blinking against the hazy Perth sky, where the late afternoon sun struggled behind a veil of clouds. Heat pressed down on her skin, mingling with the exhaustion that clung like a heavy coat. Her heart ached—bruised, hollow—but beneath the ache came a flicker of truth. She was home.

Just beyond the arrivals gate stood Clara—her personal lighthouse in a storm. She was impossible to miss, a beacon of chaotic sunshine. Her signature red hair was piled into a messy bun, strands rebelliously escaping like they always did. Oversized sunglasses sat perched on her head at a jaunty angle, and she bounced on the balls of her feet with restless energy, scanning each passenger with impatient hope.

Beside her, Jonathan leaned casually against the railing, tall and steady, the yin to Clara's riotous yang. A crooked grin tilted his mouth, and a takeaway coffee dangled easily from his hand. His calm presence felt like an anchor waiting to steady her.

But it was Clara's sign that snagged Harper's gaze first—loud, unapologetic, and very, very Clara. Bright pink cardboard. Thick black marker. Letters slightly uneven, like they'd been scrawled in a rush of righteous fury.

HARPER: OFFICIALLY DONE WITH IDIOTS.

A startled laugh slipped out of Harper before she could stop it—thin, watery, but real. It cracked something open inside her chest, a shard of light piercing through the fog. Her first laugh in days.

Clara's head snapped up at the sound. "There she is!" she squealed, abandoning all restraint, and then she was sprinting.

Harper barely managed to drop her suitcase before Clara's arms wrapped around her, fierce and unyielding. The hug was so tight it knocked the air from her lungs, a squeeze that said more than words ever could.

"There's my girl," Clara murmured, her voice thick as she held on like she had no intention of letting go.

Harper buried her face into the curve of her friend's shoulder, her throat tightening. "I missed you."

"I missed you more," Clara shot back, pulling back just enough to swipe at her own damp eyes. Then, with all the authority of someone who refused to let heartbreak win, she added, "And I brought caffeine and sarcasm—the holy duo of post-breakup survival."

Jonathan stepped forward as Clara reluctantly loosened her grip. His expression was gentle, steady. "You okay?"

Harper shook her head, though her lips curved faintly. Her eyes shimmered as she whispered, "Not really. But I think I will be."

Jonathan pressed the warm takeaway cup into her hands, the heat bleeding into her palms, grounding her. "Then we'll start with this," he said simply.

Clara immediately hooked her arm through Harper's, her grin fierce and determined. "Come on. I've got chocolate, a perfectly curated playlist of heartbreak anthems, and absolutely zero judgment. We're fixing this the proper way."

A shaky breath left Harper. Not quite a laugh. Not quite a sob. But lighter than anything she'd felt in days.

As they headed toward the car, the sting in her chest dulled, just slightly.

She wasn't okay yet.

But she wasn't alone.

And that made all the difference.

The engines hummed beneath them, a low, relentless drone that rattled through the cabin like a heartbeat Alex couldn't silence. The sleek leather seat beneath him might as well have been stone; he sat forward, elbows digging into his knees, hands locked together so tightly his knuckles were white. His gaze stayed fixed on the carpet, as if answers might be carved into the threads if he stared long enough.

Across from him, Theo nursed a tumbler of whiskey, the amber liquid catching the muted cabin light. He watched his friend with unusual restraint, as though even he knew jokes didn't belong here.

"You're awfully quiet," Theo said at last, his voice almost tentative.

Alex didn't lift his head. His voice came out low, ragged. "I lied to her. I used her. And the worst part? I didn't even realise what she meant to me until she walked away."

Theo let the silence breathe, rolling the glass slowly between his palms. "That's usually how it works," he said finally. "The people who matter... you only see it when it's almost too late."

Alex exhaled sharply, dragging both hands through his hair in a restless sweep. "It was supposed to be a game. Just a bet. I never meant for it to go this far."

Theo's eyes narrowed. He leaned back, the usual flippancy gone from his features. "Yeah, well... she was never playing."

That landed. Alex's eyes flicked up, guilt heavy in them.

Theo didn't look away. "I only spoke to her for five minutes, mate, and even I could see it—she's the real deal. Kind. Genuine. The sort of woman who deserves a hell of a lot more than some billionaire's twisted wager."

Alex's jaw tightened, his voice bitter. "I know that now."

"Then prove it," Theo said, softer this time. "Before it really is too late."

The jet tilted slightly as it began its descent, the clouds parting below to reveal the vast sweep of red earth and scattered green patches of Western Australia. Alex turned toward the window, the sight both grounding and terrifying.

"She hates me," he said quietly, the words tasting like ash.

Theo leaned forward, resting his elbows on his knees. "Then earn her forgiveness. Be the man she thought you were."

Alex turned slowly, his eyes darker than usual, sharp with determination and fear. "Why are you even helping me?"

Theo's mouth curved into something that wasn't quite a smirk, but close. "Because for once in your charmed, arrogant life, you're actually in love. And as insufferable as you usually are…" He lifted the glass in a mock salute. "I'm not completely heartless."

Alex gave him a look, half disbelieving. "You're a terrible liar."

Theo's eyes glinted. "Takes one to know one."

The plane dipped again, cabin lights flickering softly as the ground rushed closer. Alex straightened in his seat, every muscle drawn taut, nerves coiling through him like wire.

"What if I'm too late?" he murmured.

Theo drained the last of his drink and set the glass aside. His voice, when it came, carried none of its usual carelessness. "Then at least you'll know you tried. But if you don't show up? You'll regret it for the rest of your life."

Alex didn't answer. He didn't need to. The set of his jaw, the fire in his eyes, the restless beat of his pulse said it all.

He was all in.

Chapter Sixteen

Jonathan's sleek black Range Rover curved up the long, tree-lined drive of the Jameson family estate, tyres crunching softly over the immaculate gravel. The late-afternoon sun stretched low across the horizon, gilding the manicured hedges and perfectly trimmed lawns in a wash of amber light. Ahead, the grand stone house rose in quiet splendour, its tall windows glowing warmly as though the building itself were alive and waiting. The wrought-iron gate had swung open automatically as they approached, security recognising the car without hesitation—proof that this was still her family's ground, her safe harbour.

Harper sat rigid in the backseat, staring out at the familiar landscape, her heart hammering harder the closer they drew. She hadn't realised until this moment just how much she had needed this—needed them. Beside her, Clara reached across and gave her hand a gentle squeeze.

"No one here is going to judge you," Clara murmured, her voice softer than usual, stripped of its usual mischief. "They just want you home."

The SUV slowed, rolling to a smooth halt before the columned entrance. Harper's breath caught in her throat.

They were waiting.

Her parents stood side by side at the top of the broad stone steps, the picture of grace and solidarity. Her mother, elegant as always in a navy silk blouse, held herself with composure until you noticed the tremor in her hands. Her father, tall and steady, rested a hand lightly at her back, his calm presence anchoring hers.

Flanking the entrance, Julian and Nickolas leaned casually against the white stone pillars, though their relaxed postures didn't fool Harper. Protective big-brother energy radiated from both of them, the kind that said they'd already taken silent vows to make someone pay for her pain.

Behind them, Clara and Jonathan's parents lingered with warmth in their expressions—outsiders by blood, but not by heart. Jonathan's mother gave Harper a small wave, her smile both tender and knowing. His father, impeccable in his usual navy blazer and polished loafers, tipped his head in greeting, as if to say, you're safe here too.

Jonathan climbed out first and circled the car to open her door. He held out a hand, his voice low. "You ready?"

Harper nodded, though her throat was too tight to form words.

She stepped out, heels clicking against the sunlit stone. The estate sprawled around her, vast and golden, but for the first time in days, she didn't feel small.

And then—her mother moved.

Dignity forgotten, she hurried down the steps, silk blouse fluttering as she descended. She gathered Harper into her arms in a fierce embrace that carried every mile, every sleepless night, every unspoken worry.

"My darling girl," she whispered, her voice breaking. "You're safe. You're here."

Harper clung back, her tears spilling freely now, her body shaking with relief.

Her father was next. He didn't say much—he never needed to—but the way he kissed her forehead and rested a steady hand on her shoulder was more eloquent than any words.

Julian descended two steps at a time, flashing a crooked grin. "Well, if it isn't the prodigal princess."

Harper let out a shaky laugh through her tears. "Nice to see you too, Jules."

Nickolas didn't bother with jokes. He wrapped her in a firm, anchoring hug and muttered gruffly, "Say the word, and I'll fly back to Sydney to break someone's kneecaps."

Clara snorted. "Very subtle, Nicky."

The laugh that escaped Harper this time was truer—thin, watery, but real.

Clara's mum swept forward next, her cream linen ensemble crisp, her tone already decisive. "We're all staying for dinner, of course." She half-turned toward the door as though it were already settled.

Clara's dad raised a crystal decanter he'd conjured from somewhere, his grin mischievous. "We've got champagne. And whiskey. Take your pick, love."

Harper looked around at the circle that had gathered—family and found family, every one of them a shield against the storm she'd just walked through. For the first time in what felt like forever, the ache in her chest loosened.

She drew in a long, steady breath. Stood a little taller.

"Thank you," she said, voice trembling but clear. "All of you."

Her mother kissed her cheek softly, brushing a tear away with her thumb. "Come inside, darling. You're home now."

The sun hung low in the sky, washing the Jameson estate's back terrace in a soft, golden haze. The long table gleamed under its glow, dressed with crisp white linen napkins, delicate china cups, and silver tiers piled high with finger sandwiches, fruit tarts, and still-warm scones crowned with clotted cream. Laughter rippled across the gathering—her parents were recounting a story from their honeymoon in Tuscany, complete with hand gestures and sly glances, while Clara leaned in, eyes wide, mock-gasping at every scandalous detail.

Harper cradled her teacup in both hands, letting the fragrant steam curl toward her face. For the first time in days, she felt halfway human again. Safe. Sheltered. Home.

Then her father's phone buzzed against the tabletop, shattering the gentle hum of conversation.

He frowned at the screen, already rising from his seat. "That's security," he murmured, answering briskly. A few clipped words later, his eyes lifted toward Harper, sharp with concern. "There seem to be two gentlemen at the front gate. They're asking for you."

Harper's stomach dropped. She didn't need to ask who.

"No." Her voice came out tight, resolute. She set her teacup down with a decisive clink, porcelain ringing faintly. "Don't let them in."

Julian was on his feet before anyone else had time to breathe, his chair scraping back across the stone terrace. "I'll handle it."

Nickolas followed, slower but heavier, cracking his knuckles like a man warming up for a fight. "Let's go."

Jonathan rose too, calm but purposeful, his movements measured. There was a glint in his eye that told Harper he'd been waiting for this moment. "I'll come along," he said evenly. "In case things need to be… translated."

Harper's eyes widened, her pulse spiking. "No violence," she blurted, half-command, half-plea.

Julian tossed her a careless wink over his shoulder. "Wouldn't dream of it."

Clara, still sipping her tea with exaggerated poise, murmured into her cup, "That's usually a lie."

A shaky laugh bubbled out of Harper, but it didn't reach her chest. She could only watch as the three of them strode away across the terrace, shoulders squared, their combined energy sharp and unyielding. They looked less like men walking to the gate and more like soldiers advancing into battle.

Her mother reached over and laid a cool, steady hand on hers. "Let them handle it, darling," she said gently. "Sometimes all a man needs is the chance to feel useful."

Harper stared after the retreating figures, a mix of gratitude, dread, and inevitability tangling inside her. She had no idea what Alex had come to say—or whether she was ready to hear it.

But one thing was certain.

He wasn't getting past that gate without going through her brothers first.

Alex eased the car to a stop outside the sprawling estate James had directed him to. The gates loomed ahead—tall black iron woven with intricate gold detailing, glinting in the late sunlight. On either side, manicured hedges stretched in perfect symmetry, while towering eucalyptus trees whispered faintly in the breeze. Beyond the gates, the Jameson house rose like something from a glossy travel magazine— white stone walls, arched windows, steep gables. Old-world grandeur, unapologetically elegant.

Theo let out a low whistle from the passenger seat, his gaze sweeping the estate with open awe. "Bloody hell, Alex. This family isn't just comfortable—they're practically royalty."

Alex didn't answer. His hands were locked around the steering wheel, knuckles bloodless, jaw tight enough to ache. His pulse thundered in his ears, louder than the hum of the engine. "It doesn't matter," he muttered, already shoving the door open and stepping out before Theo could say more.

The gravel crunched under his shoes as he strode toward the security intercom, every step a battle to hold his composure. He pressed the button, and though his chest felt as though it might cave in, his voice came out steady, measured. "I'm here to see Harper Jameson."

A moment later, a broad man in a black security uniform stepped from the booth beside the gate. His face was cut from stone, unsmiling, eyes sharp and assessing.

"And you are?"

"Alexander Dawson."

The guard studied him for a long moment, then picked up the phone, speaking in low tones. A tense silence stretched until he finally gave a curt nod. "Someone's coming down."

Theo joined him at the gate, adjusting his cuffs with deliberate casualness. "I have a terrible feeling we're about to be punched," he murmured. "Just putting that out there."

The gates creaked open with a sound that felt more like a warning than a welcome.

Three men strode through them in unison—a wall of broad shoulders, sharp glares, and Harper's eyes staring back at him through three different faces. Protective older-brother energy radiated from them in waves, palpable and merciless.

Jonathan walked at the centre, calm but cold, his measured steps carrying a quiet authority that made the air tighten. To his left was Julian—the eldest, storm-dark and brimming with fury, every line of his tailored suit as sharp as the anger in his eyes. On Jonathan's right was Nickolas, the most athletic, arms folded across his chest, standing like a bouncer who needed only the faintest excuse to flatten someone.

Julian was the first to close the distance, his gaze slicing over Alex with surgical disdain. "Which one of you arrogant bastards made a bet on my sister?"

Theo—rarely at a loss—edged half a step back.

Alex forced himself to meet Julian's eyes. "That was me."

The air charged instantly, thick with tension.

Julian's jaw flexed. "You've got five seconds to explain why you're here before I break your nose."

Alex's voice didn't waver, though his throat was tight. "I came to see Harper. To talk to her. To apologise."

"Apologise?" Nickolas repeated, incredulous. "You think you can show up here, all smug and English, toss out a sorry, and what—she'll run back into your arms?"

Alex shook his head. "I'm not here to be smug. I'm here because I love her."

Jonathan's eyes narrowed, sharp and sceptical. "You love her?" His tone was loaded with contempt. "You humiliated her. You turned her into a wager, a pastime for your billionaire boredom—and now you claim you love her?"

Alex's chest tightened, but he held his ground. "It did begin that way. It was a mistake—a stupid, selfish mistake. But what I feel for her now? That's real. I swear it."

Julian stepped closer, his face inches from Alex's, his fury coiled and ready to strike. "Do you have any idea what she looked like when she came home? Do you know what you did to her?"

Alex swallowed hard. "I know she was hurt."

"Hurt?" Nickolas exploded, his voice a growl. "She was destroyed. Harper doesn't trust easily—she finally let someone in, and you ripped the ground out from under her. You broke her, Dawson. Like she was nothing."

"She's not nothing," Alex said fiercely. His voice cracked, raw and desperate. "She's everything. That's why I'm here."

Jonathan shook his head slowly, his voice quiet but cutting. "You don't get to stroll back in and play the hero. This isn't your redemption arc."

"I don't care about redemption," Alex shot back, his voice rising despite himself. "I just want to see her. To explain myself. Not to you. To her."

Julian folded his arms across his chest; expression carved from steel. "You think you deserve that?"

Alex's reply came without hesitation. "No. But she does."

The words hung in the air, taut as a bowstring. For a moment, no one moved. The silence was heavy, dangerous—the kind of pause before thunder splits the sky.

Then Jonathan stepped forward, eyes full of cold dismissal. "You don't belong here, rich boy. This isn't your world, and it never will be. You think money buys you access to everything—but not this. Not her. Go home."

He turned sharply, striding back toward the house. Julian followed with a last, scathing glare, while Nickolas lingered just long enough to mutter, "You're lucky she's not standing here. Because if she were, watching you get knocked flat might actually cheer her up."

Then he too was gone, their footsteps fading until the gates clanged shut once more.

Theo let out a low, stunned breath beside him. "Well. I've seen disapproving uncles. Overprotective fathers. The occasional homicidal ex. But three furious big brothers? That's a bloody new tier."

Alex didn't reply. His jaw locked tight, but his eyes burned—not with shame or despair, but with something sharper.

Determination.

He stepped closer to the gate, his voice carrying, loud and unflinching. "I'm not giving up. Not on her. I'll be here every day if I have to."

No one turned back. No one acknowledged him.

But Alex didn't need them to. He'd made worse enemies for far less. This time, he wasn't fighting for business or pride.

This time, he was fighting for the only thing that had ever truly mattered.

And he'd give everything he had to win her back.

From the terrace, Harper had heard it—the low rumble of male voices drifting faintly across the manicured lawns. Too far to catch words, but close enough to set her pulse racing. Each muted syllable felt like a pebble dropped in her chest, rippling outward until she could hardly breathe.

When at last her brothers and Jonathan reappeared, striding back up the steps without Alex in sight, something in her chest released—a knot she hadn't even realised she was holding. Relief, sharp and bittersweet.

Clara leaned closer, voice low. "Was it him?"

Harper's answer was a single, clipped nod. "It was Alex."

Her mother reached for her hand, her touch warm and steady. "Do you want to talk about it?"

Harper shook her head quickly; eyes fixed on the rim of her teacup. "Not yet."

Her father, outwardly composed as ever, lifted his cup with deliberate calm. But his gaze, steady and unflinching, found Julian's approaching figure. "Did he say anything worth hearing?"

Julian stopped beside Harper, his jaw clenched, every line of his body taut with restrained anger. "He said he's not giving up. That he'll come back every day if he has to."

Nickolas gave a sharp, humourless scoff, folding his arms across his chest. "Persistent. I'll give him that."

"I don't want him here," Harper said, her tone cool but threaded with exhaustion. "Not now. Maybe not ever."

Jonathan stepped forward, his tone steady but steel beneath. "Then say the word, Harper, and we'll make sure he gets the message. Firmly."

She managed a small, grateful smile, though her eyes shimmered. "No more theatrics. I just need… time."

Clara nudged her gently, a spark of mischief cutting through the tension. "What you need is chocolate and bad movies."

"And wine," Harper murmured, managing the faintest curve of her lips.

Clara brightened. "Now you're talking."

Her mother stood, smoothing the crease of her linen trousers, taking charge the way she always did when emotions threatened to overwhelm. "Why don't we all give Harper a little space. Clara, darling, take her inside. The rest of us will… pretend we're not strategising additional security."

As the others drifted away—Julian muttering under his breath, Nickolas still bristling with unspent energy—Harper lingered, her gaze straying toward the distant gates. The sunlight caught on the black iron, and for a fleeting moment she almost imagined Alex still standing there, waiting.

Clara looped her arm through hers. "You okay?"

Harper hesitated, then answered with quiet honesty. "No. But I'm better than I was."

Together, they turned and walked inside, leaving behind the warm evening breeze and the faint perfume of roses climbing the terrace walls.

Behind them, silence settled—broken only by Julian's low growl to Nickolas as they lingered near the steps. "If he shows up tomorrow, I'll let you answer the gate."

Nickolas cracked his knuckles with relish. "My pleasure."

Alex sat rigid in the car, knuckles white around the steering wheel, eyes locked on the grand black gates that had just closed behind Julian, Nickolas, and Jonathan. The iron and gold shimmered faintly in the fading light, a barrier both literal and metaphorical.

Theo, uncharacteristically quiet, broke the silence at last. "So… all three of them her brothers?"

Alex shook his head slowly. "No. The one who called me 'rich boy'—that's the neighbour. Jonathan."

Theo's eyebrow arched. "Let me guess. He's in love with her."

Alex's jaw tightened. "Has been… for years, I think. Unspoken, but there."

Theo whistled low, the sound carrying a mixture of admiration and worry. "Well, that certainly complicates things."

Alex leaned his head back against the leather seat, exhaling with a weight that seemed to come from deep within him. "It doesn't matter. I didn't come here to compete with another man. I came to make things right. That's all that matters."

Theo gave him a sidelong glance, cautious but probing. "I'm not sure she *wants* things made right. Because that front-line defence team? They looked ready to bury you in the rose garden with a side of regret."

Alex's eyes narrowed, but his voice remained calm, resolute. "Let them. I don't care. I'm not leaving until I've had the chance to look her in the eyes. Until I can tell her I'm sorry. Tell her I love her. Tell her none of this—*none of it*—was ever a game to me."

Theo studied him for a long moment, silent but assessing. Then he gave a slow nod. "Alright, mate. Then I guess we keep trying. Wait. Watch. Learn. And hope she lets you in."

The sun sank lower behind the sprawling estate, casting long shadows across the perfectly kept lawns. Silence settled over the car, thick with unspoken regrets, unwavering determination, and the faint, fragile hope that somehow, against all odds, it wasn't too late.

Harper and Clara were curled up on the oversized sectional in the sunroom, a classic romantic comedy flickering softly on the television. Outside, the last light of day spilled across the lawn in honeyed waves, stretching long shadows over the garden. Inside, the mood was heavy, almost tangible. The bowl of popcorn between them sat untouched, a silent witness to the quiet tension.

Clara risked a glance at Harper, who hadn't laughed once—not even during her favourite scene. She sat stiffly, arms wrapped around her knees, her gaze distant and blank.

"You okay?" Clara asked softly, almost cautiously.

Harper didn't look away from the screen. "Fine."

Clara hesitated, then reached for the remote and muted the television. The sudden silence was gentle but loaded, pressing in on them both.

"Can I ask you something?"

Harper finally turned, her eyes tired, shadowed with exhaustion and grief. "Yeah."

Clara's voice was barely above a whisper. "Do you... do you love him?"

Harper's breath caught. Her fingers curled tighter around the sleeves of her jumper, nails biting faintly into the fabric. For a long moment, she didn't answer. Then a quiet, broken laugh escaped her lips, raw and trembling.

"Yes," she whispered. "God help me, I do."

Clara reached out, her hand warm and grounding, gently taking Harper's.

"Then maybe... maybe you should hear what he has to say."

Harper's jaw clenched. Her eyes shimmered, fighting back tears that threatened to spill. "I know he made a mistake," she said hoarsely. "And maybe—eventually—I could make peace with the bet. But that's not what hurts the most."

Clara's brow furrowed, concerned. "Then what does?"

Harper looked down at her lap, voice trembling. "He had chances, Clara. So many chances to tell me the truth. He could've come clean before I fell for him. Before I trusted him. Before I—" Her voice cracked, and she shook her head. "Before he slept with me."

Clara's hand tightened over hers, steadying her.

"If he cared—really cared—wouldn't he have stopped, even once, and said, 'I need to tell you something important before we do this'?"

Harper swallowed hard, blinking rapidly, trying to force down the sting of betrayal. "I feel… violated. Like none of it meant what I thought it did. And that's what's killing me. Not the bet. Not the lie. It's that every kiss, every touch, every word he said that felt real… he still kept the truth locked away."

Clara was silent for a moment, her own eyes glossy with empathy. "I'm so sorry," she said gently. "That's not something you just brush off."

"I gave him all of me, Clara," Harper whispered, voice breaking. "And he gave me half-truths."

Clara nodded slowly, her fingers brushing Harper's. "Jonathan told me Alex said he loves you."

Harper exhaled a shaky breath. "Maybe he does. Maybe he didn't mean for it to go this far. But if he really loved me… how could he let me give myself to him like that, knowing I didn't have the whole truth?"

She wiped at her eyes with the back of her hand, trying to gather the pieces of herself. "I don't know if I can trust what we had anymore. And without trust… what's left?"

Clara tucked a loose strand of hair behind Harper's ear, her touch tender. "Maybe nothing. Or maybe everything—if he's willing to earn it back. But you don't have to decide tonight."

Harper stared out the window at the deepening sky, that endless, darkening blue that always felt like both comfort and threat. "I'm scared," she admitted quietly. "Not just of being hurt again… but of losing what I thought was real."

Clara gave her hand a comforting squeeze. "If he breaks your heart again, I'll be here with wine, chocolate, and a playlist of angry girl anthems. But Harper… sometimes love isn't about the moment someone fails you. It's about whether they fight to make it right afterward."

Harper didn't answer immediately. When she finally nodded, it was slow, tentative—a fragile flicker of hope illuminating the ache in her chest. For the first time since it all fell apart, she allowed herself to consider that maybe, just maybe, something more than heartbreak could still exist.

Chapter Seventeen

The sun was already streaming through the gauzy curtains when Harper stirred, blinking against the soft morning light. For a long moment, she simply lay there— still, quiet—listening to the gentle rustle of leaves outside her window and the faint murmur of laughter drifting from the backyard, where her brothers were likely already firing up the barbecue. The warm, comforting aroma of coffee snaked in from the kitchen, carrying with it a sense of home.

It was Christmas Day.

And her heart still ached.

She rolled onto her side, clutching the pillow as if it might anchor her to the present. The ache had not softened; it throbbed beneath her ribs—raw, restless, insistent. She missed him. God, she missed him.

Alex.

Her chest tightened at the thought of him—his laugh, the way he looked at her as if she were the only thing in the room that mattered, the teasing lilt of his voice when he called her "trouble" with that crooked, infuriating half-smile. The memory of their kiss under the mistletoe, of their stolen weekend together, of how utterly real it had felt… until it wasn't.

She blinked quickly, refusing to cry. Not today. Not on Christmas. Not when her family had done everything to lift her, to fill the void left behind—when Julian had danced around the kitchen, stirring sauces and teasing her to make her laugh, when Nickolas had cracked impossibly terrible jokes just to see her grin, when her mother had held her like she used to as a child with scraped knees, whispering comfort and warmth.

They didn't deserve her sadness.

So, Harper took a deep, steadying breath and sat up. Her hands smoothed over her soft cotton pyjama shorts as she swung her legs over the side of the bed, planting her feet firmly on the hardwood floor.

She would be brave today.

She would smile. She would hum along to the carols drifting from the living room, help with the prawns, stir cocktails with her mother, laugh at Nick's ridiculous

Santa hat, hug her family a little tighter. She would be grateful—so deeply grateful—for the family that surrounded her.

Even if her heart still throbbed in quiet rebellion.

Even if, when she allowed herself a single pause, she could feel Alex's absence pressing against her chest like a ghost.

She rose and moved to the window, pulling back the curtain just enough to take in the wide, sunlit yard below. Julian chased the dog across the lawn, barefoot and carefree, while Nickolas strung garlands along the back patio, moving with precise care. Her mother's voice floated on the air, calling something about needing more lemons for the Christmas punch.

Harper let out a small, soft smile.

She would get through this day. For them.

And maybe… for herself too.

She turned from the window, slipped into her robe, and stepped into the hallway, the scent of cinnamon and roasted tomatoes wrapping around her like a warm, familiar hug.

It was Christmas.

And despite the fracture in her heart, she was surrounded by love—steady, enduring, and real.

The sun hung high overhead, the air thick with the heady scent of eucalyptus and gardenias as Alex eased the car to a stop outside the Jameson estate gates. Cicadas buzzed lazily in the distance, the heat rising from the driveway in shimmering waves. Christmas in Perth was nothing like the cold, snow-dusted holidays he'd grown up with—but then, nothing this year had gone the way he imagined.

He tightened his grip on the small, carefully wrapped box resting on the passenger seat beside him.

He should have been inside that house, with her. Laughing alongside her family, stealing a kiss in the shade while they grilled prawns and sipped chilled wine. But instead, he was trapped behind a security gate, hoping that the words he'd scrawled inside a note would speak louder than the silence that had grown between them.

He had bought the jewellery the week before—a delicate set of sapphire and diamond necklace, bracelet, and earrings. Timeless. Elegant. The moment he saw them, he thought of her: the sparkle in her eyes, the way her face lit up when she laughed. There had never been a question. They were hers.

He pressed the call button on the gate.

"Name?" a voice crackled through.

"Alexander Dawson."

A pause. Then: "Wait there."

Minutes crawled by. The heat rose from the sun-baked pavement, cicadas singing overhead like impatient witnesses. Eventually, the front door of the house swung open, and one of Harper's brothers strode down the long gravel drive. Broad-shouldered, sun-kissed, dressed in shorts and a crisp white T-shirt—he could have been the embodiment of easy-going Aussie summer, but his expression was anything but welcoming.

"You seriously planning to be here every day?" the man asked, stopping just short of the gate.

Alex met his gaze without flinching. "I said I would be. I meant it."

The man raised a brow. "She still doesn't want to see you."

Alex's chest tightened, but he nodded. "I know."

"Which one are you?" Alex asked, curious. "Julian or Nickolas?"

A faint smirk tugged at the corner of the man's mouth. "Julian. And trust me, you're lucky it's not Nick. He's the hothead."

Alex allowed the smallest hint of a smile. "Duly noted."

Julian's eyes flicked to the wrapped box in Alex's hand. "That for her?"

"Yes," Alex said. "I bought it last week. I… saw it and thought of her eyes."

Julian studied him for a long, measured beat. Then, slowly, he reached for the box.

"She might not even open it," he said flatly.

"I know," Alex replied, his voice quiet but steady. "But I had to try. There's a card inside."

Julian glanced toward the house, then back at Alex, before letting out a soft sigh. "I'll get it to her."

Alex offered a grateful nod, though his chest still ached with anticipation.

Julian turned but paused after a few steps up the drive. "You hurt her, you know. Not just her pride. You hit something deeper."

Alex swallowed, voice low and measured. "I know. And I'll regret it for the rest of my life."

Julian lingered for a beat longer, his eyes locked on Alex's, then finally turned, and disappeared into the house.

Alex remained at the gate for a few more seconds, the heat pressing down on him like a physical weight. Then he climbed back into the car, the scent of dry grass and Christmas lunch wafting on the breeze. As he drove away, he held onto a single hope: that when Harper opened the box—if she opened it—she would see that despite everything, what he felt for her was real.

The wrapping paper still lay in cheerful scraps across the living room floor—a colourful tangle of ribbon, torn gift tags, and crumpled tissue. That morning, Harper had unwrapped a delicate gold locket from her mum, already filled with childhood photos of her and her brothers. From Nickolas, a hand-carved jewellery box. Julian had gifted her a set of luxury bath oils, accompanied by a teasing grin and a note that read, "For when you finally decide to relax."

She had smiled. Laughed, even. And meant it.

Now, the back terrace hummed with chatter and the light clink of glasses. The sun bathed the yard in golden warmth, while a gentle breeze rustled the gum trees lining the perimeter. Someone had started a Christmas playlist on a speaker, and the mingling scents of grilled seafood, eucalyptus, and lemon floated through the air.

Clara and her parents had arrived just before lunch. Clara looked effortlessly glamorous in a flowing floral maxi dress, Jonathan in tow, carrying a bottle of chilled wine and a wrapped tin of his mother's famous shortbread. Harper had hugged them all tightly, relieved they were here—Clara always brought light, wherever she went.

The two families mingled with ease, laughter flowing as naturally as the chilled rosé. Harper's mother flitted between the kitchen and terrace, making sure everyone had enough to eat. Her father sat with Jonathan and Nickolas, deep in debate over cricket scores and the fine art of backyard barbecuing.

Harper perched on the edge of a wicker lounge, sipping a cool drink, when she noticed her father step away to answer his phone. He turned slightly, speaking in a low tone. Moments later, he approached Julian, murmured something quietly, and Harper saw her brother glance her way before nodding and disappearing through the house.

Her chest tightened with a dull, heavy thud.

Alex.

He had promised he would be here every day. Maybe he truly meant it.

She lowered her gaze to her glass, swirling the ice in circles as if it could distract her from the ache rising in her chest.

Clara leaned in, whispering something about Jonathan's latest awkward attempt at poetry. Harper laughed on cue, yet her eyes flicked repeatedly toward the door where Julian had disappeared.

Alex was out there.

Waiting.

Still hoping.

And even though her heart was bruised, still tender and healing, she wasn't sure which hurt more—that he was keeping his word... or that she almost wanted him to.

Julian returned to the terrace carrying a small, neatly wrapped box. The metallic silver paper caught the sunlight as he walked toward Harper, who was still perched near Clara on the lounge.

"He said he bought it for you last week," Julian said simply, handing it over.

Harper stared at the box in her lap. Her fingers hesitated. The festive paper felt too bright, too hopeful, too impossible. She wasn't sure she wanted to open it—not here, not with everyone watching. Her chest tightened with a mixture of anticipation and dread.

Clara nudged her gently. "May as well get it over with," she said, voice teasing, though her eyes were soft with understanding.

Harper took a slow, deliberate breath and began peeling away the wrapping. The paper fell away in quiet, crinkling sheets, revealing the box beneath—a deep velvet blue. She lingered for a heartbeat before lifting the lid, almost afraid to see what was inside.

Nestled on a bed of silk lay the most exquisite necklace, bracelet, and matching drop earrings she had ever seen—sapphire and diamond, glinting like captured starlight. The sapphires mirrored her eyes so perfectly it made her chest ache. She didn't even need to read the card to understand why he had chosen them.

Julian let out a low whistle. "You have to admit, the bloke's got bloody good taste. That would've cost a small fortune."

Harper didn't answer. She simply ran a fingertip over the cool gemstones, mesmerised. They were breathtaking, thoughtful, and painfully beautiful—all of him captured in one gift.

Around her, murmurs of admiration rose. Clara whispered, her mother cooed softly, even Nickolas leaned over a glass of beer, muttering something about the "posh bastard knowing his jewellery."

But Harper's attention was on the card, still tucked neatly inside the box—plain white, her name scrawled in Alex's unmistakable handwriting.

"I'll just take it upstairs," she said quietly, almost to herself.

Clara tilted her head. "Do you want me to come with you?"

Harper gave a small, soft smile. "No… I'll be back soon."

She rose and carried the box carefully, heels clicking softly on the floorboards. Once in her room, she perched on the edge of the bed and placed the box on her bedside table. The gentle rustle of the wrapping paper sounded unnaturally loud in the quiet space.

Her hands trembled as she reached for the card. What if it undid her? What if it was everything she secretly wanted to hear—too late?

She opened it with painstaking care. The words were short. Simple. Raw.

I saw this last week and thought of your eyes.

I know it's not going to fix anything. I bought it before I wrecked everything—before I hurt you—before I stuffed up.

I wish I hadn't messed it up.

I miss you. Every minute. Every breath.

Because I love you.

Merry Christmas, Harper—Alex.

Her throat tightened as she reread the note, the weight of his words pressing into her chest. He hadn't made excuses. He hadn't begged. He had simply told the truth.

And maybe that hurt even more.

Because she loved him too.

She pressed the card to her heart and closed her eyes. The ache was still there, persistent, and raw—but for the first time in days, it no longer felt unbearable.

Chapter Eighteen

Clara sat behind the wheel of her champagne-coloured Audi, parked just outside the wrought-iron gates of the Jameson estate. Beyond the bars, the sprawling property stretched into quiet grandeur—warm, golden lights spilling from mullioned windows, the faint sparkle of Christmas decorations glinting in the fading dusk.

The manicured hedges stood still, the fountain at the centre of the circular driveway trickling softly beneath the glow of lanterns. The estate was calm. Still. Almost too quiet, as though it, too, was holding its breath, waiting.

The sky blushed lavender, streaks of gold melting into indigo as dusk settled. Warm air carried the familiar hum of cicadas from the trees, a sound that always reminded her of home.

Clara checked her phone again. He was late.

Or maybe he'd finally given up.

Six days. He had shown up every day without fail—just like he said he would. Waiting beyond the gates, sometimes pacing, sometimes perched on the hood of his car, unreadable. He never tried to force his way in. Never called out. He just… waited. Like a man determined to outlast the silence.

But today—nothing. No sign of him.

Her chest tightened, disappointment curling in her stomach like a bitter shadow.

Then—headlights.

Bright beams cut through the quiet, washing the gravel shoulder in stark light. A low growl of an engine echoed across the drive. A sleek black car emerged from the curve, polished exterior catching the last hints of daylight. It moved with smooth, deliberate purpose, as if it knew exactly where it was going.

Clara's heart thudded. This had to be him.

She stepped out of her car, heels crunching softly against the gravel. The other vehicle rolled to a halt a few metres away, engine idling in a patient purr.

The driver's door opened.

And there he was.

Alexander Dawson stepped into the fading light, looking every bit as wrecked—and resolute—as he had all week. The posture of a billionaire remained—tall, commanding—but the polish was gone. His jacket absent, sleeves rolled to the elbows. Shadowed stubble traced a jaw that had seen long, sleepless nights.

And then there were his eyes—those unmistakable green eyes. Sharp with recognition, dulled by something far more human: pain.

He looked like a man with nothing left to hide.

And everything left to fight for.

"Alex?" Clara called, stepping into the pool of light at the edge of the driveway.

His gaze flicked to her, shifting from wariness to something like curiosity.

"Clara, isn't it?"

She nodded, walking closer. "We need to talk."

His brow lifted. "Did Harper send you?"

"No," Clara replied firmly. "She doesn't know I'm here."

That caught his attention. He folded his arms, interest piqued. "Then why are you?"

Clara stopped in front of him, gaze unwavering. "Because she's my best friend. And even though I have every reason to hate you right now, I don't think you're the villain she's convinced herself you are."

He said nothing. The silence hung thick between them, heavy with tension.

"I saw her after she left Sydney," Clara continued, voice trembling slightly despite her composure. "You didn't just break her heart, Alex. You broke her. And that's not something Harper Jameson allows lightly."

His jaw tightened, throat working. When he finally spoke, his voice was low, gravelly. "I know. I hate myself for it."

Clara exhaled shakily. "Then why? Why make a bet about her?"

He looked down, fists tightening at his sides. "It wasn't about her specifically. It was a joke—a stupid challenge between friends. But the second I met her...

everything changed. I kept telling myself I'd come clean. That I'd tell her the truth. But I waited. And then I… slept with her. And it was too late. I knew I'd lose her."

Clara studied him, voice low and raw. "That's what hurts her most, Alex. Not just the bet—but the lies that followed. You had so many chances to tell her. And instead, you slept with her knowing she didn't have the full story. If you cared—really cared—wouldn't you have told her first?"

Alex's eyes shimmered. His composure cracked. "I was a coward. I didn't want to ruin the one real thing I've ever had." He lifted his gaze to hers, each word weighted with truth. "But I do care. More than I ever thought possible. I love her. And I'd give anything to go back and do it differently."

Clara's voice softened, a fraction. "She says she's not ready to see you."

"I figured," he murmured, glancing toward the estate gates. "Her brothers made that painfully clear."

Clara almost smiled. "Yeah, they're not exactly subtle."

"And your brother, Jonathan—he's not a fan either."

"My brother's been half in love with Harper since high school," she said matter-of-factly. "I used to think they'd end up together. But that hope died a long time ago."

Alex looked at her, guarded. "So why are you here, Clara?"

She didn't flinch. "Because I believe in second chances. And because I think, deep down… so does she."

The weight on his shoulders eased slightly. A flicker of hope lit his eyes—quiet, but unmistakable.

"But listen to me," Clara said, stepping closer, voice sharp and cutting through the evening air. "If you hurt her again—there won't be a PR team, a security gate, or a single lawman on this continent that can protect you. Her brothers will hunt you. So will I. And so will Jonathan."

A dry, humourless smile touched his lips. "Message received."

"She's going to a New Year's Eve party tomorrow night. At the Harrington Hotel. I'll make sure she's alone in a reception room—for five minutes, maybe less. She won't know you're coming, so if she walks out, don't take it personally."

Alex's gaze hardened. "And if she stays?"

Clara tilted her head, expression unreadable. "Then that's on you. Everything after that… it's yours to fix."

He met her eyes, sincerity etched into every line of his face. "Thank you, Clara."

"Don't make me regret this," she said quietly. Then she turned, heels clicking against the gravel, fading into the shadows.

Behind her, Alex remained at the edge of the evening light, stripped of wealth, titles, and pretence.

Just a man.

Waiting.

Hoping.

And finally, ready to fight for the woman he loved.

Harper stood before the full-length mirror, staring at her reflection as though she hardly recognised the woman looking back.

She smoothed down the silky fabric of her royal blue gown, letting the material cascade to the floor in elegant, fluid waves. The colour deepened the hue of her eyes, making them appear almost violet in the soft, warm light. The bodice hugged her curves with understated grace—elegant, effortless—the kind of beauty that didn't need to try.

Clara had insisted on this dress. "Something unforgettable," she'd said, a conspiratorial wink accompanying her words.

And she'd insisted Harper wear the jewellery Alex had given her for Christmas. The sapphire and diamond necklace, the matching bracelet, the delicate drop earrings—they sparkled as though they belonged on someone fearless. Exquisite. And yet, they felt like a question Harper wasn't sure she had the answer to.

She inhaled slowly, adjusting the slender straps on her shoulders. Her strawberry-blonde hair was swept into soft, tumbling waves and pinned at the back, with a few artful tendrils framing her face. Her makeup was subtle but deliberate: a thin sweep of eyeliner, a touch of shimmer on her cheekbones, and bold red lips that didn't tremble—even if her heart did.

She turned slightly in the mirror, studying herself from every angle.

Elegant.

Composed.

Guarded.

Exactly how she needed to be.

Still, she lifted her chin. Straightened her spine.

Clara called from the other room, voice carrying through the hallway. "You ready?"

Harper's eyes lingered on the reflection a moment longer. "Ready as I'll ever be," she murmured.

With one last glance at herself, she stepped out of the room, her gown sweeping behind her like a trail of midnight silk.

Jonathon was waiting downstairs. He'd offered to accompany her tonight—no expectations, no awkward questions. Just quiet support. Harper hadn't realised how much she needed that until she'd said yes. She was genuinely grateful.

Down the hall, Clara turned at the sound of Harper's footsteps. Her emerald-green dress shimmered under the warm hallway lights, her red hair swept into a loose chignon. She smiled, fierce and bright, like sunlight through glass.

"You look gorgeous, babe," Clara said, her words sincere, her tone carrying that rare, best-friend fierceness.

"Thanks," Harper replied, smiling. "So do you. Green is definitely your colour."

They descended the staircase together, the low hum of conversation from the main floor growing louder, wrapping around them like a warm, living current. At the foot of the stairs stood Julian and Nickolas—both in dark, tailored suits, both grinning like proud older brothers who had been waiting for this moment.

"Wow, sis," Julian said, nudging Nickolas. "You look stunning."

"Absolute knockout," Nickolas agreed, winking.

Harper rolled her eyes lightly, but the fondness in her smile betrayed her. Despite the flutter of nerves in her stomach, warmth bloomed in her chest. These were her people—her anchor in the chaos of the world.

Clara stepped forward, radiant in emerald-green. "We'll see you there," she said, linking arms with Julian and Nickolas and sweeping them both toward the front door with a playful flourish.

Then Jonathon stepped closer.

He took both of Harper's hands gently, holding her still for a moment. His gaze lingered—not possessive, not expectant, just present. Steady, unwavering.

"You look incredible, Harper," he said, voice low, sincere.

The compliment hit deeper than she anticipated. Her smile softened, but her eyes stung, tears threatening to rise—not because of Jonathon, but because even in this house full of love, she still felt the absence of someone else. Someone who had carved a different kind of space in her heart.

She squeezed Jonathon's hands, grounding herself. "Thank you. For everything."

He nodded, quiet understanding in his eyes, and offered his arm. "Shall we make an entrance?"

Harper drew a slow breath, yet a flicker of doubt tugged at her chest.

'I never meant to hurt you.'

Alex's voice, raw and fractured, echoed unbidden in her memory. She shook it off. Tonight wasn't about him. It couldn't be.

She straightened her shoulders, lifted her chin, and stepped outside.

The limousine waited at the curb, sleek lines catching the soft glow of the porch lights.

Her parents had already departed for the party, leaving her this quiet, precious moment to gather herself—just her and Jonathon, poised at the edge of the night, stepping into the unknown together.

The grand ballroom of The Harrington Hotel glittered under soft golden lights, the towering Christmas tree at its centre dripping with crystals, ribbons, and tiny twinkling ornaments. Laughter floated through the air, mingling with the gentle clink of champagne flutes, the murmur of conversation, and the soft, lilting strains of a string quartet tucked into the corner.

Alex adjusted the cuffs of his tailored tuxedo, jaw tight, eyes scanning the room with a mix of anticipation and dread. Every detail seemed magnified—the shimmer of gowns, the polished marble floor, the soft glow of candlelight reflecting off crystal chandeliers.

"You sure about this?" Theo asked, his voice quiet but firm. He stood beside Alex in a midnight-blue tuxedo that likely cost more than most people's monthly rent. "Because once she sees you, there's no turning back."

Alex didn't answer right away. Words felt useless—too small to contain the storm of anxiety, hope, and aching resolve tightening in his chest.

"This party's strictly by invitation," he said at last, his voice low and taut with restraint. "I'm… grateful for the strings you pulled."

Theo took a leisurely sip of his drink, scanning the glittering crowd as though he owned the room. "You're my best friend, mate. And whether I think you've lost your mind or not, I know what it looks like when a man's in love." He tipped his glass toward the ballroom, where laughter and music swirled together like fate itself. "This is your last shot. Don't waste it."

Alex exhaled slowly, the air catching in his chest, fingers tightening around the stem of his glass. His pulse hammered in his ears. Each passing second stretched like a taut wire, a reminder that somewhere in this crowd, she would walk in.

Harper.

Dressed in elegance, poised, guarded. Still carrying the weight of hurt and betrayal—but maybe, just maybe, still willing to hear him out.

"I won't waste it," Alex muttered, more to himself than to Theo.

Tonight wasn't about charm. It wasn't about luck. It wasn't about a game, a bet, or proving anything to anyone but himself.

Tonight was about redemption.

Tonight was about Harper Jameson.

The scent of pine and champagne filled the air, but Alex couldn't focus on anything except the ache in his chest—the hollow, gnawing ache she left behind.

He stood near the edge of the ballroom, shoulders squared, jaw tight, scanning the glittering crowd. Conversation buzzed around him like static, but it faded the instant his eyes landed on them—Clara moving gracefully between Julian and Nickolas, all three dressed to impress, radiating the kind of presence that turned heads and drew whispers in their wake.

"That's them," he murmured under his breath, more to himself than anyone else.

Theo, glass of champagne in hand, leaned in slightly, his tone casual but curious. "And who's the stunner with the brothers?"

Alex didn't even glance at him. "That's Clara. Harper's best friend."

Theo's eyebrow shot up, intrigued. "She's gorgeous."

Alex finally turned toward him, eyes narrowing in warning. "Don't even think about it. Her brother is fiercely protective—and Clara's no pushover either."

Theo grinned, entirely unbothered. "Relax, mate. I'm just observing."

Alex shook his head, half amused, half exasperated. "This is serious, Theo. Tonight isn't about your next distraction."

Theo lifted his glass in mock surrender. "Noted. Eyes on the prize."

But Alex's attention had already shifted. Back to the entrance. Back to the moment that hadn't yet arrived but could change everything. Harper hadn't walked through the doors yet—but when she did, he would be ready.

Clara weaved through the clusters of glittering guests with effortless grace until she reached Alex near the far wall. He felt his chest tighten, gaze sharpening like a man waiting for a sign he didn't dare hope for too early.

"You look lovely tonight," he said, voice low and steady, laced with genuine warmth.

Clara's lips curved into a small, knowing smile. "Careful, Dawson. Keep talking like that and I might start thinking you have a type."

Before Alex could answer, her eyes flicked to the man standing beside him. Theo stepped forward, effortless charm in every gesture, extending his hand.

"Theo Clarke," he said, his accent smooth and rich as velvet. "And you must be Clara—Harper's best friend. Alex neglected to mention you were stunning."

Clara arched an eyebrow, amusement flickering across her face, and took his hand. "And you must be trouble."

"Only in the best ways," he said with a grin. "Save me a dance?"

She tilted her head, pretending to consider it. "I'll think about it."

Alex shot Theo a warning glance, but Clara waved it off with a playful smirk, her attention returning to him, expression sobering.

"I'll let you know when she'll be going to the reception room," she said quietly, voice soft but firm. "Try to stay hidden until then. She's not stupid—if she spots you too soon, she'll bolt."

Alex nodded, jaw tightening, focus absolute.

As Clara turned to leave, she paused beside Theo. With a mischievous flick, she traced a single finger along the edge of his jawline. "I might see you later."

Then she disappeared into the crowd, her emerald gown trailing behind her like smoke—seductive, elusive, unforgettable.

"I think I'm in love," Theo murmured, eyes lingering on the spot she had occupied.

She left both men standing in her wake: one thoroughly entertained, the other silently bracing himself… waiting for the woman who held his heart to finally walk through the door.

Jonathon sat beside Harper in the quiet hum of the limousine, the city lights reflecting off the windows as the car rolled to a stop in front of the hotel. The soft rustle of fabric and the faint scent of her perfume filled the small space between them.

"You ready?" he asked, voice low, careful, as though afraid to disturb the fragile tension between them.

Harper turned to him, eyes shimmering—not with anticipation, but with something quieter, more complicated. A shadow of sadness lingered beneath the surface.

"Jonathon," she said gently, her voice soft but deliberate, "I'm sorry."

He frowned, a crease forming between his brows. "What for?"

"For this," she whispered. "I know you care about me. A lot."

He stiffened slightly, the air between them taut. "Harper…"

"I wish I felt the same way," she continued, her fingers brushing against his as if to make the words less harsh. "You're a good man."

"But not good enough," he said quietly, voice tight but steady.

"Don't say that," she murmured, wrapping her hands around his. "It's not that. It's just… my heart isn't free. It hasn't been for a long time."

Jonathon held her gaze, silent for a long beat, reading the honesty in her eyes. Then he nodded slowly, a small sigh escaping him. "It's okay, Harper. I've known for a while… I knew it was never going to happen between us."

Tears pricked her eyes. "You deserve someone who gives you everything back," she whispered. "I'm sorry I can't be that person for you."

He gave a soft, bittersweet smile, the kind that carried warmth and quiet resignation. "I just want you to be happy. No matter who you end up with."

Harper squeezed his hands, feeling the tug of gratitude and heartbreak at once. "Thank you," she said, voice barely above a whisper.

The driver opened the limousine door, and the night beyond waited like a promise and a threat all at once. Jonathon stepped out first, reaching back to offer his hand. Harper took it, her fingers soft and cool against his, grounding herself.

She looked up at him, giving a wistful, grateful smile.

He leaned down, pressing a gentle, respectful kiss to her cheek. "You look beautiful," he murmured.

"Thank you," she replied softly, her heart tightening at the honesty of it.

With her arm tucked into his, they walked together toward the grand entrance of the ballroom, heads held high, carrying a quiet ache beneath the poise, hearts full of unspoken truths and tender longing.

Chapter Nineteen

Alex stood near the bar, shoulders squared, gaze locked on the grand entrance like a man waiting for a miracle he wasn't sure he deserved.

And then—she appeared.

Harper.

On the arm of Jonathan.

Time stilled.

Beside him, Theo let out a low whistle. "No wonder you fell for her."

Alex couldn't answer. Couldn't move. Could barely breathe.

She was beyond beautiful—elegant, radiant, utterly magnetic. The royal blue gown flowed over her like it had been sculpted for her alone, every step a study in grace. Her strawberry-blonde hair was swept up into soft waves, a few artful tendrils curling around her face, catching the light with each movement.

And around her neck—his necklace.

The sapphires and diamonds he had carefully chosen shimmered against her skin, catching the chandelier light in a thousand tiny reflections. The matching bracelet and earrings sparkled with subtle perfection, a delicate echo of the deep hue of her dress. She was wearing them. She hadn't returned them. That had to mean something.

Alex's chest tightened.

She hadn't forgotten.

She hadn't completely let go.

He watched her cross the ballroom like a vision drawn from the best part of his dreams and the worst part of his regrets. She was everything he wanted. Everything he feared losing again.

And she still wasn't his. Not yet.

Alex's chest tightened further as she drew closer. How could she look even more breathtaking than he remembered? And yet—she was walking toward him on another man's arm.

They approached two older couples, stopping briefly for greetings. Harper kissed them on the cheek, her smile soft, warm, full of life. Alex recognized the resemblance—one couple had to be her parents. Her brothers, Julian and Nickolas, stood nearby, protective, and proud, watching her every move.

All he could do was wait.

Clara had promised to bring Harper to him when the time was right, but every passing second stretched like a lifetime as he watched her move through the crowd. First with her father, then her brothers, then Jonathon. She laughed, smiled, danced lightly, the room bending around her. A few other men approached, hoping for a dance, but she declined them all. She was keeping her loved ones close tonight.

And that was his fault.

Alex remained in the shadows near the bar, gripping a drink he hadn't sipped. Then, suddenly, Jonathon appeared before him. Alex tensed, bracing for confrontation, for the entire plan to unravel in a single sharp word.

"Dawson," Jonathon said, voice clipped, measured.

"Jonathon," Alex replied, calm but wary.

They held each other's gaze, two men from different paths bound by the same woman.

"I know what Clara is doing," Jonathon said, expression unreadable, tone low.

"You do?" Alex asked, cautious, heart hammering.

Jonathon stepped closer, eyes locked on his. "Yes. And if you mess this up… if you hurt her," his voice became steel, unwavering, "I will bury you."

Alex nodded solemnly. "Understood. I know you care for her."

"I do," Jonathon admitted quietly. "But she loves you. I want her to be happy. And if that's you… then I'll support her."

Alex's chest constricted. "Thank you," he said, voice low. "I hope I am."

For a moment, they simply stood there, two very different men acknowledging the same truth: Harper's happiness mattered more than pride.

Jonathon extended a hand.

Alex took it.

No more words were necessary.

Jonathon turned and disappeared into the crowd, leaving Alex alone once more.

Theo stepped up beside him, swirling the drink lazily. "This woman really inspires loyalty, doesn't she?"

Alex didn't take his eyes off the entrance. "Yes," he said softly. "She does."

At last, Clara appeared, purposeful and poised, eyes sweeping the room until they landed on him.

"Alright," she said, voice brisk yet kind. "It's time. You can go into the reception room now." She nodded toward a nearby door. "It's unlocked. Wait inside. I'll bring Harper."

Alex stepped forward, sincerity etched across his face. "Thank you, Clara. I'll never forget this."

She softened slightly. "You can repay me by making her happy. She deserves that."

He nodded silently, heart pounding like a drum.

As he walked away, Clara turned to Theo, trailing a finger lightly down his chest.

"Now don't go anywhere," she said, playful yet commanding. "I'll be back for you."

Theo grinned, eyes gleaming. "I'll be here."

And Alex moved toward the door, heart full of hope, fear, and the single, unwavering thought: Harper Jameson.

Clara returned to the ballroom and found Harper standing at the edge of the dance floor, watching her brothers laugh with their parents. The sapphire necklace sparkled against her skin, catching the soft light of the chandeliers, but her eyes held a distant, wistful sadness that made her seem almost untouchable.

"Harper," Clara said gently, resting a hand on her arm.

Harper turned, startled. "Clara?"

"There's someone who wants to see you. He's waiting."

Harper's brows drew together, a flicker of anxiety crossing her face. "Who?"

Clara didn't answer immediately. She just smiled softly, warm and reassuring. "Come with me."

Harper hesitated, her heart already thudding violently in her chest. But there was something in Clara's expression—a quiet insistence, a spark of hope—that made her legs move. She followed her best friend out of the ballroom, down a quiet corridor lined with soft carpets and warm, muted lights, until they reached a closed door.

Clara stopped and turned, eyes locking with Harper's. "Before you go in… I need to say something."

Harper's pulse quickened. "What?"

"I know you're scared," Clara said gently, her voice low and steady, "but so is he. Just… listen. Don't walk away this time unless you're absolutely certain."

Harper's breath caught in her throat. "It's Alex, isn't it?"

Clara only smiled again, soft, and certain. She reached for the doorknob and slowly pushed the door open. "Go on."

Harper stepped inside.

The room was dimly lit, quiet except for the faint hum of the city outside. Shadows pooled in the corners, emphasizing the single figure standing near the tall window, back to her.

At the sound of the door, he turned.

Alex.

Her heart skipped a beat, then stuttered.

He looked breathtaking in a classic black tuxedo, every line of him poised yet relaxed, his green eyes locking onto hers as if the rest of the world had vanished. There was something raw in his gaze—vulnerability mixed with a quiet, desperate hope, as though this moment could define everything.

She didn't speak. Neither did he.

For a long, suspended moment, they simply looked at each other. The air between them was thick with unspoken words, regrets, and promises, heavy yet fragile, waiting to be acknowledged.

Alex took a step toward her, his voice low, almost reverent.

"I wasn't sure you'd come," he murmured. "But I hoped."

Harper's eyes shimmered, her hands curling into light fists at her sides. "Clara didn't give me much choice."

He gave a faint, wry smile, tinged with relief. "Then I'll be grateful for her interference until the day I die."

Silence stretched between them, thick and fragile, heavy with all the things they had never said and all the things that still needed saying.

At last, Alex drew a slow, steadying breath. His chest rose and fell as though he were preparing for battle.

"I lied to you," he began, his voice rough with remorse. "I let my pride, my fear, and a stupid bet get in the way of the best thing that's ever happened to me. You."

She flinched, a flicker of pain tightening her features, but he didn't stop. He couldn't.

"I came to Sydney thinking love was a game—something people played to get what they wanted. I never thought it would happen to me. And then…" His voice cracked, forcing him to swallow hard. "Then I met you."

His gaze softened, reverent. "You were real. Kind. So damn strong. You challenged me, saw through me, called me out when no one else dared. And still—God, Harper—still you made me want to be better. Not richer. Not more powerful. Just better. For you."

His hand trembled slightly as he reached into his jacket pocket and pulled something out—a small, worn rectangle of plastic. His Veridian Dynamics name tag.

"I kept this," he whispered, his thumb brushing over the faded lettering. "Because the man you met while I wore this… he was more himself with you than he's ever been. You made me that man."

Harper's lips parted, eyes wide, her breath catching at the sight of the meaningless object transformed into a talisman of memory.

Alex's voice broke again. "I love you, Harper Jameson. Not the idea of you. Not the fantasy of you. You. The woman who speaks her mind, who protects the people she loves, who looks heartbreak in the face and somehow—miraculously—still chooses to care again."

He closed the distance between them until only inches separated them, his breath uneven. "I don't expect forgiveness tonight. I just needed you to know—I am not the same man. And if you give me a second chance, I'll spend the rest of my life proving I deserve it."

Harper stood utterly still, her pulse racing, the muffled hum of laughter and music from the ballroom fading into nothingness. His eyes held hers—green and desperate, shimmering with unspoken pleas.

Her voice was quiet when it came, but each word cut through the silence. "You hurt me, Alex. You made me feel like a joke… like I was just some challenge for you to win."

His expression fractured, regret etching deep lines across his face. "You were never a challenge, Harper. You were the moment everything changed."

She let out a trembling breath, her composure slipping. "Then why didn't you tell me the truth? You had chances. So many chances."

Alex opened his mouth, but no words came. His silence spoke louder than excuses ever could.

"You slept with me," she whispered, her voice breaking. "You let me give you that piece of myself—while you kept the lie. Do you have any idea what that did to me?"

He took an instinctive step closer, but she lifted a hand between them, halting him.

"I could have forgiven the bet," she said, her eyes burning, sharp with pain. "It was stupid and cruel, but maybe… maybe I could have understood it. But you knew I was falling for you. And instead of telling me, you let it happen. You let me believe it was real—while you were still hiding the worst part."

Her voice dropped to a raw whisper, stripped bare. "So, tell me, Alex. How am I supposed to believe any of it was real?"

His throat worked as he swallowed, but he couldn't look away. Couldn't defend himself. Not against her pain.

Her eyes shimmered with tears she refused to shed as she lifted her chin. "I wasn't your game piece, Alex. I was your consequence."

The words hit him like a blow, but he didn't flinch. Instead, he nodded faintly, voice low and wrecked. "You're right. You were never the bet. You were what made the bet feel like poison in my mouth the second I met you."

Her jaw tightened, her silence weighted with the ache of truth.

"I was a coward," he admitted, his voice rough with shame. "I fell in love with you, Harper. And it terrified me."

For the first time, her eyes flickered, the wall of her composure cracking.

"I kept telling myself I'd tell you," he went on, every word scraped raw. "Every time we got closer, I swore I'd come clean. But the longer I waited, the more afraid I became—afraid of losing you, afraid of proving myself right. That the moment you knew the truth, I'd be nothing to you."

A pause. Heavy. Shattering.

"I didn't hide it because I didn't care," Alex whispered. "I hid it because I cared too damn much. And I couldn't stand the thought of watching you walk away."

She swallowed hard, the hurt in her eyes softening—just enough to let a glimmer of hope shine through.

"You were right," he added, his voice breaking, ragged with honesty. "You were my consequence. The best one I've ever had."

Silence swelled between them, thick and almost tangible, heavy with everything they had left unsaid—and maybe, just maybe, the first flicker of something neither of them was ready to name.

"Say it again."

Her voice was barely more than a whisper, yet it landed in his chest like a thunderclap, reverberating through every nerve.

He knew exactly what she needed—not promises. Not excuses. Only the truth.

"I love you," he said, his voice rough, raw, and unsteady with emotion. "More than I thought I was capable of. More than I ever planned to. The time we spent together... it changed me. It opened my eyes to what my life had been missing all along."

He took a hesitant step closer, every movement measured, careful. "You're sexy. Cheeky. Brilliant. Maddening. Loyal when it matters most, fierce when you protect the people you love. You challenge me, make me laugh, make me feel like I'm more than just a name on a company letterhead. You're everything, Harper. Everything I never knew I needed—until I met you."

Her breath hitched. Her lips parted, but no words came.

His voice softened, cracked, and lingered in the space between them. "I'm not asking for a second chance because I deserve it. I don't. I'm asking because I cannot imagine my life without you in it. Please forgive me. Because I swear to you—I will never forgive myself for the way I hurt you."

The silence that followed was heavy, electric, charged with possibility and fear.

"I love you," she whispered, the words trembling on her lips, tears brimming. "God help me… I still love you."

Relief washed across his face—pure, unguarded, blinding. He took another careful step forward, closing the space between them.

But she lifted a hand.

"Wait."

He froze, heart pounding, eyes searching hers.

"But," she said, her voice steady now, firm with the steel she'd spent weeks rebuilding, "if you ever lie to me again… if you ever make me feel small, like a fool, like I don't matter—I won't come back. My heart is not built to survive you twice."

His breath caught, his own voice low and reverent. "You won't have to. Never again."

A long, tense pause stretched between them. And then, slowly, Harper stepped forward and placed her hand against his chest, right over the thundering beat of his heart.

It was racing, just like hers.

She looked up at him, and something inside her finally released—a breath she hadn't realised she'd been holding for weeks. A weight that had lodged in her chest the moment she'd walked away melted, bit by bit, into the quiet hope of now.

When he reached for her, she didn't flinch or pull away. Instead, her fingers slid into his, interlacing with reverent care—like something sacred had just been restored.

"I love you," she murmured again, words soft, fragile, yet unyielding. "Even when I tried not to. Even when I hated myself for it."

"I love you," he echoed, steady, full of truth. Not desperation this time. Not apology. Just love, as clear and essential as air.

He leaned in slowly, pausing, giving her the space to meet him halfway. Their lips met in a kiss tender at first—tentative, careful, as though both feared breaking the fragile moment.

Then her arms wound around his neck, pulling him closer, and he responded without hesitation, wrapping his arms around her waist like a man anchoring himself to the only thing in his life that had ever made sense.

The kiss deepened, unhurried, aching, as if each brush of their mouths could stitch together every broken piece of the past. It was forgiveness, hope, and longing all at once—everything they had lost and everything they had yet to find.

When they finally broke apart, breathless, trembling, their foreheads rested together. The heat of their closeness hummed with all that had been lost—and all that could still be reclaimed.

"God, I missed you," he whispered, his voice thick with longing. "It felt like a lifetime."

Her eyes shimmered, raw, and open. "It was."

He reached up, thumb brushing her cheek, tucking a loose curl behind her ear. "I thought about you every single day. Wondered where you were, what you were doing... if you still thought about me. If I'd already lost you forever."

Harper's lips curved into a bittersweet, trembling smile. "You almost did."

"But I didn't," he said, quiet but certain. "Because you're here."

"I'm here," she whispered, softly, resolutely. "Because I still believe in us. In what we had... and in what we still could have."

"I won't waste it," he promised, voice steady, eyes locked on hers. "Not one second. I'll spend every day proving I'm worthy of your heart."

She leaned in again, pressing her lips to his with a tenderness that stole his breath. Slow this time. Soft. Measured. A promise sealed in silence.

And when they finally pulled apart, it was with a shared breath and a quiet, unspoken truth:

This wasn't just a reunion.

This was a beginning.

Alex let out a slow breath, glancing toward the ballroom doors. "We better go," he said, a smirk tugging at the corner of his mouth, teasing but tender. "Time to face the music. Your brothers are terrifying, by the way."

She laughed, a soft, genuine sound that warmed his chest. "They love me."

"Yeah," he said, taking her hand, his thumb brushing over hers in a comforting, intimate gesture. "That's what I'm afraid of."

Together, they stepped into the ballroom, hand in hand, as if the weight of the world had finally lifted from their shoulders. The room glittered with golden light, the string quartet's soft, romantic melodies weaving around them like a private cocoon. Without hesitation, Alex led Harper to the centre of the dance floor.

The music swelled, and he pulled her into his arms, closer than polite society might deem respectable—but neither of them cared. Her hands rested lightly on his shoulders, delicate yet steady. His hands settled firmly at her waist, then slowly slid up her back, holding her as though he never intended to let go again.

As they moved together—slow, unhurried, perfectly in sync—he leaned in, his warm breath brushing her ear. "You're my heart, my soul... my entire world."

Harper's eyes fluttered closed, the words stitching together something fragile and broken inside her, mending it with every beat of his voice.

Then his gaze drifted to the side. Her brothers.

Julian and Nickolas stood off to the side, arms crossed, expressions rigid masks of big-brother suspicion—but just beneath, a reluctant softness. They were watching, cautious but protective, and Alex gave them a small, respectful nod—an unspoken vow of intent and sincerity.

Harper followed his gaze, letting out a soft, amused chuckle. "They're trying not to smile."

"Trying very hard," Alex murmured, a grin tugging at his lips. "I'm a brave man, but I might still need your protection."

She looked up at him, her smile radiant, teasing, full of warmth. "You already have it."

And in that moment, as they spun slowly on the polished dance floor, surrounded by friends, family, music, and the soft glow of golden lights, they weren't just dancing.

They were beginning again.

Chapter Twenty

After their second dance, Harper looked up at Alex with a soft, almost mischievous smile. "I think it's time you were properly introduced to my family."

Alex arched a brow, a faint smirk tugging at the corner of his mouth. "Are you sure that's wise? I feel like I've only just scraped through round one."

She gave a low, amused chuckle and slipped her hand into his, warm and reassuring. "You've more than earned it."

With a graceful tug, she led him through the crowd toward a small circle gathered near the open bar. Her parents were chatting with Julian and Nickolas, both of whom were already eyeing Alex with a mixture of guarded interest and quiet scrutiny.

"Mum, Dad," Harper said warmly, her voice calm but clear, carrying just enough authority to settle the moment, "this is Alexander Dawson." She turned to him, her fingers still laced with his and offered a reassuring smile. "Alex, these are my parents—William and Jenny Jameson."

Alex straightened slightly, pulling himself into a posture of polite respect, and extended his hand to William first. "It's a pleasure to meet you, sir."

William shook his hand firmly, measuring his grip. His gaze lingered on Alex a second too long—quiet, careful, evaluating. "If my daughter's sure of you," he said at last, "then you have my support."

Alex inclined his head in acknowledgment, voice steady. "Thank you, sir. That means a great deal to me."

Jenny stepped forward, her smile warm and radiant. "So, this is the man my Harper loves," she said, drawing Alex into a soft, maternal hug and planting a quick kiss on his cheek. "It's lovely to meet you, Alex."

"The pleasure's mine, Mrs. Jameson," he replied, touched by the ease of her kindness and the unspoken welcome it carried.

Just then, Harper's brothers stepped forward. Julian, broad-shouldered and serious-eyed, gave Alex a long, appraising look before extending his hand. "Julian," he said simply.

"Nickolas," added the younger brother, flashing a lopsided grin, matching his brother's grip with firm confidence. "Just so you know—we'll be watching."

"Nickolas," Harper groaned under her breath, shaking her head.

Alex chuckled, tension finally easing from his shoulders. "Fair enough," he said lightly, the smile reaching his eyes.

They stood there for a moment, an easy circle of laughter and soft conversation mingling with the hum of the party. And for the first time that evening, Alex didn't feel like an outsider in Harper's world.

He felt like he belonged.

The music drifted softly through the ballroom, warm golden lights casting a gentle, intimate glow over the gathering. Laughter and the soft clinking of glasses filled the air, but Alex's attention narrowed to a single point in the crowd—Harper.

She stood near the bar with Clara and Theo, her head thrown back in laughter at something Theo had said, her eyes sparkling in that way that always managed to knock the air from Alex's lungs. Even now, after everything, he couldn't believe she looked at him the way she did—unaware of the storm he carried for her, yet lighting up the room entirely.

He turned slightly to William Jameson, who stood beside him, nursing a scotch with quiet vigilance, a father's innate watchfulness never leaving his posture.

"Mr. Jameson," Alex said, adjusting his stance, voice steady but low, carrying both respect and sincerity. "Do you mind if we have a quiet word?"

William's eyes flicked to him, sharp and assessing, then softened into a small nod. "Of course."

They stepped away from the bustle, just far enough for some privacy near the edge of the ballroom. Alex paused, drawing in a slow, measured breath before speaking.

"I won't take much of your time," he began, voice deliberate, carrying the weight of truth. "I just… I wanted to do this properly. I wanted to show you, finally, that I understand what's at stake."

William's brow lifted slightly, his gaze steady, but he didn't interrupt.

"I know I made mistakes," Alex continued, eyes briefly flicking back to Harper. "I didn't come into Harper's life with honest intentions. But somewhere along the way, everything changed. She changed me. I fell in love with her—fully, deeply, in a way I didn't think I was capable of. Every day without her has been a reminder of what I nearly lost."

His gaze softened as it returned to Harper. She was still laughing with Clara, playfully swatting at Theo's arm. The sight—safe, radiant, alive—made his chest tighten, ache even, with longing and gratitude.

"I'd like to ask for your blessing," he said finally, turning fully back to William. "I want to marry your daughter. Not because I deserve her, but because I'll spend every day trying to. Trying to be the man she deserves."

A long silence followed. William studied him carefully, eyes calculating, weighing both words and heart.

Then, slowly, the stern line of his expression softened.

"You came all the way across the country to fix what you broke," William said, voice steady but warm. "You swallowed your pride. Faced her brothers. Faced me. That tells me more than words ever could." He exhaled, then extended his hand. "That tells me enough."

Alex grasped it firmly, gratitude and emotion coursing through him.

"You have my blessing, Alex," William said, tone open now, carrying both acceptance and pride. "Welcome to the family."

"Thank you," Alex said, his voice rougher than he intended, choked with emotion. "That means everything."

William gave him a firm clap on the shoulder. "Make her happy. That's all I ask."

Alex nodded, feeling a lump in his throat, his heart overflowing as he looked once more at the woman who had upended his life—and somehow, in doing so, made it whole.

The Harrington Hotel ballroom shimmered with effortless elegance. Crystal chandeliers sparkled overhead, scattering golden light across the polished marble floors. Ornate floral arrangements graced each table, their delicate blooms catching the glow. A live jazz band played softly in the background, the music rising and falling like a gentle tide, weaving warmth through the bustling room.

Alex made his way through the crowd, every step purposeful, his eyes locked on Harper.

She stood near the champagne tower, deep in conversation with Clara and Theo. Harper laughed at something Theo had just said, her head tilting back slightly, the soft waves of her strawberry-blonde hair catching the light with every movement. Clara gave Theo a playful shove, and he, with his usual theatrical flair, looked entirely unrepentant.

As Alex drew closer, Harper's gaze met his. A slow, radiant smile curved her lips, and she cast a teasing glance toward Theo. "Where did you find this guy?" she asked, one eyebrow arching in mock accusation.

Theo placed a hand over his chest, feigning deep offense. "Excuse you, Harper. I was born this fabulous."

"He came with my original bad decisions package," Alex said dryly, slipping an arm around Harper's waist. "Unfortunately, the return policy expired."

Clara laughed, shaking her head. "He does grow on you. Like mould."

"Charming mould," Theo added with a grin, lifting his glass in mock toast.

Harper leaned slightly into Alex, her eyes softening. "You vanished for a bit."

"I needed a quiet word with your father," Alex said, his tone low and steady.

Her expression shifted—still gentle, but curious. "You did?"

"I did."

Before she could respond, the lights in the ballroom dimmed slightly. The band transitioned into a slower, more intimate melody, and murmurs of anticipation rippled through the room.

Harper glanced toward the towering clock near the stage. "It's almost midnight."

Alex extended his hand. "Come dance with me."

She placed her hand in his without hesitation.

He led her to the centre of the dance floor, where other couples swayed in soft, gentle rhythm. The floor gleamed under the warm chandelier glow, the room pulsing with quiet joy, clinking glasses, and whispered laughter. As Alex wrapped one arm around Harper's waist, his other hand holding hers, she leaned into him, resting her head near his shoulder. Her familiar, delicate perfume drifted between them, a quiet, grounding presence.

Neither spoke at first. They simply moved together—slow, seamless, like two pieces of a puzzle finally aligned, perfectly attuned to one another.

Then Harper looked up at him, her blue eyes searching, intense and shimmering with unspoken questions. "What did you say to him?"

Alex smiled softly, brushing a lock of hair from her cheek, his fingers lingering for just a heartbeat longer than necessary. "I told him I loved you. That I made mistakes… but I will make it up to you. Every day."

She smiled, small and tender, a glimmer of relief in her expression—but before she could answer, the ballroom lights dimmed further, and the countdown began.

"Ten… nine…"

The band fell silent. Guests leaned forward, glasses raised, faces lit with eager anticipation, voices joining together in a rhythm of hope.

"…eight… seven…"

Harper's fingers tightened around his, seeking reassurance and finding it.

"…six… five… four…"

Alex leaned closer, his forehead resting lightly against hers, their breaths mingling. "You've changed everything for me," he murmured, his voice low, full of awe.

"…three… two…"

Her lips parted slightly, her eyes bright with emotion, shimmering like the confetti soon to fall.

"…one!"

The room erupted in cheers, clapping, and the jubilant pop of champagne corks. Confetti cascaded from the high ceiling, fluttering down like tiny stars caught in Harper's hair and the folds of her gown.

Alex kissed her.

It started soft, tentative, a gentle seal of the moment—but it deepened quickly, charged with weeks of tension, missteps, longing, and the undeniable truth that had quietly settled in his heart. When they finally pulled apart, the ballroom was still alive with celebration—but for them, the world had stopped, suspended in a single perfect second.

"Happy New Year," she whispered, her hand resting over his heart, feeling the steady thrum that mirrored her own.

"Happy New Year," he echoed, brushing his thumb across her cheek, his voice husky with emotion. "You make everything new."

The celebrations had begun to wind down, the last notes of jazz echoing softly through the Harrington Hotel ballroom as guests slowly filtered out. Laughter and the delicate clink of champagne glasses lingered in the air, but Alex's attention was fixed entirely on Harper.

She stood beside him near the grand staircase, cheeks flushed from the evening's excitement, heels in hand now that the night was ending. Her gown shimmered under the soft, golden lights, but it was the way she looked at him—with quiet affection and something deeper, something unspoken—that made his chest tighten.

"I think we should head out," he said quietly, leaning close so only she could hear.

Harper glanced up, her smile instant and knowing, a mixture of relief and anticipation in her eyes. "I was hoping you'd say that."

They wove their way through the thinning crowd toward the exit, passing Harper's family and Clara's as farewells were exchanged. Jenny embraced Harper warmly, while William offered Alex a nod of quiet approval.

Clara gave Harper a quick hug, whispering something that made her laugh softly. Then Jonathon stepped forward, his expression serious as he extended a hand toward Alex.

"Keep her safe," Jonathon said, his tone low but firm. "And happy."

Alex accepted the handshake with a firm grip. "I will. You have my word."

With the final goodbyes said, Alex placed a protective hand at the small of Harper's back, guiding her gently toward the elevator. The lobby had quieted, the opulence of the Harrington gleaming around them—crystal sconces catching the last flickers of light, dark wood panelling glowing warmly, and the faint scent of orchids and aged whiskey mingling in the air.

As they stopped before the lift, Harper tilted her head toward him. "You're staying here tonight?"

The elevator chimed softly, doors sliding open. Alex looked at her, eyes steady and warm, and then leaned in, kissing her—unhurried, deep, tasting faintly of champagne and promise.

"We're staying here," he murmured against her lips.

She followed him inside without hesitation.

The doors closed behind them, enclosing them in a private world broken only by the soft hum of ascent. Alex stood beside her, brushing his hand against hers, neither speaking—they didn't need to. The space between them pulsed with quiet anticipation and something infinitely sweeter: trust.

When the elevator doors opened onto the penthouse suite, Harper drew in a soft breath.

The living room glowed in warm, golden light. Vases of fresh flowers filled every corner—roses in soft blush and deep crimson, cascading white orchids, and full ivory peonies arranged with exquisite precision. Their scent lingered lightly in the air, romantic and intoxicating, blending seamlessly with the distant hum of the city skyline beyond the floor-to-ceiling windows.

She stepped forward slowly, absorbing the beauty around her. "Alex…" she breathed. "What's all this?"

He came up behind her, arms wrapping gently around her waist, his chin resting lightly on her shoulder.

"It's all for you," he whispered, his voice low and reverent. "Every last bloom."

Harper turned slightly in his arms, eyes wide with awe. "It's beautiful."

"You're beautiful," he said simply, as though it were the only truth that mattered.

Her gaze softened. "You planned this?"

He gave a small, earnest nod. "I wanted tonight to feel like a dream. Because that's what you are to me—a dream I never thought I was allowed to have."

She leaned into him, fingers resting lightly against his chest. "It feels like a fairytale."

"It's real," he said, brushing a stray curl behind her ear. "You're here. I'm here. No pretending. No hiding."

For a long moment, they simply stood there, wrapped in the quiet magic of the room, the city glittering around them, the flowers whispering their silent blessing. Time itself seemed to pause.

Slowly, Alex pulled back just enough to meet her gaze—green locking with deep blue.

Without a word, he dropped to one knee before her.

Harper's hand flew to her mouth, eyes wide, shimmering with disbelief and something deeper—hope.

He looked up at her, voice steady despite the raw emotion threading through it.

"I came to Sydney thinking love was a game I could control… that feelings made you vulnerable. But then I met you. And you changed everything."

Tears welled in her eyes, her breath hitching.

"I fell for you when you didn't fall for me. I kept falling, even when you pushed me away. And when I least deserved it… you gave me a second chance."

He opened the velvet box, revealing a sapphire-and-diamond ring, elegant and timeless—just like her.

"So now, Harper Jameson," he said softly, "will you take one more chance on me?"

Her lips parted, no words coming, just a shaky breath and shimmering tears.

"Alex…" she whispered, voice catching.

"I love you," he said, unwavering and certain. "And I want to love you for the rest of my life. Will you marry me?"

She stared for a heartbeat, then another—before collapsing to her knees, laughter and tears colliding, arms flying around his neck.

"Yes," she breathed, clutching him. "Yes. Yes—of course I will."

With hands trembling slightly, he slid the ring onto her finger, then kissed her slowly, deeply. Behind them, the city glowed, and the night seemed to hold its breath.

In that moment, there were no wagers, no fortunes, no regrets, no broken promises.

There was only them—choosing love. Choosing forever.

Epilogue

Twelve months later…

They clung to each other in the quiet aftermath, limbs entwined, breaths catching, hearts pounding in perfect tandem. Wrapped in the hush of intimacy and the lingering warmth of love, they lay together in the soft embrace of Egyptian cotton sheets, the king-sized bed tucked into the rear cabin of his private jet.

The muted hum of the engines thrummed beneath them—a steady, soothing lullaby—and outside, the sun sank low on the horizon, painting the clouds in streaks of amber, gold, and rose. The golden light filtered through the windows, casting a honeyed glow across Harper's bare shoulder, tracing the delicate curve of her collarbone and the gentle rise and fall of her chest as her breathing slowly steadied.

"I love you, sweetheart," Alex murmured, his voice roughened by emotion and the weight of everything he felt for her. He pressed a tender, reverent kiss against her skin, as if committing the moment—and her—to memory.

She smiled, blissful and still breathless, her body warm with the echo of his touch. "I love you more," she whispered, turning into him, her voice soft as silk against his chest. Her fingers traced slow, aimless circles over his skin, as if trying to anchor herself to the quiet, almost sacred magic that lingered between them.

He pulled her closer still, their bodies slotting together like two halves of the same soul. Their legs tangled beneath the sheets, his arm wrapped securely around her waist, holding her as if he might never let go.

"Six months married," he said softly, brushing his lips against her temple, "and I still can't believe you're mine."

She laughed, soft and sweet, her head resting on his shoulder, the sound like music drifting through the intimate cocoon of the jet. "I've been yours since the day you turned up at Veridian Dynamics and said you always wanted to see what Australians were like outside the travel brochures."

Alex chuckled, the memory painting a smile across his lips. "And you told me you bite less than the brochures imply. Most days." He shifted slightly, angling his body to reveal the faint red marks blooming across his shoulder. "I don't believe it."

Her laughter deepened, low and lazy, curling around him like a ribbon of warmth. She lifted her head just enough to press a playful kiss beside one of the marks. "That's what you get for falling in love with a girl from the wild outback of Sydney."

He rolled his eyes with affectionate mockery. "Remind me to file a tourist complaint."

"You'll have to take it up with HR," she teased, trailing her fingers lightly across his chest. "Though I hear the manager has a soft spot for charming foreigners."

Alex tipped her chin up and kissed her, slow, lingering, and smiling. "Lucky me."

Her eyes sparkled with teasing affection. "Your mum was sweet last weekend."

Alex sighed, gently tucking a strand of hair behind her ear. "She's grown quite fond of you."

"I love her too," Harper said softly. "Where is she off to this week?"

"On safari in Botswana, I think. She said she'd come for Christmas next year—but let's be honest, there'll probably be another adventure calling her name."

Harper shook her head, amused. "I can't wait to see everyone."

His eyes softened, warm, and steady. "I'm even looking forward to seeing our family."

She arched a brow, playful. "So, you're no longer afraid of my brothers?"

"I was never afraid," he said with mock offence, propping himself on one elbow with exaggerated dignity. "I was just… cautiously respectful of three grown men who looked like they wanted to throttle me."

She giggled, slipping closer, her hand resting lightly over his heart. "Well, at least they don't want to kill you anymore."

He leaned in, brushing his lips to hers with a tender grin. "There's that small mercy."

When they landed at Perth Airport, a sleek black limousine waited on the tarmac, the warm December sun stretching long shadows across the runway. As they drove toward the Jameson estate, Harper pressed her hand to the window, heart swelling with a mixture of excitement and contentment. The familiar eucalyptus trees, the soft golden hills, and the endless expanse of sky all whispered home, each passing mile grounding her in a sense of belonging she hadn't felt in years.

At the estate, the front doors swung open even before the car came to a full stop. William and Jenny stood on the porch, arms wide, faces alight with joy, while Clara bounced beside them, practically vibrating with excitement.

Harper barely stepped out before Clara squealed, flinging her arms around her. "You're glowing!" she said breathlessly. "Married life suits you!"

William stepped forward, clasping Alex's hand in a firm, welcoming shake. "Good to see you again, son."

Jenny followed with a warm hug, pressing a quick kiss to his cheek. "We're so happy you're here. Welcome home."

Alex stood for a moment, struck by how completely, how effortlessly, they had welcomed him. The old armour of distance and cynicism slipped a little further from his shoulders. For the first time in a long time, he didn't feel like a visitor in someone else's life. He felt like family.

Clara slid her arm through his and pressed a playful kiss to his cheek. "Julian, Nickolas, and Jonathan are in the games room, playing pool. Go on. I need girl time with your wife."

Alex glanced at Harper, giving her hand a slow, lingering squeeze. "Wish me luck."

"You'll need it," she teased, a grin tugging at her lips.

He stepped into the games room, the familiar scent of aged leather and whisky thick in the air. Soft music played in the background, blending with the sharp click of pool balls echoing off the walls.

Julian looked up and grinned. "Well, look who finally decided to bring our sister home." He crossed the room, hand outstretched. "You planning on leaving her behind this time?"

"Not a chance in hell," Alex replied, shaking firmly.

Nickolas clapped him on the shoulder. "Good to see you, mate."

Jonathan leaned casually on his cue, smirking. "Nice to see you, rich boy."

Alex rolled his eyes. "Am I ever going to live that down?"

All three men grinned, voices in perfect unison: "No."

He laughed, freely and easily, the tension of the journey melting away. Nickolas handed him a glass of whiskey, the amber liquid catching the light as they clinked their glasses together.

"Merry Christmas," Julian said, warm and easy.

"Merry Christmas," the others echoed, the words carrying a promise of family, belonging, and the kind of joy only home could bring.

Outside, Clara and Harper strolled through the sun-dappled gardens, arms linked, the warm summer breeze carrying the mingling scents of jasmine and eucalyptus. Birds chirped lazily in the background, and the sunlight danced across the petals of brightly coloured blooms.

"So," Clara said, grinning mischievously, "married life? Still madly in love with your mysterious billionaire husband?"

Harper laughed, the sound light and carefree. "Madly. Though he still steals the covers every single night."

Her phone buzzed in her hand. Harper glanced down at the screen—and stopped walking, the world narrowing around that tiny device.

"It's the doctor's office," she murmured.

Clara watched her closely as Harper answered, her voice calm but tinged with curiosity. "Hello? Yes, this is Harper Dawson."

She listened, her eyes widening, lips parting slightly. Then her expression shifted, softening, glowing, tears shimmering at the corners of her eyes.

"Thank you so much," she said, her voice thick with emotion. She hung up, standing still for a moment, stunned and awash with joy.

Clara grabbed her hand, her curiosity impossible to mask. "That smile is either very good or very scandalous. Spill."

Harper bit her lip, her eyes shining like sunlight on water. "I can't say… not yet. I need to find Alex first."

The terrace was alive with laughter and conversation, drinks in hand, the hum of family and friends filling the warm afternoon air. Harper pushed through, urgency in her step cutting through the background noise.

She reached Alex, her heart hammering. "I need to talk to you. Now."

He turned instantly, concern flickering across his face. "What's wrong, sweetheart?"

"I just got a call from the doctor."

His heart caught in his chest. "Are you… are you ill? Why didn't you tell me?"

"No," she said, shaking her head, a small, trembling smile breaking across her lips. "Alex… I'm pregnant."

He froze, disbelief flashing across his features, before hope and joy caught up with reality. "Really?"

She nodded, tears spilling over despite herself.

Then the sunlight seemed to pour directly into Alex's chest. Joy broke across his face like dawn breaking through clouds. He lifted her effortlessly into his arms and spun her, laughing, his voice rich with elation. "God, I love you, Mrs. Dawson!"

She laughed, her tears sparkling like diamonds in the summer light, clinging to him as the world spun just slightly brighter around them.

Still holding her, Alex turned to the gathering family. "We're having a baby!"

The terrace erupted into cheers. Clara squealed, hopping in excitement. Jenny clapped her hands to her mouth, laughter and tears mingling. William let out a whoop, echoing across the gardens. Harper's brothers swarmed them, ruffling hair, clapping shoulders, and offering heartfelt congratulations.

And just like that, Christmas began—not with snow or presents, but with sunlight, laughter, and the warm, perfect wonder of new beginnings, wrapped in love that had only grown stronger with time

The End

Before You Go...

If you fell for these characters and want more love stories filled with emotion, passion, and second chances, my newsletter is where I share them first.

You'll receive:

💕 Early access to new releases

💕 Exclusive reader-only content and extras

👉 **Join my reader list here:** https://alisonreidauthor.com

I'd love to welcome you.

Alison Reid

Thank you for reading Hidden Truths!

If you enjoyed this collection of irresistible heroes and heroines, keep an eye out for more upcoming romance collections by Alison Reid, including:

Alpha Kings - *A Billionaire Alpha Male Romance Collection*

Cautious Hearts - *A Trust-After-Heartbreak Romance Collection*

Dark & Dangerous - *Brooding Heroes Romance Collection*

Final Surrender - *Alpha Heroes Yielding to Love Collection*

Forbidden Hearts - *A Forbidden Love Romance Collection*

Forever Mine - *A Longing-for-Love Romance Collection*

Guarded Hearts - *A Surrender to Love Romance Collection*

Hearts & Secrets - *Small Town Romance Collection*

Hearts in Peril - *A Suspenseful Romance Collection*

Lies & Hearts - *A Lies, Secrets & Betrayal Romance Collection*

Love After Regret - *A Second-Chance Redemption Romance Collection*

Misjudged Hearts - *A Love After Judgement Romance Collection*

Torn Between Hearts - *A Love Triangle Romance Collection*

All of Alison Reid's books feature standalone stories, swoon-worthy heroes, and guaranteed happily-ever-afters.

Books by Alison Reid

A Billionaire for Christmas

A Heart in Florence

After The Storm

Always You

Before I Fell

Before the Thaw

Beneath the Lies

Billionaire Bodyguard

Billionaire Rancher

Blueprints of the Heart

Branlow

Collide

Echoes of Deception

Falling for the Billionaire

Forever Yours

Heart of the Outback

Hearts on the Line

Hidden Gem

Kept Promises

Mended Hearts

Mistaken Hearts

New Year's Eve Kiss

Quiet Danger

Reckless Hearts

Reflections of Deception

Second Glance

Shadows of the Past

Shattered Dreams

Shattered Hope, Stolen Kisses

Still Yours

The Billionaire's Accidental Legacy

The Billionaire's Bargain

The Billionaire's Mistake

The Billionaire's Regret

The Billionaire's Secret Baby

The Billionaire's Unexpected Heir

The Blood Debt

The Playboy's Surrender

The Wrong Sister

Trust in Time

Undercover Billionaire

Until you Loved Me

Vows of Vengeance

Wife in Name Only

Find all my books on Amazon:

https://www.amazon.com/author/alisonreid1970

About the Author

Alison Reid writes contemporary and small-town romance filled with heart, passion, and second-chance love stories. Her novels often feature strong heroines, irresistible heroes, and the happily-ever-afters readers adore. When she's not writing, Alison enjoys reading, spending time with her family, and imagining new love stories. She hopes her books give readers a few hours of escape, joy, and swoon-worthy romance they won't forget.

www.i...
...-product-compliance
...4829...
797*